Penguin Education

Penguin Critical Anthologies
General Editor: Christopher Ricks

Jonathan Swift

Edited by Denis Donoghue

Jonathan Swift
A Critical Anthology

Edited by Denis Donoghue
Penguin Books

Penguin Books Ltd, Harmondsworth,
Middlesex, England
Penguin Books Inc., 7110 Ambassador Road,
Baltimore, Md 21207, U.S.A.
Penguin Books Australia Ltd,
Ringwood, Victoria, Australia

First published 1971
This selection copyright © Denis Donoghue, 1971
Introduction and notes copyright © Denis Donoghue, 1971

Made and printed in Great Britain by
Hazell Watson & Viney Ltd,
Aylesbury, Bucks
Set in Monotype Bembo

Contents

6 Contents

Part Two The Developing Debate

8 Contents

13 Contents

Preface

I wish to thank Christopher Ricks and Martin Lightfoot for many valuable suggestions; and Linda O'Donnell for technical guidance during the preparation of the book. I am extremely grateful to authors and publishers who have kindly permitted their work to be reprinted here. Most regrettably, permission to reprint F. R. Leavis's essay on Swift *in toto* was not granted on this occasion, so an important moment in the history of Swift's reception is represented only by paraphrase and excerpt.

Table of Dates

Note on Quotations

In this anthology quotations from Swift's prose writings are taken
from the edition by Herbert Davis *et al.* published by Blackwell.
The individual volumes are numbered as follows:

Quotations from Swift's correspondence are taken from the
edition by Sir Harold Williams, published by the Clarendon Press,
as follows:

III   *1724–1731*, 1963.
IV   *1732–1736*, 1965.
V   *1737–1745*, 1965.

Quotations from *Journal to Stella* are taken from the edition by Sir Harold Williams, two volumes, published by the Clarendon Press, 1948.

Quotations from Swift's poems are also taken from the edition by Sir Harold Williams, three volumes, second edition, Clarendon Press, 1958.

Spelling and punctuation have been modernized, except in quotations from Swift's verse where the loss of original spelling and punctuation would make a certain difference.

Part One **Contemporaneous Criticism**

Introduction

Swift's enemies agreed with his friends on one point, that he wrote well. As he said in *Verses on the Death of Dr Swift*, he had 'some repute for prose'. His friends were delighted to find their cause defended by such a pen; his enemies affected to lament that a man should so grossly abuse his talent. But neither party descended to literary criticism: that Swift was an artist hardly appears. His first readers had a political end in view. When *A Tale of a Tub* appeared in 1704, readers did not concern themselves with the structure of the book, the relation between the story and the digressions, the problem of form, the book as part of a vigorous tradition, the relation between style and meaning. These were not then the teasing matters they have now become. Readers censured the author's attitude to religion, and were not appeased by the consideration that his glances at the Roman Catholic Church were far more damaging than those which he turned occasionally upon the Church of England. The book was a scandal. Again, the question of art did not arise when Swift emerged, some years later, as the most brilliant Tory, Harley's man, virulent in the Paper War. Perhaps there were Whig readers of the *Examiner* who acknowledged that the several essays had merit beyond their occasions, but they kept the feeling to themselves. When *Gulliver's Travels* was published in 1726, readers found it delightful, but many thought the satire too general, too severe, a libel upon mankind. This is perhaps the only question which has persisted as a matter of critical interest. What Bolingbroke thought of *Gulliver's Travels* is couched in terms which a modern reader acknowledges.

Generally, however, the question of Swift as an artist was not pursued. His friends might praise one of his poems, an essay, a pamphlet, the *Travels*, but such praise did not mean that he was accepted, like Pope, as a poet. He was not a professional writer. He was not a playwright. He was not, in the sense then current, a novelist; that is, he did not write romances, prose fictions consistent with their origin in heroic poetry. What he did, he did superbly, but his works called for little in the way of literary criticism. Writing, in such a case, was treated as a mode of politics; its origin, its methods and its ends were political questions, in the first instance. In fact, very few forms of writing in the eighteenth century were regarded as having an avowedly aesthetic existence. Critics disputed the nature of tragedy, verse, the three unities, Ancients and Moderns, Roman comedy, French plots, the propriety of introducing the Gods in a stage play: these were matters of critical debate, but few of them could be illustrated by reference to Swift. The Dean wrote well, and he put his talent at the disposal of Party. The literary question did not arise as a separable issue.

It may appear that Swift was unfortunate in his readers. A modern student of English fiction would be remarkably abstemious if he chose not to reflect upon *Gulliver's Travels*, emphasizing the art of the book and defining the particular version of fiction which it embodies. But its first readers were not primarily concerned with such questions: they translated the story into local terms, recognized the political thrusts, spotted every hit. The book was enjoyed, its jokes relished, but it was enjoyed as a masterly intervention, a dramatic *coup*.

But it is a question whether Swift was badly served by his readers. Perhaps their instincts were accurate. It is possible to discuss the development of the English novel, as Ian Watt has done in *The Rise of the Novel* (1963), without adverting much to Swift. Besides, Swift himself had virtually nothing to say on art, and thought the question of Art and Nature such a cliché that he consigned it to his *Tritical Essay upon the Faculties of the Mind*. He was content, apparently, to be regarded as a wit, a political satirist, something of an historian and a poet of sorts. He did not demand to be appreciated in other terms. When he wrote of literary things, his assumptions remained political: indeed, the relation between Swift and his readers was based upon this understanding.

A piece of writing was important in its bearing upon language and manners, rather than in itself. Language was politics, articulate.

It was inevitable, therefore, that Swift, a beleaguered Tory, should regard the English language as correspondingly abused. Like everything else, the poor language was degenerating, largely as a result of a pernicious court and a meretricious theatre. The main evil was what he called, in the *Tatler* and elsewhere, 'false refinements', Whig sophistries of manner and style. The best time in the history of the language was 'the peaceable part of King Charles the First's reign'; naturally, this was also the best time for politeness, good manners, agreeable conversation between the sexes. These conditions produced that simplicity of style which is 'the best and truest ornament of most things in human life'. Vices of style were always crimes against simplicity. In the *Letter to a Young Clergyman* Swift warns his pupil against 'hard words' and 'fine language'. He despised any overt rhetoric, any direct appeal to sentiment. In *Remarks upon Tindal's Rights of the Christian Church* he makes fun of Locke for his 'refined jargon'. He ridiculed Steele for attending to the cadences of words without consulting their meaning. To write well one must be, in Swift's estimate, a gentleman. If proof of merit is simplicity, proof of corruption is singularity, wilful and eccentric vaunting, the personal equivalent of faction. There is one style which is better than any other: a simple style, direct and unequivocal. So there is one style of life which is better than any other: the style of being an Anglican, a Tory, a gentleman. The point to make, indeed, is that Swift's rhetoric, in the matter of language, was simultaneously an essay in party politics. He wanted to enforce the moral that 'the good life' was justly represented in his terms; the fact that those terms were Anglican and Tory followed as night follows the day. When Swift wrote in those terms, he always implied that his position was sustained by the Natural Law, and that its manifestation in Tory idiom was simply in the nature of the case, God's will being what it was. Oldmixon and Mainwaring were right, then, in reading the ostensibly innocent *Proposal for Correcting, Improving and Ascertaining the English Tongue* (see p. 38) as a Tory pamphlet, an arrant piece of propaganda, not merely because it was addressed to Harley and its author proposed to pack the Academy with Tories, but because its linguistic assumptions were recognizably Tory. In the given case, Swift implied, there was a direct relation between political folly and shoddy writing: it was possible to throw a crumb of praise to Steele in the *Proposal*, but the attack delivered in *The Importance of the Guardian Considered* was based upon the understanding that a miserable Whig is bound to be a bad writer if he has the impudence to be a writer at all. Swift wanted to ascertain or fix the language, because he thought that it was changing too quickly and changing in degenerate ways. These changes, clear in linguistic terms, were moral changes at bottom; men were falling away from the Tory verities of character and opinion. Oldmixon tried to turn the force of this rhetoric back upon its inventor, comparing the Tories with 'their good friends the French, who for these three or fourscore years have been attempting to make their tongue as imperious as their power'. In 1712 a man's loyalty, as an Englishman, might easily be confounded by a few maxims upon grammar. In a context defined by language, politics, religion and history, it was not always safe to open one's mouth.

This is Swift's context. Satire, irony and invective arose from a setting in which language, politics, religion and history were not separate activities but one activity, taking these several forms. The kinds of writing in which he excelled were those offered at the intersection of his talent and his time. He understood his time in the given terms. As for his talent, he claimed to have a ready hand for irony and he knew that he had 'the satirical itch'; he would write in 'my own hum'rous biting way'. Enraged with mere men, he attacked Man, knowing that the blow would return upon finite victims: nothing remains long upon an abstraction. The values

which sustained the satire are those of simplicity, but in a special
sense. In a letter to Bolingbroke, 19 December 1719 (see p. 45),
Swift gives himself away, I think, more fully than has been
recognized. There is a trace of irony in the letter, but not enough
to deflect the feeling engaged. 'If I were to frame a romance of a
great minister's life,' Swift writes, 'he should begin it as Aristippus
has done; then be sent into exile, and employ his leisure in writing
the memoirs of his own Administration; then be recalled, invited
to resume his share of power, act as far as was decent; at last,
retire to the country, and be a pattern of hospitality, politeness,
wisdom and virtue.' Swift is trying to cheer Bolingbroke up,
telling him that genius has always been an obstacle to advancement,
since common talents are perfectly adequate for the purposes of
government. In 1719 Bolingbroke was in exile as a result of his
flight to join the Stuart Pretender in France in March 1715. But
since 1717 his reputation at home had been improving, partly
because of his *Letter to Sir William Windham* in that year, a bid for
reconciliation and forgiveness, and partly because he had turned
against the Pretender. The new king, George I, was willing to be
impressed. In fact, Bolingbroke would have been cordially recalled
in 1720 or soon thereafter, if Walpole had not returned to power in
1721. As it was, Bolingbroke was allowed to return in 1725, and
his country house at Dawley became the centre of the opposition
to Walpole for the next several years. Swift is putting a brave face
on the situation, then, but he is also recalling an earlier career,
that of Sir William Temple. Cast aside in 1670, despite his
diplomatic successes on the Continent, Temple retired to his
country house at Sheen, and occupied himself in writing his
memoirs. Macaulay was to think that Temple was too cautious to
be great, and to rebuke him for 'writing memoirs and tying up
apricots' while the nation 'groaned under oppression'. But Swift
took a different view. Clearly, he admired Temple for practising
the art of withdrawal. What Macaulay thought wretched caution,

Swift thought simplicity. Besides, it was consoling to Swift himself to establish a dignified pattern in this regard: to involve oneself in great affairs of state and then to withdraw from their vexations. Swift had done it in 1714 and he needed an endorsing rhetoric. When we think of simplicity as a moral value in Swift, we should have something like this pattern in mind; not a cloistered virtue, but a final choice, after the great world has been tasted. The best of both worlds is the Horatian conclusion. Of course this means a reduction in one's world, but such a reduction is consistent with the drift of Swift's rhetoric throughout: the good life is what remains, when all excesses have been cut away. Morality is like gardening, Temple's favourite art.

I am emphasizing the ground of communication between Swift and his first readers. He was read, we may suppose, pretty much as he wished to be read. *The Conduct of the Allies* had the kind of popular success appropriate to a major essay on a major issue. *Gulliver's Travels* transcended the divisions of party. So the way in which Swift was read by his first readers may not be as limited as we have said; it may point to something permanently valid in his reception. At least we can make one assertion: that a reading of Swift which releases him from the bonds of politics, religion and history is likely to be misleading. Having made one assertion, we may risk another: that the sense of limit which arises from contemporaneous accounts of Swift may be justified; he is a genius, 'a great English writer' (as Dr Leavis called him in the first sentence of an essay which thereafter gives a limiting account of that greatness), but his genius does not express itself in terms of plenitude, multiplicity, diversity. Swift is not great as Shakespeare is great: he is great in concentration and immediate force. He wrote nothing like *Middlemarch*, a work which invites the reader to live among its figures, consorting with surface and depth, responding to it in a wide range of idioms and reflections. To speak of George Eliot's art and then of Swift's art is not to shame one in the sight of the other, but to mark a crucial difference between the two writers: a difference in their sense of life, their sense of art, its possibilities, its bearing upon daily life. In Swift, the range of attitudes deemed possible is relatively narrow; in George Eliot, it is as wide as the sky. George Eliot's art is open to the world and its variety; Swift's art thrives on the force of concentration and pressure. We need not extend the marks of difference, they are clear enough. Their relevance, after all is to suggest that the contemporaneous response to Swift, str. and limited as it was, may have been, in its direction, sound enough.

Jonathan Swift

from 'The Publisher's Epistle to the Reader', *Letters Written by
Sir William Temple* 1700 (reprinted in *Prose Writings*, vol. 1)

It is generally believed that this author has advanced our English
tongue to as great a perfection as it can well bear; and yet, how great
a master he was of it has, I think, never appeared so much as it will in
the following letters; wherein the style appears so very different
according to the difference of the persons to whom they were addressed; either men of business, or idle; of pleasure, or serious; of
great or of less parts or abilities, in their several stations. So that one
may discover the characters of most of those persons he writes to
from the style of his letters.
(258)

Jonathan Swift

from 'The Preface of the Author' to *The Battle of the Books* 1704
(reprinted in *Prose Writings*, vol. 1)

Satire is a sort of glass, wherein beholders do generally discover
everybody's face but their own; which is the chief reason for that
kind of reception it meets in the world, and that so very few are
offended with it. But if it should happen otherwise, the danger is not
great; and I have learned from long experience never to apprehend
mischief from those understandings I have been able to provoke. For
anger and fury, though they add strength to the sinews of the body,
yet are found to relax those of the mind, and to render all its efforts
feeble and impotent.

There is a brain that will endure but one scumming: let the owner
gather it with discretion, and manage his little stock with husbandry;
but of all things, let him beware of bringing it under the lash of his
betters, because that will make it all bubble up into impertinence, and
he will find no new supply; wit without knowledge being a sort of
cream, which gathers in a night to the top, and by a skilful hand may
be soon whipped into froth; but once scummed away, what appears

underneath will be fit for nothing but to be thrown to the hogs.
(140)

Jonathan Swift

from the Preface to *A Tale of a Tub* 1704 (reprinted in *Prose Writings*, vol. 1)

'Tis a great ease to my conscience that I have writ so elaborate and useful a discourse without one grain of satire intermixed; which is the sole point wherein I have taken leave to dissent from the famous originals of our age and country. I have observed some satirists to use the public much at the rate that pedants do a naughty boy ready horsed for discipline: first expostulate the case, then plead the necessity of the rod, from great provocations, and conclude every period with a lash. Now if I know anything of mankind, these gentlemen might very well spare their reproof and correction, for there is not through all Nature another so callous and insensible a member as the world's posteriors, whether you apply to it the toe or the birch. Besides, most of our late satirists seem to lie under a sort of mistake, that because nettles have the prerogative to sting, therefore all other weeds must do so too. I make not this comparison out of the least design to detract from these worthy writers, for it is well known among mythologists that weeds have the pre-eminence over all other vegetables; and therefore the first monarch of this island, whose taste and judgement were so acute and refined, did very wisely root out the roses from the collar of the Order, and plant the thistles in their stead, as the nobler flower of the two. For which reason it is conjectured by profounder antiquaries that the satirical itch, so prevalent in this part of our island, was first brought among us from beyond the Tweed. Here may it long flourish and abound: may it survive and neglect the scorn of the world with as much ease and contempt as the world is insensible to the lashes of it. May their own dullness, or that of their party, be no discouragement for the authors to proceed; but let them remember, it is with wits as with razors, which are never so apt to cut those they are employed on, as when they have lost their edge. Besides, those whose teeth are too rotten to bite are best of all others qualified to revenge that defect with their breath. . . .

But though the matter for panegyric were as fruitful as the topics of satire, yet would it not be hard to find out a sufficient reason why the latter will be always better received than the first. For, this being bestowed only upon one or a few persons at a time, is sure to raise envy and consequently ill words from the rest, who have no share in the blessing: but satire being levelled at all, is never resented for an offence by any, since every individual person makes bold to understand it of others, and very wisely removes his particular part of the burden upon the shoulders of the world, which are broad enough and able to bear it.

(29–30, 31)

William King

from *Some Remarks on 'A Tale of a Tub'* 1704

'Why then,' cries another, 'Oliver's porter had an amanuensis at Bedlam that used to transcribe what he dictated, and may not these be some scattered notes of his master's?' To which all replied, that though Oliver's porter was crazed, yet his misfortune never let him forget that he was a Christian. One said it was a surgeon's man that had married a midwife's nurse; but though by the style it might seem probable that two such persons had a hand in it, yet since he could not name the persons, his fancy was rejected. 'I conjecture,' says another, 'that it may be a lawyer, that . . .', when, on a sudden, he was interrupted by Mr Markland the scrivener. 'No, rather by the oaths it should be an Irish evidence.' At last there stood up a sprunt young man that is secretary to our scavenger, and cries, 'What if after all it should be a parson; for who may make more free with their trade? What if I know him, describe him, name him, and how he and his friends talk of it, admire it, are proud of it.' 'Hold,' cry all the company, 'that function must not be mentioned without respect, we have enough of the dirty subject, we had better drink our coffee and talk our politics.'

(15–16)

William Wotton

from *A Defense of the Reflections upon Ancient and Modern
Learning, in Answer to the Objections of Sir W. Temple and Others,
with Observations upon the Tale of a Tub* 1705 (reprinted in A. C.
Guthkelch and D. Nichol Smith (eds.), *A Tale of a Tub,* 1920)

But I expect, Sir, that you should tell me that the *Tale*-teller falls
here only upon the ridiculous inventions of Popery; that the Church
of Rome intended by these things to gull silly superstitious people;
and to rook them of their money; that the world had been but too
long in slavery; that our ancestors gloriously redeemed us from that
yoke; that the Church of Rome therefore ought to be exposed, and
that he deserves well of mankind that does expose it.

   All this, Sir, I own to be true: but then I would not so shoot at an
enemy as to hurt myself at the same time. The foundation of the
doctrines of the Church of England is right, and came from God.
Upon this the Popes, and Councils called and confirmed by them
have built, as St Paul speaks, hay and stubble, perishable and slight
materials, which when they are once consumed that the foundation
may appear, then we shall see what is faulty and what is not. But our
Tale-teller strikes at the very root. 'Tis all with him a farce, and all a
ladle, as a very facetious poet says upon another occasion. The Father,
and the will, and his son Martin are part of the *Tale*, as well as Peter
and Jack, and are all ushered in with the common old wives' introduction, once upon a time.
(318)

Jonathan Swift

Letter to Isaac Bickerstaff, *Tatler,* no. 230   26–8 September 1710
(reprinted in *Prose Writings*, vol. 2)

From my own Apartment, 27 September

The following letter has laid before me many great and manifest
evils in the world of letters which I had overlooked; but they open to
me a very busy scene, and it will require no small care and application

to amend errors which are become so universal. The affectation of politeness is exposed in this epistle with a great deal of wit and discernment; so that whatever discourses I may fall into hereafter upon the subjects the writer treats of, I shall at present lay the matter before the world without the least alteration from the words of my correspondent.

To Isaac Bickerstaff, Esq.

Sir,

There are some abuses among us of great consequence, the reformation of which is properly your province, though, as far as I have been conversant in your papers, you have not yet considered them. These are, the deplorable ignorance that for some years hath reigned among our English writers, the great depravity of our taste and the continual corruption of our style. I say nothing here of those who handle particular sciences, divinity, law, physic, and the like; I mean, the traders in history and politics, and the *belles lettres*; together with those by whom books are not translated, but (as the common expressions are) 'done out of French, Latin' or other language, and 'made English'. I cannot but observe to you, that till of late years a Grub-Street book was always bound in sheepskin, with suitable print and paper, the price never above a shilling, and taken off wholly by common tradesmen or country pedlars, but now they appear in all sizes and shapes, and in all places. They are handed about from lapfuls in every coffee-house to persons of quality, are shown in Westminster Hall and the Court of Requests. You may see them gilt, and in royal paper, of five or six hundred pages, and rated accordingly. I would engage to furnish you with a catalogue of English books published within the compass of seven years past, which at the first hand would cost you a hundred pounds, wherein you shall not be able to find ten lines together of common grammar or common sense.

These two evils, ignorance and want of taste, have produced a third; I mean, the continual corruption of our English tongue which, without some timely remedy, will suffer more by the false refinements of twenty years past, than it hath been improved in the foregoing hundred: and this is what I design chiefly to enlarge upon, leaving the former evils to your animadversion.

But instead of giving you a list of the late refinements crept into our language, I here send you the copy of a letter I received some time ago from a most accomplished person in this way of writing, upon which I shall make some remarks. It is in these terms.

Sir,
I *cou'dn't* get the things you sent for all *about Town.* – I *thot* to *ha'* come down myself, and then *I'd ha' bro't 'um;* but I *ha'n't don't,* and I believe I *can't do't,* that's *pozz.* – *Tom*[1] begins to *g'imself airs* because *he's* going with the *plenipo's.* – 'Tis said, the *French* King will *bamboozl' us agen,* which *causes many speculations.* The *Jacks,* and others of that *kidney,* are very *uppish,* and *alert upon't,* as you may see by their *phizz's.* – *Will Hazzard* has got the *hipps,* having lost *to the tune of* five hundr'd pound, *tho* he understands play very well, *nobody better.* He has promis't me upon *rep,* to leave off play; but you know 'tis a weakness *he's* too apt to *give into, tho* he has as much wit as any man, *nobody more.* He has lain *incog* ever since. – The *mobb's* very quiet with us now. – I believe you *thot* I *banter'd* you in my last like a *country put.* – I *sha'n't* leave Town this month, &c.

This letter is in every point an admirable pattern of the present polite way of writing; nor is it of less authority for being an epistle. You may gather every flower of it, with a thousand more of equal sweetness, from the books, pamphlets and single papers, offered us every day in the coffee-houses: and these are the beauties introduced to supply the want of wit, sense, humour and learning, which formerly were looked upon as qualifications for a writer. If a man of wit, who died forty years ago, were to rise from the grave on purpose, how would he be able to read this letter? And after he had gone through that difficulty, how would he be able to understand it? The first thing that strikes your eye is the *breaks* at the end of almost every sentence; of which I know not the use, only that it is a refinement, and very frequently practised. Then you will observe the abbreviations and elisions, by which consonants of most obdurate sound are joined

---

1 Thomas Harley, cousin of the first Earl of Oxford. He was Secretary of the Treasury, and afterwards Minister at Hanover. He died in 1737.

together, without one softening vowel to intervene; and all this only to make one syllable of two, directly contrary to the example of the Greeks and Romans: altogether of the Gothic strain, and a natural tendency towards relapsing into barbarity which delights in monosyllables, and uniting of mute consonants; as it is observable in all the Northern languages. And this is still more visible in the next refinement, which consists in pronouncing the first syllable in a word that has many, and dismissing the rest; such as *phizz*, *hipps*, *mobb*, *pozz*, *rep* and many more; when we are already overloaded with monosyllables, which are the disgrace of our language. Thus we cram one syllable, and cut off the rest; as the owl fattened her mice, after she had bit off their legs to prevent their running away; and if ours be the same reason for maiming of words, it will certainly answer the end; for I am sure no other nation will desire to borrow them. Some words are hitherto but fairly split, and therefore only in their way to perfection, as *incog* and *plenipo's*: But in a short time it is to be hoped they will be further docked to *inc* and *plen*. This reflection had made me of late years very impatient for a peace, which I believe would save the lives of many brave words, as well as men. The war has introduced an abundance of polysyllables which will never be able to live many more campaigns; *speculations*, *operations*, *preliminaries*, *ambassadors*, *palisadoes*, *communication*, *circumvallation*, *battalions*, as numerous as they are, if they attack us too frequently in our coffee-houses, we shall certainly put them to flight and cut off the rear.

The third refinement observable in the letter I send you, consists in the choice of certain words invented by some *pretty fellows*; such as *banter*, *bamboozle*, *country put* and *kidney*, as it is there applied; some of which are now struggling for the vogue, and others are in possession of it. I have done my utmost for some years past to stop the progress of *mobb* and *banter*, but have been plainly borne down by numbers and betrayed by those who promised to assist me.

In the last place, you are to take notice of certain choice phrases scattered through the letter; some of them tolerable enough, till they were worn to rags by servile imitators. You might easily find them, though they were not in a different print, and therefore I need not disturb them.

These are the false refinements in our style which you ought to correct: first, by arguments and fair means; but if those fail, I think you are to make use of your authority as censor, and by an annual *index expurgatorius* expunge all words and phrases that are offensive to good sense, and condemn those barbarous mutilations of vowels and syllables. In this last point the usual pretence is, that they spell as they speak; a noble standard for language! – to depend upon the caprice of every coxcomb who, because words are the clothing of our thoughts, cuts them out, and shapes them as he pleases and changes them oftener than his dress. I believe, all reasonable people would be content that such refiners were more sparing of their words, and liberal in their syllables: On this head I should be glad you would bestow some advice upon several young readers in our churches, who coming up from the university, full fraught with admiration of our town politeness, will needs correct the style of their prayer-books. In reading the Absolution, they are very careful to say *pardons and absolves*, and in the Prayer for the Royal Family, it must be *endue'um, enrich'um, prosper'um* and *bring'um*. Then in their sermons they use all the modern terms of art, *sham, banter, mob, bubble, bully, cutting, shuffling* and *palming*, all which, and many more of the like stamp, as I have heard them often in the pulpit from such young sophisters, so I have read them in some of those sermons that have made a great noise of late. The design, it seems, is to avoid the dreadful imputation of pedantry, to show us that they know the town, understand men and manners, and have not been poring upon old unfashionable books in the university.

I should be glad to see you the instrument of introducing into our style that simplicity which is the best and truest ornament of most things in human life, which the politer ages always aimed at in their building and dress (*simplex munditiis*), as well as their productions of wit. It is manifest, that all new, affected modes of speech, whether borrowed from the court, the town or the theatre, are the first perishing parts in any language and, as I could prove by many hundred instances, have been so in ours. The writings of Hooker, who was a country clergyman, and of Parsons the Jesuit, both in the reign of Queen Elizabeth, are in a style that, with very few allowances, would not offend any present reader; much more clear and intelligible than those of Sir H. Wotton, Sir Robert Naunton, Osborn, Daniel the historian, and several others who wrote later; but being men of the court, and affecting the phrases then in fashion, they are often either not to be understood or appear perfectly ridiculous.

What remedies are to be applied to these evils I have not room to consider, having, I fear, already taken up most of your paper. Besides, I think it is our office only to represent abuses, and yours to redress them.

I am, with great respect,

Sir,

Yours, &c.

(173–7)

John Gay

from *The Present State of Wit, in a Letter to a Friend in the Country* 1711

The *Examiner* is a paper which all men who speak without prejudice allow to be well written. Though his subject will admit of no great variety, he is continually placing it in so many different lights, and endeavouring to inculcate the same thing by so many beautiful changes of expression, that men who are concerned in no party may read him with pleasure. His way of assuming the question in debate is extremely artful; and his *Letter to Crassus* is, I think, a masterpiece. . . . Soon after their first appearance, came out a paper from the other side, called the *Whig Examiner*, written with so much fire, and in so excellent a style, as put the Tories in no small pain for their favourite hero. Everyone cried, 'Bickerstaff must be the author!' and people were the more confirmed in this opinion upon its being so soon laid down; which seemed to show that it was only written to bind the *Examiners* to their good behaviour and was never designed to be a weekly paper. The *Examiners*, therefore, have no one to combat with at present but their friend the *Medley*: the author of which paper, though he seems to be a man of good sense, and expresses it luckily now and then, is, I think, for the most part, perfectly a stranger to fine writing. I presume I need not tell you that the *Examiner* carries much the more sail, as it is supposed to be written by the direction and under the eye of some great persons who sit at the helm of affairs,

and is consequently looked on as a sort of public notice which way
they are steering us.

The reputed author is Dr S[wif]t, with the assistance sometimes of
Dr Att[erbur]y and Mr P[rio]r. The *Medley* is said to be written by
Mr Old[mixo]n and supervised by Mr Mayn[warin]g, who perhaps
might entirely write those few papers which are so much better than
the rest.

Jonathan Swift

from *A Proposal for Correcting, Improving and Ascertaining the
English Tongue*   1712 (reprinted in *Prose Writings*, vol. 4)

The period wherein the English tongue received most improvement,
I take to commence with the beginning of Queen Elizabeth's reign
and to conclude with the great rebellion in forty-two. It is true, there
was a very ill taste, both of style and wit, which prevailed under King
James I; but that seems to have been corrected in the first years of his
successor who, among many other qualifications of an excellent
prince, was a great patron of learning. From that great rebellion to
this present time, I am apt to doubt whether the corruptions in our
language have not at least equalled the refinements of it; and these
corruptions, very few of the best authors in our age have wholly
escaped. During the Usurpation, such an infusion of enthusiastic
jargon prevailed in every writing, as was not shaken off in many years
after. To this succeeded that licentiousness which entered with the
Restoration, and, from infecting our religion and morals, fell to corrupt our language: which last was not like to be much improved by
those who at that time made up the Court of King Charles II; either
such who had followed him in his banishment, or who had been
altogether conversant in the dialect of those fanatic times; or young
men who had been educated in the same company; so that the Court,
which used to be the standard of propriety and correctness of speech,
was then, and I think hath ever since continued, the worst school in
England for that accomplishment, and so will remain till better care
be taken in the education of our young nobility, that they may set
out into the world with some foundation of literature, in order to

qualify them for patterns of politeness. The consequence of this defect upon our language may appear from the plays and other compositions written for entertainment within fifty years past; filled with a succession of affected phrases and new conceited words, either borrowed from the current style of the Court or from those who, under the character of men of wit and pleasure, pretended to give the law. Many of these refinements have already been long antiquated and are now hardly intelligible; which is no wonder, when they were the product only of ignorance and caprice.

I have never known this great town without one or more dunces of figure, who had credit enough to give rise to some new word and propagate it in most conversations, although it had neither humour nor significancy. If it struck the present taste, it was soon transferred into the plays and current scribbles of the week, and became an addition to our language; while the men of wit and learning, instead of early obviating such corruptions, were too often seduced to imitate and comply with them.

There is another set of men who have contributed very much to the spoiling of the English tongue: I mean the poets, from the time of the Restoration. These gentlemen, although they could not be insensible to how much our language was already overstocked with monosyllables, yet to save time and pains introduced that barbarous custom of abbreviating words to fit them to the measure of their verses; and this they have frequently done so very injudiciously as to form such harsh unharmonious sounds that none but a northern ear could endure. They have joined the most objurate consonants, without one intervening vowel, only to shorten a syllable; and their taste in time became so depraved that what was at first a poetical licence, not to be justified, they made their choice, alleging that the words pronounced at length sounded faint and languid. This was a pretence to take up the same custom in prose, so that most of the books we see nowadays are full of those manglings and abbreviations. Instances of this abuse are innumerable: what does your Lordship think of the words, 'drudg'd', 'disturb'd', 'rebuk'd', 'fledg'd' and a thousand others everywhere to be met in prose as well as verse?; where by leaving out a vowel to save a syllable we form so jarring a sound, and so difficult to utter, that I have often wondered how it could ever obtain. . . .

Several young men at the universities, terribly possessed with the fear of pedantry, run into a worse extreme; and think all politeness to consist in reading the daily trash sent down to them from hence. This they call 'knowing the world', and 'reading men and manners'. Thus furnished, they come up to town, reckon all their errors for accomplishments, borrow the newest set of phrases and, if they take a pen into their hands, all the odd words they have picked up in a coffee-house or a gaming ordinary are produced as flowers of style and the orthography refined to the utmost. To this we owe those monstrous productions which under the names of 'trips', 'spies', 'amusements' and other conceited appellations have over-run us for some years past. To this we owe that strange race of wits who tell us they write to the 'humour of the age'. And I wish I could say these quaint fopperies were wholly absent from graver subjects. In short, I would undertake to show your Lordship several pieces where the beauties of this kind are so predominant that with all your skill in languages you could never be able either to read or understand them.

But I am very much mistaken if many of these false refinements among us do not arise from a principle which would quite destroy their credit if it were well understood and considered. For I am afraid, my Lord, that with all the real good qualities of our country we are naturally not very polite.

(9–12)

John Oldmixon

from *Reflections on Dr Swift's Letter to Harley*   1712

That good old church martyr, the Earl of Strafford, was of opinion common fame was enough to hang a man, as in the case of the Duke of Buckingham, when he was impeached by the Commons for mal-practices in his Ministry, and there were no better grounds for accusing him than that everybody said so. I am quite of another mind, and let the world say what they will of anyone, I am for condemning nobody but whom the law condemns, and therefore in these reflec-tions I shall not consider so much how to please the spleen of one party, as how to expose the arrogance of another, who would lord it over us in everything, and not only force their principles upon us, but their language, wherein they endeavour to ape their good friends the French, who for these three or fourscore years have been attempting to make their tongue as imperious as their power.

This most ingenious writer has so great a value for his own judgement in matters of style that he has put his name to his letter, and a name greater than his own, as if he meant to bully us into his methods for pinning down our language and making it as criminal to admit foreign words as foreign trades, though our tongue may be enriched by the one, as much as our traffic by the other. He would have it 'corrected', 'enlarged' and 'ascertained', and who must do it? He tells you with great modesty and discernment in the twenty-seventh page, *'the choice of hands should be left to him, and he would then assign it over to the women'*, because they are softer mouthed and are more for liquids than the men, as he tried himself in a very notable experiment. I wonder a grave, serious divine, who is so well versed in college learning, should in compliment to a certain lady, whose breeding and conversation must have given her wonderful opportunities to refine our tongue, imagine that the two universities would give up so essential a branch of their privileges to the ladies, and take from them the standard of English. This puts me in mind of Fontenelle's way of learning a language, which he recommends to be by having an intrigue with some fair foreigner, and beginning with the verb 'I love, you love', etc. . . . It is a sad case, when men get a habit of saying what they please, nothing caring whether true or false. Who can without pity see our letter writer accuse the famous La Bruyère for being accessary to the declining of the French tongue by his affectation; when it is notorious that La Bruyère is the most masterly writer of that nation, and that his affectation was in the turn of his thought, which he did to strike his readers who had been too much used to dry lessons to receive any impression by them. He says he has many hundred 'new words, not to be found in the common dictionaries before his time'. I should be glad to know who are those lexicographers whose knowledge in the French tongue he prefers to La Bruyère's; since Richelet and the Academy are not of his era. I should rejoice with him if a way could be found out to 'fix our language for ever', that like the Spanish cloak it might always be in fashion; but I hope he will come into temper with the inconstancy of people's minds, of which he complains, and that we are in no fear of the invasion and conquest he talks of, comforting himself 'that the best writings may be preserved and esteemed', meaning his own and his friends', which no doubt would fare much better than Mr Locke's or Mr Hoadley's; for conquerors are not used to take much care of those that write against them.

(1-3, 13-14)

Jonathan Swift

from *The Memoirs of Martin Scriblerus*[1] 1714 (reprinted in W. A. Eddy (ed.), *Jonathan Swift: Satires and Personal Writings*, 1932)

Of the Secession of Martinus and some hints of his Travels

It was in the year 1699 that Martin set out on his travels. Thou wilt certainly be very curious to know what they were? It is not yet time to inform thee. But what hints I am at liberty to give, I will.

Thou shalt know then, that in his first Voyage he was carried by a prosperous storm, to a discovery of the remains of the ancient Pygmaean Empire.

That in his second, he was as happily shipwreck'd on the land of the Giants, now the most humane people in the world.

That in his third voyage, he discovered a whole kingdom of philosophers, who govern by the mathematics; with whose admirable schemes and projects he returned to benefit his own dear country; but had the misfortune to find them rejected by the envious Ministers of Queen Anne, and himself sent treacherously away.

And hence it is, that in his fourth voyage he discovered a vein of melancholy, proceeding almost to a disgust of his species; but, above all, a mortal detestation to the whole flagitious race of Ministers, and a final resolution not to give in any memorial to the Secretary of State, in order to subject the lands he discovered to the Crown of Great Britain.

1 The *Memoirs* were written as a collective enterprise by the members of the Scriblerus Club: Arbuthnot, Pope, Swift, Gay, Parnell, Lord Oxford and Atterbury; thus it cannot be established that Swift himself wrote this extract. [Ed.]

Now if, by these hints, the reader can help himself to a further discovery of the nature and contents of these travels, he is welcome to as much light as they afford him; I am obliged, by all the ties of honour, not to speak more openly.

But if any man shall ever see such very extraordinary voyages, into such very extraordinary nations, which manifest the most distinguishing marks of a philosopher, a politician and a legislator; and can imagine them to belong to a surgeon of a ship, or a captain of a merchantman, let him remain in his ignorance.

And whoever he be, that shall further observe, in every page of such a book, that cordial love of mankind, that inviolable regard to truth, that passion for his dear country, and that particular attachment to the excellent Princess Queen Anne; surely that man deserves to be pitied, if by all those visible signs and characters, he cannot distinguish and acknowledge the Great Scriblerus.[1]

Of the Discoveries and Works of the Great Scriblerus, made and to be made, written and to be written, known and unknown

Here therefore, at this great period, we end our first book. And here, O reader, we entreat thee utterly to forget all thou hast hitherto read, and to cast thy eyes only forward, to that boundless field the next shall open unto thee; the fruits of which (if thine, or our sins do not prevent) are to spread and multiply over this our work, and over all the face of the Earth.

In the mean time, know what thou owest, and what thou yet mayest owe, to this excellent Person, this Prodigy of our Age; who may well be called the Philosopher of Ultimate Causes, since by a sagacity peculiar to himself, he hath discovered effects in their very cause; and without the trivial helps of experiments, or observations, hath been the inventor of most of the modern systems and hypotheses.

He hath enriched Mathematics with many precise and geometrical quadratures of the circle. He first discovered the cause of gravity, and the intestine motion of fluids.

To him we owe all the observations on the parallax of the polestar, and all the new theories of the deluge.

1 *Gulliver's Travels*, here described in brief, were first intended to form part of Scriblerus's *Memoirs*. [Ed.]

He it was, that first taught the right use sometimes of the *Fuga Vacui*, and sometimes the *Materia Subtilis*, in resolving the grand phenomena of nature.

He it was that first found out the palpability of colours; and by the delicacy of his touch, could distinguish the different vibrations of the heterogeneous rays of light.

His were the projects of *Perpetuum Mobiles*, flying engines and pacing saddles; the method of discovering the longitude, by bomb-vessels, and of increasing the trade-wind by vast plantations of reeds and sedges.

(133-5)

John Oldmixon

from *Memoirs of Ireland from the Restoration to the Present Times* 1716

I have in more places than one hinted how the late Tory ministers imitated the Popish and Irish Tory managers, under King James, in their administration. There is one circumstance more which I cannot forbear mentioning, as a farther proof of it; and that is, their employing mercenary scribblers to vilify and blacken the Protestants and their religion.

The late ministers set Jonathan Swift whom they made Dean of St Patrick's, Daniel Defoe, a broken hosier, and one Oldsworth to work, to insult and abuse their predecessors who had done such great things towards reducing the exorbitant power of France that it might never be of use to the pretended son of our abdicated King. They hired these scribblers to calumniate our allies and all lovers of liberty, whether of the Church of England or any other Protestant Church. They represented them all as fanatical and seditious in the *Examiners*, *John Bulls*, etc.

(246)

Jonathan Swift

from a letter to Viscount Bolingbroke   19 December 1719 (reprinted in *Correspondence*, vol. 2)

But if I were to frame a romance of a great minister's life, he should begin it as Aristippus has done; then be sent into exile, and employ his leisure in writing the memoirs of his own administration; then be recalled, invited to resume his share of power, act as far as was decent; at last, retire to the country, and be a pattern of hospitality, politeness, wisdom and virtue. Have you not observed that there is a lower kind of discretion and regularity which seldom fails of raising men to the highest stations in the court, the church and the law? It must be so: for providence, which designed the world should be governed by many heads, made it a business within the reach of common understandings; while one great genius is hardly found among ten millions. Did you never observe one of your clerks cutting his paper with a blunt ivory knife? Did you ever know the knife to fail going the true way? Whereas, if he had used a razor or a penknife, he had odds against him of spoiling a whole sheet. I have twenty times compared the motion of that ivory implement to those talents that thrive best at court. Think upon Lord Bacon, Williams, Strafford, Laud, Clarendon, Shaftesbury, the last Duke of Buckingham; and of my own acquaintance, the Earl of Oxford and yourself: all great geniuses in their several ways; and if they had not been so great, would have been less unfortunate. I remember but one exception, and that was Lord Somers, whose timorous nature, joined with the trade of a common lawyer and the consciousness of a mean extraction, had taught him the regularity of an alderman or a gentleman-usher. But of late years I have been refining upon this thought: for I plainly see that fellows of low intellectuals, when they are gotten at the head of affairs, can sally into the highest exorbitances, with much more safety than a man of great talents can make the least step out of the way. Perhaps it is for the same reason that men are more afraid of attacking a vicious than a mettlesome horse: but I rather think it owing to that incessant envy wherewith the common rate of mankind pursues all superior natures to their own. And, I conceive, if it were left to the choice of an ass, he would rather be kicked by one of his own species, than a better. If you will recollect that I am towards six years older than when I saw you last, and twenty years duller, you will not wonder to find me abound in empty speculations: I can now express in a hundred words what would formerly have cost me ten. I can write epigrams of fifty distichs, which might be squeezed into one. I have gone the round of all my stories three or four times with the younger people, and begin them again. I give hints how significant a person I have been, and nobody believes me; I pretend to pity them, but am inwardly angry. I lay traps for people to desire I would show them some things I have written, but cannot succeed; and wreak my spite in condemning the taste of the people and company where I am. But it is with place as it is with time. If I boast of having been valued three hundred miles off, it is of no more use than if I told how handsome I was when I was young. The worst of it is that lying is of no use, for the people here will not believe one half of what is true. If I can prevail on anyone to personate a hearer and admirer, you would wonder what a favourite he grows. He is sure to have the first glass out of the bottle, and the best bit I can carve. Nothing has convinced me so much that I am of a little subaltern spirit, *inopis atque pusilli animi*, as to reflect how I am forced into the most trifling amusements to divert the vexation of former thoughts and present objects. Why cannot you lend me a shred of your mantle, or why did not you leave a shred of it with me when you were snatched from me? You see I speak in my trade, although it is growing fast a trade to be ashamed of.

(332–4)

Jonathan Swift

from a letter to Thomas Sheridan   11 September 1725 (reprinted in *Correspondence*, vol. 3)

If you are indeed a discarded courtier, you have reason to complain, but none at all to wonder; you are too young for many experiences to fall in your way, yet you have read enough to make you know the nature of man. It is safer for a man's interest to blaspheme God than to be of a party out of power, or even to be thought so. . . . Therefore sit down and be quiet, and mind your business as you should do, and contract your friendships, and expect no more from man than such an animal is capable of, and you will every day find my description of Yahoos more resembling. You should think and deal with every man as a villain, without calling him so, or flying from him or valuing him less. This is an old true lesson.

93-4)

Jonathan Swift

from a letter to Alexander Pope 29 September   25 (reprinted in *Correspondence*, vol. 3)

I have employed my time (besides ditching) in finishing correcting, amending and transcribing my *Travels*, in four parts complete, newly augmented and intended for the Press when the world shall deserve them, or rather when a printer shall be found brave enough to venture his ears. I like your schemes of our meeting after distresses and dispersions, but the chief end I propose to myself in all my labours is to vex the world rather than divert it, and if I could compass that design without hurting my own person or fortune, I would be the most indefatigable writer you have ever seen without reading. I am exceedingly pleased that you have done with translations. Lord Treasurer Oxford often lamented that a rascally world should lay you under a necessity of misemploying your genius for so long a time. But since you will now be so much better employed, when you think of the world give it one lash the more at my request. I have ever hated all nations, professions and communities, and all my love is towards individuals: for instance, I hate the tribe of lawyers, but I love councillor such a one, judge such a one, for so with physicians (I will not speak of my own trade), soldiers, English, Scotch, French; and the rest, but principally I hate and detest that animal called man, although I heartily love John, Peter, Thomas, and so forth. This is the system upon which I have governed myself many years (but do not tell), and so I shall go on till I have done with them. I have got materials towards a treatise proving the falsity of that definition *animal rationale*; and to show it should be only *rationis capax*. Upon this great foundation of misanthropy (though not Timon's manner) the whole building of my *Travels* is erected; and I never will have peace of mind till all honest men are of my opinion; by consequence you are to embrace it immediately and procure that all who deserve my esteem may do so too. The matter is so clear that it will admit little dispute. Nay, I will hold a hundred pounds that you and I agree in the point. ....

Mr Lewis sent me an account of Dr Arbuthnot's illness which is a very sensible affliction to me, who by living so long out of the world have lost that hardness of heart contracted by years and general conversation. I am daily losing friends, and neither seeking nor getting others. O, if the world had but a dozen Arbuthnots in it, I would burn my *Travels*; but however he is not without fault. There is a passage in Bede highly commending the piety and learning of the Irish in that age, where after abundance of praises he overthrows them all by lamenting that, alas, they kept Easter at a wrong time of the year. So our Doctor has every quality and virtue that can make a man amiable or useful, but alas he hath a sort of slouch in his walk. (102–4)

Jonathan Swift

from a letter to Alexander Pope   26 November 1725 (reprinted in *Correspondence*, vol. 3)

I tell you after all that I do not hate mankind; it is *vous autres* who hate them, because you would have them reasonable animals, and are angry for being disappointed. I have always rejected that definition and made another of my own. I am no more angry with [Walpole] than I was with the kite that last week flew away with one of my chickens, and yet I was pleased when one of my servants shot him two days after. This I say because you are so hardy as to tell me of your intentions to write maxims in opposition to La Rochefoucauld, who is my favourite because I found my whole character in him. However, I will read him again because it is possible I may have since undergone some alterations. (118)

Viscount Bolingbroke

from a letter to Jonathan Swift   14 December 1725 (reprinted in
Correspondence, vol. 3)

Pope and you are very great wits, and I think very indifferent
philosophers. If you despise the world as much as you pretend and
perhaps believe, you would not be so angry with it. The founder of
your sect, that noble original whom you think it so great an honour
to resemble [La Rochefoucauld], was a slave to the worst part of the
world, to the court, and all his big words were the language of a
slighted lover who desired nothing so much as a reconciliation, and
feared nothing so much as a rupture. I believe the world has used me
as scurvily as most people, and yet I could never find in my heart to
be truly angry with the simple, false, capricious thing. I should blush
alike to be discovered fond of the world or piqued at it. Your definition of *animal (capax) rationis* instead of the common one, *animal
rationale*, will not bear examination. Define but reason, and you will
see why your distinction is no better than that of the Pontiff Cotta
between *mala ratio* and *bona ratio*. But enough of this. Make us a visit
and I'll subscribe to any side of these important questions which you
please.
(121–2)

Jonathan Swift

from *Gulliver's Travels*   1726 (reprinted in *Prose Writings*, vol. 11)

We next went to the school of languages where three professors sat
in consultation upon improving that of their own country.
    The first project was to shorten discourse by cutting polysyllables
into one, and leaving out verbs and participles, because in reality all
things imaginable are but nouns.
    The other was a scheme for entirely abolishing all words what-
soever; and this was urged as a great advantage in point of health as
well as brevity. For it is plain, that every word we speak is in some
degree a diminution of our lungs by corrosion, and consequently

contributes to the shortening of our lives. An expedient was therefore offered, that since words are only names for *things*, it would be more convenient for all men to carry about them such things as were necessary to express the particular business they are to discourse on. And this invention would certainly have taken place, to the great ease as well as health of the subject, if the women, in conjunction with the vulgar and illiterate, had not threatened to raise a rebellion, unless they might be allowed the liberty to speak with their tongues, after the manner of their forefathers; such constant irreconcilable enemies to science are the common people. However, many of the most learned and wise adhere to the new scheme of expressing themselves by things, which hath only this inconvenience attending it, that if a man's business be very great, and of various kinds, he must be obliged in proportion to carry a greater bundle of things upon his back, unless he can afford one or two strong servants to attend him. I have often beheld two of those sages almost sinking under the weight of their packs, like pedlars among us; who, when they met in the streets, would lay down their loads, open their sacks and hold conversation for an hour together; then put up their implements, help each other to resume their burdens and take their leave.

But for short conversations a man may carry implements in his pockets and under his arms, enough to supply him, and in his house he cannot be at a loss. Therefore the room where company meet who practise this art, is full of all things ready at hand, requisite to furnish matter for this kind of artificial converse.

Another great advantage proposed by this invention, was that it would serve as an universal language to be understood in all civilized nations, whose goods and utensils are generally of the same kind, or nearly resembling, so that their uses might easily be comprehended. And thus ambassadors would be qualified to treat with foreign princes or ministers of state, to whose tongues they were utter strangers.

I was at the mathematical school, where the master taught his pupils after a method scarce imaginable to us in Europe. The proposition and demonstration were fairly written on a thin wafer, with ink composed of a cephalic tincture. This the student was to swallow upon a fasting stomach, and for three days following eat nothing but bread and water. As the wafer digested, the tincture mounted to his brain, bearing the proposition along with it. But the success hath not hitherto been answerable, partly by some error in the *quantum* or composition and partly by the perverseness of lads, to whom this bolus is so nauseous, that they generally steal aside, and discharge it upwards before it can operate; neither have they been yet persuaded to use so long an abstinence as the prescription requires.

(185–6)

John Arbuthnot

from a letter to Jonathan Swift   5 November 1726 (reprinted in *Correspondence*, vol. 3)

Your books shall be sent as directed. They have been printed above a month, but I cannot get my subscribers' names. I will make over all my profits to you for the property of *Gulliver's Travels*, which I believe will have as great a run as John Bunyan. Gulliver is a happy man that at his age can write such a merry work.

I made my Lord Archbishop's compliment to Her Royal Highness, who returns his Grace her thanks. At the same time Mrs Howard read your letter to herself. The Princess immediately seized on your plaid for her own use, and has ordered the young princesses to be clad in the same. When I had the honour to see her, she was reading *Gulliver* and was just come to the passage of the hobbling prince, which she laughed at. I tell you freely the part of the projectors is the least brilliant. . . .

Gulliver is in everybody's hands. Lord Scarborough, who is no inventor of stories, told me that he fell in company with a master of a ship, who told him that he was very well acquainted with *Gulliver*, but that the printer had mistaken, that he lived in Wapping and not in Rotherhith. I lent the book to an old gentleman, who went immediately to his map to search for Lilliput.

(179–80)

John Gay

from a letter to Jonathan Swift   17 November 1726 (reprinted in *Correspondence*, vol. 3)

About ten days ago a book was published here of the travels of one Gulliver, which hath been the conversation of the whole town ever since. The whole impression sold in a week, and nothing is more diverting than to hear the different opinions people give of it, though all agree in liking it extremely. 'Tis generally said that you are the author, but I am told the bookseller declares he knows not from what hand it came. From the highest to the lowest it is universally read, from the cabinet council to the nursery. The politicians to a man agree that it is free from particular reflections, but that the satire on general societies of men is too severe. Not but we now and then meet with people of greater perspicuity who are in search of particular applications in every leaf; and it is highly probable we shall have keys published to give light into Gulliver's design. Your Lord [Bolingbroke] is the person who least approves it, blaming it as a design of evil consequence to depreciate human nature, at which it cannot be wondered that he takes most offence, being himself the most accomplished of his species, and so losing more than any other of that praise which is due both to the dignity and virtue of a man. Your friend, my Lord Harcourt, commends it very much, though he thinks in some places the matter too far carried. The Duchess Dowager of Marlborough is in raptures at it: she says she can dream of nothing else since she read it; she declares that she hath now found out that her whole life hath been lost in caressing the worst part of mankind, and treating the best as her foes; and that if she knew Gulliver, though he had been the worst enemy she ever had, she would give up all her present acquaintance for his friendship. You may see by this that you are not much injured by being supposed the author of this piece. If you are, you have disobliged us and two or three of your best friends in not giving us the least hint of it while you were with us; and in particular Dr Arbuthnot who says it is ten thousand pities he had not known it, he could have added such abundance of things upon every subject. Among lady critics, some have found out that Mr Gulliver had a particular malice to maids of honour. Those of

them who frequent the Church say his design is impious and that it is an insult on providence by depreciating the works of the Creator. Notwithstanding, I am told the Princess hath read it with great pleasure. As to other critics, they think the flying island is the least entertaining; and so great an opinion the town have of the impossibility of Gulliver's writing at all below himself, that 'tis agreed that part was not writ by the same hand, though this hath its defenders too. It hath passed Lords and Commons, *nemine contradicente*, and the whole town, men, women and children are quite full of it.
(182-3)

Alexander Pope

from a letter to Jonathan Swift   16 November 1726 (reprinted in *Correspondence*, vol. 3)

I find no considerable man very angry at the book [*Gulliver's Travels*]. Some indeed think it rather too bold, and too general a satire, but none that I hear of accuse it of particular reflections (I mean no persons of consequence or good judgement: the mob of critics, you know, always are desirous to apply satire to those that they envy for being above them) so that you needed not to have been so secret upon this head. Motte received the copy (he tells me) he knew not from whence nor from whom, dropped at his house in the dark, from a hackney-coach. By computing the time I found it was after you left England, so for my part I suspend my judgement.
(181)

Jonathan Swift

from a letter to Mrs Howard   27 November 1726 (reprinted in *Correspondence*, vol. 3)

The stuffs you require are making, because the weaver piques himself upon having them in perfection, but he has read Gulliver's book, and has no conception of what you mean by returning money, for he is become a proselyte of the Houyhnhnms, whose great principle (if I rightly remember) is benevolence. And as to myself, I am rightly affronted with such a base proposal that I am determined to complain of you to Her Royal Highness, that you are a mercenary Yahoo fond of shining pebbles. What have I to do with you or your Court further than to show the esteem I have for your person, because you happen to deserve it, and my gratitude to Her Royal Highness, who was pleased a little to distinguish me; which, by the way, is the greatest compliment I ever made, and may probably be the last. For I am not such a prostitute flatterer as Gulliver; whose chief study is to extenuate the vices and magnify the virtues of mankind, and perpetually dins our ears with the praises of his country in the midst of corruptions, and for that reason alone hath found so many readers, and probably will have a pension, which I suppose was his chief design in writing. As for his compliments to the ladies, I can easily forgive him as a natural effect of that devotion which our sex always ought to pay to yours.

(187)

Alexander Pope

from *The Dunciad*   1728 (reprinted in J. Sutherland (ed.),
The Dunciad, 2nd edn, 1953)

O Thou! whatever title please thine ear,
Dean, Drapier, Bickerstaff, or Gulliver!
Whether thou chuse Cervantes' serious air,
Or laugh and shake in Rab'lais' easy chair,
Or praise the Court, or magnify Mankind,
Or thy griev'd Country's copper chains unbind;
From thy Boeotia tho' her Pow'r retires,
Mourn not, my Swift, at ought our Realm acquires,
Here pleas'd behold her mighty wings out-spread
To hatch a new Saturnian age of Lead.

(I 19–28)

Jonathan Swift

from 'The Intelligencer'   1728 (reprinted in *Prose Writings*, vol. 12)

(Of Humour) By what disposition of the mind, what influence of the stars or what situation of the climate, this endowment is bestowed upon mankind, may be a question fit for philosophers to discuss. It is certainly the best ingredient toward that kind of satire which is most useful and gives the least offence; which, instead of lashing, laughs men out of their follies and vices; and is the character that gives Horace the preference to Juvenal. And although some things are too serious, solemn or sacred to be turned into ridicule, yet the abuses of them are certainly not; since it is allowed that corruptions in religion, politics and law may be proper topic for this kind of satire.

   There are two ends that men propose in writing satire, one of them less noble than the other as regarding nothing further than the private satisfaction and pleasure of the writer; yet without any view towards personal malice. The other is a public spirit prompting men of genius and virtue to mend the world as far as they are able. And as both these ends are innocent, so the latter is highly commendable. With regard to the former, I demand whether I have not as good a title to laugh as men have to be ridiculous; and to expose vice, as another hath to be vicious. If I ridicule the follies and corruptions of a court, a ministry or a senate, are they not amply paid by pensions, titles and power; while I expect and desire no other reward than that of laughing with a few friends in a corner? Yet if those who take offence think me in the wrong, I am ready to change the scene with them, whenever they please.

(33–4)

John Oldmixon

from *The Arts of Logic and Rhetorick*   1728

This delicate author [Pope] has written a rhyming *Essay on Criticism*, and made himself merry with his brethren in a notable treatise called *The Art of Sinking*, to which he and his partner S(wif)t have

contributed, more than all the rest of their contemporary writers, if trifling and grimace are not in the high parts of writing. . . . What a precipice is it from Locke's Human Understanding to Swift's Lilliput and Profundity . . . there might have been hopes of rising again, but we sink now like ships laden with lead, and must despair of ever recovering the height from which we have fallen.
(416–17)

Jonathan Swift

from *Verses on the Death of Dr Swift* 1731 (reprinted in *Poems*, vol. 2)

In Pope I cannot read a line,
But with a sigh I wish it mine;
Yet he can in one couplet fix
More sense than I can do in six;
It gives me such a jealous fit,
I cry, 'Pox take him and his wit!'
I grieve to be outdone by Gay
In my own hum'rous biting way.
Arbuthnot is no more my friend,
Who dares to irony pretend,
Which I was born to introduce,
Refin'd it first, and shew'd its use.
St John, as well as Pultney, knows
That I had some repute for prose;
And, till they drove me out of date
Could maul a minister of state.
If they have mortify'd my pride,
And made me throw my pen aside;
If with such talents Heav'n has blest 'em,
Have I not reason to detest 'em?
    To all my foes, dear Fortune, send
Thy gifts; but never to my friend.
I tamely can endure the first;
But this with envy makes me burst. . . .
    Perhaps I may allow the Dean,

Had too much satire in his vein;
And seem'd determined not to starve it,
Because no age could more deserve it.
Yet malice never was his aim;
He lash'd the vice, but spared the name;
No individual could resent,
Where thousands equally were meant;
His satire points at no defect,
But what all mortals may correct;
For he abhorr'd that senseless tribe
Who call it humour when they gibe.
He spared a hump, or crooked nose,
Whose owners set not up for beaux.
True genuine dullness moved his pity,
Unless it offer'd to be witty.
(555, 571–2)

Jonathan Swift

from a letter to Charles Wogan   July–2 August 1732 (reprinted in
Correspondence, vol. 4)

As I am conjectured to have generally dealt in raillery and satire,
both in prose and verse, if that conjecture be right, although such an
opinion hath been an absolute bar to my rising in the world, yet that
very world must suppose that I followed what I thought to be my
talent, and charitable people will suppose I had a design to laugh the
follies of mankind out of countenance, and as often to lash the vices
out of practice. And then it will be natural to conclude that I have
some partiality for such kind of writing, and favour it in others. I
think you acknowledge that in some time of your life you turned to
the rallying part, but I find at present your genius runs wholly into
the grave and sublime, and therefore I find you less indulgent to my
way by your dislike of the *Beggar's Opera*, in the persons particularly
of Polly Peachum and Macheath; whereas we think it a very severe
satire upon the most pernicious villainies of mankind. And so you
are in danger of quarrelling with the sentiments of Mr Pope, Mr Gay

the author, Dr Arbuthnot, myself, Dr Young, and all the brethren
whom we own. Dr Young is the gravest among us, and yet his satires
have many mixtures of sharp raillery.
(53)

Voltaire

Letter 22 in *Letters Concerning the English Nation*   1733 (4th edn, 1739)

Whoever sets up for a commentator of smart sayings and repartees is
himself a blockhead. This is the reason why the works of the ingenious
Dean Swift, who hath been called the English Rabelais, will never be
well understood in France. This gentleman has the honour (in common with Rabelais) of being a priest, and like him laughs at everything. But in my humble opinion the title of the English Rabelais
which is given the Dean is highly derogatory to his genius. The
former hath interspersed his unaccountably fantastic and unintelligible book with the most gay strokes of humour, but which at the
same time hath a greater proportion of impertinence. He hath been
vastly lavish of erudition, of smut and insipid raillery. An agreeable
tale of two pages is purchased at the expense of whole volumes of
nonsense. There are but few persons, and those of a grotesque taste,
who pretend to understand and to esteem this work; for as to the rest
of the nation, they laugh at the pleasant and diverting touches which
are found in Rabelais and despise his book. He is looked upon as the
Prince of Buffoons. The readers are vexed to think that a man who
was master of so much wit should have made so wretched a use of it.
He is an intoxicated philosopher, who never writ but when he was in
liquor.

Dean Swift is Rabelais in his senses, and frequenting the politest
company. The former indeed is not so gay as the latter, but then he
possesseth all the delicacy, the justness, the choice, the good taste, in
all which particulars our giggling rural vicar Rabelais is wanting. The
poetical numbers of Dean Swift are of a singular and almost inimitable taste; true humour whether in prose or verse seems to be his
peculiar talent, but whoever is desirous of understanding him perfectly must visit the island in which he was born.
(181–2)

Jonathan Swift

from a letter to the Reverend Henry Clarke 12 December 1734
(reprinted in *Correspondence*, vol. 4)

I quarrel at your author, as I do with all writers and many of your
preachers, for their careless incorrect and improper style, which they
contract by reading the scribblers from England, where an abominable taste is every day prevailing. It is your business who are coming
into the world to put a stop to these corruptions, and recover that
simplicity which in everything of value ought chiefly to be followed.
(274)

Jonathan Swift

from a letter to William Pulteney 7 March 1737 (reprinted in
Correspondence, vol. 5)

I desire that my prescription of living may be published, which you
design to follow, for the benefit of mankind, which however I do not
value a rush, nor the animal itself as it now acts; neither will I ever
value myself as a Philanthropus, because it is now a creature (taking
a vast majority) that I hate more than a toad, a viper, a wasp, a stock,
a fox or any other that you will please to add.
(7)

Henry Fielding

from *Amelia* 1751 (reprinted in *Complete Works: Amelia*,
vol. 2, 1967)

As Booth was therefore what might well be called, in this age at
least, a man of learning, he began to discourse our author on subjects
of literature. 'I think, sir,' says he, 'that Dr Swift hath been generally
allowed, by the critics in this kingdom, to be the greatest master of
humour that ever wrote. Indeed, I allow him to have possessed most

admirable talents of this kind; and, if Rabelais was his master, I think he proves the truth of the common Greek proverb – that the scholar is often superior to the master. As to Cervantes, I do not think we can make any just comparison; for, though Mr Pope compliments him with sometimes taking Cervantes's serious air. . . .' 'I remember the passage,' cries the author:

O thou, whatever title please thine ear,
Dean, Drapier, Bickerstaff, or Gulliver;
Whether you take Cervantes' serious air,
Or laugh and shake in Rabelais' easy chair.

'You are right, sir,' said Booth; 'but though I should agree that the doctor hath sometimes condescended to imitate Rabelais, I do not re-member to have seen in his works the least attempt in the manner of Cervantes. But there is one in his own way, and whom I am con-vinced he studied above all others – you guess, I believe, I am going to name Lucian. This author, I say, I am convinced, he followed; but I think he followed him at a distance: as, to say the truth, every other writer of this kind hath done in my opinion; for none, I think, hath yet equalled him.'
(83–4)

Part Two The Developing Debate

Introduction

Commentaries on Swift, after his death in 1745, were largely
biographical: concerned with his character, his relations with
Stella and Vanessa, his participation in public life, his friendship
with the Tory wits. Early biographers attacked or defended his
reputation, but his writings were not closely examined for their
own sake; their relevance was deemed to be moral and
biographical. Of the first accounts (Orrery, 1752; Delany, 1754;
Deane Swift, 1755; Hawkesworth, 1755) only Orrery's has
anything of critical significance to offer. The question of Swift's
misanthropy, for instance, was inescapable; in such considerations,
the works were read for the light they cast upon Swift's character.[1]
The fourth Book of *Gulliver's Travels* became the classic text of
dispute. In *Conjectures on Original Composition* (1759) Edward
Young attacked it as an abomination, a blasphemy: 'he has
blasphemed a nature a little lower than that of angels and assumed
by far higher than they' (see p. 77). The same denunciation is
heard in the critical commentaries upon the *Travels* until late in the
nineteenth century: it may still be heard, now and again.

Swift's misanthropy and the obscenity of the fourth Book of
Gulliver's Travels have been standard themes, then, since the middle
of the eighteenth century. Moral philosophers denounced the
Yahoos in terms similar to Samuel Johnson's: 'he that formed
those images had nothing filthy to learn'. Thackeray's outburst is a
famous occasion in the history of nineteenth-century feeling. But
objection to the Houyhnhnms is more interesting. 'Their virtuous
qualities are only negative,' Orrery maintained; a position of great
critical moment, since it anticipates one of the most celebrated
modern essays on Swift, F. R. Leavis's: the Houyhnhnms 'may
have all the reason, but the Yahoos have all the life'. Coleridge,
too, took a severe view of the Houyhnhnms, but he thought it
more important to concentrate upon the inconsistency of the book
rather than upon its misanthropy. The debate on this matter,
started in Orrery's *Remarks*, still persists: that *Gulliver's Travels* is a

classic work is proved by the fact that every reader has his own sense of it, and the book itself is patient in every quarrel.

Of Swift's style, little was said in the years after his death; that he possessed a formidable style was commonly acknowledged, but readers did not feel inclined to pursue the matter. The style was not seriously questioned until later in the century. Two developments may be remarked. From about 1770 on, it became fashionable to set Swift's style against Addison's, and to prefer Addison's. It was a mark of the reigning sensibility to consider Swift's style hard and dry, aggressively plain, pedantic in its refusal of grace; while Addison was thought to be the model of fine writing, elegance, urbanity. The values upon which this preference depends were sponsored, indeed, by Addison himself in *Pleasures of Imagination*; in time, he did a lot to create the audience by which he was praised. John Locke did even more. Northrop Frye has called these years the Age of Sensibility. By any name, they make a period in which Swift's style was rebuked; it was, as styles go, too rigid, too objective, it did not cultivate the reasons of the heart. For sturdier reasons, Johnson criticized Swift's style: it was good for handling facts and putting things in order, for counting up to ten and getting the sum right, but for any loftier occasion it was inadequate. It might be praised, short of the highest praise. (Professor Wimsatt has considered the question of Swift and Johnson and the factors which account for Johnson's dislike of Swift's style: the relevant passage from *The Prose Style of Samuel Johnson* is given on p. 174.)

But the consideration of Swift as a novelist had not yet begun. Swift belonged to the Art of Prose, apparently, but not yet to the Art of Fiction. Indeed, the first serious account of Swift as a novelist was given by John Dunlop in his *History of Fiction* (1814), serious in the sense that it proposed a critical comparison between *Gulliver's Travels* and *Robinson Crusoe* as fictions. The comparison was welcomed by Sir Walter Scott, the same year, in his edition of

Swift. But Scott went much further than Dunlop: he emphasized Swift's power of sustaining a fictional character, his dramatic imagination. Swift's status in the development of English fiction was then acknowledged; though it may still be argued that *Gulliver's Travels* is on the margin of that development, rather than a central work. In any event, the art of fiction was just beginning to be received as a respectable concern; Swift was included in the new theme.

Meanwhile, Swift's poems were largely neglected: they could not be assimilated to the spirit of the age. Hazlitt, indeed, was the first critic to take them seriously, and his place in the criticism of Swift is important for that reason. He was not content to say that the poems achieved what they set out to achieve. It was also Hazlitt who put the question of Swift's misanthropy in perspective: the argument had gone too far. The result was that certain parts of Swift's work, long ignored, now began to receive some attention. Even the consideration of Swift's style was modified. De Quincey thought it worth saying that Gulliver's style is dull, but purposely and properly dull, since the man is a sea-captain, garrulous and prosaic. De Quincey's review (see p. 116) seems to be the first occasion on which Gulliver was represented as separate from Jonathan Swift. The separation has now become one of the axioms of modern criticism; in fact, its success in the world may already be excessive. It is quite possible to argue that Gulliver and Swift are much closer in their typical attitudes than twentieth-century readers are prepared to admit. This dispute is not settled: some readers insist that Gulliver is, from first to last, the victim of Swift's irony: others maintain that, for the most part, Swift endorses Gulliver. De Quincey's treatment of Gulliver as a fictional character is not in itself remarkable: it is consistent, for instance, with the terms of Dunlop and Scott. But it defined and then released certain possibilities in the interpretation of the *Travels*: we have not heard the last of them yet.

In the later years of the nineteenth century Swift seems to have receded somewhat from the central concerns of criticism. Perhaps he could not survive Thackeray's attack, in the common mind. Certainly the gay science of criticism had little to say of him in those years. It is significant that Henry James, voluminous on many writers, had merely a remark to offer on Swift. In the great question of the novel, Swift was not considered crucial: it was not necessary to name him with Balzac, Flaubert, George Eliot. Even in the first decades of the twentieth century, Swift's force was felt more directly in certain mythologies than in literature and criticism. For Joyce, Swift was a mythological figure. Joyce read in Marsh's Library, a few yards from St Patrick's Cathedral in Dublin, the *Prophecies* of Joachim: the occasion is given in simple terms in *Stephen Hero*, much more elaborately in *Ulysses*, where Swift's ghost haunts the early chapters. But Swift's works are not as vivid to Joyce as his presence, the risk, the fate he enacted. He is a crucial figure in Yeats's landscape, too, not only in *The Words upon the Window Pane* but wherever Yeats meditates upon the the themes of Irish history and the heroic ideal. Swift is also present in the *Four Quartets* of T. S. Eliot: the 'familiar compound ghost' of 'Little Gidding' is a compound of Dante's Brunetto Latini, Swift and the aged Yeats, their common lesson a wisdom of disenchantment. Indeed, it is not fanciful to say that in Dr Leavis's essay on 'The Irony of Swift' (in his *Determinations*), too, Swift is confronted as a figure from myth, not a great writer but a great scandal. Swift is scandalous to any critic who insists that great literature is necessarily the embodiment of 'moral grandeur'. If, as Dr Leavis elsewhere argues, the central tradition of the English novel is marked at its crucial moments by Jane Austen, George Eliot, Conrad, Henry James and D. H. Lawrence; if Lawrence is deemed, in certain essential respects, the moral culmination of the whole enterprise; and if Lawrence is exceeded in these crucial respects only by the Tolstoy of *Anna Karenina*: it is question what part, if any, Swift can be allowed to play. Dr Leavis's argument is that Swift specializes in 'negative emotions'. There are certain writings of Swift to which the more applicable word is, indeed, 'critical' rather than 'negative':

– notably, the pamphlets or pamphleteering essays in which the irony is instrumental, directed and limited to a given end. The *Argument against Abolishing Christianity* and *A Modest Proposal*, for instance, are discussable in the terms in which satire is commonly discussed: as the criticism of vice, folly or other aberration, by some kind of reference to positive standards. But even here, even in the *Argument*, where Swift's ironic intensity undeniably directs itself to the defence of something that he is intensely concerned to defend, the effect is essentially negative. The positive itself appears only negatively – a kind of skeletal presence, rigid enough, but without life or body; a necessary pre-condition, as it were, of directed negation. The intensity is purely destructive.

Swift's irony ('a matter of surprise and negation') is compared to Gibbon's (which 'habituates and reassures'). Dr Leavis's essay ends:

We have, then, in his writings probably the most remarkable expression of negative feelings and attitudes that literature can offer – the spectacle of creative powers (the paradoxical description seems right) exhibited consistently in negation and rejection. . . .

A great writer – yes; that account still imposes itself as fitting, though his greatness is no matter of moral grandeur or human centrality; our sense of it is merely a sense of great force. And this force, as we feel it, is conditioned by frustration and constriction; the channels of life have been blocked and perverted. That we should be so often invited to regard him as a moralist and an idealist would seem to be mainly a witness to the power of vanity, and the part that vanity can play in literary appreciation: *saeva indignatio* is an indulgence that solicits us all, and the use of literature by readers and critics for the projection of nobly suffering selves is familiar. No doubt, too, it is pleasant to believe that unusual capacity for egotistic animus means unusual distinction of intellect; but, as we have seen, there is no reason to lay stress on intellect in Swift. His work does indeed exhibit an extraordinary play of mind; but it is not great intellectual force that is exhibited in his indifference to the problems raised – in, for instance, the *Voyage to the Houyhnhnms* – by his use of the concept, or the word 'nature'. It is not merely that he had an Augustan contempt for metaphysics; he shared the shallowest complacencies of Augustan common sense: his irony might destroy these, but there is no conscious criticism.

He was, in various ways, curiously unaware – the reverse of clairvoyant. He is distinguished by the intensity of his feelings, not by insight into them, and he certainly does not impress us as a mind in possession of its experience.

We shall not find Swift remarkable for intelligence if we think of Blake.

In Dr Leavis's essay Swift is of the devil's party: that last sentence stands for a moral argument conducted not in this essay but in other books by Dr Leavis, especially in *D. H. Lawrence: Novelist*. Swift is the greatest figure in Dr Leavis's demonology, the brightest of those fallen angels who were damned by their own insistence. He is a scandal because he subverts the values for which, in the eyes of a morally determined critic, great literature exists. Dr Leavis's essay is famous, for good reason: the experience of reading Swift, of being affronted by him, has never been more powerfully enacted. But the argument of the essay is vulnerable, especially in its recourse to 'positive' and 'negative' as evaluative terms. Lawrence, reviewing Rozanov, said that in *The Apocalypse of Our Times*, 'we get what we have got from no Russian, neither Tolstoy nor Dostoyevsky nor any of them, a real, positive view on life'. But he immediately clarified and justified this rhetoric by appeal to Rozanov's 'vast old pagan background, the phallic' (*Phoenix*, p. 369). The reader is free to take or leave this critical argument; in any event he knows what Lawrence intends by 'a real, positive view on life'. With Dr Leavis, he is not certain, despite the rhetorical and critical emphasis in *Revaluation*, *The Great Tradition*, *The Common Pursuit* and the other books. Besides, even on the general question, Dr Leavis does not allow for the sense in which it is a mark of great literature to be subversive.

The essay deserves to be challenged in detail. For instance: much of the argument culminates in the paragraph in which Dr Leavis quotes Swift on the possession of being well deceived, 'the serene peaceful state of being a fool among knaves'. What is left, Dr Leavis asks? But there is plenty left. To be a fool among knaves is to be any of the following: Wordsworthian child, Platonic poet, king's jester, Franciscan saint, Erasmus's hero, Cervantes's knight, Horace's man of retirement, Marvell's gardener. The present editor has argued (*Jonathan Swift: A Critical Introduction*, 1969, pp. 45 ff.) that Swift means, for his 'fool', no less a personage than Temple, who gave up the busy work of politics and diplomacy and retired to his garden. This is folly in Erasmus's tradition; a perfectly coherent, indeed impregnable, form of life, set off against the vanity of successful knaves. The problem is to estimate the ingredient of irony in 'serene' and 'peaceful', if 'fool' is more respectable than Dr Leavis allowed: the logic now requires that the first two be taken as much less ironic than readers of Swift have assumed.

John Boyle, Fifth Earl of Orrery

from *Remarks on the Life and Writings of Dr Jonathan Swift* 1752

If we consider his prose works, we shall find a certain masterly conciseness in their style that has never been equalled by any other writer. The truth of this assertion will more evidently appear by comparing him with some of the authors of his own time. Of these, Dr Tillotson and Mr Addison are to be numbered among the most eminent. Addison has all the powers that can captivate and improve: his diction is easy, his periods are well turned, his expressions are flowing and his humour is delicate. Tillotson is nervous, grave, majestic and perspicuous. We must join both these characters together to form a true idea of Dr Swift: yet as he outdoes Addison in humour, he excels Tillotson in perspicuity. The Archbishop indeed confined himself to subjects relative to his profession: but Addison and Swift are more diffusive writers. They continually vary in their manner, and treat different topics in a different style. When the writings of Addison terminate in party, he loses himself extremely, and from a delicate and just comedian, deviates into one of the lowest kind. Not so Dr Swift: he appears like a masterly gladiator. He wields the sword of party with ease, justness and dexterity: and while he entertains the ignorant and the vulgar, he draws an equal attention from the learned and the great. When he is serious, his gravity becomes him. When he laughs, his readers must laugh with him. But what shall be said for his love of trifles and his want of delicacy and decorum? Errors, that if he did not contract, at least he increased in Ireland. They are without a parallel. I hope they will ever remain so. The first of them arose merely from his love of flattery, with which he was daily fed in that kingdom; the second proceeded from the misanthropy of his disposition, which induced him peevishly to debase mankind, and even to ridicule human nature itself. . . .

Swift deduces his observations from wrong principles; for in his land of Houyhnhnms he considers the soul and body in their most degenerate and uncultivated state, the former as a slave to the appetites of the latter. He seems insensible of the surprising mechanism and beauty of every part of the human composition. He forgets the fine description which Ovid gives of mankind:

Os homini sublime dedit, caelumque tueri
Jussit, et erectos ad sidera tollere vultus.

In painting Yahoos he becomes one himself. Nor is the picture which he draws of the Houyhnhnms inviting or amusing. It wants both light and shade to adorn it. It is cold and insipid. We there view the pure instincts of brutes, unassisted by any knowledge of letters, acting within their own narrow sphere, merely for their immediate preservation. They are incapable of doing wrong, therefore they act right. It is surely a very low character given to creatures in whom the author would insinuate some degree of reason, that they act inoffensively, when they have neither the motive nor the power to act otherwise. Their virtuous qualities are only negative. Swift himself, amidst all his irony, must have confessed that to moderate our passions, to extend our munificence to others, to enlarge our understanding and to raise our idea of the Almighty by contemplating his works is not only the business but often the practice and the study of the human mind.

(62–4, 188–9)

Patrick Delany

from Observations upon Lord Orrery's 'Remarks on the Life and Writings of Dr Jonathan Swift' 1754

For the rest, [Swift's] whole reasoning tends to no other purpose than to establish that principle, long since exploded in the schools, that would infer the disuse of all things most valuable and desirable in the world from their abuse: kings, ministers, laws, physic, wine, riches, love, etc. But what he means by the acuteness of his master Houyhnhnm which daily convinced him of a thousand faults in himself, whereof he had not the least perception before, and which with us would never be numbered even among human infirmities, I confess I can neither comprehend nor conceive.

Upon the whole, I am clearly of opinion that he would more

effectually have endeavoured to amend mankind by putting the virtues and the suited practice of one, even imaginary good man in a fair and amiable light than by painting the depravities of the whole species in the most odious colours and attitudes. Who would not wish rather to be the author of one *Arcadia* than fifty *Laputas*, *Lilliputs* and *Houyhnhnms*?

I am fully satisfied that exaggerated satire never yet did any good nor ever will. The only satire that can do any good is that which shows mankind to themselves in their true light, and exposes those follies, vices and corruptions of every kind in all their absurdities, deformities and horrors, which flattery, self-love and passions of any kind had hitherto hid from their eyes. That magnifying glass which enlarges all the deformed features into monstrous dimensions defeats its own purpose, for no man will ever know his own likeness in it and consequently, though he may be shocked, he will not be amended by it.

I cannot help thinking that if Swift had recovered one hour of rational reflection after the final chastisement of his total infatuation, he would have numbered his latter works among the follies of his life, and lamented himself in a strain something like those lines which I have somewhere met with:

O life how art thou made a scene,
    Of follies first and last;
Rejoicing in the present train,
    Repining at the past.

I am sick of this subject; and now have done with everything relating to Swift, except some particularities in his conduct and character which could not have fallen under your notice.
(170–72)

Deane Swift

from *An Essay upon the Life, Writings and Character of Dr Jonathan Swift* 1755

Gulliver's voyage to Lilliput, as well as the voyage to Brobdingnag, the machinery and some particular sallies of nature, wit and humour only excepted, is entirely political. His meaning throughout the whole, especially where he glances at the history of his own times, the wars of Europe and the factions of Whig and Tory, is to be found so very near the surface that it would almost be an affront to the common reason of those who are at all versed in the affairs of the world to offer at any further explication.

(217)

John Wesley

from *The Doctrine of Original Sin, According to Scripture, Reason, and Experience* 1756 (reprinted in *Works*, n.d., vol. 9)

Are Protestant nations nothing concerned in that humorous but terrible picture, drawn by a late eminent hand?

He was perfectly astonished (and who would not, if it were the first time he had heard it?) at the historical account I gave him of our affairs during the last century; protesting it was only a heap of conspiracies, rebellions, murders, massacres; the very worst effects that avarice, faction, hypocrisy, perfidiousness, cruelty, rage, madness, hatred, envy, lust, malice and ambition could produce. Even in times of peace, how many innocent and excellent persons have been condemned to death or banishment, by great ministers practising upon the corruption of judges and the malice of factions? How many villains have been exalted to the highest places of trust, power, dignity and profit! By what methods have great numbers, in all countries, procured titles of honour and vast estates! Perjury, oppression, subornation, fraud, panderism, were some of the most excusable; for many owed their greatness to sodomy or incest; others, to the prostituting of their own wives or daughters; others, to the betraying of their country, or their prince; more, to the perverting of justice to destroy the innocent (XI 132).

Well might that keen author add, 'If a creature pretending to reason can be guilty of such enormities, certainly the corruption of that faculty is far worse than brutality itself.'

Now, are Popish nations only concerned in this? Are the Protestants quite clear? Is there no such thing among them (to take one instance only) as 'perverting of justice', even in public courts of judicature? Can it not be said in any Protestant country:

There is a society of men among us, bred up from their
youth in the art of proving, according as they are paid, by
words multiplied for the purpose, that white is black and
black is white? For example, if my neighbour has a mind to
my cow, he hires a lawyer to prove that he ought to have
my cow from me. I must hire another to defend my right, it
being against all rules of law that a man should speak for
himself. In pleading, they do not dwell on the merits of the
cause, but upon circumstances foreign thereto. For instance,
they do not take the shortest method to know what title my
adversary has to my cow; but whether the cow be red or
black, her horns long or short; whether the field she grazes
in be round or square, and the like. After which, they
adjourn the cause from time to time; and in ten or twenty
years' time they come to an issue. This society, likewise, has
a peculiar cant and jargon of their own, in which all their
laws are written. And these they take special care to
multiply; whereby they have so confounded truth and
falsehood, right and wrong, that it will take twelve years to
decide, whether the field, left me by my ancestors for six
generations, belong to me or to one three hundred miles off
(XI 248–50).

Is it in Popish countries only that it can be said: 'It does not appear that any one perfection is required towards the procurement of any one station among you; much less, that men are ennobled on account of their virtue; that priests are advanced for their piety or learning, judges for their integrity, senators for the love of their country, or counsellors for their wisdom?'

But there is a still greater and more undeniable proof that the very foundations of all things, civil and religious, are utterly out of course in the Christian as well as the heathen world. There is a still more horrid reproach to the Christian name, yea, to the name of man, to all reason and humanity. There is war in the world! War between men! War between Christians! I mean, between those that bear the name of Christ, and profess to 'walk as he also walked'. Now, who can reconcile war, I will not say to religion, but to any degree of reason or common sense?

But is there not a cause? O yes: 'The causes of war,' as the same writer observes,

are innumerable. Some of the chief are these: the ambition of princes; or the corruption of their ministers: difference of opinion, as whether flesh be bread or bread be flesh, whether the juice of the grape be blood or wine, what is the best colour for a coat, whether black, white or grey, and whether it should be long or short, whether narrow or wide. Nor are there any wars so furious as those occasioned by such difference of opinions.

Sometimes two princes make a war to decide which of them shall dispossess a third of his dominions. Sometimes a war is commenced, because another prince is too strong; sometimes, because he is too weak. Sometimes our neighbours want the things which we have, or have the things which we want; so both fight, until they take ours, or we take theirs. It is a reason for invading a country, if the people have been wasted by famine, destroyed by pestilence or embroiled by faction; or to attack our nearest ally, if part of his land would make our dominions more round and compact (XI 245–6).

Another cause of making war is this: a crew are driven by a storm they know not where; at length they make the land and go ashore; they are entertained with kindness. They give the country a new name, set up a stone or rotten plank for a memorial, murder a dozen of the natives and bring away a couple by force. Here commences a new right of dominion; ships are sent, and the natives driven out or destroyed. And this is done to civilize and convert a barbarous and idolatrous people (XI 294).

But, whatever be the cause, let us calmly and impartially consider the thing itself. Here are forty thousand men gathered together on this plain. What are they going to do? See, there are thirty or forty thousand more at a little distance. And these are going to shoot them through the head or body, to stab them, or split their skulls and send most of their souls into everlasting fire, as fast as they possibly can. Why so? What harm have they done to them? O none at all! They do not so much as know them. But a man, who is King of France, has a quarrel with another man, who is King of England. So these Frenchmen are to kill as many of these Englishmen as they can, to prove the King of France is in the right. Now, what an argument is this! What a method of proof! What an amazing way of deciding controversies! What must mankind be, before such a thing as war could ever be known or thought of upon earth? How shocking, how inconceivable a want must there have been of common understanding, as well as common humanity, before any two governors, or any two nations in the universe, could once think of such a method of decision? If, then, all nations, pagan, Mahometan and Christian do, in fact, make this their last resort, what farther proof do we need of the utter degeneracy of all nations from the plainest principles of reason and virtue, of the absolute want, both of common sense and common humanity, which runs through the whole race of mankind?

In how just and strong a light is this placed by the writer cited before!

I gave him a description of cannons, muskets, pistols, swords,
bayonets; of sieges, attacks, mines, countermines,
bombardments; of engagements by sea and land; ships sunk
with a thousand men, twenty thousand killed on each side,
dying groans, limbs flying in the air; smoke, noise,
trampling to death under horses' feet; flight, pursuit, victory;
fields strewed with carcases, left for food to dogs and beasts of
prey; and, farther, of plundering, stripping, ravishing,
burning and destroying. I assured him, I had seen a hundred
enemies blown up at once in a siege, and as many in a ship,
and beheld the dead bodies drop down in pieces from the
clouds, to the great diversion of the spectators (XI 247).

Is it not astonishing, beyond all expression, that this is the naked truth; that, within a short term of years, this has been the real case in almost every part of even the Christian world? And meanwhile we gravely talk of the 'dignity of our nature' in its present state! This is really surprising, and might easily drive even a well-tempered man to say:

One might bear with men, if they would be content with those vices and follies to which nature has entitled them. I am not provoked at the sight of a pickpocket, a gamester, a politician, a suborner, a traitor, or the like. This is all according to the natural course of things. But when I behold a lump of deformity and diseases, both in body and mind, smitten with pride, it breaks all the measures of my patience; neither shall I ever be able to comprehend how such an animal and such a vice can tally together (XI 296).

And surely all our declamations on the strength of human reason, and the eminence of our virtues, are no more than the cant and jargon of pride and ignorance, so long as there is such a thing as war in the world. Men in general can never be allowed to be reasonable creatures till they know not war any more. So long as this monster stalks uncontrolled, where is reason, virtue, humanity? They are utterly excluded; they have no place; they are a name, and nothing more. (220–23)

Edward Young

from *Conjectures on Original Composition* 1759

But as nothing is more easy than to write originally wrong, originals are not here recommended, but under the strong guard of my first rule – *Know Thyself*. Lucian, who was an original, neglected not this rule, if we may judge by his reply to one who took some freedom with him. He was, at first, an apprentice to a statuary; and when he was reflected on as such, by being called Prometheus, he replied, 'I am indeed the inventor of new work, the model of which I owe to none, and if I do not execute it well, I deserve to be torn by twelve vultures instead of one.'

If so, O Gulliver, dost thou not shudder at thy brother Lucian's vultures hovering o'er thee? Shudder on! They cannot shock thee more than decency has been shocked by thee. How have thy Houyhnhnms thrown thy judgement from its seat, and laid thy imagination in the mire? In what ordure hast thou dipped thy pencil? What a monster hast thou made of the 'human face divine'?

This writer has so satirized human nature as to give a demonstration in himself, that it deserves to be satirized. But, say his wholesale admirers, few could have so written; true, and fewer would. If it required great abilities to commit the fault, greater still would have saved him from it. But whence arise such warm advocates for such a performance? From hence; before a character is established, merit makes fame; afterwards, fame makes merit. Swift is not commended for this piece, but this piece for Swift. He has given us some beauties which deserve all our praise; and our comfort is, that his faults will not become common; for none can be guilty of them, but who have wit as well as reputation to spare. His wit had been less wild if his temper had not jostled his judgement. If his favourite Houyhnhnms could write, and Swift had been one of them, every horse with him would have been an ass, and he would have written a panegyric on mankind, saddling with much reproach the present heroes of his pen. On the contrary, being born amongst men and, of consequence, piqued by many and peevish at more, he has blasphemed a nature a little lower than that of angels and assumed by far higher than they. But surely the contempt of the world is not a greater virtue than the contempt of mankind is a vice. Therefore I wonder that, though forborne by others, the laughter-loving Swift was not reproved by the venerable Dean, who could sometimes be very grave.
(61–4)

Oliver Goldsmith

from 'A History of England' 1764 (reprinted in J. W. M. Gibbs (ed.), *Works*, vol. 5, 1886)

Dean Swift was the professed antagonist of both Addison and [Steele]. He perceived that there was a spirit of romance mixed with all the works of the poets who preceded him; or, in other words, that they had drawn nature on the most pleasing side. There still, therefore, was a place left for him who, careless of censure, should describe it just as it was, with all its deformities; he therefore owes much of his fame, not so much to the greatness of his genius, as to the boldness of it. He was dry, sarcastic and severe; and suited his style exactly to the turn of his thought, being concise and nervous. (345–6)

Samuel Johnson[1]

from 'Life of Swift' 1779–81 (reprinted in G. Birkbeck Hill (ed.), *Lives of the English Poets*, vol. 3, 1905)

Swift began early [around 1700] to think, or to hope, that he was a poet, and wrote Pindaric odes to Temple, to the King and to the Athenian Society, a knot of obscure men, who published a periodical pamphlet of answers to questions sent, or supposed to be sent, by letters. I have been told that Dryden, having perused these verses, said, 'Cousin Swift, you will never be a poet'; and that this denunciation was the motive of Swift's perpetual malevolence to Dryden. . . .

Swift was not one of those minds which amaze the world with early pregnancy; his first work, except his few poetical essays, was *A Discourse of the Contests and Dissensions between the Nobles and Commons in Athens and Rome*, published (1701) in his thirty-fourth year. After its appearance, paying a visit to some bishop, he heard mention made of the new pamphlet that Burnet had written, replete with political knowledge. When he seemed to doubt Burnet's right to the work he was told by the bishop that he was 'a young man' and, still persisting to doubt, that he was 'a very positive young man'.

Three years afterward (1704) was published *A Tale of a Tub*. Of this book charity may be persuaded to think that it might be written

---

1 There are a number of inaccuracies on publication dates of several of Swift's works, in this extract. Those concerned are: *The Conduct of the Allies*, published in 1711, not, as Johnson says, 1712; *A Proposal for Correcting, Improving and Ascertaining the English Tongue*, 1712 not 1711; *A Letter to the October Club*, 1712 not 1711; *Gulliver's Travels*, 1726 not 1727. [Ed.]

by a man of a peculiar character, without ill intention; but it is certainly of dangerous example. That Swift was its author, though it be universally believed, was never owned by himself, nor very well proved by any evidence; but no other claimant can be produced, and he did not deny it when Archbishop Sharpe and the Duchess of Somerset, by showing it to the Queen, debarred him from a bishopric.

When this wild work first raised the attention of the public, Sacheverell, meeting Smalridge, tried to flatter him by seeming to think him the author; but Smalridge answered with indignation, 'Not all that you and I have in the world, nor all that ever we shall have, should hire me to write *A Tale of a Tub*.'

The digressions relating to Wotton and Bentley must be confessed to discover want of knowledge or want of integrity; he did not understand the two controversies, or he willingly misrepresented them. But wit can stand its ground against truth only a little while. The honours due to learning have been justly distributed by the decision of posterity.

The Battle of the Books is so like the *Combat des Livres*, which the same question concerning the ancients and moderns had produced in France, that the improbability of such a coincidence of thoughts without communication is not, in my opinion, balanced by the anonymous protestation prefixed, in which all knowledge of the French book is peremptorily disowned.

For some time after Swift was probably employed in solitary study, gaining the qualifications requisite for future eminence. How often he visited England, and with what diligence he attended his parishes, I know not. It was not till about four years afterwards that he became a professed author, and then one year (1708) produced *The Sentiments of a Church-of-England Man*; the ridicule of Astrology, under the name of Bickerstaff; the *Argument against Abolishing Christianity*; and the defence of the Sacramental Test.

The Sentiments of a Church-of-England Man is written with great coolness, moderation, ease and perspicuity. The *Argument against Abolishing Christianity* is a very happy and judicious irony. One passage in it deserves to be selected.

If Christianity were once abolished, how could the
free-thinkers, the strong reasoners and the men of profound

learning be able to find another subject so calculated, in all points, whereon to display their abilities? What wonderful productions of wit should we be deprived of from those whose genius, by continual practice, hath been wholly turned upon raillery and invectives against religion, and would therefore never be able to shine, or distinguish themselves, upon any other subject? We are daily complaining of the great decline of wit among us, and would take away the greatest, perhaps the only, topic we have left. Who would ever have suspected Asgill for a wit or Toland for a philosopher, if the inexhaustible stock of Christianity had not been at hand to provide them with materials? What other subject, through all art or nature, could have produced Tindal for a profound author, or furnished him with readers? It is the wise choice of the subject that alone adorns and distinguishes the writer. For had a hundred such pens as these been employed on the side of religion, they would have immediately sunk into silence and oblivion (11 36).

The reasonableness of a test is not hard to be proved; but perhaps it must be allowed that the proper test has not been chosen.

The attention paid to the papers published under the name of Bickerstaff induced Steele, when he projected the *Tatler*, to assume an appellation which had already gained possession of the reader's notice.

In the year following he wrote *A Project for the Advancement of Religion*, addressed to Lady Berkeley, by whose kindness it is not unlikely that he was advanced to his benefices. To this project, which is formed with great purity of intention and displayed with spriteliness and elegance, it can only be objected that, like many projects, it is, if not generally impracticable, yet evidently hopeless, as it supposes more zeal, concord and perseverance than a view of mankind gives reason for expecting.

He wrote likewise this year *A Vindication of Bickerstaff*, and an explanation of an *Ancient Prophecy*, part written after the facts, and the rest never completed, but well planned to excite amazement. . . .

Being not immediately considered as an obdurate Tory, he conversed indiscriminately with all the wits, and was yet the friend of

Steele who, in the *Tatler* which began in 1710, confesses the advantages of his conversation and mentions something contributed by him to his paper. But he was now emerging into political controversy; for the same year produced the *Examiner*, of which Swift wrote thirty-three papers. In argument he may be allowed to have the advantage; for where a wide system of conduct and the whole of a public character is laid open to inquiry, the accuser having the choice of facts must be very unskilful if he does not prevail; but with regard to wit, I am afraid none of Swift's papers will be found equal to those by which Addison opposed him.

Early in the next year he published *A Proposal for Correcting, Improving and Ascertaining the English Tongue, in a Letter to the Earl of Oxford*, written without much knowledge of the general nature of language and without any accurate inquiry into the history of other tongues. The certainty and stability which, contrary to all experience, he thinks attainable, he proposes to secure by instituting an academy; the decrees of which every man would have been willing, and many would have been proud to disobey, and which, being renewed by successive elections, would in a short time have differed from itself.

He wrote the same year *A Letter to the October Club*, a number of Tory gentlemen sent from the country to Parliament, who formed themselves into a club to the number of about a hundred, and met to animate the zeal and raise the expectations of each other. They thought, with great reason, that the ministers were losing opportunities, that sufficient use was not made of the ardour of the nation; they called loudly for more changes and stronger efforts, and demanded the punishment of part, and the dismission of the rest, of those whom they considered as public robbers. . . .

Swift now attained the zenith of his political importance: he published (1712) *The Conduct of the Allies*, ten days before the Parliament assembled. The purpose was to persuade the nation to a peace, and never had any writer more success. The people, who had been amused with bonfires and triumphal processions, and looked with idolatry on the general and his friends who, as they thought, had made England the arbitress of nations, were confounded between shame and rage when they found that 'mines had been exhausted and millions destroyed', to secure the Dutch or aggrandize the emperor, without any advantage to ourselves; that we had been

bribing our neighbours to fight their own quarrel; and that amongst
our enemies we might number our allies.

That is now no longer doubted, of which the nation was then
first informed, that the war was unnecessarily protracted to fill the
pockets of Marlborough, and that it would have been continued without end if he could have continued his annual plunder. But Swift
I suppose, did not yet know what he has since written, that a commission was drawn which would have appointed him general for
life, had it not become ineffectual by the resolution of Lord Cowper,
who refused the seal.

'Whatever is received,' say the schools, 'is received in proportion
to the recipient.' The power of a political treatise depends much
upon the disposition of the people: the nation was then combustible,
and a spark set it on fire. It is boasted that between November and
January eleven thousand were sold; a great number at that time,
when we were not yet a nation of readers. To its propagation certainly no agency of power or influence was wanting. It furnished
arguments for conversation, speeches for debate and materials for
parliamentary resolutions.

Yet, surely, whoever surveys this wonder-working pamphlet with
cool perusal will confess that its efficacy was supplied by the passions
of its readers; that it operates by the mere weight of facts, with very
little assistance from the hand that produced them.

This year (1712) he published his *Reflections on the Barrier Treaty*,
which carries on the design of his *Conduct of the Allies* and shows how
little regard in that negotiation had been shown to the interest of
England and how much of the conquered country had been demanded
by the Dutch.

This was followed by *Remarks on the Bishop of Sarum's Introduction
to his Third Volume of the History of the Reformation*: a pamphlet which
Burnet published as an alarm, to warn the nation of the approach of
Popery. Swift, who seems to have disliked the bishop with something
more than political aversion, treats him like one whom he is glad of
an opportunity to insult. . . .

In the midst of his power and his politics, he kept a journal of his
visits, his walks, his interviews with Ministers and quarrels with his
servant, and transmitted it to Mrs Johnson and Mrs Dingley, to whom
he knew that whatever befell him was interesting, and no accounts

could be too minute. Whether these diurnal trifles were properly exposed to eyes which had never received any pleasure from the presence of the Dean, may be reasonably doubted. They have, however, some odd attraction: the reader, finding frequent mention of names which he has been used to consider as important, goes on in hope of information; and, as there is nothing to fatigue attention, if he is disappointed he can hardly complain. It is easy to perceive, from every page, that though ambition pressed Swift into a life of bustle, the wish for a life of ease was always returning. . . .

The great acquisition of esteem and influence was made by the *Drapier's Letters* in 1724. One Wood of Wolverhampton in Stafford-shire, a man enterprising and rapacious, had, as is said, by a present to the Duchess of Munster, obtained a patent, empowering him to coin one hundred and eighty thousand pounds of halfpennies and farthings for the kingdom of Ireland, in which there was a very inconvenient and embarrassing scarcity of copper coin, so that it was possible to run in debt upon the credit of a piece of money; for the cook or keeper of an alehouse could not refuse to supply a man that had silver in his hand, and the buyer would not leave his money without change.

The project was therefore plausible. The scarcity, which was already great, Wood took care to make greater by agents who gathered up the old halfpennies; and was about to turn his brass into gold by pouring the treasures of his new mint upon Ireland, when Swift, finding that the metal was debased to an enormous degree, wrote letters, under the name of *M. B. Drapier*, to show the folly of receiving, and the mischief that must ensue, by giving gold and silver for coin worth perhaps not a third part of its nominal value.

The nation was alarmed; the new coin was universally refused; but the governors of Ireland considered resistance to the King's patent as highly criminal; and one Whitshed, then Chief Justice, who had tried the printer of the former pamphlet, and sent out the jury nine times, till by clamour and menaces they were frighted into a special verdict, now presented the Drapier, but could not prevail on the grand jury to find the bill.

Lord Carteret and the Privy Council published a proclamation, offering three hundred pounds for discovering the author of the *Fourth Letter.* Swift had concealed himself from his printers, and trusted only his butler, who transcribed the paper. The man, immediately after the appearance of the proclamation, strolled from the house, and stayed out all night and part of the next day. There was reason enough to fear that he had betrayed his master for the reward; but he came home, and the Dean ordered him to put off his livery and leave the house, 'for,' says he, 'I know that my life is in your power, and I will not bear, out of fear, either your insolence or negligence'. The man excused his fault with great submission, and begged that he might be confined in the house while it was in his power to endanger his master; but the Dean resolutely turned him out, without taking further notice of him, till the term of information had expired, and then received him again. Soon afterwards he ordered him and the rest of the servants into his presence, without telling his intentions, and bade them take notice that their fellow-servant was no longer Robert the butler, but that his integrity had made him Mr Blakeney, verger of St Patrick's, an officer whose income was between thirty and forty pounds a year; yet he still continued for some years to serve his old master as his butler.

Swift was known from this time by the appellation of 'The Dean'. He was honoured by the populace as the champion, patron and instructor of Ireland, and gained such power as, considered both in its extent and duration, scarcely any man has ever enjoyed without greater wealth or higher station.

He was from this important year the oracle of the traders and the idol of the rabble, and by consequence was feared and courted by all to whom the kindness of the traders or the populace was necessary. The Drapier was a sign; the Drapier was a health; and whichever way the eye or the ear was turned some tokens were found of the nation's gratitude to the Drapier.

The benefit was indeed great; he had rescued Ireland from a very oppressive and predatory invasion: and the popularity which he had gained he was diligent to keep by appearing forward and zealous on every occasion where the public interest was supposed to be involved. Nor did he much scruple to boast his influence; for when, upon some attempts to regulate the coin, Archbishop Boulter, then one of the Justices, accused him of exasperating the people, he exculpated himself by saying, 'If I had lifted up my finger, they would have torn you to pieces.' ...

He was now so much at ease that (1727) he returned to England where he collected three volumes of *Miscellanies* in conjunction with Pope who prefixed a querulous and apological Preface.

This important year sent likewise into the world *Gulliver's Travels*, a production so new and strange that it filled the reader with a mingled emotion of merriment and amazement. It was received with such avidity that the price of the first edition was raised before the second could be made; it was read by the high and the low, the learned and illiterate. Criticism was for a while lost in wonder: no rules of judgement were applied to a book written in open defiance of truth and regularity. But when distinctions came to be made the part which gave least pleasure was that which describes the Flying Island, and that which gave most disgust must be the history of the Houyhnhnms. . . .

He, however, permitted one book to be published, which had been the production of former years: *Polite Conversation*, which appeared in 1738. The *Directions to Servants* was printed soon after his death. These two performances show a mind incessantly attentive and, when it was not employed upon great things, busy with minute occurrences. It is apparent that he must have had the habit of noting whatever he observed; for such a number of particulars could never have been assembled by the power of recollection. . . .

When Swift is considered as an author it is just to estimate his powers by their effects. In the reign of Queen Anne he turned the stream of popularity against the Whigs, and must be confessed to have dictated for a time the political opinions of the English nation. In the succeeding reign he delivered Ireland from plunder and oppression, and showed that wit, confederated with truth, had such force as authority was unable to resist. He said truly of himself that Ireland 'was his debtor'. It was from the time when he first began to patronize the Irish that they may date their riches and prosperity. He taught them first to know their own interest, their weight and their strength, and gave them spirit to assert that equality with their fellow-subjects to which they have ever since been making vigorous advances, and to claim those rights which they have at last established. Nor can they be charged with ingratitude to their benefactor, for they reverenced him as a guardian and obeyed him as a dictator.

In his works he has given very different specimens both of sentiment and expression. His *Tale of a Tub* has little resemblance to his other pieces. It exhibits a vehemence and rapidity of mind, a copiousness of images and vivacity of diction such as he afterwards never possessed or never exerted. It is of a mode so distinct and peculiar that it must be considered by itself; what is true of that is not true of anything else which he has written.

In his other works is found an equable tenor of easy language, which rather trickles than flows. His delight was in simplicity. That he has in his works no metaphor, as has been said, is not true; but his few metaphors seem to be received rather by necessity than choice. He studied purity; and though perhaps all his structures are not exact, yet it is not often that solecisms can be found: and whoever depends on his authority may generally conclude himself safe. His sentences are never too much dilated or contracted; and it will not be easy to find any embarrassment in the complication of his clauses, any inconsequence in his connexions or abruptness in his transition.

His style was well suited to his thoughts, which are never subtilized by nice disquisitions, decorated by sparkling conceits, elevated by ambitious sentences or variegated by far-sought learning. He pays no court to the passions; he excites neither surprise nor admiration; he always understands himself, and his reader always understands him: the peruser of Swift wants little previous knowledge; it will be sufficient that he is acquainted with common words and common things; he is neither required to mount elevations nor to explore profundities; his passage is always on a level, along solid ground, without asperities, without obstruction.

This easy and safe conveyance of meaning it was Swift's desire to attain, and for having attained he deserves praise, though perhaps not the highest praise. For purposes merely didactic, when something is to be told that was not known before, it is the best mode, but against that inattention by which known truths are suffered to lie neglected it makes no provision; it instructs, but does not persuade.

By his political education he was associated with the Whigs, but he deserted them when they deserted their principles, yet without running into the contrary extreme; he continued throughout his life to retain the disposition which he assigns to the 'Church-of-England Man', of thinking commonly with the Whigs of the State, and with the Tories of the Church.

He was a churchman rationally zealous; he desired the prosperity and maintained the honour of the clergy; of the dissenters he did not wish to infringe the toleration, but he opposed their encroachments.

To his duty as Dean he was very attentive. He managed the revenues of his church with exact economy; and it is said by Delany that more money was, under his direction, laid out in repairs than had ever been in the same time since its first erection. Of his choir he was eminently careful; and, though he neither loved nor understood music, took care that all the singers were well qualified, admitting none without the testimony of skilful judges.

In his church he restored the practice of weekly communion, and distributed the sacramental elements in the most solemn and devout manner with his own hand. He came to church every morning, preached commonly in his turn, and attended the evening anthem, that it might not be negligently performed.

He read the service 'rather with a strong nervous voice than a graceful manner; his voice was sharp and high-toned, rather than harmonious'.

He entered upon the clerical state with hope to excel in preaching, but complained that, from the time of his political controversies, 'he could only preach pamphlets'. This censure of himself, if judgement be made from those sermons which have been published, was unreasonably severe.

The suspicions of his irreligion proceeded in a great measure from his dread of hypocrisy: instead of wishing to seem better, he delighted in seeming worse than he was. He went in London to early prayers lest he should be seen at church; he read prayers to his servants every morning with such dexterous secrecy that Dr Delany was six months in his house before he knew it. He was not only careful to hide the good which he did, but willingly incurred the suspicion of evil which he did not. He forgot what himself had formerly asserted, that hypocrisy is less mischievous than open impiety. Dr Delany, with all his zeal for his honour, has justly condemned this part of his character.

The person of Swift had not many recommendations. He had a kind of muddy complexion, which, though he washed himself with oriental scrupulosity, did not look clear. He had a countenance sour and severe, which he seldom softened by any appearance of gaiety. He stubbornly resisted any tendency to laughter.

To his domestics he was naturally rough; and a man of a rigorous temper, with that vigilance of minute attention which his works discover, must have been a master that few could bear. That he was disposed to do his servants good on important occasions is no great mitigation; benefaction can be but rare, and tyrannic peevishness is perpetual. He did not spare the servants of others. Once, when he dined alone with the Earl of Orrery, he said, of one that waited in the room, 'That man has, since we sat to the table, committed fifteen faults.' What the faults were Lord Orrery, from whom I heard the story, had not been attentive enough to discover. My number may perhaps not be exact.

In his economy he practised a peculiar and offensive parsimony, without disguise or apology. The practice of saving being once necessary, became habitual, and grew first ridiculous and at last detestable. But his avarice, though it might exclude pleasure, was never suffered to encroach upon his virtue. He was frugal by inclination but liberal by principle; and if the purpose to which he destined his little accumulations be remembered, with his distribution of occasional charity, it will perhaps appear that he only liked one mode of expence better than another, and saved merely that he might have something to give. He did not grow rich by injuring his successors, but left both Laracor and the Deanery more valuable than he found them.

With all this talk of his covetousness and generosity it should be remembered that he was never rich. The revenue of his Deanery was not much more than seven hundred a year.

His beneficence was not graced with tenderness or civility; he relieved without pity, and assisted without kindness, so that those who were fed by him could hardly love him.

He made a rule to himself to give but one piece at a time, and therefore always stored his pocket with coins of different value.

Whatever he did, he seemed willing to do in a manner peculiar to himself, without sufficiently considering that singularity, as it implies a contempt of the general practice, is a kind of defiance which justly provokes the hostility of ridicule; he therefore who indulges peculiar habits is worse than others, if he be not better.

Of his humour a story told by Pope may afford a specimen:

Dr Swift has an odd, blunt way that is mistaken by strangers for ill-nature. 'Tis so odd, that there's no describing it but by facts. I'll tell you one that first comes into my head. One evening Gay and I went to see him: you know how intimately we were all acquainted. On our coming in, 'Heyday, gentlemen (says the Doctor), what's the meaning of this visit? How came you to leave all the great Lords, that you are so fond of, to come hither to see a poor Dean.' 'Because we would rather see you than any of them.' 'An, anyone that did not know [you] so well as I do, might believe you. But since you are come I must get some supper for you, I suppose.' 'No, Doctor, we have supped already.' 'Supped already? That's impossible! Why, 'tis not eight o'clock yet. That's very strange; but, if you had not supped, I must have got something for you. Let me see, what should I have had? A couple of lobsters; ay, that would have done very well; two shillings – tarts, a shilling: but you will drink a glass of wine with me, though you supped so much before your usual time only to spare my pocket?' 'No, we had rather talk with you than drink with you.' 'But if you had supped with me, as in all reason you ought to have done, you must then have drunk with me. A bottle of wine, two shillings – two and two is four, and one is five: just two-and-sixpence a-piece. There, Pope, there's half-a-crown for you, and there's another for you, sir; for I won't save any thing by you, I am determined.' This was all said and done with his usual seriousness on such occasions; and, in spite of every thing we could say to the contrary, he actually obliged us to take the money.

In the intercourse of familiar life he indulged his disposition to petulance and sarcasm, and thought himself injured if the licentiousness of his raillery, the freedom of his censures or the petulance of his frolics were resented or repressed. He predominated over his companions with very high ascendancy, and probably would bear none over whom he could not predominate. To give him advice was, in the style of his friend Delany, 'to venture to speak to him'. This customary superiority soon grew too delicate for truth; and Swift, with all his penetration, allowed himself to be delighted with low flattery.

On all common occasions he habitually affects a style of arrogance, and dictates rather than persuades. This authoritative and magisterial language he expected to be received as his peculiar mode of jocularity; but he apparently flattered his own arrogance by an assumed imperiousness, in which he was ironical only to the resentful, and to the submissive sufficiently serious.

He told stories with great felicity, and delighted in doing what he knew himself to do well. He was therefore captivated by the respectful silence of a steady listener, and told the same tales too often.

He did not, however, claim the right of talking alone; for it was his rule, when he had spoken a minute, to give room by a pause for any other speaker. Of time, on all occasions, he was an exact computer, and knew the minutes required to every common operation.

It may be justly supposed that there was in his conversation, what appears so frequently in his letters, an affectation of familiarity with the great, an ambition of momentary equality sought and enjoyed by the neglect of those ceremonies which custom has established as the barriers between one order of society and another. This transgression of regularity was by himself and his admirers termed greatness of soul. But a great mind disdains to hold anything by courtesy, and therefore never usurps what a lawful claimant may take away. He that encroaches on another's dignity puts himself in his power: he is either repelled with helpless indignity or endured by clemency and condescension.

Of Swift's general habits of thinking, if his letters can be supposed to afford any evidence, he was not a man to be either loved or envied. He seems to have wasted life in discontent, by the rage of neglected pride and the languishment of unsatisfied desire. He is querulous and fastidious, arrogant and malignant; he scarcely speaks of himself but with indignant lamentations, or of others but with insolent superiority when he is gay, and with angry contempt when he is gloomy. From the letters that pass between him and Pope it might be inferred that they, with Arbuthnot and Gay, had engrossed all the understanding and virtue of mankind, that their merits filled the world; or that there was no hope of more. They show the age involved in darkness, and shade the picture with sullen emulation.

When the Queen's death drove him into Ireland he might be allowed to regret for a time the interception of his views, the extinction of his hopes and his ejection from gay scenes, important employment and splendid friendships; but when time had enabled reason to prevail over vexation the complaints, which at first were natural, became ridiculous because they were useless. But querulousness was now grown habitual, and he cried out when he probably had ceased to feel. His reiterated wailings persuaded Bolingbroke that he was really willing to quit his deanery for an English parish; and Bolingbroke procured an exchange which was rejected, and Swift still retained the pleasure of complaining.

The greatest difficulty that occurs, in analysing his character, is to discover by what depravity of intellect he took delight in revolving ideas from which almost every other mind shrinks with disgust. The ideas of pleasure, even when criminal, may solicit the imagination; but what has disease, deformity and filth upon which the thoughts can be allured to dwell? Delany is willing to think that Swift's mind was not much tainted with this gross corruption before his long visit to Pope. He does not consider how he degrades his hero by making him at fifty-nine the pupil of turpitude, and liable to the malignant influence of an ascendant mind. But the truth is that Gulliver had described his Yahoos before the visit, and he that had formed those images had nothing filthy to learn.

I have here given the character of Swift as he exhibits himself to my perception; but now let another be heard who knew him better. Dr Delany, after long acquaintance, describes him to Lord Orrery in these terms:

My Lord, when you consider Swift's singular, peculiar and most variegated vein of wit, always rightly intended (although not always so rightly directed), delightful in many instances, and salutary, even where it is most offensive; when you consider his strict truth, his fortitude in resisting oppression and arbitrary power; his fidelity in friendship, his sincere love and zeal for religion, his uprightness in making right resolutions, and his steadiness in adhering to them; his care of his church, its choir, its economy, and its income; his attention to all those that preached in his cathedral, in order to their amendment in pronunciation and style; as also his remarkable attention to the interest of his successors, preferably to his own present emoluments; [his] invincible patriotism, even to a country which he did not love; his very various, well-devised, well-judged and extensive charities throughout his life, and his whole fortune (to say nothing of his wife's) conveyed to the same Christian purposes at his death – charities from which he could enjoy no honour, advantage nor satisfaction of any kind in this world. When you consider his ironical and humorous, as well as his serious schemes, for the promotion of true religion and virtue; his success in soliciting for the 'First Fruits' and 'Twentieths', to the unspeakable benefit of the established Church of Ireland; and his felicity (to rate it no higher) in giving occasion to the building of fifty new churches in London.

All this considered, the character of his life will appear like that of his writings; they will both bear to be reconsidered and re-examined with the utmost attention, and always discover new beauties and excellences upon every examination.

They will bear to be considered as the sun, in which the brightness will hide the blemishes; and whenever petulant ignorance, pride, malice, malignity or envy interposes to cloud or sully his fame, I will take upon me to pronounce that the eclipse will not last long.

To conclude – no man ever deserved better of any country than Swift did of his. A steady, persevering, inflexible friend; a wise, a watchful and a faithful counsellor, under many severe trials and bitter persecutions, to the manifest hazard both of his liberty and fortune.

He lived a blessing, he died a benefactor, and his name will ever live an honour to Ireland.

In the poetical works of Dr Swift there is not much upon which the critic can exercise his powers. They are often humorous, almost always light, and have the qualities which recommend such compositions, easiness and gaiety. They are, for the most part, what their author intended. The diction is correct, the numbers are smooth and the rhymes exact. There seldom occurs a hard-laboured expression or a redundant epithet; all his verses exemplify his own definition of a good style, they consist of 'proper words in proper places'.

To divide this collection into classes, and show how some pieces are gross and some are trifling, would be to tell the reader what he knows already and to find faults of which the author could not be ignorant, who certainly wrote often not to his judgement, but his humour.

It was said, in a preface to one of the Irish editions, that Swift had never been known to take a single thought from any writer, ancient or modern. This is not literally true; but perhaps no writer can easily be found that has borrowed so little, or that in all his excellences and all his defects has so well maintained his claim to be considered as original.
(1-66)

James Harris

from *Philosophical Inquiries* 1781

Misanthropy is so dangerous a thing, and goes so far in sapping the very foundation of morality and religion, that I esteem the last part of Swift's *Gulliver* (that I mean relative to his Houyhnhnms and Yahoos) to be a worse book to peruse than those which we forbid as the most flagitious and obscene. One absurdity in this author (a wretched philosopher, though a great wit) is well worth remarking: in order to render the nature of men odious, and the nature of beasts amiable, he is compelled to give human characters to his beasts, and beastly characters to his men; so that we are to admire the beasts, not for being beasts, but amiable men; and to detest the men, not for being men, but detestable beasts.

Whoever has been reading this unnatural filth, let him turn for a moment to a *Spectator* of Addison, and observe the philanthropy of that classical writer; I may add, the superior purity of his diction, and his wit.
(537)

Joseph Warton

from *An Essay on the Genius and Writings of Pope*,
vols. 1 and 2   1782

We do not, it should seem, sufficiently attend to the difference there
is betwixt a man of wit, a man of sense and a true poet. Donne and
Swift were undoubtedly men of wit and men of sense: but what
traces have they left of pure poetry? . . .

[Pope's letters] contain, it must be allowed, many interesting
particulars; but they are tinctured and blemished with a great share
of vanity and self-importance, and with too many commendations of
his own integrity, independency and virtue. Pope, Swift and Bolingbroke appear by the letters to have formed a kind of haughty trium-
virate, in order to issue forth proscriptions against all who would not
adopt their sentiments and opinions. And by their own account of
themselves, they would have the reader believe that they had engrossed and monopolized all the genius and all the honesty of the age
in which, according to their opinion, they had the misfortune to live.
(407)

Hugh Blair

from *Lectures on Rhetoric and Belles Lettres*, vol. 2   1783

The difference between a dry and plain writer is that the former is
incapable of ornament and seems not to know what it is; the latter
seeks not after it. He gives us his meaning in good language, distinct
and pure; any further ornament he gives himself no trouble about;
either because he thinks it unnecessary to his subject or because his
genius does not lead him to delight in it, or because it leads him to
despise it.

This last was the case with Dean Swift, who may be placed at the
head of those that have employed the plain style. Few writers have
discovered more capacity. He treats every subject which he handles,
whether serious or ludicrous, in a masterly manner. He knew, almost
beyond any man, the purity, the extent, the precision of the English

language; and therefore, to such as wish to attain a pure and correct style, he is one of the most useful models. But we must not look for much ornament and grace in his language. His haughty and morose genius made him despise any embellishment of this kind as beneath his dignity. He delivers his sentiments in a plain downright positive manner, like one who is sure he is in the right; and is very indifferent whether you be pleased or not. His sentences are commonly negligently arranged; distinctly enough as to the sense, but without any regard to smoothness of sound; often without much regard to compactness or elegance. If a metaphor or any other figure chanced to render his satire more poignant, he would perhaps vouchsafe to adopt it when it came in his way, but if it tended only to embellish and illustrate, he would rather throw it aside. Hence, in his serious pieces, his style often borders upon the dry and unpleasing; in his humorous ones, the plainness of his manner sets off his wit to the highest advantage. There is no froth nor affection in it; it seems native and unstudied; and while he hardly appears to smile himself, he makes his reader laugh heartily.

(22–3)

James Beattie

from a letter to Dr Porteus 21 October 1785 (reprinted in *Letters*, vol. 2, 1819–21)

I read lately Sheridan's *Life of Swift*. It is panegyric from beginning to end. Swift had many good as well as great qualities, but his character was surely, upon the whole, very exceptionable. Mr Sheridan, however, will not admit that he had any fault. Even his brutality to Stella on her deathbed, which undoubtedly hastened her dissolution, his biographer endeavours to apologize for; and he has a great deal of very unsatisfactory reasoning on the subject of the Yahoos. The question is not whether *that* man is not a very odious animal who finds his own likeness in those filthy beings; but whether Swift did not intend his account of them as a satire on human nature, and an oblique censure of providence itself in the formation of the human body and soul. That this was Swift's meaning is to me as evident as that he wrote the book: and yet I do not find my own likeness in the Yahoos. I only know, for I think I could prove, that Swift wished it to be understood as his opinion that the human species and the Yahoo are equally detestable.

(132)

James Boswell

from *Life of Johnson*   1791 (in G. Birkbeck Hill (ed.), *Life of Johnson*, revised by L. F. Powell, 1953)

Friday, 24 March 1775. Johnson was in high spirits this evening at the club, and talked with great animation and success. He attacked Swift, as he used to do upon all occasions. The *Tale of a Tub* is so much superior to his other writings that one can hardly believe he was the author of it. 'There is in it such a vigour of mind, such a swarm of thoughts, so much of nature and art and life.' I wondered to hear him say of *Gulliver's Travels*, 'When once you have thought of big men and little men, it is very easy to do all the rest.' I endeavoured to make a stand for Swift, and tried to rouse those who were much more able to defend him, but in vain. Johnson at last, of his own accord, allowed very great merit to the inventory of articles found in the pockets of the Man Mountain, particularly the description of his watch, which it was conjectured was his God, as he consulted it upon all occasions. He observed that 'Swift put his name to but two things (after he had a name to put), *The Plan for the Improvement of the English Language* and the last *Drapier's Letter*'.

(595)

Thomas Wallace

from 'An Essay on the Variations of English Prose, from the Revolution to the Present Time', *Transactions of the Royal Irish Academy*, vol. 6   1797

Should it be doubted, whether the improvement of style which took place in the time of Addison – that variation which substituted uniform and correct neatness in composition for what was loose, inaccurate and capricious – be justly attributed to him, the doubt will vanish when it is remembered that in no work prior to his time is an equal degree of accuracy or neatness to be found, and even among those periodical papers to which the most eminent of his contemporary writers contributed, the Clio of Addison stands eminently conspicuous. It was, indeed, from the productions of this classic and copious mind that the public seems to have caught the taste for fine writing which has operated from that time to the present, and which has given to our language perhaps the greatest degree of elegance and accuracy of which it is susceptible – for if anything is yet to be added to the improvement of the English style, it must be more nerve and muscle, not a nicer modification of form or feature:

... sectantem levia, nervi
Deficiunt animique:

While Addison was communicating to English prose a degree of correctness with which it had been, till his time, unacquainted, Swift was exemplifying its precision and giving a standard for its purity. Swift was the first writer who attempted to express his meaning without subsidiary words and corroborating phrases. He nearly laid aside the use of synonyms in which even Addison had a little indulged, and without being very solicitous about the structure or harmony of his periods, seemed to devote all his attention to illustrate the force of individual words. Swift hewed the stones, and fitted the materials for those who built after him; Addison left the neatest and most finished models of ornamental architecture.

(58–9)

William Godwin

from *The Enquirer: Reflections on Education, Manners and Literature* 1797

What is the tendency of *Gulliver's Travels*, particularly of that part which relates to the Houyhnhnms and Yahoos? It has frequently been affirmed to be to inspire us with a loathing aversion to our species and fill us with a frantic preference for the society of any class of animals, rather than of men. A poet of our own day [Hayley], as a suitable remuneration for the production of such a work, has placed the author in hell, and consigned him to the eternal torment of devils. On the other hand it has been doubted whether, under the name of Houyhnhnms and Yahoos, Swift has done anything more than ex- hibit two different descriptions of men, in their highest improvement and lowest degradation; and it has been affirmed that no book breathes more strongly a generous indignation against vice, and an ardent love of everything that is excellent and honourable to the human heart.

There is no end to an enumeration of controversies of this sort. (133–4)

Walter Scott

from *Memoirs of Jonathan Swift* 1814 (reprinted in *The Works of Jonathan Swift*, vol. 1, 1883)

He possessed, indeed, in the highest perfection, the wonderful power of so embodying and imaging forth 'the shadowy tribes of mind', that the fiction of the imagination is received by the reader as if it were truth. Undoubtedly the same keen and powerful intellect, which could sound all the depths and shallows of active life, stored his mind with facts drawn from his own acute observation and thus sup- plied with materials the creative talent which he possessed; for although the knowledge of the human mind may be, in a certain extent, intuitive and subsist without extended acquaintance with the living world, yet that acquaintance with manners, equally remarkable

in Swift's productions, could only be acquired from intimate familiarity with the actual business of the world.

In fiction he possessed, in the most extensive degree, the art of
verisimilitude – the power, as we observed in the case of *Gulliver's
Travels*, of adopting and sustaining a fictitious character, under every
peculiarity of place and circumstance. A considerable part of this
secret rests upon minuteness of narrative. Small and detached facts
form the foreground of a narrative when told by an eye-witness.
They are the subjects which immediately press upon his attention, and
have, with respect to him as an individual, an importance which they
are far from bearing to the general scene in which he is engaged; just
as a musket-shot, passing near the head of a soldier, makes a deeper
impression on his mind than all the heavy ordnance which has been
discharged throughout the engagement. But to a distant spectator all
these minute incidents are lost and blended in the general current of
events; and it requires the discrimination of Swift, or of Defoe, to
select, in a fictitious narrative, such an enumeration of minute incidents as might strike the beholder of a real fact, especially such a one
as has not been taught, by an enlarged mind and education, to generalize his observations. I am anticipated in a sort of parallel which I
intended to have made between the romances of Gulliver and Robinson Crusoe by the ingenious author of the *History of Fiction*, whose
words I adopt with pleasure, as expressing an opinion which I have
been long induced to hold. After illustrating his proposition, by
showing how Crusoe verifies his narrative of a storm, through means
of a detail of particular incidents, he proceeds:

Those minute references immediately lead us to give credit to the
whole narrative, since we think they would hardly have been mentioned unless they had been true. The same circumstantial detail of
facts is remarkable in *Gulliver's Travels*, and we are led on by them
to a partial belief in the most improbable narrations.[1]

The genius of Defoe has never been questioned, but his sphere of
information was narrow; and hence his capacity of fictitious invention was limited to one or two characters. A plain sailor, as Robinson
Crusoe, a blunt soldier, as his supposed 'Cavalier', a sharper in low

[1] John Dunlop, *The History of Fiction*, vol. 3, 1814, p. 400.

life, like some of his other fictitious personages, were the only dis-
guises which the extent of his information permitted him to assume.
In this respect he is limited, like the sorcerer in the Indian tale, whose
powers of transformation were confined to assuming the likeness of
two or three animals only. But Swift seems, like the Persian dervish,
to have possessed the faculty of transfusing his own soul into the body
of anyone whom he selected; of seeing with his eyes, employing
every organ of his sense and even becoming master of the powers of
his judgement. Lemuel Gulliver the traveller, Isaac Bickerstaff the
astrologer, the Frenchman who writes the *New Journey to Paris*, Mrs
Harris, Mary the cook-maid, the grave projector who proposes a plan
for relieving the poor by eating their children, and the vehement
Whig politician who remonstrates against the enormities of the
Dublin signs, are all persons as distinct from each other as they are in
appearance from the Dean of St Patrick's. Each maintains his own
character, moves in his own sphere and is struck with those circumstances which his situation in life, or habits of thinking, have rendered
most interesting to him as an individual.

The proposition I have ventured to lay down respecting the art of
giving verisimilitude to a fictitious narrative, has a corollary resting
on the same principles. As minute particulars, pressing close upon the
observation of the narrator, occupy a disproportionate share of his
narrative and of his observation, so circumstances more important in
themselves, in many cases, attract his notice only partially, and are
therefore but imperfectly detailed. In other words, there is a distance
as well as a foreground in narrative, as in natural perspective, and the
scale of objects necessarily decreases as they are withdrawn from the
vicinity of him who reports them. In this particular, the art of Swift
is equally manifest. The information which Gulliver acquires from
hearsay is communicated in a more vague and general manner than
that reported on his own knowledge. He does not, like other voya-
gers into Utopian realms, bring us back a minute account of their
laws and government, but merely such general information upon
these topics as a well-informed and curious stranger may be reasonably
supposed to acquire during some months' residence in a foreign
country. In short, the narrator is the centre and mainspring of the
story, which neither exhibits a degree of extended information such
as circumstances could not permit him to acquire, nor omits those

minute incidents which the same circumstances rendered of importance to him, because immediately affecting his own person. (456–60)

Francis Jeffrey

from a review of 'Scott's Edition of Swift', *Edinburgh Review*, vol. 27, no. 53 September 1816

By far the most considerable change which has taken place in the world of letters, in our days, is that by which the wits of Queen Anne's time have been practically brought down from the supremacy which they had enjoyed, without competition, for the best part of a century. When we were at our studies, some twenty-five years ago, we can perfectly remember that every young man was set to read Pope, Swift and Addison, as regularly as Virgil, Cicero and Horace. [Jeffrey then considers Swift, attacking him as a low-bred underling, a parvenu, a traitor to the Whig cause, despicable in his relations with Varina, Stella and Vanessa.]

With these impressions of his personal character, perhaps it is not easy for us to judge quite fairly of his works. Yet we are far from being insensible to their great and very peculiar merits. Their chief peculiarity is, that they were almost all what may be called occasional productions, not written for fame nor for posterity, from the fullness of the mind, or the desire of instructing mankind, but on the spur of the occasion, for promoting some temporary and immediate object, and producing a practical effect, in the attainment of which their sole importance centred. With the exception of the *Tale of a Tub, Gulliver, Polite Conversation* and about half a volume of poetry, this description will apply to almost all that is now before us; and it is no small proof of the vigour and vivacity of his genius that posterity should have been so anxious to preserve these careless and hasty productions, upon which their author appears to have set no other value than as means for the attainment of an end. The truth is, accordingly, that they are very extraordinary performances; and, considered with a view to the purposes for which they were intended, have probably never been equalled in any period of the world. They were written

with great plainness, force and intrepidity – advance at once to the matter in dispute – give battle to the strength of the enemy and never seek any kind of advantage from darkness or obscurity. Their distinguishing feature, however, is the force and the vehemence of the invective in which they abound; the copiousness, the steadiness, the perseverance and the dexterity with which abuse and ridicule are showered upon the adversary. This, we think, was, beyond all doubt, Swift's great talent and the weapon by which he made himself formidable. He was, without exception, the greatest and most efficient *libeller* that ever exercised the trade; and possessed, in an eminent degree, all the qualifications which it requires: a clear head, a cold heart, a vindictive temper, no admiration of noble qualities, no sympathy with suffering, not much conscience, not much consistency, a ready wit, a sarcastic humour, a thorough knowledge of the baser parts of human nature and a complete familiarity with everything that is low, homely and familiar in language. These were his gifts; and he soon felt for what ends they were given. Almost all his works are libels; generally upon individuals, sometimes upon sects and parties, sometimes upon human nature. Whatever be his end, however, personal abuse, direct, vehement, unsparing invective, is his means. It is his sword and his shield, his panoply and his chariot of war. In all his writings, accordingly, there is nothing to raise or exalt our notions of human nature – but everything to vilify and degrade.
(44–5)

Thomas Holcroft

from *The Life of Thomas Holcroft, Written by Himself* 1816
(reprinted in E. Colby (ed.), *The Life of Thomas Holcroft, Written by Himself*, 1925)

[Of a friend] He even lent me books to read: among which were *Gulliver's Travels* and the *Spectator*, both of which could not but be to me of the highest importance. I remember after I had read them he asked me to consider and tell him which I liked best: I immediately replied, 'there was no need of consideration, I liked *Gulliver's Travels* ten times the best.' 'Aye', said he, 'I would have laid my life on it; boys and young people always prefer the marvellous to the true.' I acquiesced in his judgement which, however, only proved that neither he nor I understood *Gulliver*, though it afforded me infinite delight.

(90)

Samuel Taylor Coleridge

from 'On Rabelais, Swift and Sterne' 1818 (reprinted in T. M. Raysor (ed.), *Coleridge's Miscellaneous Criticism*, 1936)

The great defect of the Houyhnhnms is not its misanthropy, and those who apply this word to it must really believe that the essence of human nature, that the *anthropos misoumenos*, consists in the shape of the body. Now, to show the falsity of this was Swift's great object; he would prove to our feelings and imagination, and thereby teach *practically* that it is reason and conscience which give all the loveliness and dignity not only to man, but to the shape of man; that deprived of these, and yet retaining the understanding, he would be the most loathsome and hateful of all animals; that his understanding would manifest itself only as malignant cunning, his free will as obstinacy and unteachableness. And how true a picture this is, every madhouse may convince any man; a brothel where highwaymen meet will convince every philosopher. But the defect of the work is its inconsistency; the Houyhnhnms are not rational creatures, that is, creatures of perfect reason; they are not progressive; they have servants without any reason for their natural inferiority or any explanation how the difference acted; and, above all, they, that is Swift himself, have a perpetual affectation of being wiser than their Maker, and of eradicating what God gave to be subordinated and used: the maternal and paternal affection. There is likewise a true Yahooism in the constant denial of the existence of love, as not identical with friendship, and yet always distinct and very often divided from lust. The best defence is that it is a satire; still, it would have been felt a thousand times more deeply if reason had been truly portrayed, and a finer imagination would have been evinced if the author had shown the effects of the possession of reason and the moral sense on the outward form and gestures of the horses. In short, critics in general complain of the Yahoos; I complain of the Houyhnhnms. . . .

. . . the work, which I still think the highest effort of Swift's genius, unless we should except *A Tale of a Tub*. Then I would put *Lilliput*; next *Brobdingnag*; and *Laputa* I would expunge altogether. It is a wretched abortion, the product of spleen and ignorance and self-conceit. (128–30)

William Hazlitt

from *Lectures on the English Poets* 1818 (reprinted in A. R. Waller and A. Glover (eds.), *Collected Works*, vol. 5, 1902)

Swift's reputation as a poet has been in a manner obscured by the greater splendour, by the natural force and inventive genius of his prose writings; but if he had never written either *A Tale of a Tub* or *Gulliver's Travels*, his name merely as a poet would have come down to us, and have gone down to posterity with well-earned honours. His *Imitations of Horace*, and still more his *Verses on the Death of Dr Swift*, place him in the first rank of agreeable moralists in verse. There is not only a dry humour, an exquisite tone of irony, in these productions of his pen, but there is a touching, unpretending pathos, mixed up with the most whimsical and eccentric strokes of pleasantry and satire. His *Description of the Morning in London*, and of a *City Shower*, which were first published in the *Tatler*, are among the most delightful of the contents of that very delightful work. Swift shone as one of the most sensible of the poets; he is also distinguished as one of the most nonsensical of them. No man has written so many lack-a-daisical, slip-shod, tedious, trifling, foolish, fantastical verses as he, which are so little an imputation on the wisdom of the writer; and which, in fact, only show his readiness to oblige others and to forget himself. He has gone so far as to invent a new stanza of fourteen and sixteen syllable lines for Mary the cook-maid to vent her budget of nothings and for Mrs Harris to gossip with the deaf old housekeeper. Oh, when shall we have such another Rector of Laracor! *A Tale of a Tub* is one of the most masterly compositions in the language, whether for thought, wit or style. It is so capital and undeniable a proof of the author's talents, that Dr Johnson, who did not like Swift, would not allow that he wrote it [but see p. 79]. It is hard that the same performance should stand in the way of a man's promotion to a bishopric, as wanting gravity, and at the same time be denied to be his, as having too much wit. It is a pity the Doctor did not find out some graver author, for whom he felt a critical kindness, on whom to father this splendid but unacknow-ledged production. Dr Johnson could not deny that *Gulliver's Travels* were his; he therefore disputed their merits, and said that after the first idea of them was conceived, they were easy to execute; all the rest followed mechanically. I do not know how that may be; but the mechanism employed is something very different from any that the author of *Rasselas* was in the habit of bringing to bear on such occasions. There is nothing more futile, as well as invidious, than this mode of criticizing a work of original genius. Its greatest merit is supposed to be in the invention; and you say, very wisely, that it is not *in the execution*. You might as well take away the merit of the invention of the telescope, by saying that, after its uses were explained and understood, any ordinary eyesight could look through it. Whether the excellence of *Gulliver's Travels* is in the conception or the execution, is of little consequence; the power is somewhere, and it is a power that has moved the world. The power is not that of big words and vaunting common places. Swift left these to those who wanted them; and has done what his acuteness and intensity of mind alone could enable anyone to conceive or to perform. His object was to strip empty pride and grandeur of the imposing air which external circumstances throw around them; and for this purpose he has cheated the imagination of the illusions which the prejudices of sense and of the world put upon it, by reducing everything to the abstract predicament of size. He enlarges or diminishes the scale, as he wishes to show the insignificance or the grossness of our overweening self-love. That he has done this with mathematical precision, with com-plete presence of mind and perfect keeping, in a manner that comes equally home to the understanding of the man and of the child, does not take away from the merit of the work or the genius of the author. He has taken a new view of human nature, such as a being of a higher sphere might take of it; he has torn the scales off his moral vision; he has tried an experiment upon human life and sifted its pretensions from the alloy of circumstances; he has measured it with a rule, has weighed it in a balance, and found it, for the most part, wanting and worthless – in substance and in show. Nothing solid, nothing valuable is left in his system but virtue and wisdom. What a libel is this upon mankind! What a convincing proof of misanthropy! What presumption and what *malice prepense*, to show men what they are, and to teach them what they ought to be! What a mortifying stroke aimed at national glory, is that unlucky incident of Gulliver's wading across the channel and carrying off the whole fleet of Blefuscu! After that, we have only to consider which of the contending parties was in the right. What a shock to personal vanity is given in the account of Gulliver's nurse Glumdalclitch! Still, notwithstanding the disparagement to her personal charms, her good nature remains the same amiable quality as before. I cannot see the harm, the misanthropy, the immoral and degrading tendency of this. The moral lesson is as fine as the intellectual exhibition is amusing. It is an attempt to tear off the mask of imposture from the world; and nothing but imposture has a right to complain of it. It is, indeed, the way with our quacks in morality to preach up the dignity of human nature, to pamper pride and hypocrisy with the idle mockeries of the virtues they pretend to, and which they have not; but it was not Swift's way to cant morality, or anything else; nor did his genius prompt him to write unmeaning panegyrics on mankind!

I do not, therefore, agree with the estimate of Swift's moral or intellectual character, given by an eminent critic, who does not seem to have forgotten the party politics of Swift. I do not carry my political resentments so far back: I can at this time of day forgive Swift for having been a Tory. I feel little disturbance (whatever I might think of them) at his political sentiments, which died with him, considering how much else he has left behind him of a more solid and imperishable nature! If he had, indeed, (like some others) merely left behind him the lasting infamy of a destroyer of his country, or the shining example of an apostate from liberty, I might have thought the case altered.

The determination with which Swift persisted in a preconcerted theory, savoured of the morbid affection of which he died. There is nothing more likely to drive a man mad, than the being unable to get rid of the idea of the distinction between right and wrong, and an obstinate, constitutional preference of the true to the agreeable. Swift was not a Frenchman. In this respect he differed from Rabelais and Voltaire. They have been accounted the three greatest wits in modern times; but their wit was of a peculiar kind in each. They are little beholden to each other; there is some resemblance between Lord Peter in *A Tale of a Tub*, and Rabelais' Friar John; but in general they are all three authors of a substantive character in themselves. Swift's wit (particularly in his chief prose works) was serious, saturnine and practical; Rabelais' was fantastical and joyous; Voltaire's was light, sportive and verbal. Swift's wit was the wit of sense; Rabelais', the wit of nonsense; Voltaire's, of indifference to both. The ludicrous in Swift arises out of his keen sense of impropriety, his soreness and impatience of the least absurdity. He separates, with a severe and caustic air, truth from falsehood, folly from wisdom, 'shows vice her own image, scorn her own feature'; and it is the force, the precision and the honest abruptness with which the separation is made, that excites our surprise, our admiration and laughter. He sets a mark of reprobation on that which offends good sense and good manners, which cannot be mistaken, and which holds it up to our ridicule and contempt ever after. His occasional disposition to trifling (already noticed) was a relaxation from the excessive earnestness of his mind. *Indignatio facit versus.* His better genius was his spleen. It was the biting acrimony of his temper that sharpened his other faculties. The truth of his perceptions produced the pointed coruscations of his wit; his playful irony was the result of inward bitterness of thought; his imagination was the product of the literal, dry, incorrigible tenaciousness of his understanding. He endeavoured to escape from the persecution of realities into the regions of fancy, and invented his Lilliputians and Brobdingnagians, Yahoos and Houyhnhnms, as a diversion to the more painful knowledge of the world around him: *they* only made him laugh, while men and women made him angry. His feverish impatience made him view the infirmities of that great baby the world, with the same scrutinizing glance and jealous irritability that a parent regards the failings of its offspring; but, as Rousseau has well observed, parents have not on this account been supposed to have more affection for other people's children than their own. In other respects, and except from the sparkling effervescence of his gall, Swift's brain was as 'dry as the remainder

biscuit after a voyage'. He hated absurdity – Rabelais loved it, exaggerated it with supreme satisfaction, luxuriated in its endless varieties, rioted in nonsense, 'reigned there and revelled'.
(109–12)

Lord Byron

from a letter to John Murray 10 October 1819 (reprinted in R. E. Prothero (ed.), *Works: Letters and Journals*, vol. 4, 1900)

[Byron is referring to an anonymous writer in the *Edinburgh Magazine*, August, 1819, who denounced *Don Juan* as 'a filthy and impious poem'.]

What would he say of the grossness without passion, and the misanthropy without feeling, of *Gulliver's Travels*?
(385)

Arthur Schopenhauer

from *Die Welt als Wille und Vorstellung* 1819 (reprinted in *The World as Will and Idea*, vol. 1, trans. R. B. Haldane and J. Kemp, 1883)

Allegory has an entirely different relation to poetry from that which it has to plastic and pictorial art, and although it is to be rejected in the latter, it is not only permissible but very serviceable to the former. For in plastic and pictorial art it leads away from what is perceptibly given, the proper object of all art, to abstract thoughts; but in poetry the relation is reversed; for here what is directly given in words is the concept, and the first aim is to lead from this to the object of perception, the representation of which must be undertaken by the imagination of the hearer. If in plastic and pictorial art we are led from what is immediately given to something else, this must always be a conception, because here only the abstract cannot be given directly; but a conception must never be the source, and its communication must never be the end of a work of art. In poetry, on the contrary, the conception is the material, the immediately given, and therefore we may very well leave it, in order to call up perceptions which are quite different, and in which the end is reached. Many a conception or abstract thought may be quite indispensable to the connexion of a poem, which is yet, in itself and directly, quite incapable of being perceived; and then it is often made perceptible by means of some example which is subsumed under it. This takes place in every trope, every metaphor, simile, parable and allegory, all of which differ only in the length and completeness of their expression. Therefore, in the arts which employ language as their medium, similes and allegories are of striking effect. How beautifully Cervantes says of sleep in order to express the fact that it frees us from all spiritual and bodily suffering: 'It is a mantle that covers all mankind.' How beautifully Kleist expresses allegorically the thought that philosophers and men of science enlighten mankind, in the line: 'Those whose midnight lamp lights the world.' How strongly and sensuously Homer describes the harmful Ate when he says: 'She has tender feet, for she walks not on the hard earth, but treads on the heads of men.' How forcibly we are struck by Menenius Agrippa's fable of the belly and the limbs, addressed to the people of Rome when they seceded. How beautifully Plato's figure of the Cave, at the beginning of the seventh book of *The Republic*, expresses a very abstract philosophical dogma. The fable of Persephone is also to be regarded as a deeply significant allegory of philosophical tendency, for she became subject to the nether world by tasting a pomegranate. This becomes peculiarly enlightening from Goethe's treatment of the fable, as an episode in the *Triumph der Empfindsamkeit*, which is beyond all praise. Three detailed allegorical works are known to me, one, open and avowed, is the incomparable *Criticón* of Balthasar Gracián. It consists of a great rich web of connected and highly ingenious allegories, that serve here as the fair clothing of moral truths, to which he thus imparts the most perceptible form, and astonishes us by the richness of his invention. The two others are concealed allegories, *Don Quixote* and *Gulliver's Travels*. The first is an allegory of the life of every man, who will not, like others, be careful, merely for his own welfare, but follows some objective, ideal end, which has taken possession of his thoughts and will; and certainly, in this world, he has then a strange appearance. In the case of Gulliver we have only to take everything physical as spiritual or intellectual, in order to see what the 'satirical rogue', as Hamlet would call him, meant by it. Such, then, in the poetical allegory, the conception is always the given, which it tries to make perceptible by means of a picture; it may sometimes be expressed or assisted by a painted picture. Such a picture will not be regarded as a work of art, but only as a significant symbol, and it makes no claim to pictorial, but only to poetical worth. Such is that beautiful allegorical vignette of Lavater's, which must be so heartening to every defender of truth: a hand holding a light is stung by a wasp, while gnats are burning themselves in the flame above; underneath is the motto:

And although it singes the wings of the gnats,
Destroys their heads and all their little brains,
      Light is still light;
And although I am stung by the angriest wasp,
      I will not let it go.

To this class also belongs the gravestone with the burnt-out, smoking candle, and the inscription:

When it is out, it becomes clear
Whether the candle was tallow or wax.

Finally, of this kind is an old German genealogical tree, in which the last representative of a very ancient family thus expresses his determination to live his life to the end in abstinence and perfect chastity, and therefore to let his race die out; he represents himself at the root of the high-branching tree cutting it over himself with shears. In general all those symbols referred to above, commonly called emblems, which might also be defined as short painted fables with obvious morals, belong to this class. Allegories of this kind are always to be regarded as belonging to poetry, not to painting, and as justified thereby; moreover, the pictorial execution is here always a matter of secondary importance, and no more is demanded of it than that it shall represent the thing so that we can recognize it. But in poetry, as in plastic art, the allegory passes into the symbol if there is merely an arbitrary connexion between what it presented to perception and the abstract significance of it. For as all symbolism rests, at bottom, on an agreement, the symbol has this among other disadvantages, that in time its meaning is forgotten, and then it is dumb. Who would guess why the fish is a symbol of Christianity if he did not know? Only a Champollion; for it is entirely a phonetic hieroglyphic. Therefore, as a poetical allegory, the Revelation of John stands much in the same position as the reliefs with *Magnus Deus sol Mithra*, which are still constantly being explained. (310-13)

Lord Byron

from *Don Juan* 1819-24 (reprinted in E. H. Coleridge (ed.), *Works: Poetry*, vol. 6, 1903)

They accuse me – *Me* – the present writer of
   The present poem – of – I know not what –
A tendency to under-rate and scoff
   At human power and virtue, and all that;
And this they say in language rather rough. –
   Good God! I wonder what they would be at!
I say no more than hath been said in Dante's
Verse, and by Solomon and by Cervantes

By Swift, by Machiavel, by Rochefoucault,
   By Fénelon, by Luther, and by Plato;
By Tillotson, and Wesley, and Rousseau,
   Who knew this life was not worth a potato.
(VII 3-4)

Anonymous

from a review of Byron's *Don Juan*, Cantos III, IV and V, *Monthly Review*, vol. 52 September 1821

The spirit of these passages will give our readers a pretty correct idea of the cynical sorties in which the poet delights to indulge. And, in truth, we see no reason for visiting him with a very heavy penalty of indignation, if he ventures to speak of human beings and human affairs in this strain of bitter sarcasm. Compare these cantos with the works of Swift. There is nothing in them which presents our nature in so degraded and disgusting a point of view as the latter laboured to place it in. His works are a tissue of wit, misanthropy and something coarser, yet he was a dignitary of the church, and of unimpeached character. And why not allow his jest to Lord Byron?

(126)

Samuel Taylor Coleridge

from *Table Talk*   1830 (published in H. N. Coleridge (ed.), *Specimens of the Table Talk of Coleridge*, 1874)

Swift was *anima Rabelaisii habitans in sicco* – the soul of Rabelais dwelling in a dry place.

 Yet Swift was rare. Can anything beat his remark on King William's motto, *Recepit, non rapuit* – 'that the receiver was as bad as the thief'.

(98)

I think Swift adopted the name of Stella, which is a man's name, with a feminine termination, to denote the mysterious epicene relation in which poor Miss Johnson stood to him.

(106)

Robert James Mackintosh

from *Memoirs of the Life of Sir James Mackintosh, Edited by his Son*, vol. 2   1835

Among the men of letters of his age, some indeed filled higher stations but none played a more important part than Jonathan Swift. Without being distinguished by imagination, subtlety, comprehension or refinement, he possessed a degree of masterly and correct good sense, almost as rare as genius; if indeed we be authorized to withhold the name of genius from so large a measure of any important mental power. Wit was in him not so much the effort or the sport of fancy as the keen edge of that exquisite good sense which laid bare the real ridicule and deformity existing in human life. The distinguishing feature of his moral character was a strong sense of justice, which disposed him to exact with rigour, as well as in general scrupulously to observe, the duties of society. These powerful feelings, exasperated probably by some circumstances of his own life, were gradually formed into an habitual and painful indignation against triumphant wrong, which became the ruling principle of his character and writings. His anger and disgust extended to every physical and moral deformity which human effort could remove; and it cannot be doubted that his severity materially corrected many of them. But the race of man cannot be viewed with benevolence unless their frailties are regarded with an indulgent and merciful eye. The honest indignation of Swift impaired his benevolence, and even affected the justness of his estimate of human nature. His hatred of hypocrisy sometimes drove him to a parade of harshness, which made his character appear to be less amiable than it really was. His friendships were faithful, if not tender; and his beneficence was active, though it rather sprang from principle than feeling. No stain could be discoverable in his private conduct, if we could forget his intercourse with one unfortunate, and with one admirable, woman.

His style is, in its kind, one of the models of English composition; it is proper, pure, precise, perspicuous, significant, nervous; deriving a certain dignity from a masterly contempt of puerile ornaments; in which every word seems to convey the intended meaning with the decision of the writer's character; not adapted, indeed, to express nice distinctions of thought or shades of feeling, or to convey those new and large ideas which must be illustrated by imagery; but qualified beyond any other to discuss the common business of life in such a manner as to convince and persuade the generality of men; and, where occasion allows it, meriting in its vehement plainness the praise of the most genuine eloquence. His verse is only, apparently, distinguished by the accident of measure; it has no quality of poetry and, like his prose, is remarkable for sense and wit.

He was educated in the family of Sir W. Temple, and he learned from that illustrious statesman not only habits of correct writing but the principles of liberty which he never avowedly relinquished. His

first connexions were with the Whigs, who seem to have treated him with a slight which, with a consciousness of his extraordinary powers, he very justly resented. He unfortunately suffered himself to be betrayed by his just resentment into a coalition with their opponents, without sufficiently considering that to retain right principles in mere abstraction was no atonement for co-operation with their enemies. But it must not be forgotten that in this unhappy change he broke no confidence; that he long resisted the tendency of political separation to dissolve friendship; and that when he at last yielded, instead of persecuting old friends, as so often happens, he used all his influence to serve them. He soon made his value felt by those whom he quitted, as well as by those whom he joined. During the administration of Lord Oxford, he was one of the most effective writers who ever influenced popular opinion. He had always been an ecclesiastical Tory, even while he was a political Whig, though it must be owned that his zeal appeared to be rather for the church than for religion. His retirement to Ireland dissolved his connexion with the political world, and left him at liberty to apply those just and generous principles of his youth to the condition of his own unfortunate country: to rouse a national indignation against misgovernment and thus to deserve a place among her highest benefactors.
(176–8)

Thomas Babington Macaulay

from 'Sir William Temple' 1838 (reprinted in *Critical and Historical Essays*, vol. 3, 1900)

Swift retained no pleasing recollection of Moor Park. And we may easily suppose a situation like his to have been intolerably painful to a mind haughty, irascible and conscious of pre-eminent ability. Long after, when he stood in the Court of Requests with a circle of gartered peers round him, or punned and rhymed with cabinet ministers over Secretary St John's *Monte-Pulciano*, he remembered, with deep and sore feeling, how miserable he used to be for days together when he suspected that Sir William had taken something ill. He could hardly believe that he, the Swift who chid the Lord Treasurer, rallied the

Captain General and confronted the pride of the Duke of Buckinghamshire with pride still more inflexible, could be the same being who had passed nights of sleepless anxiety in musing over a cross look or a testy word of a patron. 'Faith,' he wrote to Stella, with bitter levity, 'Sir William spoiled a fine gentleman.' Yet in justice to Temple we must say that there is no reason to think that Swift was more unhappy at Moor Park than he would have been in a similar situation under any roof in England. We think also that the obligations which the mind of Swift owed to that of Temple were not inconsiderable. Every judicious reader must be struck by the peculiarities which distinguish Swift's political tracts from all similar works produced by mere men of letters. Let any person compare, for example, the *Conduct of the Allies*, or the *Letter to the October Club* with Johnson's *False Alarm* or *Taxation No Tyranny*, and he will be at once struck by the difference of which we speak. He may possibly think Johnson a greater man than Swift. He may possibly prefer Johnson's style to Swift's. But he will at once acknowledge that Johnson writes like a man who has never been out of his study. Swift writes like a man who has passed his whole life in the midst of public business and to whom the most important affairs of state are as familiar as his weekly bills.

Turn him to any cause of policy,
The Gordian knot of it he will unloose,
Familiar as his garter.

The difference, in short, between a political pamphlet by Johnson and a political pamphlet by Swift is as great as the difference between an account of a battle by Mr Southey and the account of the same battle by Colonel Napier. It is impossible to doubt that the superiority of Swift is to be, in a great measure, attributed to his long and close connexion with Temple.

(258–9)

Thomas De Quincey

from 'Schlosser's Literary History of the Eighteenth Century'
1847 (reprinted in D. Masson (ed.), *Collected Writings*, vol. 11, 1890)

Schlosser, however, is right in a graver reflection which he makes
upon the prevailing philosophy of Swift, namely, that 'all his views
were directed towards what was *immediately* beneficial; which is the
characteristic of savages'. This is undeniable. The meanness of Swift's
nature, and his rigid incapacity for dealing with the grandeurs of the
human spirit, with religion, with poetry or even with science when
it rose above the mercenary practical, is absolutely appalling. His
own Yahoo is not a more abominable one-sided degradation of
humanity than is he himself under this aspect. . . .

As to the *style* of Swift, Mr Schlosser shows himself without sensibility in his objections. . . . Schlosser thinks the style of Gulliver
'somewhat dull'. This shows Schlosser's presumption in speaking
upon a point where he wanted, first, original delicacy of tact and,
secondly, familiar knowledge of English. Gulliver's style is *purposely*
touched slightly with that dullness of circumstantiality which besets
the excellent, but somewhat dull, race of men – old sea-captains. Yet
it wears only an aerial tint of dullness; the felicity of this colouring in
Swift's management is that it never goes the length of actually
wearying, but only of giving a comic air of downright Wapping and
Rotherhithe verisimilitude.

(14, 16)

William Makepeace Thackeray

from *English Humourists of the Eighteenth Century* 1851
(reprinted in *Works*, vol. 10, 1888)

As for the humour and conduct of this famous fable, I suppose there
is no person who reads but must admire; as for the moral, I think it
horrible, shameful, unmanly, blasphemous; and giant and great as
this Dean is, I say we should hoot him. Some of this audience mayn't
have read the last part of *Gulliver*, and to such I would recall the

advice of the venerable Mr Punch to persons about to marry, and say, 'Don't'. When Gulliver first lands among the Yahoos, the naked howling wretches clamber up trees and assault him, and he describes himself as 'almost stifled with the filth which fell about him'. The reader of the fourth part of *Gulliver's Travels* is like the hero himself in this instance. It is Yahoo language: a monster gibbering shrieks, and gnashing imprecations against mankind – tearing down all shreds of modesty, past all sense of manliness and shame; filthy in word, filthy in thought, furious, raging, obscene....

Treasures of wit and wisdom, and tenderness, too, must that man have had, locked up in the caverns of his gloomy heart, and shown fitfully to one or two whom he took in there. But it was not good to visit that place. People did not remain there long, and suffered for having been there. He shrank away from all affections sooner or later. Stella and Vanessa both died near him, and away from him. He had not heart enough to see them die. He broke from his fastest friend, Sheridan; he slunk away from his fondest admirer, Pope. His laugh jars on one's ear after seven-score years. He was always alone – alone and gnashing in the darkness, except when Stella's sweet smile came and shone upon him. When that went, silence and utter night closed over him. An immense genius: an awful downfall and ruin. So great a man he seems to me, that thinking of him is like thinking of an empire falling.

(406, 414–15)

Walter Bagehot

from 'The First Edinburgh Reviewers' 1855 (reprinted in N. St John-Stevas (ed.), *The Collected Works of Walter Bagehot*, vol. 1, 1965)

Sydney Smith is often compared to Swift; but this only shows with how little thought our common criticism is written. The two men have really nothing in common, except that they were both high in the church, and both wrote amusing letters about Ireland. Of course, to the great constructive and elaborative power displayed in Swift's longer works, Sydney Smith has no pretension; he could not have written *Gulliver's Travels*; but so far as the two series of Irish letters goes, it seems plain that he has the advantage. Plymley's letters are true; the treatment may be incomplete – the Catholic religion may have latent dangers and insidious attractions which are not there mentioned – but the main principle is sound; the common sense of religious toleration is hardly susceptible of better explanation. Drapier's letters, on the contrary, are essentially absurd; they are a clever appeal to ridiculous prejudices. Who cares now for a disputation on the evils to be apprehended a hundred years ago from adulterated halfpennies especially when we know that the halfpennies were not adulterated, and that if they had been, those evils would never have arisen? Any one, too, who wishes to make a collection of currency crotchets, will find those letters worth his attention. No doubt there is a clever affectation of common sense as in all of Swift's political writings, and the style has an air of business; yet, on the other hand, there are no passages which any one would now care to quote for their manner and their matter; and there are many in 'Plymley' that will be constantly cited, so long as existing controversies are at all remembered. The whole genius of the two writers is emphatically opposed. Sydney Smith's is the ideal of popular, buoyant, riotous fun; it cries and laughs with boisterous mirth; it rolls hither and thither like a mob, with elastic and commonplace joy. Swift was a detective in a dean's wig: he watched the mob; his whole wit is a kind of dexterous indication of popular frailties; he hated the crowd; he was a spy on beaming smiles, and a common informer against genial enjoyment. His whole essence was a soreness against mortality; show him innocent mirth, he would say: 'How absurd!' He was painfully wretched, no doubt, in himself: perhaps, as they say, he had no heart; but his mind, his brain, had a frightful capacity for secret pain; his sharpness was the sharpness of disease; his power the sore acumen of morbid wretchedness. It is impossible to fancy a parallel more proper to show the excellence, the unspeakable superiority of a buoyant and bounding writer.

(336–7)

Walter Savage Landor

Untitled poem 1863 (reprinted in S. Wheeler (ed.), *Complete Works: Poems*, vol. 15, 1935)

Will nothing but from Greece or Rome
Please me? is nothing good at home?
Yes; better; but I look in vain
For a Molière or La Fontaine.
Swift in his humour was as strong
But there was gall upon his tongue.
Bitters and acids may excite,
Yet satisfy not appetite.

(209)

H. A. Taine

from *Histoire de la littérature anglaise*, vol. 3 1864 (translated by H. van Laun as *History of English Literature*, vol. 3, 1871)

Such was this great and unhappy genius, the greatest of the classical age, the most unhappy in history, English throughout, whom the excess of his English qualities inspired and consumed, having this intensity of desires, which is the main feature of the race, the enormity of pride which the habit of liberty, command and success has impressed upon the nation, the solidity of the positive mind which habits of business have established in the country; precluded from power and action by his unchecked passions and his intractable pride; excluded from poetry and philosophy by the clear-sightedness and narrowness of his common sense; deprived of the consolations offered by contemplative life, and the occupation furnished by practical life; too superior to embrace heartily a religious sect or a political party, too narrow-minded to rest in the lofty doctrines which conciliate all beliefs, or in the wide sympathies which embrace all parties; condemned by his nature and surroundings to fight without loving a cause, to write without taking a liking to literature, to think without feeling the truth of any dogma, warring as a *condottiere* against all parties, a misanthrope disliking all men, a sceptic denying all beauty and truth. But those very surroundings, and this very nature, which expelled him from happiness, love, power and science, raised him, in this age of French imitation and classical moderation, to a wonderful height where, by the originality and power of his inventions, he is the equal of Byron, Milton and Shakespeare, and shows pre-eminently the character and mind of his nation. Sensibility, a positive mind and pride forged for him a unique style, of terrible vehemence, withering calmness, practical effectiveness, hardened by scorn, truth and hatred, a weapon of vengeance and war which made his enemies cry out and die under its point and its poison. A pamphleteer against opposition and government, he tore or crushed his adversaries with his irony or his sentences, with the tone of a judge, a sovereign and a hangman. A man of the world and a poet, he invented a cruel pleasantry, funereal laughter, a convulsive gaiety of bitter contrasts; and whilst dragging the mythological trappings, as if it were rags he was obliged to wear, he created a personal poetry by painting the crude details of trivial life, by the energy of a painful grotesqueness, by the merciless revelation of the filth we conceal.

(254–5)

Matthew Arnold

from *Culture and Anarchy* 1869 (reprinted in R. H. Super (ed.), *Complete Prose Works*, vol. 5, 1965)

But the point of view of culture, keeping the mark of human perfection simply and broadly in view, and not assigning to this perfection, as religion or utilitarianism assigns to it, a special and limited character, this point of view, I say, of culture is best given by these words of Epictetus: 'It is a sign of $\dot{a}\varphi\upsilon\dot{\iota}a$,' says he – that is, of a nature not finely tempered,

to give yourselves up to things which relate to the body; to make, for instance, a great fuss about exercise, a great fuss about eating, a great fuss about drinking, a great fuss about walking, a great fuss about riding. All these things ought to be done merely by the way: the formation of the spirit and character must be our real concern.

This is admirable; and, indeed, the Greek word εὐφυΐα, a finely tempered nature, gives exactly the notion of perfection as culture brings us to conceive it: a harmonious perfection, a perfection in which the characters of beauty and intelligence are both present, which unites 'the two noblest of things' – as Swift, who of one of the two, at any rate, had himself all too little, most happily calls them in his *The Battle of the Books*, 'the noblest of things, *sweetness and light*'. The εὐφυής is the man who tends towards sweetness and light; the ἀφυής, on the other hand, is our Philistine. The immense spiritual significance of the Greeks is due to their having been inspired with this central and happy idea of the essential character of human perfection; and Mr Bright's misconception of culture, as a smattering of Greek and Latin, comes itself, after all, from this wonderful significance of the Greeks having affected the very machinery of our education, and is in itself a kind of homage to it.
(98–9)

John Ruskin

from the Preface to *Sesame and Lilies*   1871 (reprinted in *Works*, vol. 1, 1887)

Yet if anyone, skilled in reading the torn manuscripts of the human soul, cares for more intimate knowledge of me, he may have it by knowing with what persons in past history I have most sympathy.

I will name three.

In all that is strongest and deepest in me – that fits me for my work, and gives light or shadow to my being, I have sympathy with Guido Guinicelli.

In my constant natural temper, and thoughts of things and of people, with Marmontel.

In my enforced and accidental temper, and thoughts of things and of people, with Dean Swift.

Anyone who can understand the natures of those three men can understand mine.
(xxviii)

Henry James

from a review of Taine's *English Literature*   1872 (reprinted in
M. Shapira (ed.), *Henry James: Selected Criticism*, 1963)

A phrase of very frequent occurrence with M. Taine, and very whole-some in its frequency, is *la grande invention*; his own tendency is to practise it. In effort and inclination, however, he is nothing if not impartial; and there is something almost touching in the sympathetic breadth of his admiration for a tone of genius so foreign to French tradition as the great Scriptural inspiration of Bunyan and of Milton. To passionate vigour he always does justice. On the other hand, when he deals with a subject simply because it stands in his path, he is far less satisfactory. His estimate of Swift is a striking example of his tendency to overcharge his portrait and make a picture at all hazards. Swift was a bitter and incisive genius, but he had neither the volume nor the force implied in M. Taine's report of him.
(19)

Edward John Trelawny

from *Records of Shelley, Byron and the Author*   1878

As [Byron] was dismounting he mentioned two odd words that would rhyme. I observed on the felicity he had shown in this art, repeating a couplet out of *Don Juan*; he was both pacified and pleased at this, and putting his hand on my horse's crest, observed, 'If you are curious in these matters, look in Swift. I will send you a volume; he beats us all hollow; his rhymes are wonderful.'
(31)

W. E. H. Lecky

from *History of England in the Eighteenth Century* 1878
(reprinted 1883)

The position of Swift at this time [1714] is well worthy of attention, for his judgement was that of a man of great shrewdness as well as great genius, and he probably represented the feelings of many of the more intelligent members of his party. Though a fierce, unscrupulous and singularly scurrilous political writer, he was not, in the general character of his politics, a violent man,[1] and the inconsistency of his political life has been very grossly exaggerated. It was almost inevitable that a young man, brought up as Secretary to Sir W. Temple, should enter public life with Whig prepossessions. It was almost equally inevitable that a High-Church divine should, in the party conflicts under Queen Anne, ultimately gravitate to the Tories. Personal ambition, no doubt, as he himself very frankly admitted, contributed to his change, but there was nothing in it of that complete and scandalous apostasy of which he has often been accused. From first to last an exclusive Church feeling was his genuine passion. It appeared fully, though in a very strange form, in *A Tale of a Tub* which was published as early as 1704. It appeared still more strongly in his *Project for the Reformation of Manners*, in his *Sentiments of a Church-of-England Man*, in his *Argument against Abolishing Christianity*, in his 'Letter to a Member of Parliament concerning the Sacramental Test'; all of which were published at the time when he was ostensibly a Whig. It appeared not less clearly many years afterwards in his Irish tracts, written at a period when it would have been eminently conducive to the objects he was aiming at to have rallied all religions in opposition to the Government. In the latter part of the reign of Anne political parties were grouped, much more than in the previous reign, by ecclesiastical considerations; and, after the impeachment of Sacheverell, the Tory party had become, before all

---

1 His genuine political opinion was expressed by him in one very happy and characteristic sentence: 'Whoever has a true value for Church and State should avoid the extremes of Whig for the sake of the former, and the extremes of Tory on account of the latter' – *The Sentiments of a Church-of-England Man*.

things, the party of the Church. On the other hand, Swift never appears to have wavered in his attachment to the Protestant line; and there is not the smallest evidence that he had at any period of his life the slightest communication with St Germain's. His position in the party was a very prominent one. He was, without exception, the most effective political writer in England at a time when political writing was of transcendent importance. His influence contributed very much to that generous and discriminating patronage of literature which was the special glory of the Tory ministry of Anne. To his pen we owe by far the most powerful and most rational defence of the Peace of Utrecht that has ever been composed; and although, like the other writers of his party, he wrote much in a strain of disgraceful scurrility against Marlborough, it is at least very honourable to his memory that he disapproved of, and protested against, the conduct of the ministers in superseding that great general in the midst of the war.[1]

In the crisis which we are considering, he strongly urged upon them to reconcile themselves with the elector; and he came over specially from Ireland in order to compose the differences in the cabinet. Having failed in his attempt, he retired to the house of a friend in Berkshire, and there wrote a remarkable appeal to the nation, which shows clearly his deep sense of the dangers of the time. Though he was much more closely connected, both by personal and political sympathy, with Oxford than with Bolingbroke, he now strongly blamed the indecision and procrastination of the former, and maintained that the party was in such extreme and imminent danger that nothing but the most drastic remedies could save it. The great majority of the nation, he maintained, had two wishes. The first was, 'that the Church of England should be preserved entire in all her rights, powers and privileges; all doctrines relating to government discouraged which she condemns; all schisms, sects and heresies discountenanced' (VIII 88). The second was, the maintenance of the Protestant succession in the House of Brunswick, 'not for any partiality to that illustrious house further than as it hath had the

1 *Journal to Stella*, 7 January 1712. In one of his letters to Steele, dated 27 May 1713, he says: 'As to the great man [Marlborough] whose defence you undertake, though I do not think so well of him as you do, yet I have been the cause of preventing 500 hard things said against him'.

honour to mingle with the blood royal of England, and is the nearest branch of our regal line reformed from Popery' (VIII 90). He proceeded, in language which showed some insincerity or some blindness, to deny the existence of any considerable Jacobitism outside the non-juror body, maintaining that the supporters of the theory of passive obedience could have no difficulty in supporting a line which they found established by law, and were not at all called upon by their principles to enter into any historical investigation of the merits of the revolution. But the danger of the situation lay in the fact that the heir to the throne had completely failed to give any assurance to the nation that he would support that Church party to which the overwhelming majority of the nation was attached; that he had, on the contrary, given all his confidence to the implacable enemies of that party – to the Whigs, Low Churchmen and Dissenters. Swift maintained that the only course that could secure the party was the immediate and absolute exclusion of all such persons from every description of civil and military office. The whole government of the country, in all its departments, must be thrown into the hands of Tories, and it would then be impossible to displace them. This was necessary because the Whigs had already proved very dangerous to the constitution in Church and State, because they were highly irritated at the loss of power,

but principally because they have prevailed, by misrepresentations and other artifices, to make the successor look upon them as the only persons he can trust. Upon which account they cannot be too soon or too much disabled; neither will England ever be safe from the attempts of this wicked confederacy until their strength and interest shall be so far reduced that for the future it may not be in the power of the Crown, although in conjunction with any rich and factious body of men, to choose an ill majority in a House of Commons (VIII 89).

He at the same time urged that the Elector should be peremptorily called upon by the Queen to declare his approbation of the policy of the Queen's ministers, and to disavow all connexion with the Whigs.

It must be owned that this pamphlet showed very little of that extreme subservience to royal authority for which the Tory party had been so often reproached. The policy indicated, if openly avowed, might have led to a civil war, and Bolingbroke probably showed much wisdom in inducing Swift to withhold the publication. Though caring only for the ascendency of the Tory party, Bolingbroke had by this time gone so far in the direction of Jacobitism that it was difficult to recede, and the policy of the Government tended more and more to a restoration of the Stuarts. Yet Oxford opposed to the last any step which amounted to an irrevocable decision, and at the time when Parliament was prorogued nothing had been arranged. Many military and civil appointments had, indeed, been made in the interest of the Pretender, but nothing had been done to induce the Queen to invite him over, or to determine formally the conditions on which he might mount the throne, or the plan of operations after the death of the Queen. The leaders in France became more and more convinced of the insincerity of Oxford. Berwick and Torcy wrote to him representing that the Queen's death might happen very shortly, and asking for a distinct account of his measures to secure in that case the interests of the legitimate heir, as well as of the steps the Prince himself should take; but they could obtain no other answer than that, if the Queen now died, the affairs both of the Stuarts and of the Government were ruined without resource. France was so exhausted after the late struggle that she could not venture, at the risk of another war, to support the Pretender by force of arms; and it was also an unfortunate circumstance for his cause that about this time Berwick, who was one of its chief supports, received a command in Catalonia.

The object of the Jacobites under these circumstances was to displace Oxford, and they had no great difficulty in accomplishing it. The influence which his good private character and his moderate and compromising temperament once gave him in the country had been rapidly waning. His party were disgusted with his habitual indecision. The Queen had to complain of many instances of gross and scandalous disrespect; but the influence which at last turned the scale was that of Lady Masham. She was now wholly in the interests of the Jacobites. She had quarrelled violently with Oxford about a pension and, at the request of the Jacobite leaders, she used her great influence with the Queen to procure his dismissal. Seldom has it been given to a woman wholly undistinguished by birth, character, beauty or intellect to affect so powerfully the march of affairs. Her influence, though by no means the sole, was undoubtedly a leading, cause of the change of ministry in 1710, which saved France from almost complete ruin and determined the Peace of Utrecht. Her influence in 1714 all but altered the order of succession in England, and with it the whole course of English politics. On 27 July, after a long and violent altercation in the cabinet, Oxford was dismissed, the Queen resumed the white staff of Treasurer, and Bolingbroke became Prime Minister. (196–201)

Leslie Stephen

from *English Literature and Society in the Eighteenth Century*   1904
(The Ford Lectures, 1903)

Swift is one of the most impressive of all literary figures, and I will not touch upon his personal peculiarities. I will only remark that in one respect he agrees with his friend Addison. He emphasizes, of course, the aspect over which Addison passes lightly; he scorns fools too heartily to treat them tenderly and do justice to the pathetic side of even human folly. But he, too, believes in culture – though he may despair of its dissemination. He did his best, during his brief period of power, to direct patronage towards men of letters, even to Whigs; and tried, happily without success, to found an English Academy. . . .

The growing sense that there was something wrong about the political system which Pope turned to account was significant of coming changes. The impression that the evil was entirely due to Walpole personally was one of the natural illusions of party warfare, and the disease was not extirpated when the supposed cause was removed. The most memorable embodiment of the sentiment was Swift. The concentrated scorn of corruption in the *Drapier's Letters* was followed by the intense misanthropy of *Gulliver's Travels.* The singular way in which Swift blends personal aversion with political conviction, and the strange humour which conceals the misanthropist under a superficial playfulness, veils to some extent his real aim. But Swift showed with unequalled power and in an exaggerated form the conviction that there was something wrong in the social order, which was suggested by the conditions of the time and was to bear fruit in later days. Satire, however, is by its nature negative; it does not present a positive ideal, and tends to degenerate into mere hopeless pessimism. Lofty poetry can only spring from some inner positive enthusiasm. (77–8, 119–20)

T. S. Eliot

from 'Andrew Marvell'   1921 (reprinted in *Selected Essays*, 1951)

Out of that high style developed from Marlowe through Jonson (for Shakespeare does not lend himself to these genealogies) the seventeenth century separated two qualities: wit and magniloquence. Neither is as simple or as apprehensible as its name seems to imply, and the two are not in practice antithetical; both are conscious and cultivated, and the mind which cultivates one may cultivate the other. The actual poetry, of Marvell, of Cowley, of Milton and of others, is a blend in varying proportions. And we must be on guard not to employ the terms with too wide a comprehension; for like the other fluid terms with which literary criticism deals, the meaning alters with the age, and for precision we must rely to some degree upon the literacy and good taste of the reader. The wit of the Caroline poets is not the wit of Shakespeare, and it is not the wit of Dryden, the great master of contempt, or of Pope, the great master of hatred, or of Swift, the great master of disgust. (293)

James Joyce

from *Ulysses*   1922 (reprinted 1947)

Houses of decay, mine, his and all. You told the Clongowes gentry you had an uncle a judge and an uncle a general in the army. Come out of them, Stephen. Beauty is not there. Nor in the stagnant bay of Marsh's library where you read the fading prophecies of Joachim Abbas. For whom? The hundredheaded rabble of the cathedral close. A hater of his kind ran from them to the wood of madness, his mane

foaming in the moon, his eyeballs stars. Houyhnhnm, horse-nostrilled. The oval equine faces. Temple, Buck Mulligan, Foxy Campbell. Lantern jaws. Abbas father, furious dean, what offence laid fire to their brains?
(36)

T. S. Eliot

from '*Ulysses*, Order, and Myth', *Dial*, vol. 75   November 1923

[Richard Aldington] finds the book, if I understand him, to be an invitation to chaos, and an expression of feelings which are perverse, partial and a distortion of reality. But unless I quote Mr Aldington's words I am likely to falsify. 'I say, moreover,' he says, 'that when Mr Joyce, with his marvellous gifts, uses them to disgust us with mankind, he is doing something which is false and a libel on humanity.' It is somewhat similar to the opinion of the urbane Thackeray upon Swift. 'As for the moral, I think it horrible, shameful, unmanly, blasphemous; and giant and great as this Dean is, I say we should hoot him.' (This, of the conclusion of the voyage to the Houyhn-hnms – which seems to me one of the greatest triumphs that the human soul has ever achieved.) It is true that Thackeray later pays Swift one of the finest tributes that a man has ever given or received: 'So great a man he seems to me that thinking of him is like thinking of an empire falling.'
(481)

André Breton

from *Manifeste du surréalisme*   1924 (reprinted in 1969; translated for this volume by Denis Donoghue)

Certainly, not to consider our conclusions too glibly, there are many writers who could pass as surrealists, beginning with Dante and – on his better days – Shakespeare. . . .

Swift is surrealist in wickedness.
Sade is surrealist in sadism.
Chateaubriand is surrealist in exoticism.
Constant is surrealist in politics.
Hugo is surrealist when he is not foolish.
Desbordes-Valmore is surrealist in love.
Bertrand is surrealist in the past.
Rabbe is surrealist in death.
Poe is surrealist in adventure.
Baudelaire is surrealist in morals.
Rimbaud is surrealist in the practical experience of life, etc.
Mallarmé is surrealist in confidences.
Jarry is surrealist in absinth.
Nouveau is surrealist in the kiss.
Saint-Pol-Roux is surrealist in the symbol.
Fargue is surrealist in atmosphere.
Vaché is surrealist in ego.
Reverdy is surrealist of himself.
Saint-John Perse is surrealist, aloof.
Roussel is surrealist in the anecdote.
Etc.

I insist that these writers are not always surrealist in the sense in which I distinguish, in each of them, certain preconceived ideas which, very naïvely indeed, they hold. They held them because they had not heard the surrealist voice which continued to sound on the eve of death and above the storms; because they were not content merely to orchestrate the marvellous score. As instruments, they were too proud; that is why they did not always produce a harmonious sound. (38–40)

But what if my own 'tradition' – highly circuitous, I agree, but at least my own – passes through Heraclitus, Abélard, Eckhardt, Retz, Rousseau, Swift, Sade, Lewis, Arnim, Lautréamont, Engels, Jarry and a few others? I have made for myself a system of co-ordinates, a system which runs contrary to my personal experience, but seems to me nevertheless to contain many possibilities for the future. (166)

T. S. Eliot

from 'The Oxford Jonson', *Dial*, vol. 85   July 1928

Messrs Herford and Simpson bring out very well the capital importance of *Sejanus* in the preparation of Jonson for writing *Volpone* and
The Alchemist and *The Silent Woman*:

Closely as *Sejanus* is modelled upon history, none of Jonson's
dramas is more Jonsonian in conception and execution. If he
alters little in his historical materials, it is partly because
history in some important points played as it were into his
hands, providing both a kind of action and a prevailing
quality of character singularly suited to his genius and to his
art. The advance in coherence upon any of the Humour
plays, after the first, is enormous; upon *Every Man in His
Humour* itself, it is considerable. He was entering in fact upon
a new phase of his art. The immense constructive grip soon
to be shown in *Volpone* and *The Alchemist* is already
approached, as their dramatic situation is anticipated.

The resemblances between *Sejanus* and *Volpone* are particularized, and
the criticism of the former closes with this paragraph:

On the whole, *Sejanus* is the tragedy of a satirist – of one
who felt and saw more intensely the vices and follies than
the sorrows of men, and who, with boundless power of
scorn, was poorly endowed in pity. He could draw the
plotting of bad men, their savage vengeance, their ruinous
fall; he could draw the fatuities and mishaps of fools; but
the delusions which jangle and overthrow a noble nature lay
beyond his sphere. Jonsonian tragedy suffers from an inner
poverty in the humanities of the heart – analogous to the
wilful bareness of style which masks the poetic core of the
tragedy of Ibsen. But the imagination is nevertheless
impressed by this sombre fabric of verdureless flint and
granite, too arid and savage to leave any coign of vantage for
sympathy.

This is good criticism, though the analysis could be carried farther. For it does not explain the fact that the satire of Swift, with equal power of scorn, equal perception of folly, stupidity and evil, moves our feeling as nothing of Jonson's can do. The last chapter of the voyage to the Houyhnhnms is, in its kind, more terrible satire than anything Jonson ever wrote, yet it can move us to pity and a kind of purgation. We feel everywhere the tragedy of Swift himself, we never feel any tragedy about Jonson. Jonson nevertheless remains for us a great personality, as was Swift; but this personality is largely given through the tradition about the man, and nowhere completely in his work; and Swift on the other hand is wholly a terrific personality *in* his work. What is the difference? It is not to say that Swift was a greater man, or a greater artist, than Jonson; nor can we say in return that Jonson's was a keener intellect than Swift's. But the work of Swift came out of deeper and intenser emotion.

What is repellent to many readers in the plays of Jonson, or what at least leaves them indifferent, is perhaps this fact that the satire fails of the first intensity, by not seeming to come out of deep personal feeling. By the consistency of the point of view, the varied repetition of the same tone, by artistic constructive skill, Jonson does create the illusion of a world, and works a miracle of great satire without great emotion behind it. But it is not a world in which any one can live for long at a time, though it is one from the study of which every writer can profit.

(67–8)

D. H. Lawrence

from the Introduction to *Pansies*   1929 (reprinted in E. D. McDonald (ed.), *Phoenix: The Posthumous Papers of D. H. Lawrence*, 1936)

We can't have the consciousness haunted any longer by repulsive spectres which are no more than poor simple scapegoat words representing parts of man himself; words that the cowardly and unclean mind has driven out into the limbo of the unconscious, whence they return upon us looming and magnified out of all proportion, frightening us beyond all reasons. We must put an end to that. It is the self divided against itself most dangerously. The simple and natural 'obscene' words must be cleaned up of all their depraved fear-associations, and readmitted into the consciousness to take their natural place. Now they are magnified out of all proportion, so is the mental fear they represent. We must accept the word arse as we accept the word face, since arses we have and always shall have. We can't start cutting off the buttocks of unfortunate mankind, like the ladies in the Voltaire story, just to fit the mental expulsion of the word.

This scapegoat business does the mind itself so much damage. There is a poem of Swift's which should make us pause. It is written to Celia, his Celia – and every verse ends with the mad, maddened refrain: 'But – Celia, Celia, Celia shits!' Now that, stated baldly, is so ridiculous it is almost funny. But when one remembers the gnashing insanity to which the great mind of Swift was reduced by that and similar thoughts, the joke dies away. Such thoughts poisoned him, like some terrible constipation. They poisoned his mind. And why, in heaven's name? The *fact* cannot have troubled him, since it applied to himself and to all of us. It was not the fact that Celia shits which so deranged him, it was the *thought*. His mind couldn't bear the thought. Great wit as he was, he could not see how ridiculous his revulsions were. His arrogant mind overbore him. He couldn't even see how much worse it would be if Celia didn't shit. His physical sympathies were too weak, his guts were too cold to sympathize with poor Celia in her natural functions. His insolent and sicklily squeamish mind just turned her into a thing of horror, because she was merely natural and went to the w.c. It is monstrous! One feels like going back across all the years to poor Celia, to say to her: 'It's all right, don't you take any notice of that mental lunatic.'

And Swift's form of madness is very common today. Men with cold guts and over-squeamish minds are always thinking those things and squirming. Wretched man is the victim of his own little revulsions, which he magnifies into great horrors and terrifying taboos. We are all savages, we all have taboos. The Australian black may have the kangaroo for his taboo. And then he will probably die of shock and terror if a kangaroo happens to touch him. Which is what I would call a purely unnecessary death. But modern men have even more dangerous taboos. To us, certain words, certain ideas are taboo, and if they come upon us and we can't drive them away, we die or go mad with a degraded sort of terror. Which is what happened to Swift. He was such a great wit. And the modern mind altogether is falling into this form of degraded taboo-insanity. I call it a waste of sane human consciousness. But it is very dangerous, dangerous to the individual and utterly dangerous to society as a whole. Nothing is so fearful in a mass-civilization like ours as a mass insanity.

The remedy is, of course, the same in both cases: lift off the taboo. The kangaroo is a harmless animal, the word shit is a harmless word. Make either into a taboo, and it becomes more dangerous. The result of taboo is insanity. And insanity, especially mob-insanity, mass-insanity, is the fearful danger that threatens our civilization. There are certain persons with a sort of rabies, who live only to infect the mass. If the young do not watch out, they will find themselves, before so very many years are past, engulfed in a howling manifestation of mob-insanity, truly terrifying to think of. It will be better to be dead than to live to see it. Sanity, wholeness, is everything. In the name of piety and purity, what a mass of disgusting insanity is spoken and written. We shall have to fight the mob, in order to keep sane, and to keep society sane.

T. S. Eliot

from 'Cyril Tourneur' 1930 (reprinted in *Selected Essays*, 3rd edn, 1951)

[Eliot's theme is the 'loathing and horror of life itself' in *The Revenger's Tragedy*.]

The Revenger's Tragedy, then, is, in this respect, quite different from any play by any minor Elizabethan; it can, in this respect, be compared only to *Hamlet*. Perhaps, however, its quality would be better marked by contrasting it with a later work of cynicism and loathing, *Gulliver's Travels*. No two compositions could be more dissimilar. Tourneur's 'suffering, cynicism and despair', to use Collins's[1] words, are static; they might be prior to experience, or be the fruit of but little; Swift's is the progressive cynicism of the mature and dis-

1. John Churton Collins, editor of Tourneur. [Ed.]

appointed man of the world. As an objective comment on the world, Swift's is by far the more terrible. For Swift had himself enough pettiness, as well as enough sin of pride, and lust of dominion, to be able to expose and condemn mankind by its universal pettiness and pride and vanity and ambition; and his poetry, as well as his prose, attests that he hated the very smell of the human animal. We may think as we read Swift, 'how loathesome human beings are'; in reading Tourneur we can only think, 'how terrible to loathe human beings so much as that'. For you cannot make humanity horrible merely by presenting human beings as consistent and monotonous maniacs of gluttony and lust.

(190)

W. B. Yeats

from the Introduction to *The Words upon the Window-Pane*   1934 (reprinted in *Explorations*, 1962)

Swift haunts me; he is always just round the next corner. Sometimes it is a thought of my great-great-grandmother, a friend of that Archbishop King who sent him to England about the 'First-Fruits', sometimes it is St Patrick's, where I have gone to wander and mediate, that brings him to mind, sometimes I remember something hard or harsh in O'Leary or in Taylor, or in the public speech of our statesmen, that reminds me by its style of his verse or prose. Did he not speak, perhaps, with just such an intonation? This instinct for what is near and yet hidden is in reality a return to the sources of our power, and therefore a claim made upon the future. Thought seems more true, emotion more deep, spoken by someone who touches my pride, who seems to claim me of his kindred, who seems to make me a part of some national mythology, nor is mythology mere ostentation, mere vanity if it draws me onward to the unknown; another turn of the gyre and myth is wisdom, pride, discipline. I remember the shudder in my spine when Mrs Patrick Campbell said, speaking words Hofmannsthal put into the mouth of Electra, 'I too am of that ancient race':

Swift has sailed into his rest:
Savage indignation there
Cannot lacerate his breast.
Imitate him if you dare,
World-besotted traveller; he
Served human liberty.

'In Swift's day men of intellect reached the height of their power, the greatest position they ever attained in society and the State. . . . His ideal order was the Roman Senate, his ideal men Brutus and Cato; such an order and such men had seemed possible once more.' The Cambridge undergraduate [a character in Yeats's *The Words upon the Window-Pane*] into whose mouth I have put these words may have read similar words in F. S. Oliver, 'the last brilliant addition to English historians', for young men such as he read the newest authorities; probably Oliver and he thought of the influence at court and in public life of Swift and of Leibniz, of the spread of science and of scholarship over Europe, its examination of documents, its destruction of fables, a science and a scholarship modern for the first time, of certain great minds that were medieval in their scope but modern in their freedom. I must, however, add certain thoughts of my own that affected me as I wrote. I thought about a passage in the Grammont *Memoirs* where some great man is commended for his noble manner, as we commend a woman for her beauty or her charm; a famous passage in the *Appeal from the New to the Old Whigs* commending the old Whig aristocracy for their intellect and power and because their doors stood open to like-minded men; the palace of Blenheim, its pride of domination that expected a thousand years, something Asiatic in its carved intricacy of stone.
   'Everything great in Ireland and in our character, in what remains of our architecture, comes from that day . . . we have kept its seal longer than England.' The overstatement of an enthusiastic Cambridge student, and yet with its measure of truth. The Battle of the Boyne overwhelmed a civilization full of religion and myth, and brought in its place intelligible laws planned out upon a great blackboard, a capacity for horizontal lines, for rigid shapes, for buildings, for attitudes of mind that could be multiplied like an expanding bookcase: the modern world, and something that appeared and

perished in its dawn, an instinct for Roman rhetoric, Roman elegance.
It established a Protestant aristocracy, some of whom neither called
themselves English[1] nor looked with contempt or dread upon conquered Ireland. Indeed the battle was scarcely over when Molyneux,
speaking in their name, affirmed the sovereignty of the Irish Parliament.[2] No one had the right to make our laws but the King, Lords
and Commons of Ireland; the battle had been fought to change not
an English but an Irish Crown; and our Parliament was almost as
ancient as that of England. It was this doctrine[3] that Swift uttered in
the *Fourth Drapier's Letter* with such astringent eloquence that it
passed from the talk of study and parlour to that of road and market,
and created the political nationality of Ireland. Swift found his
nationality through the *Drapier's Letters*, his convictions came from
action and passion, but Berkeley, a much younger man, could find it
through contemplation. He and his fellow-students but knew the
war through the talk of the older men. As a boy of eighteen or
nineteen he called the Irish people 'natives' as though he were in
some foreign land, but two or three years later, perhaps while still
an undergraduate, defined the English materialism of his day in three

1 Nor were they English: the newest arrivals soon intermarried with an older
stock, and that older stock had intermarried again and again with Gaelic Ireland.
All my childhood the Coopers of Markree, County Sligo, represented such
rank and fashion as the County knew, and I had it from my friend the late
Bryan Cooper that his supposed Cromwellian ancestor, being childless, adopted
an O'Brien; while local tradition thinks that an O'Brien, promised the return
of her confiscated estate if she married a Cromwellian soldier, married a
Cooper and murdered him three days after. Not, however, before he had
founded a family. The family of Yeats, never more than small gentry, arrived,
if I can trust the only man among us who may have seen the family tree before
it was burnt by Canadian Indians, 'about the time of Henry VII'. Ireland,
divided in religion and politics, is as much one race as any modern country.
2 'Until 1691 Roman Catholics were admitted by law into both Houses of
Legislature in Ireland' (J. G. S. MacNeill, *Constitutional and Parliamentary History of Ireland*, Dublin, 1917, p. 10).
3 A few weeks ago the hierarchy of the Irish Church addressed, without any
mandate from Protestant Ireland, not the Irish people as they had every right
to, even in the defence of folly, but the Imperial Conference, and begged that
the Irish courts might remain subservient to the Privy Council. Terrified into
intrigue where none threatened, they turned from Swift and Molyneux. I
remind them that when the barons of the Irish Court of Exchequer obeyed the
English Privy Council in 1719 our ancestors clapped them into jail. (1931.)

profound sentences, and wrote after each that 'we Irish' think otherwise – 'I publish . . . to know whether other men have the same ideas
as we Irishmen' – and before he was twenty-five had fought the
Salamis of the Irish intellect. The Irish landed aristocracy, who knew
more of the Siege of Derry and the Battle of the Boyne delineated on
vast tapestries for their House of Lords by Dublin Huguenots, than
of philosophy, found themselves masters of a country demoralized
by generations of war and famine and shared in its demoralization.
In 1730 Swift said from the pulpit that their houses were in ruins and
no new building anywhere, that the houses of their rack-ridden
tenants were no better than English pigsties, that the bulk of the
people trod barefoot and in rags. He exaggerated, for already the
Speaker, Connolly, had built that great house at Celbridge where slate,
stone and furniture were Irish, even the silver from Irish mines; the
new Parliament House had perhaps been planned; and there was a
general stir of life. The old age of Berkeley passed amid art and music,
and men had begun to boast that in these no country had made such
progress; and some dozen years after Berkeley's death Arthur Young
found everywhere in stately Georgian houses scientific agricultural-
ists, benefactors of their countryside, though for the half-educated,
drunken, fire-eating, impoverished lesser men he had nothing but
detestation. Goldsmith might have found likeable qualities, a capacity
for mimicry[1] perhaps, among these lesser men, and Sir Jonah Bar-
rington made them his theme, but, detestable or not, they were out
of fashion. Miss Edgeworth described her *Castle Rackrent* upon the
title page of its first edition as 'the habits of the Irish squirearchy
before 1782'. A few years more and the country people would have
forgotten that the Irish aristocracy was founded, like all aristocracies,
upon conquest, or rather, would have remembered, and boasted in
the words of a medieval Gaelic poet, 'We are a sword people and we
go with the sword.' Unhappily the lesson first taught by Molyneux
and Swift had been but half learnt when the test came – country
gentlemen are poor politicians – and Ireland's 'dark insipid period'
began. During the entire eighteenth century the greatest landowning
family of the neighbourhood I best knew in childhood sent not a
single man into the English army and navy, but during the nineteenth

1 He wrote that he had never laughed so much at Garrick's acting as at somebody in an Irish tavern mimicking a Quaker sermon.

century one or more in every generation; a new absenteeism, foreseen by Miss Edgeworth, began; those that lived upon their estates bought no more fine editions of the classics; separated from public life and ambition they sank, as I have heard Lecky complain, 'into grass farmers'. Yet their genius did not die out; they sent everywhere administrators and military leaders, and now that their ruin has come (what resolute nation permits a strong alien class within its borders?) I would, remembering obscure ancestors that preached in their churches or fought beside their younger sons over half the world, and despite a famous passage of O'Grady's, gladly sing their song.

He foresaw the ruin to come, Democracy, Rousseau, the French Revolution; that is why he hated the common run of men – 'I hate lawyers, I hate doctors,' he said, 'though I love Dr So-and-so and Judge So-and-so' – that is why he wrote *Gulliver*, that is why he wore out his brain, that is why he felt *saeva indignatio*, that is why he sleeps under the greatest epitaph in history.

A Discourse of the Contests and Dissensions between the Nobles and Commons in Athens and Rome, published in 1701 to warn the Tory Opposition of the day against the impeachment of ministers, is Swift's one philosophical work. All states depend for their health upon a right balance between the One, the Few and the Many. The One is the executive, which may in fact be more than one – the Roman republic had two consuls – but must for the sake of rapid decision be as few as possible; the Few are those who through the possession of hereditary wealth, or great personal gifts, have come to identify their lives with the life of the State, whereas the lives and ambitions of the Many are private. The Many do their day's work well, and so far from copying even the wisest of their neighbours affect 'a singularity' in action and in thought; but set them to the work of the State and every man Jack is 'listed in a party', becomes the fanatical follower of men of whose characters he knows next to nothing, and from that day on puts nothing into his mouth that some other man has not already chewed and digested. And furthermore, from the moment of enlistment thinks himself above other men and struggles for power until all is in confusion. I divine an Irish hatred of abstraction likewise expressed by that fable of Gulliver among the inventors and men of science, by Berkeley in his *Commonplace Book*, by Goldsmith in the satire of *The Good-Natured Man*, in the picturesque, minute observation of *The Deserted Village*, and by Burke in his attack upon mathematical democracy. Swift enforced his moral by proving that Rome and Greece were destroyed by the war of the Many upon the Few; in Rome, where the Few had kept their class organization, it was a war of classes, in Greece, where they had not, war upon character and genius. Miltiades, Aristides, Themistocles, Pericles, Alcibiades, Phocion, 'impeached for high crimes and misdemeanours . . . were honoured and lamented by their country as the preservers of it, and have had the veneration of all ages since paid justly to their memories'. In Rome parties so developed that men born and bred among the Few were compelled to join one party or the other and to flatter and bribe. All civilizations must end in some such way, for the Many obsessed by emotion create a multitude of religious sects but give themselves at last to some one master of bribes and flatteries and sink into the ignoble tranquillity of servitude. He defines a tyranny as the predominance of the One, the Few or the Many, but thinks that of the Many the immediate threat. All states at their outset possess a ruling power seated in the whole body as that of the soul in the human body, a perfect balance of the three estates, the king some sort of chief magistrate, and then comes 'a tyranny: first either of the Few or the Many; but at last infallibly of a single person'. He thinks the English balance most perfect in the time of Queen Elizabeth, but that in the next age a tyranny of the Many produced that of Cromwell, and that, though recovery followed, 'all forms of government must be mortal like their authors', and he quotes from Polybius, 'those abuses and corruptions, which in time destroy a government, are sown along with the very seeds of it' and destroy it 'as rust eats away iron, and worms devour wood'. Whether the final tyranny is created by the Many – in his eyes all Caesars were tyrants – or imposed by foreign power, the result is the same. At the fall of liberty came 'a dark insipid period through all Greece' – had he Ireland in his mind also? – and the people became, in the words of Polybius, 'great reverencers of crowned heads'.

Twenty-two years later Giambattista Vico published that *Scienza Nuova* which Mr James Joyce is expounding or symbolizing in the strange fragments of his *Work in Progress*. He was the opposite of

Swift in everything, a humble, peaceful man, son of a Neapolitan bookseller and without political opinions; he wrote panegyrics upon men of rank, seemed to admire all that they did, took their gratuities and yet kept his dignity. He thought civilization passed through the phases Swift has described, but that it was harsh and terrible until the Many prevailed, and its joints cracked and loosened, happiest when some one man, surrounded by able subordinates, dismissed the Many to their private business, that its happiness lasted some generations until, sense of the common welfare lost, it grew malicious and treacherous, fell into 'the barbarism of reflection', and after that into an honest, plain barbarism accepted with relief by all, and started upon its round again. Rome had conquered surrounding nations because those nations were nearer than it to humanity and happiness; was not Carthage already almost a democratic state when destruction came? Swift seemed to shape his narrative upon some clairvoyant vision of his own life, for he saw civilization pass from comparative happiness and youthful vigour to an old age of violence and self-contempt, whereas Vico saw it begin in penury like himself and end as he himself would end in a long inactive peace. But there was a greater difference: Swift, a practical politician in everything he wrote, ascribed its rise and fall to virtues and vices all could understand, whereas the philosophical Vico ascribed them to 'the rhythm of the elemental forms of the mind', a new idea that would dominate philosophy. Outside Anglo-Saxon nations where progress, impelled by moral enthusiasm and the Patent Office, seems a perpetual straight line, this 'circular movement', as Swift's master, Polybius, called it, has long been the friend and enemy of public order. Both Sorel and Marx, their eyes more Swift's than Vico's, have preached a return to a primeval state, a beating of all down into a single class that a new civilization may arise with its Few, its Many and its One. Students of contemporary Italy, where Vico's thought is current through its influence upon Croce and Gentile, think it created, or in part created, the present government of one man surrounded by just such able assistants as Vico foresaw. Some philosopher has added this further thought: the classes rise out of the matrix, create all mental and bodily riches, sink back, as Vico saw civilization rise and sink, and government is there to keep the ring and see to it that combat never ends. These thoughts in the next few generations, as elaborated by Oswald

Spengler, who has followed Vico without essential change, by Flinders Petrie, by the German traveller Frobenius, by Henry Adams, and perhaps by my friend Gerald Heard, may affect the masses. They have already deepened our sense of tragedy and somewhat checked the naïver among those creeds and parties who push their way to power by flattering our moral hopes. Pascal thought there was evidence for and against the existence of God, but that if a man kept his mind in suspense about it he could not live a rich and active life, and I suggest to the Cellars and Garrets that though history is too short to change either the idea of progress or the eternal circuit into scientific fact, the eternal circuit may best suit our preoccupation with the soul's salvation, our individualism, our solitude. Besides we love antiquity, and that other idea – progress – the sole religious myth of modern man, is only two hundred years old.

Swift's pamphlet had little effect in its day; it did not prevent the impeachment and banishment a few years later of his own friends; and although he was in all probability the first – if there was another 'my small reading cannot trace it' – to describe in terms of modern politics the discord of parties that compelled revolutionary France, as it has compelled half a dozen nations since the war, to accept the 'tyranny' of a 'single person', it was soon forgotten; but for the understanding of Swift it is essential. It shows that the defence of liberty boasted upon his tombstone did not come from political disappointment (when he wrote it he had suffered none); and what he meant by liberty. Gulliver, in those travels written twenty years later, calls up from the dead 'a sextumvirate to which all the ages of the world cannot add a seventh': Epaminondas and Socrates, who suffered at the hands of the Many; Brutus, Junius Brutus, Cato the Younger, Thomas More, who fought the tyranny of the One; Brutus with Caesar still his inseparable friend, for a man may be a tyrant without personal guilt.

Liberty depended upon a balance within the State, like that of the 'humours' in a human body, or like that 'unity of being' Dante compared to a perfectly proportioned human body, and for its sake Swift was prepared to sacrifice what seems to the modern man liberty itself. The odds were a hundred to one, he wrote, that 'violent zeal for the truth' came out of 'petulancy, ambition or pride'. He himself might prefer a republic to a monarchy, but did he open his mouth upon the subject would be deservedly hanged. Had he religious doubts he was not to blame so long as he kept them to himself, for God had given him reason. It was the attitude of many a modern Catholic who thinks, though upon different grounds, that our civilization may sink into a decadence like that of Rome. But sometimes belief itself must be hidden. He was devout; had the Communion Service by heart; read the Fathers and prayed much, yet would not press the mysteries of his faith upon any unwilling man. Had not the early Christians kept silent about the divinity of Christ; should not the missionaries to China 'soften' it? He preached as law commanded; a man could save his soul doubtless in any religion which taught submission to the Will of God, but only one State could protect his body; and how could it protect his body if rent apart by those cranks and sectaries mocked in *A Tale of a Tub*? Had not French Huguenots and English Dissenters alike sinned against the State? Except at those moments of great public disturbance, when a man must choose his creed or his king, let him think his own thoughts in silence.

What was this liberty bought with so much silence, and served through all his life with so much eloquence? 'I should think,' he wrote in the *Discourse*,

that the saying, *vox populi, vox dei,* ought to be understood of the universal bent and current of a people, not the bare majority of a few representatives, which is often procured by little arts, and great industry and application; wherein those who engage in the pursuits of malice and revenge are much more sedulous than such as would prevent them (1 225).

That *vox populi* or 'bent and current', or what we even more vaguely call national spirit, was the sole theme of his *Drapier's Letters*; its right to express itself as it would through such men as had won or inherited general consent. I doubt if a mind so contemptuous of average men thought, as Vico did, that it found expression also through all individual lives, or asked more for those lives than protection from the most obvious evils. I remember J. F. Taylor, a great student of Swift, saying 'individual liberty is of no importance, what matters is national liberty'.

The will of the State, whether it build a cage for a dead bird or remain in the bird itself, must always, whether interpreted by Burke or Marx, find expression through some governing class or company identified with that 'bent and current', with those 'elemental forms', whether by interest or training. The men of Swift's day would have added that class or company must be placed by wealth above fear and toil, though Swift thought every properly conducted State must limit the amount of wealth the individual could possess. But the old saying that there is no widsom without leisure has somewhat lost its truth. When the physical world became rigid; when curiosity inherited from the Renaissance, and the soul's anxiety inherited from the Middle Ages, passed, man ceased to think; his work thought in him. Spinoza, Leibniz, Swift, Berkeley, Goethe, the last typical figure of the epoch, recognized no compulsion but the 'bent and current' of their lives; the Speaker, Connolly, could still call out a posse of gentlemen to design the façade of his house, and though Berkeley thought their number too great, that work is still admired; Swift called himself a poor scholar in comparison with Lord Treasurer Harley. Unity of being was still possible though somewhat over-rationalized and abstract, more diagram than body; whereas the best modern philosophers are professors, their pupils compile notebooks that they may be professors some day; politicians stick to their last or leave it to plague us with platitudes; we poets and artists may be called, so small our share in life, 'separated spirits', words applied by the old philosophers to the dead. When Swift sank into imbecility or madness his epoch had finished in the British Isles, those 'elemental forms' had passed beyond him; more than the 'great Ministers' had gone. I can see in a sort of nightmare vision the 'primary qualities' torn from the side of Locke, Johnson's ponderous body bent above the letter to Lord Chesterfield, some obscure person somewhere inventing the spinning-jenny, upon his face that look of benevolence kept by painters and engravers, from the middle of the eighteenth century to the time of the Prince Consort, for such as he, or, to simplify the tale:

Locke sank into a swoon;
The Garden died;
God took the spinning-jenny
Out of his side.

'That arrogant intellect free at last from superstition': the young man's overstatement full of the unexamined suppositions of common speech. I saw Asia in the carved stones of Blenheim, not in the pride of great abstract masses, but in that humility of flowerlike intricacy – the particular blades of the grass; nor can chance have thrown into contiguous generations Spinoza and Swift, an absorption of the whole intellect in God, a fakir-like contempt for all human desire; 'take from her', Swift prayed for Stella in sickness, 'all violent desire whether of life or death'; the elaboration and spread of Masonic symbolism, its God made in the image of a Christopher Wren; Berkeley's declaration, modified later, that physical pleasure is the *summum bonum*, heaven's sole reality, his counter-truth to that of Spinoza.

In judging any moment of past time we should leave out what has since happened; we should not call the Swift of the *Drapier's Letters* nearer truth because of their influence upon history than the Swift who attacked in *Gulliver* the inventors and logicians; we should see certain men and women as if at the edge of a cliff, time broken away from their feet. Spinoza and the Masons, Berkeley and Swift, speculative and practical intellect, stood there free at last from all prepossessions and touched the extremes of thought; the Gymnosophists of Strabo close at hand, could they but ignore what was harsh and logical in themselves, or the China of the Dutch cabinet-makers, of *The Citizen of the World*: the long-settled rule of powerful men, no great dogmatic structure, few great crowded streets, scattered unprogressive communities, much handiwork, wisdom wound into the roots of the grass.

'I have something in my blood that no child must inherit.' There have been several theories to account for Swift's celibacy. Sir Walter Scott suggested a 'physical defect', but that seems incredible. A man so outspoken would have told Vanessa the truth and stopped a tragic persecution, a man so charitable would have given Stella the protection of his name. The refusal to see Stella when there was no third person present suggests a man that dreaded temptation; nor is it compatible with those stories still current among our country people of Swift sending his servant out to fetch a woman, and dismissing that servant when he woke to find a black woman at his side. Lecky suggested dread of madness – the theory of my play – of madness already present in constant eccentricity; though, with a vagueness born from distaste of the theme, he saw nothing incompatible between Scott's theory and his own. Had Swift dreaded transmitting madness he might well have been driven to consorting with the nameless barren women of the streets. Somebody else suggests syphilis contracted doubtless between 1699 when he was engaged to Varina and some date soon after Stella's arrival in Ireland. Mr Shane Leslie thinks that Swift's relation to Vanessa was not platonic,[1] and that whenever his letters speak of a cup of coffee they mean the sexual act; whether the letters seem to bear him out I do not know, for those letters bore me; but whether they seem to or not he must, if he is to get a hearing, account for Swift's relation to Stella. It seems certain that Swift loved her though he called it by some other name, and she him, and that it was platonic love.

Thou, Stella, wert no longer young,
When first for thee my harp I strung:
Without one word of Cupid's darts,
Of killing eyes or bleeding hearts;
With friendship and esteem possest,
I ne'er admitted Love a guest.
In all the habitudes of life,
The friend, the mistress, and the wife,
Variety we still pursue,
In pleasure seek for something new;
Or else comparing with the rest,
Take comfort that our own is best;
(The best we value by the worst,
As tradesmen show their trash at first:)
But his pursuits are at an end,
Whom Stella chooses for a friend.
(*Poems*, II 728)

If the relation between Swift and Vanessa was not platonic there must have been some bar that affected Stella as well as Swift. Dr

---

1 Rossi and Hone take the same view, though uncertain about the coffee. When I wrote, their book had not appeared.

Delany is said to have believed that Swift married Stella in 1716 and found in some exchange of confidences that they were brother and sister, but Sir William Temple was not in Ireland during the year that preceded Swift's birth, and so far as we know Swift's mother was not in England.

There is no satisfactory solution. Swift, though he lived in great publicity, and wrote and received many letters, hid two things which constituted perhaps all that he had of private life: his loves and his religious beliefs.

'Was Swift mad? Or was it the intellect itself that was mad?' The other day a scholar in whose imagination Swift has a pre-eminence scarcely possible outside Ireland said: 'I sometimes feel that there is a black cloud about to overwhelm me, and then comes a great jet of life; Swift had that black cloud and no jet. He was terrified.' I said, 'Terrified perhaps of everything but death', and reminded him of a story of Dr Johnson's.[1] There was a reward of £500 for the identification of the author of the *Drapier's Letters*. Swift's butler, who had carried the manuscript to the printer, stayed away from work. When he returned, Swift said, 'I know that my life is in your hands, but I will not bear, out of fear, either your insolence or negligence.' He dismissed the butler, and when the danger had passed, he restored him to his post, rewarded him, and said to the other servants, 'No more Barclay, henceforth Mr Barclay.' 'Yes,' said my friend, 'he was not afraid of death but of life, of what might happen next; that is what made him so defiant in public and in private and demand for the State the obedience a Connacht priest demands for the Church.' I have put a cognate thought into the mind of John Corbet. He imagines, though but for a moment, that the intellect of Swift's age, persuaded that the mechanicians mocked by Gulliver would prevail, that its moment of freedom could not last, so dreaded the historic process that it became in the half-mad mind of Swift a dread of parentage: 'Am I to add another to the healthy rascaldom and knavery of the world?' Did not Rousseau within five years of the death of Swift publish his *Discourse upon Arts and Sciences* and discover instinctive harmony not in heroic effort, not in Cato and Brutus,

1 Sheridan has a different version, but as I have used it merely to illustrate an argument I leave it as Dr Johnson told it.

not among impossible animals – I think of that noble horse Blake drew for Hayley – but among savages, and thereby beget the *sansculottes* of Marat? After the arrogance of power the humility of a servant.

(345–63)

Part Three **Modern Views**

Introduction

The first point to make about modern criticism of Swift is that
there is a lot of it. It would be a Laputan exercise to determine
whether he has been the occasion of more comment than, say,
Donne or Joyce. It is permissible, however, to find the critical
corpus daunting. No reader worth his salt continues daunted for
long, of course, and it is always possible to feel that one's own
reading of *A Tale of a Tub* is novel. In principle, this feeling is
justifiable. It is only prudent to acknowledge, at the same time,
that modern views of Swift have been exceedingly diverse.
Daunting or not, this diversity is attractive. Earlier criticism of
Swift is lively, but much of it runs upon established lines. One of
the engaging marks of twentieth-century criticism is the latitude of
contexts which it discovers; historical, psychological, philosophical,
linguistic, political, religious. Swift has been found relevant to these
several contexts, and crucial to some of them. The result is that
some modern commentaries on Swift are, indeed, novel. There is
nothing in earlier criticism to put beside William Empson's remarks
on Swift, for instance, brief as they are and marginal to his
official argument.

The main tendency of modern criticism has been to seek a more
plausible balance of interests, where Swift is concerned. Readers
feel, on the whole, that the critical problem is to accommodate the
entire work in their sense of Swift, rather than to argue that his
essential quality is found in one or two books. That he contains
multitudes is the quality we tend to emphasize: or at least we feel
that Swift is much more capacious than early accounts of him
would suggest. Irvin Ehrenpreis refers to 'that partnership of
preacher and clown which is Swift's special mark'. Louis A.
Landa argues that everything in Swift is compatible with his role
as a Christian divine: he speaks of 'the essentially Christian
philosophy of the fourth voyage', Swift's hostility to the
benevolists, his sense of sinful man. But it is clear that Mr Landa
would agree with Mr Ehrenpreis about the clown. There is no

quarrel: both scholars want to give an account of Swift in which his diversity is recognized, his quality of mind a kind of paradox. The problem is to make a just place for everything.

The next problem is to maintain a reasonable balance between Swift as an Augustan writer, immured in his time, and Swift in some sense our contemporary. It is easier to convert Swift into modern terms than to extend the same office to, say, Pope or Johnson. In a recent spoof, a bogus fifth book of *Gulliver's Travels*, Matthew Hodgart established Gulliver at the end as a figure from the works of Samuel Beckett, his endgame played in a bin, scribbling, scribbling. . . . The conceit is entirely natural, as John Fletcher has shown (see Select Bibliography). In another version of modernity Robert Martin Adams represented Swift as cousin to Kafka; a relation defined with great persuasive power in *Strains of Discord*. That Swift is ruefully at home in the Age of Marshall McLuhan is shown in several books by Mr McLuhan's former colleague, Hugh Kenner; two excerpts from these studies are included in the present volume (see p. 264 and p. 422). One point is worth underlining: that Mr Kenner finds it relevant to discuss *A Tale of a Tub* in a book which is strictly concerned with Flaubert, Joyce and Beckett. Swift shines, apparently, in the Gutenberg galaxy.

Some of the most brilliant modern criticism has been incited by Swift's *Tale*. Indeed, it often appears that the *Tale* has displaced *Gulliver's Travels* from the centre of critical interest: it is Swift's most problematic work, and therefore the work most congenial to the modern reader; all the better if it remains imperfectly understood. Readers continue to disagree about the *Travels*, but they do not feel of this work, as they feel of the *Tale*, that it is inexhaustible. At the same time, scholars emphasize that the *Tale*, however odd it appears, is not a freak of nature; it has cousins in sixteenth- and seventeenth-century literature, especially, and particular kinship with works by Erasmus, More and Marvell.

The appreciation of Swift's poems has been tardy, and some readers refuse to be convinced. G. Wilson Knight thinks that Dryden was right, that Swift would never be a poet. But the other view has been presented, in recent years, with great verve. F. W. Bateson's claim is perhaps astonishing ('one of the great English poets: I prefer him to Pope') but it is made with a formidable show of cause. Many readers have probably agreed with Johnson that Swift's poems are, for the most part, what their author intended: the remark cannot be faulted, unless some evidence of enthusiasm is sought. But Mr Bateson's case has been strengthened recently by several scholars, notably Geoffrey Hill, Marius Bewley and C. J. Horne.

As for *Gulliver's Travels*, the commentaries included here should give a reasonably accurate impression of the ways in which modern scholar-critics read the work. Arthur E. Case's study of the personal and political satire has been extremely influential. Deane Swift said in his *Essay upon the Life, Writings and Character of Dr Jonathan Swift* (1755) that the meaning of Lilliput and Brobdingnag 'is entirely political'. Swift's meaning 'throughout the whole, especially where he glances at the history of his own times, the wars of Europe and the factions of Whig and Tory, is to be found so very near the surface that it would almost be an affront to the common reason of those who are at all versed in the affairs of the world to offer at any further explication'. Professor Case has offered a further explication, and few readers are likely to feel affronted. Ronald Crane's study of the *Travels* has been universally praised (see p. 363): it is a remarkable example of the relation between scholarship and criticism, admirable in both respects. The scholarly evidence is decisive: that Swift turned the logical manuals upside down and discovered, in that outrageous perspective, the form of his most defiant satire, is entirely appropriate to our sense of his imagination. He delighted in confronting one perspective with another. C. J. Rawson's essay (see p. 385) is an excellent example of recent scholarship, especially valuable because it exerts critical pressure upon several dearly held orthodoxies. Mr Kenner, a critical ironist, a wit, invokes the work of Alan M. Turing for the better understanding of the work of Jonathan Swift; Turing (1912–54), 'the Spinoza of computers'. The idea is that the reader reads *Gulliver's Travels*, that is, inspects the behaviour of Lemuel Gulliver in a frame of mind similar to that in which he, the reader, plays Turing's Game. Mr Kenner has already stated the rules of the game on page 121 of *The Counterfeiters*:

One player is a machine; it is trying to pass itself off as a person. Another is a person, trying to make it clear that he *is* a person. The third is an observer, trying to decide which is which. All communication is by electric teletypewriter, with the observer in a separate room.

If I understand Mr Kenner's theme, Gulliver is 'the Compleat Empiricist', but so also is the reader: both adopt 'what is essentially Turing's strategy, situating themselves outside of a man to see what could be found out about him by observing his behaviour.' The reader observes Gulliver's behaviour because he is not given anything else to observe. Now read on.

The Setting

J. C. Beckett

'Swift as an Ecclesiastical Statesman', in H. A. Cronne, T. W. Moody and D. B. Quinn (eds.), *Essays in British and Irish History in Honour of James Eadie Todd* 1949

The sincerity of Swift's religion has been a matter of controversy from his own day to ours. The gibe of his contemporary, Smedley, that he

> . . . might a bishop be in time
> Did he believe in God

echoes the tradition that it was Queen Anne's pious horror of *A Tale of a Tub* which prevented Swift's elevation to the episcopal bench. This interpretation of Swift's religious position has been elaborated by later writers and as elaborately confuted. But final decision in such a dispute is impossible. The evidence of what a man really believed is bound to be of such a nature that our interpretation of it will depend upon our estimate of the man himself; and in fact all the writers on Swift's personal religion have, consciously or unconsciously, approached the subject with their minds made up.

This essay is not an attempt to refight an old battle with modern weapons. But there is an aspect of Swift's religious life which (so far as the present writer is aware) has never been clearly set out, and which, while it may serve to illuminate his personal religious convictions, can be treated independently of them. As an Anglican priest Swift was not only a minister of religion, he was also an official of a large and influential organization. How did Swift regard this organization? What part did he take in its life? What connexions can be traced between his life as a churchman and his life as a politician and a man of letters? These are some of the questions to which an answer must now be attempted.

Swift took his orders in 1694, but a very brief experience of parochial life in the north of Ireland sent him back to Moor Park. He still had literary ambitions; he might hope to combine his clerical calling with some political or diplomatic office; Temple or some other patron might provide for him in England. The death of Temple in 1699 and Swift's acceptance of the vicarage of Laracor, in the diocese of Meath, early in the following year may be taken to mark the temporary abandonment of any scheme of promotion outside the regular routine of church preferment. Such preferment, if it was to equal Swift's hopes and his value of himself, could come only from the government. The circumstances of the time compelled him to look to the favour of a political party and, in the uneasy coalition which ruled England during the early years of Queen Anne, Swift's chief friends were the Whigs, to whom his *Discourse of the Contests and Dissensions between the Nobles and the Commons in Athens and Rome* (published in 1701) had commended him. But though the Whigs were in office they were not in power, and after a visit to England in 1703–4 Swift remained in Ireland for three and a half years. His return to London at the end of 1707, primarily on a mission for the Irish Church, was probably connected with the change in the balance of parties, which in the following year brought the Whigs completely into power.

It was now that Swift might hope to gain something from his friendship with Whig leaders. But that prospect made it necessary for him to consider carefully his attitude to Whig policy. Promotion would come only at the price of political support. Swift wanted to make it clear that the extent of that support must be determined by a stronger duty to the Church. To set out the limits within which he was willing to serve a party cause, and perhaps also to warn his Whig friends of the danger of arousing Church opposition, he published, in 1708, *The Sentiments of a Church-of-England Man, with Respect to Religion and Government*. In this we have the basic expression of Swift's views on the relations of Church and State, but it must be read in relation to its context and it must be supplemented from his other writings. Its main purpose, like that of all Swift's works, was an immediate one. As Herbert Read says:

All that Swift wrote is empirical, experimental, *actuel*. It is impossible to detach it from circumstances; we must consider each book or pamphlet in relation to its political intention (*Collected Essays in Literary Criticism*).

Swift contended that though there were two political parties there was only one Church, which was not tied to either of them.[1] She had certain political principles of her own, by which to test competing policies, and on one of the most urgent questions of the day – the treatment of Protestant dissenters – *The Sentiments of a Church-of-England Man* gives a clear and consistent opinion. In doing this it was impossible to avoid raising the fundamental question of the relations of Church and State; and though it is pretty clear that Swift disliked arguing about abstract principles, he did not hesitate to answer the question as far as the occasion required. It is because this answer was not the main purpose of the pamphlet, and because, in giving it, Swift had in mind that he was writing an eirenicon and not a challenge, that we must expand and supplement the scheme of Church–State relationship here expressed.

Such an investigation is the more necessary because some of the statements in *The Sentiments of a Church-of-England Man*, taken in isolation, can be easily misunderstood. Thus, Professor Looten writes:

Sa volonté de conjuguer les deux pouvoirs est si arrêtée que jamais pour légitimer l'existence et la mission de l'église il n'invoque son droit divin ou son origine surnaturelle. On dirait qu'il ne la conçoit qu'en marge et en fonction de l'état. (*La Pensée Religieuse de Swift*)[2]

Not only is the general trend of this contrary to explicit statements in the *Remarks upon Tindal's 'Rights of the Christian Church'*, but the last sentence attributes to Swift a conception of the Church and State directly contrary to that which he laboured to establish. For Swift held clearly, though carefully, the doctrine that the Church's power

---

1 'A Church of England man may with prudence and a good conscience, approve the professed principles of one party more than the other, according as he thinks they best promote the good of Church and State' (*The Sentiments of a Church-of-England Man*).
2 His desire to combine the two powers is so steadfast that he never invokes either the Church's divine right or her supernatural origin in order to justify her existence and mission in the world. The impression is that he only views her as a marginal function of the State.

was derived directly from Christ and his apostles.[1] But he made no attempt to consider this in its wider applications. He barely mentions the possible state of affairs under a heathen government. He thinks it necessary to enter some defence of the conception of the Church as a world-wide corporation.[2] He is satisfied to deal with the particular case immediately present – that of the Church of England.

The line of argument used is significant. Swift was, and always remained, essentially a Whig in politics, tied to the principles of the revolution and opposed to absolute rule, either by one or by many. But the traditional High-Church scheme did not fit easily into this pattern. That scheme had developed during the seventeenth century. By the end of Elizabeth's reign the Church of England was free from the immediate danger of a papal restoration imposed from without; but Papal propaganda in England continued, and the pressure of the Puritans, whether avowed dissenters or nominally within the church, grew stronger. Against this double attack it was necessary to build up a moral defence not only of doctrine but also, and more urgently, of jurisdiction. A solid basis had been laid in Hooker's *Laws of Ecclesiastical Polity*, but his arguments required expansion and particular application. The great problem was to show on what authority the jurisdiction of the Church rested. The circumstances of the English Reformation, the Act of Supremacy, and the Thirty-Seventh Article of religion all pointed to the crown; but any doctrine of royal supremacy required to be justified, not only against Rome but against Geneva, both ever ready to detect and condemn erastianism. To avoid secularizing the Church the Anglican theologians had to sanctify the monarchy and to claim that the Church and the State were but different aspects of the same commonwealth. To maintain such a position

1 'But as the supreme power can certainly do ten thousand things more than it ought, so there are several things which some people may think it can do, although it really cannot . . . because the law of God [i.e. of the Church] hath otherwise decreed; which law, although a nation may refuse to receive it, cannot alter in its own nature. But the Church of England is no creature of the civil power, either as to its polity or its doctrines. The fundamentals of both were deduced from Christ and his apostles . . .' (*Remarks upon Tindal's 'Rights of the Christian Church'*).

2 'Here we must show the necessity of the Church being a corporation all over the world: to avoid heresies and preserve fundamentals and hinder corrupting of scripture, etc.' (*Remarks*).

after the Restoration, when the dissenters formed a considerable section of the population, was difficult. The revolution made it impossible: the Church had to choose between the king and the nation. In this dilemma, the non-jurors, who stuck to the letter of their theory, were compelled to experience its logical result in their extrusion from their benefices; for Church and nation could not represent the same commonwealth if they had different kings. Not unnaturally, the non-jurors saw in this exercise of state authority that Erastianism round which they and their predecessors had been steering so careful a course for over a century.

The witness of the non-jurors made it necessary for those churchmen who had accepted the revolution to reconsider the basis of the Church's authority. It was the need to do this which sharpened the demand that convocation should be allowed to function. Bishop King, of Derry, who wanted the Irish Church to enjoy the same privileges as the English, put the matter succinctly:

The first article in Magna Carta is that the Church of England shall be free, and that freedom can consist in nothing but in choosing the ecclesiastical constitutions by which she is governed in convocations. . . . If the Church once come to have her constitutions altered without convocations, which are her legal representatives, she is no more free but an absolute slave, and our religion would in earnest be what the papists call it, a parliamentary religion (Bishop King to Southwell, 21 December 1697, Trinity College, Dublin, MS N3.1, p. 149).

But the meeting of convocation could not settle the question, for it met by royal authority, and could transact business only by royal licence. Yet the revolution had shown that if the Church possessed any divine right it must be separable from that of hereditary monarchy; or else the non-jurors were, as they claimed to be, the true Church of England. Swift's common sense revolted from a conclusion which would have branded the bulk of the nation as schismatics.[1] But he

1 The attempt to continue the schism by consecrating a new non-juring bishops aroused Swift's contempt: '. . . a parcel of obscure zealots in London, who, as we hear, are setting up a new Church of England by themselves' (Swift to Archbishop King, 13 November 1716).

was equally unwilling to accept the opposite extreme, that the Church had no divine right at all. His task was to reconcile such a divine right in the Church with his own Whig principles in politics. As in his political theory he goes back to a social contract by which power passed from the many to the few, so here he goes back to the period at which the State embraced Christianity. Characteristically, he is concerned not with individual conversions but with an official transaction between the rulers of the State and the rulers of the Church, by which the former received the doctrines and practices of the Church 'as a divine law . . . and consequently, what they could not justly alter, any more than the common laws of nature' (*Remarks*). Clearly, the relations of Church and State in England were based on such a contract. The supreme power (which for Swift was the legislature) (*Sentiments*) was morally bound to support the doctrine and discipline of the Church; but this doctrine and discipline, being part of the law of God, were, unlike the law of the state, immutable.

Up to this point, Swift's arguments seem to make directly for that kind of ecclesiastical independence, that *imperium in imperio*, which has provided one of the recurring problems of political life for many centuries. Of one obvious solution, later epitomised in the phrase 'a free Church in a free State', he speaks with contempt; the idea of a clergy supported by the alms of the people was repugnant to him (*Remarks*). On the other hand, he could not logically quarrel with the existing constitution of the established Church in England and Ireland, to the defence of which all his efforts were directed. He finds a way out of the difficulty by distinguishing between the church's power, and liberty to use that power. The former comes directly from God, the latter from the civil authority.

And, therefore, although the supreme power can hinder the clergy or Church from making any new canons, or executing the old; from consecrating bishops, or refuse those they do consecrate; or, in short, from performing any ecclesiastical office, as they may from eating, drinking, and sleeping; yet they cannot themselves perform those offices, which are assigned to the clergy by our saviour and his apostles; or, if they do, it is not according to the divine institution, and consequently null and void (II 77).

This theory of Church–State relationship was designed to fit existing circumstances, to salve the divine right of the Church, without challenging too openly the power of the state or reflecting upon the principles of the revolution. To adapt the phrase which Swift applied to his *Modest Proposal*, it was 'calculated' for England and Ireland in the reign of Queen Anne. The expression of it in *The Sentiments of a Church-of-England Man* is modified by the immediate political problem, but the enlargements in Swift's other writings on the Church, in the *Examiner*, and in his correspondence, follow logically from the principles there laid down.

One part of Swift's theorizing on Church and State was of immediate practical importance. He agreed with Hobbes that there must be an absolute authority in the State; but unlike Hobbes he placed this absolute authority in the legislature and not in the executive part of the government.[1] The legislature could do no wrong. It was by its authority that the Church of England was established[2] and the legislature could at will establish paganism or Popery or Presbyterianism instead. The safety of the Church, therefore, required that her enemies should be excluded from the legislature and from all places of political influence. This was the essential basis of Swift's opposition to the Protestant dissenters, both in England and in Ireland. He was ready to ridicule their religious peculiarities, but his arguments against them did not arise from a theological horror of schism. He had no objection to toleration, provided the dissenters were not left free to proselytize or to acquire political power. It is significant that he was much less alarmed about possible danger from the Roman Catholics, even in Ireland where they formed the vast majority of the population, because their political power was so completely gone that they could not be a danger to the Established Church.

Swift's determination to exclude Protestant dissenters from political influence brought him into opposition with the Whigs almost as soon as they had secured control of the Government. The great grievance of the dissenters was the Sacramental Test, and they looked to their

1 Hobbes 'perpetually confounds the executive with the legislative power' (*Sentiments*).
2 But Swift carefully distinguishes between 'established' and 'founded': '. . . what is contained in the idea of *established*? Surely not existence. Doth *establishment* give *being* to a thing?' (*Remarks*).

political allies to remove it. But the Test had stood in England since 1673 and was regarded by the Church party as their main security; a direct attack upon it would be unpopular and probably unsuccessful. In the meantime, its full rigour was somewhat modified by the practice of occasional conformity, which the Tories had vainly attempted to suppress in 1703. But in Ireland the Sacramental Test was a new thing, imposed for the first time in 1704 by the action of the English government; and though the Church party had welcomed it as a protection against the powerful Presbyterian population in Ulster, the latter were naturally hopeful that a Whig ministry would remove it. Swift, like many other churchmen, was convinced that the attack upon the Sacramental Test in Ireland would be merely a preparation for a similar attack in England.

As early as 1707 there had been some sort of move in the Irish commons to repeal the test, a move which had been inspired, or at least encouraged, by the English ministry. It met with strong opposition, and Archbishop King's account shows how readily the government gave in for the sake of securing peace:

You can hardly imagine what a healing measure this has proved, and how far it has prevailed to oblige those that were in great animosities against one another, to comply in all reasonable proposals; whereas, if the repeal of the Test had been insisted on, it would have broken all in pieces, and made them form parties on principles which before were founded only on personal quarrels (Archbishop King to Annesley, 16 August 1707).

In the following year the situation was different. The English government was now clearly committed to an effort at repealing the Test in Ireland, even before the choice of Lord Wharton as the new Lord Lieutenant advertised the fact to the world. All this was matter of the greatest importance to Swift. As a Whig, he might now hope to secure preferment, but he could not conceal his anxiety about the ministry's ecclesiastical policy; especially since he was a sort of ambassador from the Irish Church and so must be drawn into the government's policy for Ireland. In the opening paragraph of *The Sentiments of a Church-of-England Man* he had expressed his attitude to party loyalty: 'A wise and a good man may indeed be sometimes induced to comply with a number, whose opinion he generally approves, although it be perhaps against his own. But this liberty should be made use of upon very few occasions, and those of small importance, and then only with a view of bringing over his own side another time to something of greater and more public moment.' But the first occasion on which he had to test the strength of his own influence with the Whig leaders provided a disappointment. Swift's journey to England in 1707 had been undertaken with the approval of Archbishop King, of Dublin, for the purpose of soliciting for the Irish Church a grant of the 'First Fruits' and 'Twentieth Parts' similar to the grant made by the queen to the English Church some years earlier. He was coldly received by the treasurer (Godolphin), put off with vague assurances, puzzled by obscure hints, and finally made to understand that the government was prepared to make the grant provided the Irish Church would accept the removal of the Sacramental Test.

Once more Swift felt it necessary to make his position clear and to warn his Whig friends of the dangers involved in their ecclesiastical policy. The *Letter from a Member of Parliament in Ireland to a Member of Parliament in England, Concerning the Sacramental Test* was published in December 1708, shortly after Wharton's appointment as Lord Lieutenant. It is a natural corollary to *The Sentiments of a Church-of-England Man*, for the scheme of Church–State relationship described in the latter would be valid only so long as establishment was a reality. The core of the argument in the *Letter Concerning the Sacramental Test* is that the removal of the Test would virtually establish Presbyterianism in Ireland as a rival church; and there is a clear hint that the Government has in mind a similar policy for England. Another pamphlet, the *Letter to a Member of Parliament in Ireland, upon the Choosing a New Speaker There*, also published in 1708, went over much the same ground. But already the Whigs were beginning to waver in their determination. When Swift first informed Archbishop King of the appointment of Wharton as Lord Lieutenant he added a character of the man who was generally expected to go as his secretary: 'One, Mr Shute ... a young man, but reckoned the shrewdest head in Europe; and the person in whom the Presbyterians chiefly confide. ... As to his principles, he is truly a moderate man, frequenting the Church and the Meeting indifferently'. But before Wharton set out, a change in the government's attitude was reflected in the substitution of Addison for Shute.

Mr Addison, who goes over as first secretary, is a most excellent person; and being my most intimate friend, I shall use all my credit to set him right in his notions of persons and things. I spoke to him with great plainness upon the subject of the Test; and he says he is confident my Lord Wharton will not attempt it, if he finds the bent of the nation against it (*Correspondence*, 1 127–8).

And the archbishop himself soon received similar assurances from the Lord Lieutenant's friends of his intention to keep the 'government of State and Church on the same foot as they are.' So although Wharton repeatedly urged upon the Irish parliament the need for unity among Protestants, he made no open attack upon the Sacramental Test. By the end of 1710 the Tories were once more in power in England and Wharton had been replaced by Ormond. For the next four years the dissenters, both in England and in Ireland, were on the defensive.

Swift had maintained in *The Sentiments of a Church-of-England Man* that he was in favour of toleration for existing sects, provided that they were excluded from political power and prevented from proselytizing; and he seems to have himself acted on this principle. He took no part in the repressive measures against the Protestant dissenters which were planned and carried out during the last years of Queen Anne. In Ireland, the great aim of the High-Church party, the suspension of the *regium donum* of £1200 a year paid to the Ulster presbyterians, was achieved in 1714. In England, controversy centred round the Occasional Conformity Bill, which eventually became law in 1711. On the *regium donum* question Swift says nothing; and though he mentions the Occasional Conformity Bill from time to time, and must certainly have known what was going on, there is nothing to show that he supported it. He may have been partly influenced by the recollection of his non-committal attitude to the same question in 1703; but it is more reasonable to see here a logical carrying out of the principles laid down in *The Sentiments of a Church-of-England Man*.

His attitude to the dissenters was not an aggressive one, and while their expansion seemed to be effectively checked and their political power curbed he was content to leave them in peace.

Swift's transfer of his allegiance from the Whigs to the Tories in 1710 arose largely from his dissatisfaction with the Whigs' ecclesiastical policy. It was not merely their failure to carry through the grant of the 'First Fruits' to the Irish Church which had alienated him, but also their attempt to remove the Sacramental Test, first in Ireland and then in England, and their tolerant attitude towards writers whom Swift regarded as deistical or atheistical. Naturally, he expected preferment from his new allies, the professed patrons of the Church; but after many disappointments in England he had to accept the deanery of St Patrick's, Dublin. Here he retired in 1714, when the Whigs returned to power; and such political influence as he retained was confined almost exclusively to Ireland. But his policy in ecclesiastical matters was unchanged. Whether in England or in Ireland, the Established Church stood in the same relation to the State and had to face the same threat from the Protestant dissenters. The changes of 1714 necessarily diminished the political influence of the Church, and Swift was not prepared to challenge the new government. The Presbyterians naturally rejoiced, the *regium donum* was restored, the Occasional Conformity Act, which was on the point of being extended to Ireland, was repealed, and in 1719 the Irish parliament at last granted a legal toleration to Protestant dissenters. To all this Swift said nothing. Even a visit to Ulster in 1722 did not draw from him any public comment on the activities of the Presbyterians. But once the question of repealing the Sacramental Test was raised again, he came forward to defend it.

The new struggle was fought out in the Irish Parliament and the Irish council in 1732 and 1733. At one stage Swift regarded the cause as lost. In November 1733, he wrote to Ford:

It is reckoned that the test will be repealed. It is said that £30,000 have been returned from England; and £20,000 raised here from servants, labourers, farmers, squires, whigs, etc., to promote the good work. Half the bishops will be on their side. Pamphlets pro and con fly about ... but we all conclude the affair desperate. For the money is sufficient among us to abolish Christianity itself. All the people in power are determined for the repeal . . . (*Correspondence*, IV 210–11).

But he had over-estimated the danger; the Irish Government – directed by Primate Boulter rather than by the Lord Lieutenant – hesitated to force on a policy so distasteful to the bulk of the House of Commons. By the end of the year the repeal project had been shelved. It is hard to estimate the importance of Swift's contribution to this result. His pamphlets simply go over the old ground once again, and the country gentlemen who refused to be cajoled or frightened by Boulter or Dorset did not need to have their opinions and their prejudices expressed for them. Swift was arguing for a cause which would have triumphed without him. But his vigour may have made the government's surrender more speedy and probably helps to account for its completeness. He was on the alert from the beginning. The first signs of danger arose in England and Swift discussed with his printer, Motte, the idea of reprinting his *Letter Concerning the Sacramental Test*, announcing at the same time that 'if the same wicked project [of repealing the test] shall be attempted here, I shall so far suspend my laziness as to oppose it to the utmost'. Though the pamphlets which this 'suspension of laziness' produced show no development of thought on the question of Protestant dissenters, one of them does lay stress on an aspect of the matter which Swift was usually content to pass over very lightly. One of the *Queries Wrote by Dr J. Swift in the Year 1732* is this:

'Whether any clergyman . . . if he think his own profession most agreeable to holy scriptures, and this primitive church, can really wish in his heart, that all sectaries should be put on an equal foot with the churchmen, in point of civil power and employments?'

The emphasis on theological differences and the direct appeal to the clergy probably arose from the fear that the clergy themselves were no longer solidly against repealing the test. Probably, too, it was this which he had in mind when he complained that 'those who by their function, their conscience, their honour, their oaths and the interest of their community are most bound to obstruct such a ruin to the church, will be the great advocates for it (Swift to Motte, 9 December 1732).

Though the project for repealing the Sacramental Test in Ireland was dropped, and not renewed during Swift's lifetime, his fear of the dissenters remained. In 1736 he complained of 'the insolence of the dissenters, who, with their pupils the atheists, are now wholly employed in ruining the Church and have entered into public associations subscribed and handed about publicly for that purpose.'[1] But his alarm for the Church during these years did not arise exclusively from the dissenters. The gentlemen of the Irish House of Commons, though they had consistently defended the sacramental test, were not inclined to allow their support of the Church to interfere with their incomes. They considered tithes a heavy burden, and found a welcome prospect of relief in the argument that no tithe was due from grazing land (tithe of agistment). The question was hotly debated, and in 1735 the commons passed a resolution against the collection of the tithe of agistment. Though this had no legal force it was, in fact, acted upon, and clerical incomes suffered accordingly. Such a move touched Swift on one of his tenderest points. The rights of his order were to him even dearer than his own, or rather, he could not consider them apart; and this attack seemed to him to threaten the ruin of the Church:

I have given up all hopes of church or Christianity. A certain author, I forget his name, hath writ a book, I wish I could see it, that the Christian religion will not last above three hundred and odd years. He means there will always be Christians, as there are Jews; but it will no longer be a national religion; and there is enough to justify the scripture, that the gates of hell shall not prevail against it. As to the Church, it is equally the aversion of both kingdoms: you for the quakers' tithes, we for grass, or agistment as the term of art is (Swift to Ford, 22 June 1736; *Correspondence*, IV 505).

1 This linking together of 'dissenters' and 'atheists' or 'free-thinkers' was usual with Swift. After he joined the Tories he added 'Whigs'. In 1711 he writes of the dissenters and 'their comrades, the Whigs and free-thinkers' (*Examiner*, no. 36, 12 April 1711). The alliance was a natural one, but Swift undoubtedly hoped to damn the dissenters and Whigs by their company.

Swift's loyalty to his order appears at every stage of his ecclesiastical activity. Of humanity in general he wrote, in a famous passage, that he despised and hated it in the mass, while loving individuals. His attitude to the clergy was almost the reverse: there were few of them with whom he was on consistently friendly terms, but he never lost an opportunity of supporting their cause. In seeking the grant of the 'First Fruits' for the Irish Church he was concerned chiefly with the benefit to the poorer clergy, and slackness on the part of the officials who might be expected to forward the affair he interpreted as indifference towards clerical interests. Of one such he wrote, in a letter to Archbishop King, that he 'would not give threepence to save all the established clergy in both kingdoms from the gallows'. He was concerned about the material welfare of the clergy both as an end in itself, and because he was convinced that their poverty reduced them to contempt, and deprived them of their proper place in society. It is not unreasonable to see here a close connexion between Swift's personal character and his ecclesiastical policy. Few men were quicker to take offence or to detect an insult, and he was inclined to regard himself as open to attack in the person of each individual clergyman or in the clergy as a body. His opinion on the position of the clergy is temperately expressed in *The Sentiments of a Church-of-England Man*: '. . . he does not see how that mighty passion for the Church, which some men pretend, can well consist with those indignities, and that contempt they bestow on the persons of the clergy. . . '. Later, in the *Examiner* (no. 21), he speaks more strongly: 'For several years past there hath not, I think, in Europe, been any society of men upon so unhappy a foot as the clergy of England.' Swift was thinking of the lower clergy. In spite of his support of episcopacy as a form of church government, his love of independence made it difficult for him to accept episcopal authority. With Bishop Evans of Meath, who was his diocesan as vicar of Laracor, he quarrelled bitterly; and even with Archbishop King his relations were sometimes strained. But in his vigorous support of the lower houses of the English convocations against the upper, he was careful to point out that 'a dislike to the proceedings of any of their lordships, even to the number of a majority, will be purely personal, and not turned to the disadvantage of the order'. After his retirement to Ireland in 1714 he had stronger grounds of opposition to the bishops, for they were often Englishmen and almost always Whigs: 'It is happy for men that I know the persons of very few bishops, and it is my constant rule, never to look into a coach; by which I avoid the terror that such a sight would strike me with.' When, in 1733, two bills, one for compelling incumbents to reside and build houses on their glebes, the other for the division of large benefices, passed the Irish House of Lords, with the support of almost all the bishops, Swift wrote bitterly of 'those two abominable bills, for enslaving and beggaring the clergy, which took their birth from hell'; and asserted that the bishops who supported them had mostly done so 'with no other view, bating farther promotion, than a premeditated design, from the spirit of ambition and love of arbitrary power, to make the whole body of the clergy their slaves and vassals, until the day of judgement, under the load of poverty and contempt'. This furious sensitiveness touching his order seems to have grown on him in later years, and was probably increased by his feeling of powerlessness.

Swift's work as an ecclesiastical statesman cannot be easily summarized or accurately estimated. His career was made up of broken patches. He entered late upon the political world, and was thrown in with a party which, on grounds both personal and of principle, he could not long stand by. Later he won favour and influence in a party which he could honourably serve but which, in spite of his efforts, was ruined by internal dissension. He was exiled to Ireland, where he could exercise only indirect influence on the course of government, through his powerful friends or through the mob. So Swift's work for the Church was neither that of a scholar nor that of an experienced administrator. He was essentially a man of action, but his hopes of taking an effective part in directing the affairs of the Church and of the nation were constantly thwarted, and he was forced to find an outlet in the vigorous administration of his little kingdom of the liberties of St Patrick's and in defending its independence against the archbishop's seneschal. The same love of action appears in his writings on Church and State, every one of which is related to some immediate problem. More than this, he wrote for power and place. It would probably be possible to find some personal motive behind every pamphlet; and though Swift never allowed such motives to pervert his principle, the bitterness of his attacks upon the Whigs for their ill-treatment of the Church owed something to political expediency and, in his later life, to disappointed ambition.

This element of partisanship is the ruling factor in Swift's achievement as an ecclesiastical statesman. On the one hand it weakened his influence within the Church. Those who already suspected his orthodoxy were not reconciled by the violence and apparent instability of his party attachment. Thus, though the grant of the 'First Fruits' and 'Twentieth Parts' to the Irish Church in 1711 was largely due to Swift's patient negotiation, the bishops felt it wiser to give the credit to the Duke of Ormond, or to the Queen herself. On the other hand, it was just because he was both a clergyman and an active member of a political party that Swift was compelled to face the problem of an Established Church in a parliamentary state. It was not in his nature to produce a complete system; he solved problems and answered difficulties as they arose. But in doing so he laid down principles, briefly examined in this paper, which form an important contribution to Anglican thought on the relations of Church and State, and might have guided the church into a middle way between the fantastic unrealities of the non-jurors and the blank Erastianism of the Hanoverian bishops.

(135–52)

General Estimates

R. P. Blackmur

from 'D. H. Lawrence and Expressive Form' 1935 (reprinted in *Form and Value in Modern Poetry*, 1957)

As a poet, and only to a less degree as a novelist, Lawrence belongs to that great race of English writers whose work totters precisely where it towers, collapses exactly in its strength: work written out of a tortured Protestant sensibility and upon the foundation of an incomplete, uncomposed mind: a mind without defenses against the material with which it builds and therefore at every point of stress horribly succumbing to it. Webster, Swift, Blake and Coleridge – perhaps Donne, Sterne and Shelley, and on a lesser plane Marston, Thomson (of the *Dreadful Night*) and Beddoes – these exemplify, in their different ways, the deracinated, unsupported imagination, the mind for which, since it lacked rational structure sufficient to its burdens, experience was too much. Their magnitude was inviolate, and we must take account of it not only for its own sake but also to escape its fate; it is the magnitude of ruins – and the ruins for the most part of an intended life rather than an achieved art.
(253)

Kenneth Burke

from *Attitudes Towards History* 1937 (rev. edn, 1959)

The element of dramatic *personality* in essayistic *ideas* cannot be intelligently discerned until we recognize that names (for either dramatic characters or essayistic concepts) are shorthand designations for certain fields and methods of action. Perhaps Samuel Butler was both *on* the track and *off* it when he said that 'Men and women exist only as the organs and tools of the ideas that dominate them' (on the track, in so far as he recognized the integral relationship between people and ideas, but off it in so far as, under the stimulus of idealism, he took the ideas as causally prior).

In line with such thinking, we cannot say enough in praise of the concept, 'the socialization of losses', as a pun for liquidating the false rigidity of concepts and for inducing quick convertibility from moralistic to economic categories. The operation of this salvation device in the investment field has its counterpart in the 'curative' doctrine of 'original sin' whereby a man 'socializes' his personal loss by holding that *all* men are guilty. It suggests, for instance, the ingredient of *twisted tragedy* behind Swift's satire, whereby he uses such thinking, not to *lift himself up*, but to *pull all mankind down* (the author himself being caught in the general deflation). 'I have ever hated all nations, professions and communities; and all my love is towards individuals. . . . But principally I hate and detest that animal called man, although I heartily love John, Peter, Thomas, and so forth.'

In men as different as Malraux and Whitehead, we see the essentially religious attempt to *socialize* one's loneliness, though Whitehead stresses purely idealistic strategies in the accomplishment of this, whereas Malraux seeks the corrective 'dialectically' in collective action, in accordance with Marx's formula for the socialization of losses, to the effect that 'I am not alone as a victim; I am in a *class* of victims.' Swift, being essentially religious, was essentially tragic; but over-individualistic emphases turned the tragic scapegoat into a satiric scapegoat, thereby turning a device for solace into a device for indictment. Lack of religiosity is a convenience; but religion gone wrong is a major disaster.

(312–13)

G. Wilson Knight

from 'Swift' 1939 (reprinted in *Poets of Action*, 1967)

Swift does not, normally, give any impression of actual savagery. He writes as though well above his subject, with a deadly ease and serenity of statement. Which brings us to his famous irony: *A Modest*

Proposal is only the most celebrated instance of a continual technique. Irony says one thing while aiming to make the reader think its opposite, so that the reader himself produces the required thought from his own mind. This is, of course, the secret of persuasion in general of which rhetorical questions are the crudest, and irony the most concentrated, form. Swift, by commenting on his carefully invented situations with a quietly exaggerated respect to conventional values, releases in the reader a sudden revulsion from those values. What we call 'control' in any art is similar, being the technique of leaving certain things out, the use of suggestion, relying on the reader's, or in acting the spectator's, ability to do the rest. It is therefore easy to see why lack of it may offend, though it is equally clear that since few readers normally do their share, the more violent artist may on occasion have as good a case as the other. Pope seems to be aiming always at couplet-rhyme, his thought not stressed, to be received almost by mistake with a half-awareness, with the unfortunate result that we have taken him at his face value. Jesus speaks in parable to awake, rather than inject, the thought required, to release an automatic recognition. All symbolism takes you to the threshold, no more. Swift's irony is, compared with those, scarcely profound, nor can it be missed, but its nature poignantly condenses a universal truth: that to force people's minds may be less valuable than to engage their co-operation; as when Dryden, by masking his attack on Buckingham through the character of Zimri, makes his audience itself perform the act of recognition before weighing its justice, which is by then already admitted. All this relates closely to Swift's use of sensory symbolisms: the one is allied with the other, mad schemes chosen which lend themselves to ironic comment; and as we have already observed, his use of size relies on raising judgements instinctive to the reader. Swift *proves* nothing. The general result is an especially powerful effect with an appearance of effortless ease that impresses with a sense of necessity and truth, and causes us to think the author an intellectual giant, though there is little close thinking, as such, in these works. He is not exactly an emotional giant either; and yet he certainly seems to be a giant of some sort. In Lilliput Gulliver's size may be taken to symbolize some Gargantuan sense of superiority, as perhaps the vast stature of Satan symbolizes Milton's; some wish-fulfilment in material terms of that ease and mastery he feels within him, yet can only attain in literature. It has been observed that in Brobdingnag we tend to see Gulliver as tiny, still identifying ourselves with the big people; which, if it be so, might reflect a similar identification in the writer. The cat and thrush we may see, for a short while, as vast, but not the men; though there are other possible reasons for this.

The richest negative profundities, Milton's Hell or Webster's charnel-mongering, are absent from Swift; and, perhaps, from Pope. A certain dark intensity is left unexperienced: Pope's *Dunciad* satirizes the mentally absurd, asses his symbol; Swift's Yahoos are ape-pigs, corresponding to a more physical disgust. Pope's appears the more healthy, and clearly, in view of his other work, the more just. Certainly Swift's concentration on ordure suggests a limitation. Three sense-complexes may trouble the growing human organism: ordure, sex, death. Two organic negations seem to enclose a positive, but the sequence, I think, exists. The first normally gets, and some would say deserves, slight attention, though we may remember that excretion is a miniature death in its expulsion of poisons, and that all sensory reactions to it hold interest in reference to death itself. Sexual troubles of one sort or another are the natural playground for adult agonies, and their solution seems to condition understanding of the final mystery. Much of our horror at death is, at bottom, a physical repulsion, and may be related to both the earlier stages. It seems that Swift, on this plane of analysis, was stuck at the first obstacle and we may suspect a corresponding limitation in his gospel. He is rather like Apemantus in *Timon of Athens*.

Nevertheless, his apparent suffering elevates him far above the more smug and contented satirists. Moreover, his symbolic schemes aim at a deeper, more emotional redirection, as I have shown, than would a more facile surface argument lacking sensory-appeal. He is not merely 'intellectual'; but his strong sense-aversions, which we may, in view of their overpowering emphasis, suppose to be, originally at least, troubling elements in his own life, are fundamentally a denial of the poetic essence, and it is to his credit that he so finely reversed that denial to poetic account. We can say either (a) that his psychological peculiarities prevented his finding a positive and dynamic pattern, and that his thwarted genius did the best it could, by wrenching nausea to prophetic standard; or (b) that in this age of simultaneous respect to and repudiation of the heroic tradition such a man was best equipped for literary genius, since satire alone conditioned that entwining of symbol and story necessary to the greatest works. But our view must be measured against the comparable but different development of Pope. Though he is merciless to the main activities of Western civilization, Swift respects the heroic traditions of Greece and Rome; and this sympathy is reflected into his own narrative skill and even sentence construction, wherein the best points are continually being made through lucid statements of action. Most great writers express somewhere or other the best possible unconscious commentary, whether critical or appraising, on their own work. Here is Swift's, from *The Battle of the Books*:

For anything else of genuine that the Moderns may pretend to, I cannot recollect; unless it be a large vein of wrangling and satire, much of a nature and substance with the spider's poison; which, however they pretend to spit wholly out of themselves, is improved by the same arts, by feeding upon the insects and vermin of the age. As for us the Ancients, we are content with the bee to pretend to nothing of our own, beyond our wings and our voice, that is to say, our flights and our language. For the rest, whatever we have got, has been by infinite labour and search, and ranging through every corner of nature; the difference is, that, instead of dirt and poison, we have rather chosen to fill our hives with honey and wax, thus furnishing mankind with the two noblest of things, which are sweetness and light (1 151).

The beautiful handling of the symbol contrasts strongly with Arnold's prostitution of it in *Culture and Anarchy*. Swift here glimpses, if insecurely, a positive human excellence not incomparable with Pope's; and his satire, like Pope's, is directed against an age poisoned by petty wrangling; it is satire against satire. If the medicine is strong, so was, or is, the disease. Moreover, though this passage may today be read as self-condemnation, its beautiful strength and precision of statement, relying almost entirely on concrete nouns and active verbs with scarcely an adjective to assist, range Swift in the company rather of those ancients whose art he describes.

(173–6)

W. K. Wimsatt, Jr

from *The Prose Style of Samuel Johnson* 1941

Johnson's dislike of mere fact would perhaps not have been so clearly recorded for us were it not for his extreme dislike of the prose of another writer whose style was the antipodes of his own. Perhaps some personal rancor at times stimulated Johnson to the criticism of Swift, but the criticism is too clear and too often reiterated to leave a doubt either that Swift's style was really offensive to Johnson or that there was an esthetic reason. At best Swift's style is for Johnson but an adequate vehicle for an inferior burden. In the *Life of Swift*:

This easy and safe conveyance of meaning it was Swift's desire to attain, and for having attained he deserves praise, though perhaps not the highest praise. For purposes merely didactic, when something is to be told that was not known before, it is the best mode, but against that inattention by which known truths are suffered to lie neglected it makes no provision; it instructs, but does not persuade (*Lives*, p. 52).[1]

In Boswell's *Life* Johnson says of those who like and those who dislike Swift's style: 'Both agree that Swift has a good neat style; but one loves a neat style, another loves a style of more splendour.' (*Life*, vol. 2, pp. 191–2).[2] There are yet other passages where Johnson is less kind – where he explains in an unreserved, unmistakable, concrete manner, what he dislikes in Swift's writing. In the *Life of Swift* he says of *The Conduct of the Allies*:

Surely, whoever surveys this wonder-working pamphlet with cool perusal will confess that its efficacy was supplied by the passions of its readers; that it operates by the mere weight of facts, with very little assistance from the hand that produced them (*Lives*, p. 19).

Of the same pamphlet he had earlier said:

1 References to Johnson's 'Life of Swift' are from the G. Birkbeck Hill edition of Johnson's *Lives of the English Poets*, vol. 3, Clarendon Press, 1905. See pp. 78–93. [Ed.]
2 References to Boswell's *Life of Johnson* are from the G. Birkbeck Hill edition, vols. 1–4, Clarendon Press, 1934. [Ed.]

Swift has told what he had to tell distinctly enough, but that is all. He had to count ten, and he has counted it right (*Life*, vol. 2, p. 65).

At Mrs Thrale's once he argued with a gentleman on the same subject.

At length you *must* allow me, said the gentleman, that there are *strong facts* in the account of the four last years of Queen Anne: 'Yes surely Sir (replies Johnson), and so there are in the Ordinary of Newgate's account.'[1]

Plainness of fact, not as opposed to fiction, but as opposed to elaboration – this must be understood as the opposite of what John-son admired in writing. Swift comes no nearer to merit by the in-ventions of *Gulliver's Travels*. 'When once you have thought of big men and little men, it is very easy to do all the rest' (*Life*, vol. 2, p. 319). What *Gulliver's Travels* and the 'Ordinary of Newgate's Account' have in common is that they deal with things, a constant succession of different things, not different aspects of the same things. It is the difference between multiplication for range ('the prince and princess') and multiplication for emphasis ('the constituent and fundamental principle'). The 'so many *things*, almost in an equal number of *words*' of Sprat had been no vain exhortation to Johnson's predecessors. It had become a real and conscious rule. Swift himself praised the style of the Brobdingnagians thus: 'Their style is clear, masculine and smooth, but not florid; for they avoid nothing more than multiplying unnecessary words, or using various expressions.' And this was precisely the aim of Johnson, to multiply words, to use various expressions, to deal not in things but in thoughts about

1 G. Birkbeck Hill (ed.), *Johnsonian Miscellanies*, vol. 1, Clarendon Press, 1897, vol. 1, p. 188. He says almost the same thing in the conversation on *The Conduct of the Allies* (*Life*, vol. 2, p. 65). For further comments on Swift's style see *Lives*, p. 51, and *Life*, vol. 1, p. 452, vol. 2, pp. 318–19 and vol. 5, p. 44. In *Rambler* no. 122 he writes: 'Some have doubted whether an *Englishman* can stop at that mediocrity of style, or confine his mind to that even tenour of imagination which narrative requires.'

Addison, a writer plain and neat but much less so than Swift, receives Johnson's considered praise. But Mrs Piozzi says: 'It was notwithstanding observable enough (or I fancied so), that he never did like, though he always thought fit to praise it.'

things. In this he is nearer to the romantic essayists than to the neo-classic. His is the more meditative, more poetic style. It pauses and develops the aspects and relations of things, works them into a thought pattern, attracts into the pattern reflections of other things.

The need for elaboration was one of the consequences of the taste for generality. There were two kinds of subject matter: things, such as Swift dealt with, which had to be new things in order to claim attention; and general truths, which being general and true must be already known and which hence must be enforced or recommended. This enforcement or recommendation was the proper scope of literary art.

The task of an author is, either to teach what is not known,
or to recommend known truths by his manner of adorning
them; either to let new light in upon the mind, and open
new scenes to the prospect, or to vary the dress and situation
of common objects, so as to give them fresh grace and more
powerful attractions, to spread such flowers over the regions
through which the intellect has already made its progress, as
may tempt it to return, and take a second view of things
hastily passed over or negligently regarded.

This occurs in *Rambler* no. 3, where Johnson is explaining the plan o his work – the second alternative, 'to recommend known truths by his manner of adorning them'. In *Adventurer* no. 115 we find this distinction between the modes of writing repeated. If an author 'treats of science and demonstration', he must have a 'style clear, pure, nervous and expressive'. But 'if his topics be probable and persuasory', he must 'recommend them by the super-addition of elegance and imagery ... display the colours of varied diction, and pour forth the music of modulated periods'. In *Rambler* no. 152: 'Among the critics in history it is not contested whether truth ought to be preserved, but by what mode of diction it is best adorned.'[1]

It will be noted that Johnson is an ornamentalist, at least in his terminology. But it is likely that no great writer, or even able hack writer, was ever an ornamentalist in more than terminology. As a feat

[1] The same conception may be seen in Johnson's criticism of devotional poetry. 'The paucity of its topics enforces perpetual repetition, and the sanctity of the matter rejects the ornaments of figurative diction' (*Lives*, p. 310).

of composition or as a concrete critical state of mind, ornamentalism is perhaps impossible. When Johnson speaks of things and their ornamentation, we should have no difficulty in recognizing that he is talking about things and aspects of, or ideas about, things. This is all he can be talking about. Both the things and the ideas about them are included in what we call meaning. Since Johnson was not concerned with our particular problem, he was content to look on things, truths or facts, as solid 'meaning' (though he did not employ the term) and on notional modulations as 'ornament'. We need not then quarrel with his theory while describing it, but must recognize what it means in our own terms.

His most direct statement in defence of his system of elaboration refers to a passage of narration in the *Western Islands*. If *things must* be his reason for writing, his main theme, they can yet be adorned with clustered notions. Lord Monboddo wrote to Boswell that Johnson's language was too rich.

Johnson. Why, Sir, this criticism would be just, if in my style, superfluous words, or words too big for the thoughts, could be pointed out; but this I do not believe can be done. For instance; in the passage which Lord Monboddo admires, 'We were now treading that illustrious region', the word *illustrious*, contributes nothing to the mere narration; for the fact might be told without it: but it is not, therefore, superfluous; for it wakes the mind to peculiar attention, where something of more than usual importance is to be presented. 'Illustrious!' – for what? and then the sentence proceeds to expand the circumstances connected with Iona. . . . (*Life*, vol. 3, pp. 173–4).

Johnson is giving the reason that justifies all epithetical or non-restrictive modification. When we use any word to tell not what thing we mean but only under what aspect we mean it, we have taken the first step away from plain style. The second step is to multiply the aspects under which we refer to a single object. The third, and extreme Johnsonian, step is to multiply aspects (or words apparently expressing different aspects) so that within the range of relevance they overlap – which is 'multiplication for emphasis'. (98–101)

C. S. Lewis

from 'Addison' in *Essays on the Eighteenth Century Presented to
David Nichol Smith* 1945

I have used the word 'amiability'. Should we go further and say
'charity'? I feel that this Christian word, with its doctrinal implications, would be a little out of place when we are speaking of Addison's
essays. About the man, as distinct from the work, I will not speculate.
Let us hope that he practised this theological virtue. The story that he
summoned Lord Warwick to his deathbed *to see how a Christian can
die* is ambiguous; it can be taken either as evidence of his Christianity
or as a very brimstone proof of the reverse. I give no vote: my concern is with books. And the essays do not invite criticism in terms of
any very definite theology. They are everywhere 'pious'. Rational
Piety, together with Polite Letters and Simplicity, is one of the hall-
marks of the age which Addison was partly interpreting but partly
also bringing into existence. And Rational Piety is by its very nature
not very doctrinal. This is one of the many ways in which Addison
is historically momentous. He ushers in that period – it is just now
drawing to a close – in which it is possible to talk of 'piety' or (later)
'religion' almost in the abstract; in which the contrast is no longer
between Christian and pagan, the elect and the world, orthodox and
heretic, but between 'religious' and 'irreligious'. The transition cannot be quite defined: absence of doctrine would have to become itself
doctrinal for that to be possible. It is a change of atmosphere, which
every reader of sensibility will feel if he passes suddenly from the
literature of any earlier period to that of the eighteenth century.
Hard rocks of Calvinism show up amidst the seemingly innocuous
surface of an *Arcadia* or a *Faerie Queene*; Shakespearian comedy
reckons on an audience who will at once see the point of jokes about
the controversy on Works and Faith. Here also, no doubt, it is difficult
to bring Addison to a point. Perhaps the most illuminating passage is
the essay on 'Sir Roger at Church', and specially the quotation from
Pythagoras prefixed to it – 'Honour first the immortal gods according to the established mode.' That is the very note of Rational Piety.
A sensible man goes with his society, according to local and ancestral
usage. And he does so with complete sincerity. Clean clothes and the

sound of bells on Sunday morning do really throw him into a mood of sober benevolence, not 'clouded by enthusiasm' but inviting his thoughts to approach the mystery of things.

In this matter of Rational Piety one must not draw too sharp a contrast between Addison and the Tories. They are infected with it themselves, and Swift quotes with equal approval the pagan maxim about worshipping 'according to the laws of the country'. But I think there is *some* contrast. The Tories are a little nearer than Addison to the old period with its uncompromising creeds. Pope's Romanism is not nearly so superficial as some have supposed, and the 'Pantheism' of the *Essay on Man* owes a good deal of its notoriety to critics who would make a very poor shape at defining pantheism. He made an edifying end, and he perhaps understands the conflict in Eloise's mind – it is not simply a conflict of virtue and vice – better than Addison would have done. Swift is harder to classify. There is, to be sure, no doubt of his churchmanship, only of his Christianity, and this, of itself, is significant. If Swift were (as I do not think he is) primarily a Church-of-England man, only secondly a Christian, and not 'pious' or 'religious' at all, we might say that in Addison's writings the proportions are reversed. And some things would lend colour to such an interpretation of Swift. In the *Sentiments* his religion seems to be purely political. 'I leave it among the divines to dilate upon the danger of schism, as a spiritual evil, but I would consider it only as a temporal one.' Separation from the established worship, 'though to a new one that is more pure and perfect', is dangerous. More disquieting still are the tormented aphorisms of *Thoughts on Religion*. To change fundamental opinions is ordinarily wicked 'whether those opinions be true or false', and 'The want of belief is a defect that ought to be concealed when it cannot be overcome.' Some parts of *Gulliver* seem inconsistent with any religion – except perhaps Buddhism. The *Further Thoughts on Religion* open with the assertion that the Mosaic account of creation is 'most agreeable of all other to probability' and immediately cite – the making of Eve out of Adam's rib! Is it possible that this should not be irony? And yet there is much to set on the other side. His priestly duties were discharged with a fidelity rare in that age. The ferocity of the later *Gulliver* all works up to that devastating attack on Pride which is more specifically Christian than any other piece of ethical writing in the century, if we except William Law. The prayers offered at Stella's deathbed have a scholastic firmness in their implied moral theology. ('Keep her from both the sad extremes of presumption and despair.' 'Forgive the sorrow and weakness of those among us who sink under the grief and terror of losing so dear and useful a friend.') The sermon 'On the Trinity', taken at its face value, preaches a submission of the reason to dogma which ought to satisfy the sternest supernaturalist. And I think it should be taken at its face value. If we ever think otherwise, I believe the explanation to lie in that peculiar ungraciousness which Swift exercised upwards as well as downwards. He gave alms 'without tenderness or civility', so that 'those who were fed by him could hardly love him'. As below, so above. He practises obedience without humility or meekness, takes his medicine with a wry face. But the alms, however given, were hard cash, and I think his acceptance of Christian doctrine is equally real, though offered (as it were) under protest, as if he were resentful of Heaven for putting him in such a ridiculous position. There is a tension and discomfort about all this, but that very tension suggests depths that Addison never knew. It is from those depths that Swift is writing when he says there can be no question in England of any but a nominal Christianity – 'the other having been for some time wholly laid aside by general consent as utterly inconsistent with our present schemes of wealth and power'. This is a far cry from Mr Spectator's pleasing reflections on the Royal Exchange.

As I am a great lover of mankind, my heart naturally overflows with pleasure at the sight of a happy and prosperous multitude, insomuch that at many public solemnities I cannot forbear expressing my joy with tears that have stolen down my cheeks. For this reason I am wonderfully delighted to see such a body of men thriving in their own private fortunes, and at the same time promoting the public stock; or, in other words, raising estates for their own families, by bringing into their country whatever is wanting, and carrying out of it whatever is superfluous.

Compared with this, Swift's remark is like a scorching wind from the hermitages of the Thebaid.

Addison is never blasphemous or irreverent; Swift can be both.

That, I think, helps to confirm the kind of distinction I am drawing between them. Swift still belongs, at any rate in part, to the older world. He would have understood Rochester in both of Rochester's phases better than he could understand Addison. Rochester unconverted was a Bad Man of the old, thoroughgoing kind,

He drunk, he fought, he whored,
He did despite unto the Lord.

Rochester converted was a deathbed penitent. One cannot imagine Mr Spectator or Sir Andrew emulating him in either achievement. (3–6)

Louis A. Landa

from 'Jonathan Swift', *English Institute Essays 1946*　1947

Commentators who observe manifestations of a disordered intellect in the fourth voyage have not thought to question the intellect behind the third voyage, yet we know now that the third was composed in point of time after the fourth. And these commentators have nothing but praise for the vigor, the keenness, the sanity and the humanity of the mind that produced the *Drapier's Letters*, yet we have reasonable assurance that Swift completed the draft of Part IV of *Gulliver* in January of 1724 and was at work on the first of the *Drapier's Letters* in February.

Another procedure of which the critics of Swift are fond deserves to be scanned: the habit of taking an isolated statement or an isolated incident and giving it undue significance to support their prepossessions. In a recent study of Swift, in many respects of more than ordinary perceptiveness, the author considers Part IV of *Gulliver* as an embodiment of the tragic view of life. In so doing he passes from the work to the facts or presumed facts of Swift's life to enforce his interpretation, adducing as evidence the report of Swift's manner, in his later years, of bidding friends good-bye: 'Good night, I hope I shall never see you again.' If Swift really used this remark, if he used it seriously, some weight may be attached to it; but I should want to know to whom he used it and in what tone or spirit. It sounds very much like his usual banter, his manner of friendly insult and quite genial vituperation which so often distinguishes his letters to friends who understood his ironic turn and his liking for the inverted compliment. How can we rely on such casual remarks or possibly know what weight to give them? But such a remark is related to Swift's habit of reading certain parts of the Book of Job to prove that he hated life, and is made to seem of a piece with the fourth voyage of *Gulliver's Travels*. This is typical of the commentators who have culled from Swift's letters, from the biographies, and from other documents all the presumed evidence of gloom and misanthropy in order to uncover what they have a strong prepossession to uncover, the essential misery of his existence. This is the way to prove, in support of the interpretation of the fourth voyage, that 'Swift's life was a long disease, with its disappointments, its self-torture, its morbid recriminations.'

But a matter of statistical balance is involved here: the facts listed and weighted heavily have been too much of one complexion. Too much has been made of the last years of Swift's life, when he bothered less to conceal his moods and his irritations – and when he seemed to get a certain satisfaction in talking about his ailments. I should like to see some biographer counter the gloomy approach by emphasizing Swift's zest for life, his vitality and the playfulness of his mind. There is ample evidence in his letters – and in what we know of his activities – of high spirits, good humor and daily satisfactions. Such a study might very well, without distortion, evidence an unexpected mathematical balance between happiness and unhappiness.

I should not want to be put into the position of denying Swift a considerable pessimism and a fair share of misanthropy. These qualities, however, were not so raw or so unassimilated or so crudely operative in his daily existence as has been often represented. The manner in which these personal qualities have been used to explain *Gulliver* deserves to be questioned. It has been an overly simple process of equating biographical fact and artistic statement, of viewing the work as a transcription of the author's experiences or as a precise and complete representation of his personal philosophy – or as a final explanation of his personality. There is an obvious danger in seeing an artistic or imaginative construction as mere duplication. *Gulliver's Travels* is a work of mingled fantasy and satire; it is

Utopian literature, highly allusive and symbolic, charged with hidden meanings and projected to a level several removes from the real world of its author. [11]

To leaven the biographical approach other questions deserve attention. What are the artistic necessities of a work of this type? What are the esthetic principles, quite apart from other considerations, that shape the work? To what extent is there a compromise between these principles and the conscious or the undeliberate tendency of the author to reflect his experiences and his personality?

If the biographical approach to Swift has been crudely used or overemphasized in certain respects, there are other respects in which biographical considerations of critical value have been left almost wholly unexplored. The most significant of these seems to me to be Swift's profession as a Christian divine. Is there in this some clue to an explanation of Part IV of *Gulliver*? If a reading of the sermons can be trusted, the eighteenth-century divine relished his duty to expatiate on the evils and corruptions of this world and the inadequacies of this life. He seemed to enjoy measuring the imperfections before him against a higher set of values. Swift, I think, would have held an optimistic divine to be a contradiction in terms; and his own pessimism is quite consonant with the pessimism at the heart of Christianity. One of Swift's sermons begins as follows:

The Holy Scripture is full of expressions to set forth the
miserable condition of man during the whole progress of his
life; his weakness, pride and vanity, his unmeasurable desires,
and perpetual disappointments; the prevalency of his passions,
and the corruptions of his reason, his deluding hopes and his
real, as well as imaginary, fears . . . his cares and anxieties,
the diseases of his body, and the diseases of his mind. . . .
And the wise men of all ages have made the same reflections
(*On the Poor Man's Contentment; Prose Writings*, IX 190).

If Swift had written his own comment on *Gulliver's Travels*, he might very well have used the words of this sermon. *Gulliver's Travels* certainly is full of expressions to set forth the miserable condition of man – his weakness, pride and vanity, his unmeasurable desires, the prevalency of his passions and the corruptions of his reason – and so on through the catalogue. Indeed, Swift's few sermons and those of other eighteenth-century divines could easily be used to annotate *Gulliver's Travels*. It is difficult for me to believe that a contemporary could fail to see the affinity between the fourth voyage – or the whole of *Gulliver* – and many of the conventional sermons on human nature and the evils of this life. Swift's emphasis on depraved human nature and his evaluation of man's behavior are certainly *not* at odds with Christian tradition. There is no need to ascribe such views solely to personal bitterness or frustrations or melancholia. His thinking and status as a divine had an effect much more profound than is generally recognized. A good case can be made for Part IV of *Gulliver* as being in its implications Christian apologetics, though of course in nontheological terms; in a sense it is an allegory which veils human nature and society as a Christian divine views them. It is by indirection a defense of the doctrine of redemption and man's need of grace.

Only an occasional commentator has recognized and stressed the essentially Christian philosophy of the fourth voyage. The first was Swift's relative, Deane Swift, who declared that the Christian conception of the evil nature of man is the 'groundwork of the whole satyre contained in the voyage to the Houyhnhnms'. Then this cousin of Jonathan Swift, this lesser Swift, delivers himself of a catalogue of vices worthy of his great cousin:

Ought a preacher of righteousness [he asks], ought a watchman of the Christian faith ... to hold his peace ... when avarice, fraud, cheating, violence, rapine, extortion, cruelty, oppression, tyranny, rancour, envy, malice, detraction, hatred, revenge, murder, whoredom, adultery, lasciviousness, bribery, corruption, pimping, lying, perjury, subornation, treachery, ingratitude, gaming, flattery, drunkenness, gluttony, luxury, vanity, effeminacy, cowardice, pride, impudence, hypocrisy, infidelity, blasphemy, idolatry, sodomy and innumerable other vices are as epidemical as the pox, and many of them the notorious characteristics of the bulk of mankind? (*An Essay upon the Life, Writings and Characters of Dr Jonathan Swift*, 1755, pp. 219–20).

'Dr Swift,' he adds, 'was not the first preacher, whose writings import this kind of philosophy.' Surely those clergymen who week after week exposed the deceitfulness of the human heart would have agreed with Deane Swift.

It seems to be true, as T. O. Wedel[1] has pointed out, that Swift's view of human nature was opposed to certain contemporary attitudes in which the passions of men were looked on kindly and in which the dignity of human nature was defended in such a way that the doctrine of original sin lost its efficacy. In his *Reasonableness of Christianity* (1695) John Locke could deny, without raising much serious protest, that the fall of Adam implies the corruption of human nature in Adam's posterity. It is this same current of thought that later in the century disturbed John Wesley, who complains in one of his sermons (no. 38, 'Original Sin') that 'not a few persons of strong understanding, as well as extensive learning, have employed their utmost abilities to show, what they termed, "the fair side of human nature in Adam's posterity"'. 'So that,' Wesley continues, 'it is now quite unfashionable to say anything to the disparagement of human nature; which is generally allowed, notwithstanding a few infirmities, to be very innocent, and wise, and virtuous.' Is it not significant, when Wesley comes to write his treatise on *The Doctrine of Original Sin* (1756), that he should turn to Swift, to Part IV of *Gulliver* for quotations? In this treatise Wesley refers scornfully to those 'who gravely talk of the dignity of our nature', and then quotes several times from what he calls 'a late eminent hand'. The 'late eminent hand' is Swift's, whose words from Part IV of *Gulliver* describing man as 'a lump of deformity and disease, both in body and mind, smitten with pride' Wesley has seized on. Wesley refers again and again to the 'many laboured panegyrics ... we now read and hear on the dignity of human nature'; and he raises a question which is, I think, a clue to Swift. If men are generally virtuous, what is the need of the doctrine of Redemption? This is pretty much the point of two sermons by Swift, where he is obviously in reaction to the panegyrics on human nature which came from Shaftesbury and the benevolists, from the defenders of the Stoic wise man, and from proponents of the concept of a man of honor. Swift sensed the

[1] For the relationship between Swift and Wesley stated in this paragraph see an article to which I am much indebted, T. O. Wedel, 'On the Philosophical Background of *Gulliver's Travels*', *Studies in Philology*, vol. 23, 1926, pp. 434–50.

danger to orthodox Christianity from an ethical system or any view of human nature stressing man's goodness or strongly asserting man's capacity for virtue. He had no faith in the existence of the benevolent man of Shaftesbury and the anti-Hobbists, the proud, magnanimous man of the Stoics, or the rational man of the deists; his man is a creature of the passions, of pride and self-love, a frail and sinful being in need of redemption. The very simple and wholly unoriginal strain of apologetics in Swift's sermons is based upon an attitude common in traditional Christian thought; and to my way of thinking Swift the clergyman repeats himself in *Gulliver's Travels*.

(28–35)

William Empson

from 'The English Dog', *The Structure of Complex Words* 1951

If one considers the richness of the intuitive poetry, of the emotional life the language took for granted, in the seventeenth century, it is surprising that the eighteenth could make so much of its more narrow material, could base so much poetry on a doggish mock-heroic. It was the simplicity of this feeling, on the other hand, which let them prune down so far towards rationalizing their emotional life without killing the tree. But there was a danger of killing it. A surprising number of the great writers went mad, and most of them feared to; indeed, the more you respect reason the more you must fear the irrational. Thus another use was found for the dog in the way it stood for the unconscious; for the source of the impulses that keep us sane, and may mysteriously fail as in drought. Its process of thought is a mystery, but the results are homely and intelligible; it makes what we do not know about the roots of our own minds seem cheerful and not alarming. Swift, for example, kept himself sane for as long as he did on secret doses of this feeling (and on the collection of beggars to whom he gave the money gained by cheese-paring); its good humour and humility are somehow at the back of and make endurable the most regal solvents of his irony. Yet he would shy very decidedly from the humanist application, and his ideal animal is the pointless 'calculating horse' (the horse as generous has a point all right, but not the horse as Cold Reason).

The humanist application corresponds to the hearty use of these words, as the rationalist one does to the patronizing use. Of course humanism was a complicated affair, and the term has not always been used to mean what I mean here; I am using it for something vaguely anti-Christian. The reason the early humanist put so much weight on learning correct Latin and reading classical literature in bulk was – not exactly to put the anti-Christian idea across under cover, but to put it across in a way that would allow the pupil to digest it within Christianity; as something that applied to life in a different way, rather than conflicted. The fundamental novelty was an idea that 'Man is no longer an abortive deity, born in sin, necessarily incomplete in the world, but the most triumphant of the animals'. To call him a dog playfully is thus to insist on his rights; he is better than a dog, but has the same reasons for being cheerful. It brings in a sort of pastoral feeling to do this; that there is a sweetness or richness in the simple thing, that to cut yourself off from it would be folly, that it holds *in posse* all later values; also the fact that you need to remind yourself of it may show how encouragingly far it has been left behind. The essential here is that you can start building yourself into a man, and not hate yourself, on the basis of being that kind of animal; the trouble about evolution was that one could not feel the same about monkeys.

There was, indeed, a widespread feeling towards evolution before Darwinism, such as both uses of dog-sentiment would suggest. Bentley claimed rather absurdly to find an example of it in Milton, and said 'he remembered this senseless notion spread about'; Coleridge speaks of 'that absurd notion of Pope's *Essay on Man*, of man's having progressed from an orang-outang state'.

Still as one brood, and as another rose,
These natural love maintain'd, habitual those;
The last, scarce ripen'd into perfect man,
Saw helpless him from whom their life began.

Sure enough, these laboriously obscure lines can hardly mean anything but the development of men from unreasoning creatures – what is a natural sentiment to us, for instance, was not so to the first brood. There is a more dangerous hint a few lines later, that the idea of good was developed only because it 'preserved the kind'. The striking thing, however, is that critics were so ready to pick up a hint of this line of thought. The fact that monkeys were so like men was 'sadly humbling' to Boswell; Monboddo only dared to say what many had suspected, and Johnson agreed he was not a fool. Swift might fall back on the Houyhnhnm in accepting this about the Yahoo, but that was a refusal of humanity; the only real animal to use was the dog. And, indeed, it is comforting to reflect that this apparent evasion was to a great extent the truth. Whatever the spiritual quality we dislike in monkeys may be, there is no positive evidence that our common ancestors shared it; and even if they did, for a much greater period of time they were straightforward mammals like a dog or a squirrel. Even our ancestral reptile, in the pictures, is made to stand up on its legs and look about it like a puppy. There is a curious agreement, at any rate, that if we are animals this is the kind of animal we would like to be.

(169–70)

Louise Bogan

'Hypocrite Swift', *Collected Poems 1923–1953*   1956

Hypocrite Swift now takes an eldest daughter.
He lifts Vanessa's hand. Cudsho, my dove!
Drink Wexford ale and quaff down Wexford water
But never love.

He buys new caps; he and Lord Stanley ban
Hedge-fellows who have neither wit nor swords.
He turns his coat; Tories are in; Queen Anne
Makes twelve new lords.

The town mows hay in hell; he swims in the river;
His giddiness returns; his head is hot.
Berries are clean, while peaches damn the giver
(Though grapes do not).

Mrs Vanhomrigh keeps him safe from the weather.
Preferment pulls his periwig askew.
Pox takes belittlers; do the willows feather?
God keep you.

Stella spells ill; Lords Peterborough and Fountain
Talk politics; the Florence wine went sour.
Midnight: two different clocks, here and in Dublin,
Give out the hour.

On walls at court, long gilded mirrors gaze.
The parquet shines; outside the snow falls deep.
Venus, the Muses stare above the maze.
Now sleep.

Dream the mixed, fearsome dream. The satiric word
Dies in its horror. Wake, and live by stealth.
The bitter quatrain forms, is here, is heard,
Is wealth.

What care I; what cares saucy Presto? Stir
The bed-clothes; hearten up the perishing fire.
Hypocrite Swift sent Stella a green apron
And dead desire.

Norman O. Brown

from 'The Excremental Vision', *Life Against Death:
The Psychoanalytical Meaning of History* 1959

The thesis of this chapter is that if we are willing to listen to Swift we will find startling anticipations of Freudian theorems about anality, about sublimation, and about the universal neurosis of mankind. To anticipate objections, let me say that Swiftian psychoanalysis differs from the Freudian in that the vehicle for the exploration of the unconscious is not psychoanalysis but wit. But Freud himself recognized, in *Wit and the Unconscious*, that wit has its own way of exploring the universal neurosis of mankind.

Psychoanalysis is apparently necessary in order to explicate the 'noxious compositions'; at least the unpsychoanalysed neurotic appears to be incapable of correctly stating what these poems are about. These are the poems which provoke Murry to ecstasies of revulsion – 'nonsensical and intolerable', 'so perverse, so unnatural, so mentally diseased, so humanly *wrong*'. What Murry is denouncing is the proposition that woman is abominable because she is guilty of physical evacuation. We need not consider whether the proposition deserves such denunciation, for the simple reason that it comes from Murry's imagination, not Swift's. Murry, like Strephon and the other unfortunate men in the poems, loses his wits when he discovers that Celia shits, and thus unconsciously bears witness to the truth of Swift's psychological insight. Any mind that is at all open to the antiseptic wisdom of psychoanalysis will find nothing extraordinary about the poems, except perhaps the fact that they were written in the first half of the eighteenth century. For their real theme – quite obvious on a dispassionate reading – is the conflict between our animal body, appropriately epitomized in the anal function, and our pretentious sublimations, more specifically the pretensions of sublimated or romantic-platonic love. In every case it is a 'goddess', 'so divine a creature', 'heavenly Chloe', who is exposed; or rather what is exposed is the illusion in the head of the adoring male, the illusion that the goddess is all head and wings, with no bottom to betray the sublunary infirmities.

The peculiar Swiftian twist to the theme that Celia shits is the notion that there is some absolute contradiction between the state of being in love and an awareness of the excremental function of the beloved. Before we dismiss this idea as the fantasy of a diseased mind, we had better remember that Freud said the same thing. In an essay written in 1912 surveying the disorder in the sexual life of man, he finally concludes that the deepest trouble is an unresolved ambivalence in the human attitude toward anality:

We know that at its beginning the sexual instinct is divided
into a large number of components – or rather it develops
from them – not all of which can be carried on into its final
form; some have to be surpassed or turned to other uses
before the final form results. Above all, the coprophilic
elements in the instinct have proved incompatible with our

esthetic ideas, probably since the time when man developed an upright posture and so removed his organ of smell from the ground; further, a considerable proportion of the sadistic elements belonging to the erotic instinct have to be abandoned. All such developmental processes, however, relate only to the upper layers of the complicated structure. The fundamental processes which promote erotic excitation remain always the same. Excremental things are all too intimately and inseparably bound up with sexual things; the position of the genital organs – *inter urinas et faeces* – remains the decisive and unchangeable factor. The genitals themselves have not undergone the development of the rest of the human form in the direction of beauty; they have retained their animal cast; and so even today love, too, is in essence as animal as it ever was.

Again, in *Civilization and its Discoveries*, Freud pursues the thought that the deepest cause of sexual repression is an organic factor, a disbalance in the human organism between higher and lower functions:

The whole of sexuality and not merely anal erotism is threatened with falling a victim to the organic repression consequent upon man's adoption of the erect posture and the lowering in value of the sense of smell; so that since that time the sexual function has been associated with a resistance not susceptible of further explanation, which puts obstacles in the way of full satisfaction and forces it away from its sexual aim towards sublimations and displacements of libido. . . . All neurotics, and many others too, take exception to the fact that '*inter urinas et faeces nascimur*'. . . . Thus we should find, as the deepest root of the sexual repression that marches with culture, the organic defense of the new form of life that began with the erect posture.

Those who, like Middleton Murry, anathematize Swift's excremental vision as unChristian might ponder the quotation from St Augustine that Freud uses in both these passages.

That Swift's thought is running parallel with Freud's is demonstrated by the fact that a fuller explication of the poems would have to use the terms 'repression' and 'sublimation'. It is of course not ignorance but repression of the anal factor that creates the romantic illusions of Strephon and Cassinus and makes the breakthrough of the truth so traumatic. And Swift's ultimate horror in these poems is at the thought that sublimation – that is to say, all civilized behavior – is a lie and cannot survive confrontation with the truth. In the first of his treatments of the theme (*The Lady's Dressing Room*, 1732) he reasons with Strephon that sublimation is still possible:

Should I the Queen of Love refuse,
Because she rose from stinking ooze?

Strephon should reconcile himself to:

Such order from confusion sprung,
Such gaudy tulips rais'd from dung.
(*Poems*, II 530)

But in *Strephon and Chloe* (1734) sublimation and awareness of the excremental function are presented as mutually exclusive, and the conclusion is drawn that sublimation must be cultivated at all costs, even at the cost of repression:

Authorities both old and recent
Direct that women must be decent:
And, from the spouse each blemish hide
More than from all the world beside . . .
On sense and wit your passion found,
By decency cemented round.
(*Poems*, II 593)

In *Cassinus and Peter*, the last of these poems, even this solution is exploded. The life of civilized sublimation, epitomized in the word 'wit', is shattered because the excremental vision cannot be repressed. The poem tells of two undergraduates –

Two college sophs of *Cambridge* growth
Both special wits, and lovers both –

and Cassinus explains the trauma which is killing him:

Nor wonder how I lost my wits;
Oh! *Celia, Celia, Celia* shits.
(*Poems*, II 593, 597)

That blessed race of horses, the Houyhnhnms, are free from the illusions of romantic-platonic love, or rather they are free from love. 'Courtship, love, presents, joyntures, settlements, have no place in their thoughts; or terms whereby to express them in their language. The young couple meet and are joined, merely because it is the determination of their parents and friends: it is what they see done every day; and they look upon it as one of the necessary actions in a reasonable being.' If the Houyhnhnms represent a critique of the genital function and genital institutions of mankind, the Yahoos represent a critique of the anal function.

The Yahoos represent the raw core of human bestiality; but the essence of Swift's vision and Gulliver's redemption is the recognition that the civilized man of Western Europe not only remains Yahoo but is worse than Yahoo – 'a sort of animals to whose share, by what accident he could not conjecture, some small pittance of reason had fallen, whereof we made no other use than by its assistance to aggravate our natural corruptions, and to acquire new ones which nature had not give us'. And the essence of the Yahoo is filthiness, a filthiness distinguishing them not from Western European man but from all other animals: 'Another thing he wondered at in the Yahoos, was their strange disposition to nastiness and dirt; whereas there appears to be a natural love of cleanliness in all other animals.' The Yahoo is physically endowed with a very rank smell – 'the stink was somewhat between a *weasel* and a *fox*' – which, heightened at mating time, is a positive attraction to the male of the species. The recognition of the rank odor of humanity stays with Gulliver after his return to England: 'During the first year I could not endure my wife or children in my presence, the very smell of them was intolerable'; when he walked the street, he kept his nose 'well stopped with rue, lavender or tobacco-leaves'. The Yahoo eating habits are equally filthy: 'There was nothing that rendered the Yahoos more odious, than their undistinguishing appetite to devour everything that came in their way, whether herbs, roots, berries, corrupted flesh of animals, or all mingled together.'

But above all the Yahoos are distinguished from other animals by their attitude towards their own excrement. Excrement to the Yahoos is no mere waste product but a magic instrument for self-expression and aggression. This attitude begins in infancy: 'While I held the odious vermin in my hands, it voided its filthy excrements of a yellow liquid substance, all over my clothes.' It continues in adulthood: 'Several of this cursed brood getting hold of the branches behind, leaped up into the tree, from whence they began to discharge their excrements on my head.' It is part of the Yahoo ritual symbolizing the renewal of society: when the old leader of the herd is discarded, 'his successor, at the head of all the Yahoos in that district, young and old, male and female, come in a body, and discharge their excrements upon him from head to foot'. Consequently, in the Yahoo system of social infeudation, 'this *leader* had usually a favourite *as like himself* as he could get, whose employment was to *lick his master's feet and posteriors, and drive the male* Yahoos *to his kennel*'. This recognition that the human animal is distinguished from others as the distinctively excremental animal stays with Gulliver after his return to England, so that he finds relief from the oppressive smell of mankind in the company of his groom: 'For I feel my spirits revived by the smell he contracts in the stable.' Swift does not, as Huxley says he does, hate the bowels, but only the human use of the bowels.

This demonic presentation of the excremental nature of humanity is the great stumbling block in *Gulliver's Travels* – an esthetic lapse, crude sensationalism, says Quintana; a false libel on humanity, says Middleton Murry, 'for even if we carry the process of stripping the human to the limit of imaginative possibility, we do not arrive at the Yahoo. We might arrive at his cruelty and malice; we should never arrive at his nastiness and filth. That is a gratuitous degradation of humanity; not a salutary, but a shocking one.' But if we measure Swift's correctness not by the conventional and complacent prejudices in favor of human pride which are back of Quintana's and Murry's strictures, but by the ruthless wisdom of psychoanalysis, then it is quite obvious that the excremental vision of the Yahoo is substantially identical with the psychoanalytical doctrine of the extensive role of anal erotism in the formation of human culture.

According to Freudian theory the human infant passes through a stage – the anal stage – as a result of which the libido, the life energy of the body, gets concentrated in the anal zone. This infantile stage of anal erotism takes the essential form of attaching symbolic meaning to the anal product. As a result of these symbolic equations the anal product acquires for the child the significance of being his own child or creation, which he may use either to obtain narcissistic pleasure in play, or to obtain love from another (feces as gift), or to assert independence from another (feces as property), to to commit aggression against another (feces as weapon). Thus some of the most important categories of social behavior (play, gift, property, weapon) originate in the anal stage of infantile sexuality and – what is more important – never lose their connexion with it. When infantile sexuality comes to its catastrophic end, nonbodily cultural objects inherit the symbolism originally attached to the anal product, but only as second-best substitutes for the original (sublimations). Sublimations are thus symbols of symbols. The category of property is not simply transferred from feces to money; on the contrary, money is feces, because the anal erotism continues in the unconscious. The anal erotism has not been renounced or abandoned but repressed.

One of the central ambiguities in psychoanalytical theory is the question of whether the pregenital infantile organizations of the libido, including the anal organization, are biologically determined. We have elsewhere taken the position that they are not biologically determined but are constructed by the human ego, or rather that they represent that distortion of the human body which *is* the human ego. If so, then psychoanalysis concurs with Swift's thesis that anal erotism – in Swift's language, 'a strange disposition to nastiness and dirt' – is a specifically human privilege; on the other hand, psychoanalysis would differ from Swift's implication that the strange disposition to nastiness and dirt is biologically given. It comes to the same thing to say that Swift errs in giving the Yahoos no 'pittance of reason' and in assigning to reason only the transformation of the Yahoo into the civilized man of Western Europe. If anal organization is constructed by the human ego, then the strange disposition to nastiness and dirt is a primal or infantile manifestation of human reason. Swift also anticipates Freud in emphasizing the connexion between anal erotism and human aggression. The Yahoos's filthiness is manifested primarily in excremental aggression: psychoanalytical theory stresses the interconnexion between anal organization and human aggression to the point of labeling this phase of infantile sexuality the anal-sadistic phase. Defiance, mastery, will to power are attributes of human reason first developed in the symbolic manipulation of excrement and perpetuated in the symbolic manipulation of symbolic substitutes for excrement.

The psychoanalytical theory of anal erotism depends on the psychoanalytical theory of sublimation. If money etc. are not feces, there is not much reason for hypothesizing a strange human fascination with excrement. By the same token it is hard to see how Swift could have come by his anticipation of the doctrine of anal erotism if he did not also anticipate the doctrine of sublimation. But Swift did anticipate the doctrine of sublimation. Full credit for perceiving this goes to William Empson. Referring to *A Tale of a Tub* and its appendix, *The Mechanical Operation of the Spirit*, Empson writes:

It is the same machinery, in the fearful case of Swift, that betrays not consciousness of the audience but a doubt of which he may himself have been unconscious. 'Everything spiritual and valuable has a gross and revolting parody, very similar to it, with the same name. Only unremitting judgement can distinguish between them'; he set out to simplify the work of judgement by giving a complete set of obscene puns for it. The conscious aim was the defence of the Established Church against the reformers' Inner Light; only the psychoanalyst can wholly applaud the result. Mixed with his statement, part of what he satirized by pretending (too convincingly) to believe, the source of his horror, was 'everything spiritual is really material; Hobbes and the scientists have proved this; all religion is really a perversion of sexuality'.

The source of Swift's horror, according to Empson, is the discovery of that relation between higher and lower, spiritual and physical, which psychoanalysis calls sublimation. Swift hit upon the doctrine of sublimation as a new method for the psychological analysis of religion, specifically religious enthusiasm. His new method sees religious enthusiasm as the effect of what he calls the 'mechanical operation of the spirit'. At the outset he distinguishes his psychology of religion from traditional naturalistic psychology, which treats religious enthusiasm as 'the product of natural causes, the effect of strong imagination, spleen, violent anger, fear, grief, pain, and the like.' If you want a distinctive label for Swift's new psychology of religion, it can only be called psychoanalysis. The first step is to define religious enthusiasm as 'a lifting up of the soul or its faculties above matter'. Swift then proceeds to the fundamental proposition that 'the corruption of the senses is the generation of the spirit'. By corruption of the senses Swift means repression, as is quite clear from his explanation:

Because the senses in men are so many avenues to the fort of reason, which in this operation is wholly blocked up. All endeavours must be therefore used, either to divert, bind up, stupify, fluster and amuse the senses, or else to justle them out of their stations; and while they are either absent, or otherwise employed or engaged in a civil war against each other, the spirit enters and performs its part (1 176).

The doctrine that repression is the cause of sublimation is vividly implied in the analogy which Swift sets up for the 'mechanical operation of the spirit':

Among our ancestors, the Scythians, there was a nation, called Longheads, which at first began by a custom among midwives and nurses, of moulding, and squeezing and bracing up the heads of infants; by which means, nature shut out at one passage, was forced to seek another, and finding room above, shot upwards, in the form of a sugar-loaf (1 175).

Swift affirms not only that the spirit is generated by repression of bodily sensuousness, but also, as is implied by the analogy of the Scythian Longheads, that the basic structure of sublimation is, to use the psychoanalytical formula, displacement from below upward. Displacement from below upward, conferring on the upper region of the body a symbolic identity with the lower region of the body, is Swift's explanation for the Puritan cult of large ears: the ear is a symbolic penis. According to psychoanalysis, displacement of the genital function to another organ is the basic pattern in conversion hysteria. 'Conversion hysteria genitalizes those parts of the body at which the symptoms are manifested'; maidenly blushing, for example, is a mild case of conversion hysteria – that is, a mild erection of the entire head. According to Swift's analysis of the Puritans: 'The proportion of largeness, was not only looked upon as an ornament of the outward man, but as a type of grace in the inward. Besides, it is held by naturalists, that if there be a protuberancy of parts in the *superior* region of the body, as in the ears and nose, there must be a parity also in the *inferior*.' Hence, says Swift, the devouter Sisters 'looked upon all such extraordinary dilatations of that member, as protrusions of zeal, or spiritual excrescencies' and also 'in hopes of conceiving a suitable offspring by such a prospect'. By this road Swift arrives at Freud's theorem on the identity of what is highest and lowest in human nature. In Freud's language: 'Thus it is that what belongs to the lowest depths in the minds of each one of us is changed, through this formation of the ideal, into what we value highest in the human soul.' In Swift's language:

Whereas the mind of Man, when he gives the spur and
bridle to his thoughts, never stops, but naturally sallies out
into both extreams of high and low, of good and evil; his
first flight of fancy, commonly transports him to ideas of
what is most perfect, finished and exalted; till having soared
out of his own reach and sight, not well perceiving how near
the frontiers of height and depth, border upon each other;
With the same course and wing, he falls down plum into the
lowest bottom of things; like one who travels the east into
the west; or like a straight line drawn by its own length into
a circle (199).

Such is the demonic energy with which Swift pursues his vision that twice, once in *A Tale of a Tub* and once in *The Mechanical Operation of the Spirit*, he arrives at the notion of the unity of those opposites of all opposites, God and the Devil.

Men,
pretending ... to extend the dominion of one invisible
power, and contract that of the other, have discovered a gross
ignorance in the natures of good and evil, and most horribly
confounded the frontiers of both. After men have lifted up

the throne of their divinity to the *coelum empyraeum*; ... after
they have sunk their *principle of evil* to the lowest centre ...
I laugh aloud, to see these reasoners, at the same time,
engaged in wise dispute, about certain walks and purlieus,
whether they are in the verge of God or the Devil, seriously
debating, whether such and such influences come into men's
minds, from above or below, or whether certain passions and
affections are guided by the evil Spirit or the good. ... Thus
do men establish a fellowship of Christ with Belial, and such
is the analogy they make between *cloven tongues*, and *cloven
feet* (I 180).

Empson has shown how and by what law of irony the partially
disclaimed thought is Swift's own thought.

As we have argued elsewhere, psychoanalysis finds far-reaching
resemblances between a sublimation and a neurotic symptom. Both
presuppose repression; both involve a displacement resulting from
the repression of libido from the primary erogenous zones. Thus the
psychoanalytic theory of sublimation leads on to the theory of the
universal neurosis of mankind. In the words of Freud:

The neuroses exhibit on the one hand striking and far-reaching
points of agreement with ... art, religion and philosophy. But
on the other hand they seem like distortions of them. It might
be maintained that a case of hysteria is a caricature of a work
of art, that an obsessional neurosis is a caricature of religion
and that a paranoic delusion is a caricature of a philosophical
system.

Swift develops his doctrine of the universal neurosis of mankind
in the 'digression concerning the original, the use and improvement
of madness in a commonwealth', in *A Tale of a Tub*. Here Swift
attributes to madness 'the greatest actions that have been performed
in the world, under the influence of single men; which are, *the
establishment of new empires by conquest: the advance and progress of new
schemes in philosophy; and the contriving, as well as the propagating of
new religions*'. Psychoanalysis must regret the omission of art, but
applaud the addition of politics, to Freud's original list; Freud
himself added politics in his later writings. And Swift deduces the

universal neurosis of mankind from his notion of sublimation; in his words:

For the *upper region* of Man, is furnished like the *middle region* of the air; the materials are formed from causes of the widest difference, yet produce at last the same substance and effect. Mists arise from the earth, steams from dung hills, exhalations from the sea, and smoke from fire; yet all clouds are the same in composition, as well as consequences: and the fumes issuing from a jakes, will furnish as comely and useful a vapour, as incense from an altar. Thus far, I suppose, will easily be granted me; and then it will follow, that as the face of nature never produces rain, but when it is overcast and disturbed, so human understanding, seated in the brain, must be troubled and overspread by vapours, ascending from the lower faculties, to water the invention, and render it fruitful (1 102).

After a witty review of kings, philosophers and religious fanatics Swift concludes: 'If the *moderns* mean by *madness*, only a disturbance or transposition of the brain, by force of certain *vapours* issuing up from the lower faculties; then has this *madness* been the parent of all these mighty revolutions, that have happened in *empire*, in *philosophy* and in *religion*.' And Swift ends the digression on madness with a humility and consistency psychoanalysis has never known, by applying his own doctrine to himself:

Even I myself, the author of these momentous truths, am a person whose imaginations are hard-mouthed and exceedingly disposed to run away with his *reason*, which I have observed from long experience to be a very light rider, and easily shook off; upon which account, my friends will never trust me alone, without a solemn promise, to vent my speculations in this, or the like manner, for the universal benefit of human kind (1 114).

Swift, as we have seen, sees in sublimation, or at least certain kinds of sublimation, a displacement upward of the genital function. So much was implied in his attribution of genital significance to the Puritans' large ears. He makes a similar, only more elaborately obscene, derivation of the nasal twang of Puritan preachers. He also speaks of 'certain sanguine brethren of the first class', that 'in the height and *orgasmus* of their spiritual exercise it has been frequent with them . . . ; immediately after which they found the *spirit* to relax and flag of a sudden with the nerves, and they were forced to hasten to a conclusion'. Swift explains all these phenomena with his notion of sublimation:

The seed or principle, which has ever put men upon *visions* in things *invisible*, is of a corporeal nature. . . . The spinal marrow, being nothing else but a continuation of the brain, must needs create a very free communication between the superior faculties and those below: and thus the *thorn in the flesh* serves for a *spur* to the *spirit* (1 188).

Not only the genital function but also the anal function is displaced upward, according to Swift. The general theorem is already stated in the comparison of the upper region of Man to the middle region of the air, in which 'the fumes issuing from a jakes, will furnish as comely and useful a vapour, as incense from an altar'. The idea is developed in the image of religious enthusiasts as Aeolists, or worshipers of wind. Swift is here punning on the word 'spirit', and as Empson says, 'The language plays into his hands here, because the spiritual words are all derived from physical metaphors.' Psychoanalysis, of course, must regard language as a repository of the psychic history of mankind, and the exploration of words, by wit or poetry or scientific etymology, as one of the avenues into the unconscious. At any rate, Swift's wit, pursuing his 'physicological scheme' for satirical anatomy, 'dissecting the carcass of humane nature', asks where all this windy preaching comes from, and his answer gives all the emphasis of obscenity to the anal factor:

At other times were to be seen several hundreds linked together in a circular chain, with every man a pair of bellows applied to his neighbour's breech, by which they blew up each other to the shape and size of a *tun*; and for that reason, with great propriety of speech, did usually call their bodies, their *vessels*. When by these and the like performances, they were grown sufficiently replete, they would immediately depart, and disembogue for the public good, a plentiful share of their acquirements into their disciples chaps (1 96).

Another method of inspiration involves a barrel instead of a bellows:

Into this *barrel*, upon solemn days, the priest enters; where, having before duly prepared himself by the methods already described, a secret funnel is also conveyed from his posteriors, to the bottom of the barrel, which admits of new supplies of inspiration from a *northern* chink or cranny. Whereupon, you behold him swell immediately to the shape and size of his *vessel*. In this posture he disembogues whole tempests upon his auditory, as the spirit from beneath gives him utterance; which issuing *ex adytis*, and *penetralibus*, is not performed without much pain and gripings (1 98).

Nor is Swift's vision of sublimated anality limited to religious preaching or *A Tale of a Tub*. In *Strephon and Chloe* the malicious gossip of women is so explained:

You'd think she utter'd from behind
Or at her mouth were breaking wind.
(*Poems*, 11 592)

And more generally, as Greenacre observes, there is throughout Swift 'a kind of linking of the written or printed word with the excretory functions'. When Swift writes in a letter to Arbuthnot, 'Let my anger break out at the end of my pen', the psychoanalytically uninitiated may doubt the psychoanalytical interpretation. But Swift makes references to literary polemics (his own literary form) as dirt throwing (compare the Yahoos). More generally he meditates that 'mortal man is a broomstick', which 'raiseth a mighty dust where there was none before; sharing deeply all the while in the very same pollutions he pretends to sweep away'. In the *Letter of Advice to a Young Poet*, he advocates the concentration of writers in a Grub Street, so that the whole town be saved from becoming a sewer: 'When writers of all sizes, like freemen of cities, are at liberty to throw out their filth and excrementitious productions, in every street as they please, what can the consequence be, but that the town must be poisoned and become such another jakes, as by report of great

travellers, Edinburgh is at night.' This train of thought is so characteristically Swift's that in the *Memoirs of Martinus Scriblerus*, now
thought to have been written by Pope after talks with Arbuthnot
and Swift, the story of Scriblerus's birth must be an inspiration of
Swift's: 'Nor was the birth of this great man unattended with
prodigies: he himself has often told me, that on the night before he
was born, Mrs Scriblerus dreamed she was brought to bed of a huge
ink-horn, out of which issued several large streams of ink, as it had
been a fountain. This dream was by her husband thought to signify
that the child should prove a very voluminous writer.' Even the
uninitiated will recognize the fantasy, discovered by psychoanalysis,
of anal birth.

It would be wearisome to rehearse the parallels to Swift in psychoanalytical literature. The psychoanalysts, alas, think they can dispense
with wit in the exploration of the unconscious. Fenichel in his
encyclopedia of psychoanalytical orthodoxy refers to the 'anal-
erotic nature of speech' without intending to be funny. Perhaps it
will suffice to quote from Ferenczi's essay on the proverb 'Silence is
golden' (for Ferenczi the proverb itself is one more piece of evidence
on the anal character of speech):

That there are certain connexions between anal erotism and
speech I had already learnt from Professor Freud, who told me
of a stammerer all whose singularities of speech were to be
traced to anal fantasies. Jones too has repeatedly indicated in
his writings the displacement of libido from anal activities
to phonation. Finally I too, in an earlier article ['On Obscene
Words'] was able to indicate the connexion between musical
voice-culture and anal erotism.

Altogether Ernest Jones's essay on 'Anal-Erotic Character Traits'
leaves us with the impression that there is no aspect of higher culture
uncontaminated by connexions with anality. And Swift leaves us
with the same impression. Swift even anticipates the psychoanalytical
theorem that an anal sublimation can be decomposed into simple
anality. He tells the story of a furious conqueror who left off his
conquering career when 'the *vapour* or *spirit*, which animated the
hero's brain, being in perpetual circulation, seized upon that region
of the human body, so renowned for furnishing the *zibeta occidentalis*,

and gathering there into a tumour, left the rest of the world for that time in peace'.

The anal character of civilization is a topic which requires sociological and historical as well as psychological treatment. Swift turns to the sociology and history of anality in a poem called *A Panegyrick on the Dean*. The poem is written as if by Lady Acheson, the lady of the house at Market Hill where Swift stayed in 1729–30. In the form of ironic praise, it describes Swift's various roles at Market Hill, as Dean, as conversationalist with the ladies, as butler fetching a bottle from the cellar, as dairymaid churning butter. But the Dean's greatest achievement at Market Hill was the construction of 'two temples of magnific size,' where:

In sep'rate cells the he's and she's
Here pay their vows with *bended knees*,

to the 'gentle Goddess *Cloacine*'. As he built the two outhouses, Swift seems to have mediated on the question of why we are ashamed of and repress the anal function:

Thee bounteous Goddess *Cloacine*,
To temples why do we confine?

The answer he proposes is that shame and repression of anality did not exist in the age of innocence (here again we see how far wrong Huxley's notion of Swift's 'hatred of the bowels' is):

When *Saturn* ruled the skies alone
That *golden* age, to *gold* unknown;
This earthly Globe to thee assign'd
Receiv'd the gifts of all Mankind.

After the fall – the usurpation of Jove – came '*gluttony* with greasy paws,' with her offspring 'lolling *sloth*', 'pale *dropsy*', 'lordly *gout*', 'wheezing *asthma*', 'voluptuous *ease*, the child of *wealth*':

This bloated harpy sprung from Hell
Confin'd Thee Goddess to a cell.

The corruption of the human body corrupted the anal function and alienated the natural Cloacine:

... unsav'ry vapours rose,
Offensive to thy nicer nose.

The correlative doctrine in psychoanalysis is of course the equation of money and feces. Swift is carried by the logic of the myth (myth, like wit, reaches into the unconscious) to make the same equation: the age of innocence, 'the *golden* age, to *gold* unknown', had another kind of gold. The golden *age* still survives among the swains of Northern Ireland –

Whose off'rings plac't in golden ranks,
Adorn our crystal river's banks.

But the perspectives now opening up are too vast for Swift, or for us:

But, stop ambitious Muse, in time;
Nor dwell on subjects too sublime.
(*Poems*, III 887–96)

(186–201)

J. V. Cunningham

from *The Exclusions of a Rhyme*   1960

With a Copy of Swift's Works

Underneath this pretty cover
Lies Vanessa's, Stella's lover.
You that undertake this story
For his life nor death be sorry
Who the Absolute so loved
Motion to its zero moved,
Till immobile in that chill
Fury hardened in the will,
And the trivial, bestial flesh
In its jacket ceased to thresh,
And the soul none dare forgive
Quiet lay, and ceased to live.
(85)

Georg Lukács

from the Foreword to *Werke*, vol. 6   1964 (trans. in
G. Lichtheim, *Lukács*, 1970; reproduced here with slight
alterations)

The contrast between the novel of the eighteenth and that of the
nineteenth century is immediately apparent. But this antithesis does
not apply – or at any rate only with considerable reservations – to
Swift. With Swift, that is to say, not only is there no conscious expression of the socio-historical *hic-et-nunc*: it is formally set aside.
There is an entire human epoch with whose most general conflicts
(or with the hackneyed features of whose time) Man as such is confronted. That is what is nowadays known as *condition humaine*, but
this overlooks the fact that in Swift the discussion is not concerned
with Man as such but with his fate in a historically determined
society. Swift's unique originality reveals itself in the fact that his
view of society prophetically encompasses an entire epoch. In our
time only Kafka provides something like an analogy, in that with
him an entire age of inhumanity is set in motion as the counterpart of
the Austrian (Bohemian–German – Jewish) individual during the
closing stage of the reign of Francis Joseph. Thus his universe which –
formally, but only formally – can be interpreted as *condition humaine*,
acquires a profound and shattering truth; in contrast to those which,
lacking this kind of historical background, lacking such a foundation
and such a perspective, concentrate upon the bare, abstract – and thus
misconceived in its abstraction – generality of human existence, and
which infallibly end in complete emptiness, Nothing. This Nothing
may clothe itself in existentialist or other ornaments, it none the less
remains, in contrast to Swift and Kafka, an empty Nothing.

(103)

Irvin Ehrenpreis

'Swift and the Comedy of Evil', in B. Vickers (ed.), *The World of Jonathan Swift* 1968

Comedy and evil used to seem hard to mix. Only a few authors have in the past represented a successful villain, at the height of his evil career, as the main figure in a purely comic episode. Often enough, evil in defeat has suffered ridiculous humiliations. Equally often, an audience could watch petty vice and harmless obsessions become the occasion for elaborate farce. But unmitigated badness remained in general a figure for tragedy, melodrama, invective. If one thinks of Shakespeare's Iago, Racine's Nero or George Eliot's Grandcourt, one can hardly imagine them in a comic setting without softening their monsterhood or enlarging their humanity.

Among the exceptions to this rule are parts of works by a few celebrated satirists. In these rare, brilliant scenes a successful villain appears at the centre of a detached piece of comedy with no loss of his frightening power to embody evil. For one example, I recall Juvenal's picture of the self-deified Domitian, holding a high council in order to determine the best means of cooking a fish. The action grows monumentally absurd as the supreme advisors of the despot of the world quickly enter, cringing, to meet as a cabinet and offer their judgement whether or not the chef should cut the turbot up because the available vessels are too small to hold it entire. As one would expect, the furious poet stays outside the scene, making the emperor and his cronies into figures quite separate from himself; and he speaks almost like a reporter or moral commentator who, with all his anger, never feels responsible for the frightfulness he may have to describe. At the same time, Domitian is no way reduced by Juvenal's episode. The *pallor amicitiae*, the servility, haste and loquacity of his corrupt ministers, while they devote their full intelligence to the contemptible question, only darken the abominations of their master.

Of course, Satan himself took the first of all comic roles. Excluded from the range of our sympathy, he may have terrified us by his power; yet we laughed at the tricks he played on his stupid, irrational victims. I suggest that their foolishness has been essential to his comic operations. Since the absurd is a necessary element in humour, those ages which called irrationality evil could not regard rationality as an object of ridicule; and the satirists of imperial Rome agreed with those of King Charles and King George when they treated reason as coterminous with virtue. To show how the same lesson could be applied in another country, let me refer to the peripety of *Tartuffe*. Act four, scene five, of Molière's masterpiece is the famous courtship of Elmire by Tartuffe, with Orgon listening under a table. The comedy of the episode invariably succeeds. Even clumsy actors can hardly prevent an audience from feeling delight when Elmire signals to her stupefied husband and he fails to halt the process of seduction. Yet the satanic Tartuffe suffers no diminution. 'J'ai de quoi confondre et punir l'imposture', he announces, after retreating from Orgon's arms; and he walks off with his sinister dignity intact. Like Domitian and Satan, he will not laugh at himself, because for him the drama is tragic. This self-absorbed lack of moral intelligence seems at last determined by the *ir*rationality of a complete villain, for the great satirists gave reason dominion over moral as well as narrowly intellectual issues. Both Tartuffe and Domitian must fail to recognize the absurdity of their entanglements if they are not to see the malignity of their actions. At the same time, a character like Orgon must be more than an innocent victim or butt. Our laughter remains only partly sympathetic: we feel some degree of contempt for his co-operation in his own ruin, and we hesitate to identify ourselves with him.

In Brecht's play, *The Resistible Rise of Arturo Ui*, there is another instance of the same sort. Ui, a gangster whose life becomes an allegory of Hitler's progress, reaches the peak of his criminal achievements and then decides to have lessons in the arts of oratory and public deportment. The scene that follows is like a vaudeville turn, with the straight man taken by Ui and the end man by a broken-down actor who teaches him elocution. Every piece of instruction is farcical, and Ui accepts each one as sagacious. When the tutor declares that the properest way for Ui to manage his hands, during a speech, is to hold them over his private parts, the audience giggles, but the gangster obeys. Yet the scene does not make Ui less ominous. On the contrary, the more unreasonable he grows, the more terrifying he seems. Brecht also follows the example of Molière and Juvenal in excluding himself from any responsibility for the triumph of vice. Like most playwrights he seems no more than the historian of the events he shows us. Similarly, the gangsters and grocers who become Ui's victims seem willing tools or foolish weaklings. Like Domitian's counsellors, they discourage sympathy.

The effect I have been describing seems to me among the deepest ends of satire. In a reader's memory the crimes of a Domitian or a Tartuffe are too vivid for them to be put aside. These men can only seem objects of detestation. At the same time, the comedy of the scenes I have reviewed is detached, almost a free fantasy, never involving the villain's enormities. How, then, can a reader avoid a continuous, guilt-ridden sense of ignoring horrors which ought to obliterate any humorous aspect of a literary work? So long as the humour is compelling, I think he cannot.

If these principles appear elementary, let me complicate them now with some examples from the prose of Jonathan Swift. In 1712 appeared his *Letter of Thanks from My Lord Wharton to the Lord Bishop of St Asaph*. A year and a half earlier, Swift's art had conferred immortality on Thomas, Earl of Wharton when the satirist wrote, 'He is a Presbyterian in politics, and an atheist in religion; but he chooses at present to whore with a Papist' (III 179). Elsewhere, Swift describes his lordship in language drawn from Milton's representation of Satan (III 8); and he worked hard to have the Earl impeached for treason. Constantly in Swift's political essays, Wharton manifests himself as the supreme Whig and supreme villain, a compound of the filthiest vices, devoid of patriotism, charity, or religion. Since Wharton's father had been a parliamentary Presbyterian, Swift, as a devoted churchman and constitutional monarchist, could trace the son's political corruption to his ancestry: 'He has imbibed his father's principles in government, but dropped his religion, and took up no other in its stead: excepting that circumstance, he is a firm Presbyterian' (VII 10). When Swift blamed the Earl for defecating on the high altar of Gloucester Cathedral, there were protests; so the journalist apologized in print: 'it was neither in the Cathedral, nor City, nor County of *Gloucester*, but some other church of that Diocese' (III 57, 69).

Now I take up my chosen passage from Swift's *Letter of Thanks from my Lord Wharton to the Bishop of St Asaph*. The whole pamphlet is a satire on a Whig bishop for his wretched prose and worse venality as exhibited in the half-dozen paragraphs of a composition praising the old, ousted Whig administration. In the pamphlet the author pretends to be the Earl of Wharton writing to Bishop Fleetwood and congratulating his grace on these remarks. According to this mock-Wharton, the Bishop had never believed that the English people should live under a true monarchy or obey their rightful king unless his majesty gave in to every caprice of the mob. Addressing Fleet-wood himself, the mock-Wharton continues: 'This [i.e. republican-ism] you say is the opinion of Christ, St Peter and St Paul: and, faith I am glad to hear it; for I never thought the prigs had been Whigs before' (VI 152). In a tribute to Fleetwood's style the mock-Wharton fixes on some episcopal regrets for the fall of the Whigs, regrets which the satirist inevitably links to a sympathy with the Presby-terians in their Nonconformist meeting-houses. I quote:

Oh Exquisite! How pathetically does your Lordship complain
of the downfall of Whiggism, and Daniel Burges's meeting-
house! The generous compassion your Lordship has shown
upon this tragical occasion, makes me believe your Lordship
will not be unaffected with an accident that had like to have
befallen a poor whore of my acquaintance about that time,
who being big with Whig, was so alarmed at the rising of the
mob, that she had like to have miscarried upon it; for the
logical jade presently concluded (and the inference was
natural enough) that if they began with pulling down
meeting-houses, it might end in demolishing those houses of
pleasure, where she constantly paid her devotion (VI 154).

Without determining the ultimate literary value of Swift's perfor-mance in this pamphlet, I will say the humour is not easily withstood. Whether or not we know who Wharton was and what Swift thought of him, the burlesque of a rake praising an ambitious clergyman has its comic power. Adding to that general effect the identification of Wharton as a diabolical villain, can anyone who laughs escape the guilt of seeming indifferent to crimes that ought to excite indignation?

If my question sounds like an effort merely to place Swift in a class with Juvenal, Molière and Brecht, let me now try to distinguish him. Those authors, like most creators of satire or comedy, avoided bringing themselves directly into their work; so far from accepting a part of the responsibility for the triumph of evil, they covertly absolved themselves of blame. No historian or paid journalist could be further from involvement (except as a judge) in the events he retails.

But it is a well-known mark of the workings of Swift's imagination that he loves to speak in a parody of people he detests; and so he assigns himself in fantasy the very role of the character he means to attack. It is also typical of Swift that when he does attack a man's character, he blackens it to a depth where the villainy seems to have no mitigation. Whether he ever even attempts the subtle, controlled characterization of an evildoer that Dryden produces in the character of Achitophel, seems doubtful. If we may trust Swift, each one of his enemies aspires to the condition of Satan. In denigrating Wharton, therefore, just as in assuming his identity, Swift merely follows what to him are normal procedures.

If we now digress and search for the emotional or psychological origin of such procedures, we may speculate along familiar lines: are we to deny that in producing his flavoursome fantasies of atheistic whoremongering, the rigidly moral and devout Dr Swift enjoyed some *frissons* of ambiguous self-indulgence? I suspect that the comical parody of Lord Wharton gave Swift a delicious chance to leap in fantasy over the steep walls of his own ethical judgement. The contemplation of pure evil in a human shape released Swift's imagination till he could slip inside the diabolical nature and taste its sensations. Yet it was as the private, weak victim of such public monsters that he deliberately issued his ferocious political satires. In childhood he had been the half-orphaned son of an impoverished widow, and had suffered continually the bitter sensation of powerlessness to resist the will of those who took charge of him. As the adult moralist and patriot he made his pen an instrument for punishing traitors like Wharton, too great to be attacked openly.

Whatever may have been the hidden spring of Swift's impulse, its visible effect becomes a brilliant feature of his rhetoric. Instead of standing aloof, like most satirists, he plunges into the prospect of evil, establishing himself in the immediate foreground of the scene. For the reader, the consequence seems an exact, required direction for the flow of guilt which the comedy of evil produces. There is no comfortable outlet to relieve the reader's uneasiness, because every element of the absorbing comical situation forces him to share in the devil's work. In Swift's hoaxes and satires the victims are under attack as well as the criminals – the Ireland that helps England make men into beasts, the superstitious customers of quack astrologers, the tasteless readers of hack authors. Juvenal, Molière and Brecht excite our indignation and may even drive us toward action; but we are free, in their work, to join the high, mountain view of the cities of the plain. With them as with Swift we cannot hide in the abominable villains or contemptible victims. Yet we do retire by an instinct of revulsion to the consciousness of the poet, sheltering ourselves in his detachment or his outrage.

But when we recoil from Swift's comedy, we face a disquieting mirror. The author himself looks like the villain, and we find our reflection in both. If the scene he presents makes us uneasy, any meditation sharpens our guilt. Swift was always ready to imitate directly the irrationality on which rests his conception of evil. As early as *A Tale of a Tub* he admits his own complicity, writing, 'even, I myself, the author of these momentous truths, am a person, whose imaginations are hard-mouthed, and exceedingly disposed to run away with his *reason*, which I have observed from long experience, to be a very light rider, and easily shook off' (1 114). On the contrary, Pope, in his magnificent denunciations of social corruption, regularly excepts himself:

Yes, I am proud; I must be proud to see
Men not afraid of God, afraid of me.
(*Epilogue to the Satires*, 208–9)

I suppose Pope's many disabilities kept him from risking the sacrifice of dignity which could result from admitting that he had a hand in the sins he condemns. But by excluding his own case, he can only invite us to exclude ours. Swift, by risking more, wins more.

The greatness of Swift's whole achievement as a satirist can be expressed in terms of this comedy of impersonated evil, which forces us not simply to grow indignant but also to admit we helped perpetrate the crime we deplore. Thanks to the dramatic qualities of Swift's ironical style, such an analysis is far from limited to those works in which he adopts the name or reputation of a known villain.

To suggest what may be happening, his tone by itself is enough. For Swift, it was natural to employ the cynical voice of a debauchee when describing the vileness that every honest priest wishes to eradicate. Although the reader feels disgust, he will hardly look to the author for comfort, because Swift sounds comically acquiescent in the scandal. Cannot the much-quoted, oddly detachable sentence in the *Digression on Madness* – 'Last week I saw a woman *flayed*, and you will hardly believe, how much it altered her person for the worse' (I 109) – be understood this way? Must not this amusing speaker be both irrational and evil to ignore the agony he has witnessed? If this is so, does not the wit of the sentence delight the reader to the point of making him feel guilty for appearing indifferent to the fate of the wretched woman?

It is hardly worthwhile to glance at works like the *Digression on Madness* or *A Modest Proposal*, because this pattern so obviously fits them. But I shall notice the most disquieting mixture of humour and guilt in Swift's works. How successful the last part of *Gulliver's Travels* really is, we may doubt. But that the author means to identify the Yahoos with evil, irrationality *and* essential human nature as well, seems plain enough. What has offended most of those whom Swift nauseates in his masterpiece is this identity; and the method employed by several of his defenders has been to dwell on the comic implications of the fourth voyage. When Gulliver bathes in a river, and narrowly escapes being ravished by a female Yahoo – who relaxes her passionate embrace only because the sorrel nag drives her away – it may seem pedantic to look for anything but farce in the episode. Yet Gulliver insists that the lust of the young animal proves his own membership in the same species. Since Swift has been at pains to express Gulliver's revulsion from the Yahoos, the laughing reader is, in a sense, trapped between sympathetic humour and punitive ridicule; for to accept the black-haired Yahoo is to accept the most sickening bestiality; but to reject her is to reject oneself. Perhaps in no other work has Swift made the foundation of his moral distinctions so visible. Villain, victim, author and reader are all united in the great, hideous teetering between laughter and outrage. Gulliver reiterates and bellows his conviction that the reader is a Yahoo like himself, that we all share in creating the satanic evil we abominate. In his reformer's zeal and comic humiliation he exemplifies that partnership of preacher and clown which is Swift's special mark. Surely Swift's pessimism concerning human nature deepened the amused consciousness of his own weakness; for the irrationality of the devil who desires to ruin man is at least equalled by the irrationality of the priest who hopes to save him.

(213–19)

A Tale of a Tub

Herbert Davis

'Literary Satire – The Author of *A Tale of a Tub*'   1946 (reprinted in *Jonathan Swift: Essays on his Satire and Other Studies*, 1964)

'Tis own'd he was a *Man of Wit* –,
Yet many a *foolish thing* he writ –;
And, sure he must be *deeply* learn'd –!
That's more than ever I discern'd –;
I know his *nearest Friends* complain
He was too *airy* for a *Dean* –.

Before the publication of *A Tale of a Tub* in 1704, Swift had appeared in his own person in the world of letters only as an editor of the *Letters of Sir William Temple*. The first two volumes were printed in 1700 with a dedication in which he humbly presents them to his Most Sacred Majesty William III, describing himself as a domestic chaplain to his Excellency the Earl of Berkeley, one of the Lords Justices of Ireland. A third volume was printed in 1703. But he evidently felt that in his role as a satirist he would be hampered and restricted if he were to appear in this way, wearing a parson's gown and associated with such respectable connexions. There had been, indeed, in the seventeenth century, a splendid tradition among the most reverend and eminent divines in their controversial treatises about serious matters which would seem to sanction, as Anthony Collins pointed out in his *Discourse Concerning Ridicule*, the use of 'insult, buffoonery, banter, ridicule, irony, mockery and bitter railing'; and after the Restoration this tendency was further encouraged by a Court audience led by 'a King who had a disposition to banter and ridicule everybody' and 'some of the greatest droles and wits that any age ever produced'. But tastes were changing at the end of the century, and Swift himself was then under the influence of Sir William Temple, who had solemnly and vigorously denounced the taste for satire, and had probably prevented Swift from publishing *The Battle of the Books* in 1698.

At any rate we know that Swift put aside this and other satirical papers of his own which he had been working at in 1696-7, and took precautions that when they did appear he would not necessarily be involved, until he could see what sort of reception they would have. He felt that he needed for his purpose the fullest freedom to range at will over the whole field of letters, for he wished to make sport with all the foibles of the Grub-Street brotherhood as well as the societies of Gresham and of Wills, the hack writers and fashionable poets, the virtuosos and the wits, and 'to expose the numerous *corruptions* in religion and learning [which] might furnish matter for a satire, that would be useful and diverting'. He chose therefore to appear as an unknown young gentleman of taste and learning dedicated to the high task of serving the Church and the State by diverting the attacks of the wits who occupy themselves in picking holes in the weak sides of religion and government; and in such a task – which he claimed should win him the approval of all good men – he would be justified in letting loose all his powers to expose the shams of the time and to make merry at the expense of all hypocrites and dullards. But his attack must be made 'in a manner, that should be altogether new, the world having been already too long nauseated with endless repetitions upon every subject' (1 1).

The author of *A Tale of a Tub* is presented to us as at the maturity of his powers – 'his invention at the height, and his reading fresh in his head ... a young gentleman much in the world, and wrote to the taste of those who were like himself' (1 1). He is not without a certain youthful insolence, contemptuous alike of stupidity, dullness and pedantry, addressing himself to those who have enough wit to appreciate irony, and enough knowledge to recognize parody. He has had sufficient experience to know that he need not be afraid of those who will be provoked to anger and fury by his satire. They deserve only his scorn:

There is a *brain* that will endure but one *scumming*: let the owner gather it with discretion, and manage his little stock with husbandry; but of all things, let him beware of bringing it under the *lash* of his *betters*; because, that will make it all

bubble up into impertinence, and he will find no new supply:
wit, without knowledge, being a sort of *cream*, which gathers in
a night to the top, and by a skilful hand, may be soon *whipped*
into *froth*; but once scummed away, what appears underneath
will be fit for nothing, but to be thrown to the hogs.

This is still in the manner of the seventeenth century in the true line of
wit; the vivid image of the whipped cream, possibly picked up from
his reading of François de Callières, who had used it simply as a
symbol for writing 'large in appearance but little in substance', but
here elaborated and played with and worked to the utmost, until the
froth vanishes and we are left with another even more powerful
image of the skimmed milk fit only for the hogs. A careful contemporary reader would have recognized the method, and might have
been reminded of another fantastic image of scorn in a popular satire
of the preceding generation, which the author of *A Tale of a Tub*
admired and referred to, *The Rehearsal Transprosed* by Andrew
Marvell. He also is describing the brain of his adversary:

You have, contrary to all architecture and good economy,
made a snow-house in your upper room, which indeed was
philosophically done of you, seeing you bear your head so
high as if it were in or above the middle region, and so you
thought it secure from melting. But you did not at the same
time consider that your brain is so hot, that the wit is dissolved
by it, and is always dripping away at the icicles of your
nose. But it freezes again, I confess, as soon as it falls down;
and hence it proceeds that there is no passage in my book,
deep or shallow, but with a chill and key-cold conceit you can
ice it in a moment, and slide sheer over it without scratches.

There is the same playful extravagance and exuberant gaiety in these
conceits, but Swift's sentences show an economy and strength, and a
power of invention – to use the phrase of the time – which seems to
me to justify his claim that his wit was all his own. He speaks of
having read Marvell with pleasure, and evidently took good heed of
his warnings addressed to those who would take upon themselves the
envious and dangerous employment of being writers.

For indeed, whosoever he be that comes in print, whereas he might have sate at home in quiet, does either make a treat, or send a challenge to all readers; in which cases, the first, it concerns him to have no scarcity of provisions, and in the other, to be completely armed; for, if anything be amiss on either part, men are subject to scorn the weakness of the attack, or laugh at the meanness of the entertainment.

There is no scarcity of entertainment in the fare Swift provides, no lack of weapons for the attack. The manner of his attack may seem at first sight very conventional, for it was a favourite conceit of the time to refer to the custom of seamen to throw out a tub when they meet a whale to divert it from attacking the ship. It must have been well known to all Swift's readers, as it occurs in such popular books as this satire of Marvell's I have been referring to: 'I only threw i t out like an empty cask to amuse him, knowing that I had a *whale* to deal with ...', and again in the prefatory remarks to the reader in Francis Osborn's *Works*, which had reached a seventh edition in 1673: '... in imitation of seamen, I may perhaps by design have cast out some empty stuff, to find play for the whale-mouthed gapers after levity; lest they should spoil the voyage'. Swift's parable is very obvious, where the whale symbolizes Hobbes's *Leviathan* and the ship in danger the Commonwealth, though again he does not miss the opportunity to enlarge the conceit, rather confusing the picture, as the waters round the Leviathan positively seethe with tubs, namely 'Schemes of religion and government, whereof a great many are hollow, and dry, and empty, and noisy, and wooden and given to rotation' (I 24). He will himself provide for the purpose *A Tale of a Tub*. Again neither the phrase nor its use as a title is new. Instances are given in the Guthkelch and Nichol Smith edition, to which I am indebted throughout, of its common use in the sixteenth and seventeenth centuries, in the sense of 'an idle discourse', or as explained in the title of a lost work 'a gallimaufry of merriment'. Swift hooks the two ideas together and has a title for a gallimaufry of merriment in which he can make fun of everything that catches his fancy not only as he looks around him in the world of contemporary controversy, but as he looks back across the troubled waters of the Revolution and the Commonwealth and the Civil War to the serene shores of that age immediately before the troubles which he always regarded with longing and pride as the time of England's highest glory both in life and in letters.

For the real object of Swift's satire in the *Tale* is the corruption he saw in English letters during the latter half of the seventeenth century, destroying what he felt had been its finest achievements. This belief is repeatedly stated, and never modified. He first stated it in the *Tatler*, dated 28 September 1710, satirizing current affectations of language, and clearly setting forth what he regarded as the standards of good taste in English, namely that simplicity which is unaffected by modish fashions, such as 'the writings of Hooker, who was a country clergyman, and of Parsons the Jesuit, both in the reign of Queen Elizabeth ... much more clear and intelligible than those of Sir H. Wotton, Sir Robert Naunton, Osborn, Daniel the historian, and several others who wrote later; but being men of the Court, and affecting the phrases then in fashion; they are often either not to be understood, or appear perfectly ridiculous' (II 177).

He stated it very plainly in his *Letter to the Lord Treasurer*, emphasizing the corruptions in language 'from the Civil War to this present time'; first, the enthusiastic jargon prevailing during the usurpation, and then the licentiousness which entered with the Restoration, which from infecting religion and morals fell to corrupt the language, as shown in 'the plays and other compositions, written for entertainment' during the next fifty years (IV 10 ff.). He stated it again in *A Letter to a Young Clergyman*, written in Ireland ten years later, and again in a slightly different form in the *Essay on Conversation*, as, for example: 'I take the highest period of politeness in England (and it is of the same date in France) to have been the peaceable part of King Charles I's reign' (V 94).

It is obvious from this on which side Swift would find himself in the controversy between the ancients and the moderns which had been sharpened by the recent claims for precedence made on behalf of the latest discoveries and developments in the world of science and letters. He was indeed inclined to be unduly sceptical of the importance and value of the new sciences and more aware of the corruptions than of the improvements in modern learning. He was not therefore led into the fray entirely to defend Sir William Temple against the attacks made on his *Essay upon the Ancient and Modern Learning*, although this episode provided him with an excuse to join with the Christ Church wits against Bentley and Wotton. At the same time it forced him to uphold a very weak case, as Temple had stated it in his Essay, and he was obliged to rely on the effectiveness of the literary devices he used to get the better of his opponents. The main device is indicated by the title – *A Full and True Account of the Battle Fought last Friday, Between the Ancient and the Modern Books in St James's Library*. This looked like an imitation of François de Callières's *Histoire poétique de la guerre nouvellement déclarée entre les anciens et les modernes*, though Swift afterwards said he had never heard of it. But there were many advantages in handling the subject in a mock-heroic fashion as a battle between the actual volumes in the King's Library, which Bentley had confessed was in a state of dirt and confusion. The Homeric conflict takes place 'on the plains of St James's Library' – a phrase which is just enough to carry us into a mock-heroic world remote from the actual controversy and the arguments over the genuineness of the Epistles of Phalaris. In this world Swift can play with the reader as he will; he has only to oppose Dryden to Virgil, describing Dryden's steed and his arms in Hudibrastic fashion:

Behold, upon a sorrel gelding of a monstrous size, appeared a foe, issuing from among the thickest of the enemy's squadrons; but his speed was less than his noise; for his horse, old and lean, spent the dregs of his strength in a high trot, which though it made slow advances, yet caused a loud clashing of his armour, terrible to hear.

. . . the Helmet was nine times too large for the head, which appeared situated far in the hinder part, even like the lady in a lobster, or like a mouse under a canopy of state or like a shrivelled beau from within the penthouse of a modern periwig (I 157).

In similar fashion he describes Bentley and Wotton 'like two mongrel curs prowling around' who steal the armour of Phalaris and Aesop while they are asleep, and the final exploit of Boyle who appears like a young lion, and hunts the two of them until finally his lance pierces them together:

As, when a skilful cook has trussed a brace of *woodcocks*, he,
with iron skewer, pierces the tender sides of both, their legs
and wings close pinioned to their ribs; so was this pair of
friends transfixed, till down they fell, joined in their lives,
joined in their deaths (1 164).

If this were all, however, we should feel that Swift had done no
more than provide a trivial diversion to draw attention away from
the real conflict. But again in the midst of the allegory, as in the *Tale*,
he introduces a digression: and a very fitting one, as the dispute was
also concerned with Aesop, who was praised by Temple as the most
ancient of the ancients and was recognized by all ages as the greatest
master in this kind. Very fitly also in the dirt of St James's Library,
Swift discovers a large spider's web, in which a bee, entering through
a broken pane of the window, has become entangled. This occasions
a dispute between them which is then interpreted by Aesop, who had
listened to them 'with a world of pleasure' (1 150-51).

The fable and the interpretation of it are Swift's real contribution
to the debate between the ancients and the moderns; and it is not
surprising that a hundred and fifty years later, when the debate had
taken another form, Swift's phrase 'sweetness and light' was carried
as a banner by a young apostle of culture as he advanced against the
hosts of the Philistines. It was also a triumphant vindication of the
art of Aesop, no matter what Bentley had done to his title page and
half of his leaves. The fable is made out of a proverb, evidently
common, as it is frequently turned to literary use in the seventeenth
century: 'Where the bee sucks honey, the spider sucks poison.'
Here we can observe it expanding into a lovely form, as it is dramatized in Bentley's library, and elaborated with mock-heroic language,
and finally interpreted as a symbol of the dispute between the
ancients and the moderns:

For, pray Gentlemen, was ever any thing so *modern* as th e*spider*
in his air, his turns and his paradoxes? He argues in the behalf
of *you* his brethren, and himself, with many boastings of his
native stock, and great genius; that he spins and spits wholly
from himself, and scorns to own any obligation or assistance
from without. Then he displays to you his great skill in
architecture, and improvement in the mathematics ... yet, if

the materials be nothing but dirt, spun out of your own entrails (the guts of *modern* brains) the edifice will conclude at last in a *cobweb*: the duration of which, like that of other *spiders'* webs, may be imputed to their being forgotten or neglected, or hid in a corner. . . . As for *us*, the ancients, we are content with the *bee*, to pretend to nothing of our own, beyond our *wings* and our *voice*: that is to say, our *flights* and our *language*; for the rest, whatever we have got, has been by infinite labour, and search, and ranging through every corner of nature: the difference is, that instead of *dirt* and *poison*, we have rather chose to fill our hives with *honey* and *wax*, thus furnishing mankind with the two noblest of things, which are *sweetness* and *light* (1 151).

It was a nice compliment to Temple to use the bee as the symbol of the Ancients; for some of Swift's readers would remember Temple's *Essay on Poetry*, where he compares the poet's art with the activities of the bees in a passage which Swift in the last sentence condensed with great precision:

[Bees] must range through fields, as well as gardens, choose such flowers as they please, and by proprieties and scents they only know and distinguish: they must work up their cells with admirable art, extract their honey with infinite labour, and sever it from the wax, with such distinction and choice, as belongs to none but themselves to perform or to judge.

Some of Swift's readers would also remember this passage to which Professor F. P. Wilson drew my attention, in Bacon's *Novum Organum*:

The men of experiment are like the ant; they only collect and use; the reasoners resemble spiders, who make cobwebs out of their own substance. But the bee takes a middle course; it gathers its material from the flowers of the garden and of the field, but transforms and digests it by a power of its own. Not unlike this is the true business of philosophy.

In the *Battle of the Books* Swift shows what side he is on, and he succeeds by his wit and humour, and by the power of his style. But he does not reveal there as he does in the *Tale* the extent of the preparation he had undertaken so that in offering entertainment to his readers, he should not be criticized for any scarcity of provisions. As an undergraduate at Trinity College he had had no great reputation as a scholar; but we happen to have some interesting information about his reading during those years when he was planning and working on the *Tale*.

The list of his studies for the year 1697 indicates the breadth and variety of his reading including, in addition to French and English authors, the *Iliad* and the *Odyssey*, Virgil twice, Lucretius three times, Horace, Cicero's Epistles, Petronius, Lucius Florus three times, Diodorus Siculus, Cyprian, Irenaeus and Sleidan's commentaries. 'This,' says Professor Nichol Smith, 'gives only a fraction of the reading that went to the making of the *Tale*', but 'it admits us, as it were, to a secret view of Swift's habits of mind when he was gaining his full powers, and Swift never wrote anything that gives a greater sense of sheer power than some of the later sections of the *Tale*'.

It is unlike the rest of his writings, because it is so literary, so full of echoes from his reading, and so concerned with the world of letters, the world that at that time he knew best, because he had been living entirely in it. For he had been exercising himself in the art of writing as well as filling his mind. The *Tale* represents only a very small portion of all that he had written during the last ten years of the century. He had begun with a number of experiments in verse – Pindaric odes in which he seems to have wished to compete with Cowley and experiments in heroic verse like the Lines addressed to Congreve, not much less restrained in manner. He soon discovered that such forms would not fit the kind of thing he wanted to say, and contemptuously turned away from these poetic exercises, not even including them in any of his later collections of verse. Nevertheless there is to be observed in them a force and energy, struggling with the too voluminous folds of flowing rhetoric and showing the ferment of thought in which he lived. In his attack on the extravagancies of the previous age, he benefited by these struggles in which he had won his freedom as perhaps every young writer has to do from the prevailing forces round about him, in order to shape his art to fit his own individual purpose. These Odes, addressed to the King,

to Sir William Temple, to Archbishop Sancroft and the Epistle to
Mr Congreve begin in a dignified strain of compliment, and were
evidently intended to serve the same purpose as those later presented
by Congreve on suitable occasions as an offering to the King on his
taking of Namur, or lamenting the death of our late gracious Queen
Mary of ever blessed memory. But unlike the cool marbled smoothness of Congreve's lines, Swift's gather a tempestuous motion and
quickly become roughened by moods of anger and satire, and he
breaks off apologizing for his unfitting outbursts:

Perish the Muse's hour, thus vainly spent
In satire, to my Congreve's praises meant;
In how ill season her resentments rule,
What's that to her if mankind be a fool?
(*Poems*, 1 48)

And in the last of these poems addressed to Temple in December
1693, he renounces the Muse as a delusion and a deceit:

Troubling the crystal fountain of the sight,
Which darts on poets' eyes a trembling light;
Kindled while reason sleeps, but quickly flies,
Like antic shapes in dreams, from waking eyes:
(*Poems*, 1 54).

The experience, which he describes with such force in this poem,
where he turns away forever from the fond delusions of a youthful
poet's romantic dreams, is the source of the irony and gives a sort of
personal colouring to the triumphant scepticism of the digression on
madness in the *Tale*, where human happiness is defined as 'a perpetual
possession of being well deceived', and the same struggle between
fancy and reason is examined:

But when a man's fancy gets astride on his reason, when
imagination is at cuffs with the senses, and common
understanding, as well as common sense, is kicked out of doors;
the first proselyte he makes, is himself (1 108).

I have tried to indicate briefly how well prepared Swift was in
1697, as a young man of thirty, for the role of the author of *A Tale*

of a Tub, not only by his hard reading and study and contemplation, but also by the vigorous exercise of his imagination and his skill in the various forms of his art. Now I should like to examine the *Tale* itself to try and show the devices he used to gather into it so much of the spirit of the century that was nearing its close, its enthusiasm, its pedantry, its shams, its conceits, and all the richness and extravagance and variety of its strange faiths and hopes and delusions. For the paradox is – and it would miss its purpose if it were not paradoxical – that the work is a product of the seventeenth century, entirely characteristic in form and manner, and at the same time a repudiation and criticism of all the most vigorous literary fashions of the previous sixty years.

For example in its outward shape and form it obviously resembles the work of those writers whom Swift repudiates, rather than the work of those like Hooker and Parsons, whose style he admired. And it is equally unlike himself, as Dr Johnson pointed out, going so far as to question indeed whether Swift could have written it: 'It has so much more thinking, more knowledge, more power, more colour, than any of the works which are indubitably his.' This impression that the *Tale* is unlike Swift in having more colour, more evidence of his reading and knowledge of literature, is due to the fact that he has put into it so much material from the world of letters in order to make play with it and to shake himself free from it. It is also due to the element of parody in its whole design, a feature indeed constant in Swift's satire and he would say inevitably so, because he believed that it would be impossible for any satirist to imagine or create affectations which could serve his purpose as well as those plentifully to be found in life or literature. And parody to be perfect should be as close to the original as possible. Therefore since certain affectations in the world of letters usually appeared in certain particular places, e.g. in dedications, or digressions, or prefaces, or 'to the readers', what could be more fitting than to fit out the *Tale* with all these appendages, so that the proper place would be available to exhibit and expose such follies? In order to make sure that his method would not be misunderstood by later readers, Swift was careful in the apology, which he added as a further preface in 1710, to explain exactly what he was doing and who were his victims.

There is one thing which the judicious reader cannot but have observed, that some of those passages in this discourse, which appear most liable to objection are what they call parodies, where the author personates the style and manner of other writers, whom he has a mind to expose. I shall produce one instance, it is in the [42nd] page. Dryden, L'Estrange and some others I shall not name, are here levelled at, who having spent their lives in faction, and apostacies, and all manner of vice, pretended to be sufferers for loyalty and religion. So Dryden tells us in one of his prefaces of his merits and suffering, thanks God that he *possesses his soul in Patience*: in other places he talks at the same rate, and L'Estrange often uses the like style, and I believe the reader may find more persons to give that passage an application: but this is enough to direct those who may have overlooked the author's intention (1 3–4).

As a sample of Dryden's complaints, I will quote a sentence from his *Discourse Concerning Satire*:

But being encouraged only with fair words by King Charles II, my little salary ill paid, and no prospect of a future subsistence, I was then discouraged in the beginning of my attempt; and now age has overtaken me, and want, a more insufferable evil, through the change of the times, has wholly disenabled me.

But Dryden provided even better material in his translation of the *Works of Virgil*, which appeared in the summer of 1697, while Swift was probably working on the *Tale*. The volume was printed by Tonson in a handsome folio, adorned with a hundred sculptures, and a list of names of the subscribers to the cuts, each subscription being five guineas; with a separate list of the second subscribers. It was divided into three parts, containing the *Eclogues*, the *Georgics* and the *Aeneid*, each part equipped not only with separate prefaces or observations, but also with separate dedications – to Lord Clifford, the Earl of Chesterfield and the Marquis of Normandy. Swift did not miss his opportunity: 'Our famous Dryden has ventured to proceed a point farther, endeavouring to introduce also a multiplicity of *godfathers*; which is an improvement of much more advantage, upon a very obvious account' (1 43). It was such a good example that he would try it himself and therefore divided his treatise into forty sections and approached forty Lords of his acquaintance to stand, but they all made their excuses.

But in the postscript to the reader, Swift found a lovely sample of Dryden's further acknowledgements to more godfathers for all the encouragement and aids he had received in the course of his work, starting with the assistance granted by the Almighty in the beginning, prosecution and conclusion of his studies, and ending with his obligations to the whole faculty of medicine, especially to those two ornaments of their profession, Dr Guibbons and Dr Hobbs. And finally he assures the reader that his work will be judged in after ages to be no dishonour to his native country, whose language and poetry he has added to in the choice of words and in the harmony of numbers. This Swift notes as an excellent method of advertisement: 'Our Great Dryden . . . has often said to me in confidence, that the world would have never suspected him to be so great a poet, if he had not assured them so frequently in his prefaces, that it was impossible they could either doubt or forget it.'

Finally all such affectations as are found scattered throughout these prefaces and addresses to the reader, 'all these wonderful civilities (as Swift calls them) that have passed of late years between the nation of authors and that of readers' are gathered up in the extravagant travesty of the tenth section of *A Tale of a Tub*, where the author offers his humble thanks to his Majesty, and both Houses of Parliament, the Lords of the Privy Council, the judges, clergy, gentry and yeomanry of the land, etc. for their approbation; expresses his happiness that Fate has flung him into so blessed an age for the mutual felicity of authors and booksellers, who produce and sell their wares so easily, and promises entire satisfaction for every class of readers, the superficial, the ignorant and the learned, and ends with throwing out some bait for the latter group, by dropping some dark hints and innuendoes of hidden meanings and profound mysteries, in the hope – as the learned commentator puts it in a final note – of setting curious men a-hunting through indexes, and inquiring for books out of the common road. I may add that there are probably very few of us who have tried to edit or comment on this *Tale* who have not been tricked in this manner, and I can only commend to any of you who may be looking for a subject for research with unlimited possibilities, that you should investigate the qualities of *Acamoth*, which you may, or may not, find illuminated in the work of the dark authors of the seventeenth century.

The method of parody is also used in the ridicule of Bentley and Wotton, which occurs in the digression on critics when he sets out gravely to search for particular descriptions of the true critic in the writings of the ancients, and brings together very much in the manner of Bentley a series of quotations proving that these ancients generally fixed upon the same hieroglyph, as the subject was too dangerous to be treated except by types and figures. Thereupon the symbol of the ass is introduced with the help of two quotations from Pausanias. 'But Herodotus, holding the very same *hieroglyph*, speaks much plainer and almost *in terminis*. . . . Upon which relation Ctesias yet refines, etc.' (I 60). And even the three maxims which provide a devastating close for the chapter are ornamented with a number of similitudes, in which the prevalent witty conceit is sharpened so that it may become an effective weapon for satire. I will instance only the first of these where the irony is so nicely balanced that an early compositor added a negative which has confused the sentence as it now stands in many editions:

Criticism, contrary to all other faculties of the intellect, is ever held the truest and best, when it is the very *first* result of the *critic's* mind: as fowlers reckon the first aim for the surest, and seldom fail of missing the mark, if they stay [not] for a second (I 63).

I have spoken at such length about the parody in the book, because it explains its unlikeness to much of Swift's later work, and because it is, I think, the source of that extraordinary richness and variety in the style which is so much concerned with an examination of the books of the previous generation that inevitably it preserves so many of their tricks and mannerisms. But it contains also quite clearly and fully devloped the qualities which most distinctively mark Swift's satire, 'an irony which runs through the thread of the whole book' and a sardonic wit which is a perfect vehicle for a scepticism not less profound and not less complete than that which perhaps more plainly and nakedly reveals itself in his latest writings.

Consider for instance his answer to the problem why satire is likely to be less dull than panegyric. The solution, he says, is easy and natural.

For, the materials of panegyric being very few in number, have been long since exhausted: for, as health is but one thing and has been always the same, whereas diseases are by thousands, besides new and daily additions; so, all the virtues that have been ever in mankind, are to be counted upon a few fingers, but his follies and vices are innumerable, and time adds hourly to the heap (I 30).

That last phrase is so characteristic. It prevents the sentence from falling flat, like some stale drab moralist's jibe. It thrusts it home, revealing the endless possibility of mankind's follies mounting higher hour by hour. It reminds us of the *Dedication to Prince Posterity*, where beneath the gay raillery of his tone as he bears witness to the actual reputation of his illustrious contemporaries at the minute he is writing, there can be heard the theme of time and mortality, and his sentences are caught for a moment and held by that insistent rhythm which had been dominant for a hundred years: ' I inquired after them among readers and booksellers, but I inquired in vain, the *memorial of them was lost among men, their place was no more to be found*: and I was laughed to scorn' (I 21). And then inexorably other echoes float into his mind and bring him more images for his purpose, and, as we read, his sentences are disturbed and rock a little beneath the powerful swell of this very different rhetoric:

Sometime we see a cloud that's dragonish;
A vapour sometime like a bear or lion,
A tower'd citadel, a pendent rock,
A forked mountain, or blue promontory
With trees upon't, that nod unto the world,
And mock our eyes with air; thou hast seen these signs;
They are black vesper's pageants.
                    Ay, my lord.
That which is now a horse, even with a thought
  The rack dislimbs.

Here is what Swift makes of it. I do not quote it as an example of parody, but to show his mind in this way also enriched by his reading, and subduing it to his purpose.

If I should venture in a windy day, to affirm to Your Highness, that there is a large cloud near the *horizon* in the form of a *bear*, another in the *zenith* with the head of an *ass*, a third to the westward with claws like a *dragon*; and Your Highness should in a few minutes think fit to examine the truth, 'tis certain, they would all be changed in figure and position, new ones would arise, and all we could agree upon would be, that clouds there were, but that I was grossly mistaken in the *zoography* and *topography* of them (1 21).

Professor Sherburn has drawn attention to a striking aspect of the *Tale*, often overlooked, as it reveals Swift's 'dislike of the deluding powers of perverted reason', or, more specifically, his dislike of proselytizing, of people who wish to force their opinions upon others.

Whoever hath *an ambition to be heard in a crowd* – so, with contempt, begins his Introduction to the *Tale*; and in the climactic Digression on Madness, the lunatics are the founders of states by conquest, the founders of new systems of philosophy, and the founders of sects in religion.

This is very true, but even in this there is an element of irony, which I think Swift was not unaware of, though it was at his own expense. For he also had an ambition, and a very powerful ambition, to be heard, and while he makes fun of those who exalt themselves above the crowd by mounting upon one of those three wooden machines for the use of orators who desire to talk much without interruption, he has nevertheless devised his own Tub to provide a platform for his own special wit and genius. And it cannot be denied that he has sometimes endeavoured to satisfy the 'whale-mouthed gapers after levity', and has taken advantage of 'the liberty of these times, which hath afforded wisdom a larger passport to travel, than was ever able formerly to be obtained, when the world kept her fettered in an implicit obedience, by the three-fold cord of custom, education and ignorance'. Even when Swift is most directly attacking the sects, and may be in part influenced by his own experience among the Presbyterians in Ireland, he is still writing not as a churchman or a politician, but as a wit and as a man of letters. That is perhaps the fundamental difference between the *Tale* and the roughest controversial satires of the bishops and their opponents. They are always at certain points protected and restrained by their official status. But the author of the *Tale* is completely free, unhampered by political or practical considerations. He is concerned with words; his wit is conceit; and he did not always realize perhaps the power and the effect of the weapons he was using.

In his handling of the allegory of the three brothers, for instance, he is inclined to dramatize their actions rather in the manner of the contemporary stage, and their language and gestures remind us of the world of Sir Novelty Fashion and Lord Foppington. And the symbol of the coats, meaning 'the Doctrine and Faith of Christianity', is full of obvious dangers, though it not only lends itself to the necessary dramatization, but also may be neatly reversed and elaborated into a satire on the real religion of the fashionable world, its god the tailor and its sytem of belief according to which the universe is a large suit of clothes and man himself but a micro-coat, the acquirements of his mind furnishing an exact dress: 'Is not religion a *cloak*, honesty a *pair of shoes*, worn out in the dirt, self-love a *surtout*, vanity a *shirt*, and conscience a *pair of breeches*?' (I 47). The whole of this passage is like a string of puns and conceits held together by a thread of irony. The dangers of Swift's satire on the corruptions of religion, whether in the allegory itself, or in the account of the sect of the Aeolists and the Fragment on the mechanical operation of the Spirit, arise out of the verbal play of his wit, which does not hesitate to make a sort of punning game with all the words which had become, it is true, soiled and bent by the usage they had received at the hands of hypocrites and fanatics, but which had nevertheless also been upon the lips of saints and prophets and remained for the devout Christian sacred symbols of his faith. It is not merely that the book contains 'several youthful sallies', or that 'no one opinion can fairly be deduced from it, which is contrary to religion or morality' – it is rather that the author of *A Tale of a Tub* with an audience of 'the greatest droles and wits that any age ever produced', set out to establish his reputation among them by out-distancing them all in the variety of his drollery and the reach and penetration of his wit.

In this he succeeded. None of them went farther in their probing, none of them journeyed farther in the exploration of a rationalist's complete scepticism, none of them opened their minds so freely and without prejudice to all that was being thought and said, none of them – not even Sir Thomas Browne – more eloquently expressed that experience of following the mind of man through all its magnificent and fantastic vagaries during the century. Here Swift shows what he could have done, had he wished to write like them. Here is a *tour de force*, a superb imitation of their most exalted rhetorical periods, soaring into the empyrean in circling parodies of their favourite cosmic images, only to burst at last into an explosive flash of wit, as he compares man's fancy to the brightly plumaged bird of paradise that was reputed to live only in the heights of the air.

And, whereas the mind of Man, when he gives the spur and
bridle to his thoughts, never stops, but naturally sallies out into
both extreams of high and low, of good and evil; his first flight
of fancy, commonly transports him to ideas of what is most
perfect, finished and exalted; till having soared out of his
own reach and sight, not well perceiving how near the
frontiers of height and depth, border upon each other; with
the same course and wing, he falls down plum into the
lowest bottom of things; like one who travels the east into
the west; or like a straight line drawn by its own length into
a circle. Whether a tincture of malice in our natures, makes us
fond of furnishing every bright idea with its reverse; or,
whether reason reflecting upon the sum of things, can, like
the sun, serve only to enlighten one half of the globe, leaving
the other half, by necessity, under shade and darkness: or,
whether fancy, flying up to the imagination of what is
highest and best, becomes over-shot, and spent, and weary
and suddenly falls like a dead bird of paradise, to the ground
(I 99).

But no one has more lightly tossed aside these metaphysical conjectures to argue triumphantly in the cause of reason and common sense, ironically exposing the delusions of the imagination, and the dangers of all philosophical anatomizing, and showing the wisdom of contenting ourselves with the superficies of things, only to bring us to this conclusion: 'This is the sublime and refined point of felicity, called, *the possession of being well deceived*; the serene, peaceful state of being a fool among knaves' (1 110). And no one has gone quite so far not even that 'absolute Lord of Wit', the Earl of Rochester, who was indeed quite unhampered in his profanity and little concerned with man's dignity – as the author of *A Tale of a Tub* when he recommends as a very noble undertaking to Tory members of the House of Commons that they should appoint a commission (who shall be empowered to send for persons, papers and records) to examine into the merits of every student and professor in Bedlam, so that they might be properly used for all the offices in the state, ecclesiastical, civil and military. Various suitable candidates are vividly described and their special fitness for various occupations indicated; and the irony is pressed home in a characteristically thorough manner, by the evident manifestation that 'all would very much excel, and arrive at great perfection in their several kinds'. In case anyone should doubt this, the author of these momentous truths modestly claims to have had the happiness of being for some time a worthy member of that honourable society, and by that one plain instance clinches his argument, admitting gravely that he is 'a person, whose imaginations are hard-mouthed, and exceedingly disposed to run away with his *reason*', which he had observed 'from long experience, to be a very light rider, and easily shook off'.

Dr Johnson relates that 'when this wild work first raised the attention of the public, Sacheverell, meeting Smalridge, tried to flatter him by seeming to think him the author; but Smalridge answered with indignation, "Not all that you and I have in the world nor all that ever we shall have, should hire me to write the *Tale of a Tub*"'. Perhaps there is some reason for such an attitude, not because the *Tale* is sometimes unconventional, or even profane; but because it reveals so fully through all the parody and wit and irony the intellectual experience of the author. Though there were chasms in the manuscript, where we are told certain passages were omitted, the book as printed gives the impression of holding nothing back. It is in the tradition of the century that was closing as it was written; it is in the direct line of wit, and it may not be altogether extravagant to say that it makes an effective epilogue, and leaves the stage clear for a new and rather different set of actors. And perhaps it almost meets on a different level the requirements of one of the most notable wits in the company for whom Swift wrote, the Duke of Buckingham, who at the end of the century challenged his generation to produce another writer of such sincerity, as he who from the beginning of the century had exercised so much influence in England – the incomparable Montaigne. 'Yet,' he says, 'whenever any great wit shall incline to the same free way of writing, I almost dare assure him of success; for besides the agreeableness of such a book, so very sincere a temper of mind needs not blush to be exposed as naked as possible.' In spite of all their differences and in spite of the novelty and originality of *A Tale of a Tub* and the violence and exuberance which make it so unlike the tone and manner of Montaigne, it was nevertheless written by one who was inclined to 'the same free way of writing' and of 'so very sincere a temper of mind' that it reveals as nakedly and as fearlessly as possible the intellectual experience of a man of letters, who had reached the age of thirty a little before the turn of the century together with what might not too fancifully be called the first generation of the modern world.

(106–25)

Robert Martin Adams

from 'Swift and Kafka', *Strains of Discord* 1958

Although the world of satire is traditionally a world of disorganization and dislocation, it is typically seen by an eye which knows something better and which can emphasize the disorder by contrasting it with an understood or remembered order, a standard of excellence somehow known or implied. For this reason, mock-heroic is one of the natural modes of satire. It has sometimes been observed, however, that the effect of constant mock-heroic juxtaposition is to exalt dullness, or duplicity, into a heroic quality. It has not so often been emphasized that satire may also dissolve the order which ostensibly serves as a foil for disorder, leaving the author and reader bewildered amid a glare of glittering, cutting incongruities. An example of such satire, many-faceted and sharp-edged, is Jonathan Swift's *A Tale of a Tub*, with its appendages *The Battle of the Books* and *The Mechanical Operation of the Spirit*. It is a bold, hard, angular engine, which still cannot be carelessly handled without danger of a slash.

Swift's hydra-headed satire is in many respects a work peculiar to its time. The ancients-versus-moderns controversy, around which much of the satire is grouped, was strictly ephemeral. The sort of reading which Swift's book implied (like that which it attacks) was already outmoded; important objects of his satire, the fanatic preachers, were essentially creatures of the dying century. The very manner of the book which is shapeless, rhapsodic, stuffed with learning and authorial crotchets, clearly derives from that wonderful, crazy century which had produced *The Anatomy of Melancholy* and William Prynne, *Pseudodoxia Epidemica* and the Fifth Monarchy Men – not to mention *Don Quixote*. Thus, the 'corruptions in religion and learning' against which the author leveled his lance were in outward form at least those of a bygone or bygoing day. But *A Tale of a Tub* is not to be understood as a mechanical derivation from the social circumstances of the time, much less as a collection of intellectual factors piled together in a basket of 'moral realism'. If there is one thing clear about Swift, it is the high tension at which his mind operated, its impatient energy, its tendency to dominate and use intellectual materials. His prose, even when polished to a high gloss, is always muscular; and its muscles are always at work. His jokes, his games, his private languages and little societies, his paradoxes, and all the dramatic contrasts of his life, which furnish such rich material for the biographer, the dramatist and the purveyor of avowed or unavowed fiction, are also evidence of an emotional and intellectual turbulence which made him the theater of an endless struggle. He did not develop placidly, one more chain-linked bacillus on a neo-Stoic string; his mind was torn by agonies of conflict before he possessed the ideological framework to explain or the symbolic dress in which to clothe it; and his book is the expression quite as much of a temperament as of an era. One illustration of this fact derives from a contrast between *A Tale of a Tub* and *Gulliver's Travels. Gulliver* is much the more polished performance; it has a clarity of outline and concept which is scarcely broken, and a steady progression of symbols. The ragged edges of Swift's fury have been buried within a deliberately smooth, deceptive surface, like broken glass set in concrete. *A Tale of a Tub*, on the other hand, is all hard, raw, self-assured and fantastic in its angled bravado. It lacks a good deal in scheme and symbols, in shape and structure – not that the book fails to exploit its own lacks in these regards; because it is committed to so little, it makes all the more capital of its freedom to mock structure as well as lack of structure – but for this very reason it exposes more nakedly the bare bones and quivering nerves of Swift's logical and emotional conflicts. One cannot help feeling that in *A Tale of a Tub* Swift was reaching into the deepest, and most immediate, background of frustrations, which were partly psychological and partly philosophical but which determined and involved his whole existence as an individual. If his reading, as he declared, was all fresh in his head, so also were his angers and humiliations; and out of the two he created a work altogether original – one which he flung on the counters of a shopkeeping nation with the rage of a man who finds he has been handed a counterfeit coin.

One of the key scenes of *A Tale of a Tub*, which gave contemporary opinion one of its rudest shocks, shows Peter establishing for his brothers the doctrine of transubstantiation. He carves them a couple of pieces of bread and pretends that it is mutton. After some discussion:

'What, then, My Lord,' replied the first, 'it seems this is a
shoulder of mutton all this while.' 'Pray, sir,' says Peter, 'eat
your vittles and leave off your impertinence, if you please, for I am
not disposed to relish it at present.' But the other could not
forbear being overprovoked at the affected seriousness of
Peter's countenance. 'By G—, My Lord,' said he, 'I can only say
that to my eyes and fingers and teeth and nose it seems to be
nothing but a crust of bread.' Upon which, the second put in
his word: 'I never saw a piece of mutton in my life so nearly
resembling a slice from a twelve-penny loaf.' 'Look ye,
gentlemen,' cries Peter in a rage, 'to convince you what a
couple of blind, positive, ignorant, wilful puppies you are, I will
use but this plain argument: By G—, it is true, good, natural
mutton as any in Leaden-Hall market, and G— confound you both
eternally, if you offer to believe otherwise' (I 73).

Peter's outburst of hysterical rage is in the dominant key of *A Tale of a Tub*; like the weaver of the Preface, he speaks in the thick, choked accents of violent fury – a fury which at once perpetrates and exposes a gross, outrageous fraud. If we suppose one of the central concerns of the book to be the discovery and rejection of fraud, it will appear as the expression of a temperament and a function only secondarily determined by social circumstance and prudential motives. Swift denounces in *A Tale of a Tub* the two forms of fraud and corruption that time and circumstance had rendered most obnoxious. But the relish with which he goes about his denunciations and the lengths to which he carries them express a purely personal need. So much intense and peculiar pleasure seemed to lie in the uprooting of deceit and corruption that truth and health, even if found, could only have appeared as a disappointment.

But this denunciation of fraud, while an overriding concern of the author, is not the principle on which *A Tale of a Tub* is organized. Neither can the book be wholly described as an exposé of the innocent who pretends to be its author, important as this theme doubtless is. Although its surface is flauntingly and defiantly incoherent, *A Tale of a Tub* is, I think, chiefly held together by a pair of images which achieve explicit statement only in a fragment never fully incorporated in the book itself, though constantly associated with it. *The Mechanical Operation of the Spirit* places in opposition two concepts, the machine and the spirit, which had been deeply involved in the history of the seventeenth century and in the experience of Jonathan Swift. These two concepts are also, and singularly, themes common to the story of Jack, Peter and Martin, to the digressions, and to the (no less than five) comments prefatory to *A Tale of a Tub*. The wind and the machine are of central, summary importance to Swift, his book, and his time; he is equally hostile to both, and, though he generally uses one to mock the other, he sometimes plays audaciously at identifying them.

The 'spirit' for which Swift feels such antipathy is a quality that takes many forms; in one of his formal moments the author distinguishes manifestations of the spirit according to their origin, as the products of divine inspiration, diabolic possession, inner motives (imagination, anger, fear, grief, pain, etc.) or mechanical manipulation. But the spirit shows itself in all sorts of ways which cannot be so strictly catalogued: in self-importance (the greedy importunity of the bookseller, the lofty airs of the starving author, the alleged delusions of Descartes); in dogmatic ignorance; in esoteric doctrines, numerology and elaborate word spinnings; in the deliberate vagaries of digression counterdigressed by digression; in the pretensions of the modern age over the ancients; in the interpretive triumph of the three brothers over their father's will; in military conquests; in the lucky victory of the madman over the sane.

What precisely is the spirit? It is agitated air, 'a redundancy of vapours', whether denominated enthusiasm, hysteria or inspiration; its exponents are the learned Aeolists, a set of inflated gapers after air; it is the effective cause of conquests and systems, of faction and madness. Its normal seat is in the lungs, the belly and the genitals; denied adequate expression here, it may rise to the brain and afflict that organ with a vapor. What the difference is between overt, acknowledged madness and those forms of undeclared madness which are socially rewarded Swift half offers to make clear; but the explanation dissolves into a *Hiatus in MS*, and the satiric edge of his wit is turned against all forms of wind, because all make or are capable of making, man turbulent and fantastic.

For the brain in its natural position and state of serenity
disposes its owner to pass his life in the common forms,
without any thought of subduing multitudes to his own
power, his *reasons* or his *visions*; and the more he shapes his
understanding by the pattern of human learning, the less he is
inclined to form parties after his particular notions, because
that instructs him in his private infirmities, as well as in the
stubborn ignorance of the people. But when a man's fancy gets
astride on his reason, when imagination is at cuffs with the
senses, and common understanding as well as common sense is
kicked out of doors, the first proselyte he makes is himself,
and when that is once compassed the difficulty is not so great
in bringing over others – a strong delusion always operating
from *without* as vigorously as from *within* (1 108).

The function and title of the book are themselves involved in the image of the spirit as an explosive 'redundancy of vapours'; the wits of the age having been found to threaten the Church and State, a project for diverting their energies was sought; and as whales are given a tub to play with in order to divert them from attacking a ship, so *A Tale of a Tub* was produced to divert the wits who, puffed up with modern presumption and armed with sharp weapons from Hobbes's *Leviathan*, were becoming dangerous. Thus the mechanical excitement and mechanical manipulation of wind into one social form or another become the predominant images of Swift's satire; and while no more precise definitions are made of the sort of wind or the sort of social form satirized, the nature of the wind or spirit particularly is pretty clear. The weight of Swift's attack lies against the private spirit, the irrational personal conviction of logical rightness, physical authority or spiritual justification.

How heavy that weight lies may be realized when one notes the vast arsenal of satiric weapons with which Swift assaults the spirit and its manifestations. He persistently implies that all forms of inspiration are of the two lower varieties – neither divine nor diabolic in origin, but the product of imaginative self-indulgence or of deliberate mechanical manipulation, of lust, filth, greed or folly. Thus he explains an imperial conquest as the effect of an unsatisfied erection, imputes pulpit eloquence to sexual excitement, and bitterly derogates all forms of enthusiasm by equating the winds which puff them up.

Mists arise from the earth, steams from dunghills,
exhalations from the sea, and smoke from fire; yet all clouds
are the same in composition, as well as consequences; and the
fumes issuing from a jakes will furnish as comely and useful
a vapour as incense from an altar (1 102).

All clouds are the same, in composition as well as consequences; that is to say, all clouds and vapors are degrading to human nature. Sex and excrement are the unremitting associates of spiritual inspiration, the mechanical foundations on which enthusiasms are founded and to which they inevitably revert. No more terrible and degrading association is open to Swift's imagination. The preacher whose canting reaches its height in an act of physical orgasm; the prince whose urge to conquest derives from unexpended semen; the Aeolists, who worship in circles 'with every man a pair of bellows applied to his neighbour's breech'; the female priests, ancient and modern, 'whose organs were understood to be better disposed for the admission of those oracular gusts'; the Aeolian admiration for belching (especially, by a fine touch of art, through the nose) and for the ancient institution of barrels, from which air is introduced, through funnels, to the breech – all bespeak an aversion which, for Swift, amounted almost to phobia. The similarity that Swift affects to discover between Jack and Peter, the church of Geneva and that of Rome, is founded upon their mutual susceptibility to wind, 'the frenzy and the spleen of both having the same foundation'. And for Swift no more repulsive view of the human species is conceivable that that of the inflated and presumptuous Aeolist.

But though the primary edge of *A Tale of a Tub* is directed against the windy Aeolists and their most picturesque exemplars, the fanatic sectarians, the book's emotional structure is not that of an author secure in his possession of 'that natural position and state of security' which enables a man 'to pass his life in the common forms'. One could look for no better example of the placid, adjusted man than Swift's great enemy William Wotton, whose reaction to *A Tale of a Tub* was one of unqualified horror. Although Swift's theological blasphemies may have been exaggerated, his raging contempt for the whole race of moderns can scarcely be overstated; and surely this implies, on the face of it, a considerable contempt for the 'common forms'. Indeed, a treatise so fantastic, sardonic and derisive as *A Tale of a Tub* could scarcely culminate in a calm conformity; the expenditure of so much nervous ingenuity merely to endorse the 'common forms' would be at the least a paradox, akin to that by which the fourth book of *Gulliver* may be read as the most passionate denunciation of passion ever penned. Undoubtedly *A Tale of a Tub* partakes of this paradoxical character; and Swift (or at least his author-mask) is explicit in his recognition of the fact:

Even I myself, the author of these momentous truths, am a
person whose imaginations are hard-mouthed and
exceedingly disposed to run away with his *reason,* which I
have observed from long experience to be a very light rider,
and easily shook off (1 114).

But there is a further complexity to *A Tale of a Tub*; the problem is not simply that the satiric attack includes, in some measure, as its object the author himself; it is that the point of view from which one satire is launched is itself the object of a second attack, and the common forms' into which the sane and ordinary mind placidly fits are ridiculed under the aspect of a machine.

The story of Jack, Peter and Martin, the Calvinist, Roman Catholic and Lutheran churches, is ostensibly a story in which the reasonable *via media* of the Church of England is upheld against the superstition of Rome and the crude, violent inspirations of the sects. The satire upon the philosophers of wind, likewise, tends to support the reasonable, common-sense judgement of the enlightened, unprejudiced few. But Martin's placid responses to Jack are ridiculed as the tricky devices of a cunning debater; and the three machines, of ladder, pulpit and stage itinerant, are presented as the types of all modern authorship – grotesque devices of elevation to facilitate the puffing of air into a multitude. Here once more the author introduces himself and his own book within the framework of the satire, describing his present production as a work of the stage itinerant; and indeed, there is no evident principle (save *obiter dictum*) by which any work or author could be exempted from the satire. Swift's hatred of the moderns (which is a principle more vital to him than love of the ancients) seems to allow no room for exceptions, no escape from primitive presumption and mechanical craft.

Not only is the machine a frequent device for controlling the escape of redundant vapor (as most schemes of religion and government resemble tubs in being 'hollow and dry and empty and noisy and wooden and given to rotation'); machines may also be used to excite the more pretentious and windy spiritual activities. Under the cover of spiritual aims, carnal energies are gratified; by mechanical devices, excess spiritual wind is diverted into useful channels. The relation of wind and machine is reciprocal; schemes and projects are the mere complements of fanaticism and enthusiasm. This of course is the history of Protestant sectarianism in a nutshell; the energy of the saints, diverted to secular projects and mechanical improvements, gave rise to that eighteenth-century outlook for which philosophy and religion are both in different ways too exalted names but which is very adequately described as Franklinism. The application of religious zeal to business ends is the essence of Franklinism, as of the 'modern spirit' which Swift hated. Because his Tory principles involved a deep-seated preference for the slow, traditional forms of a landed aristocracy over the sharper, more competitive, turbulent and individualist ways of the money men, Swift despised all 'getting ahead'; and he hated individual passion or appetite more even than wind and machines because it was the determining agent of both.

Standing apart from 'discipline-directed' as from 'system-directed' man, Swift saw, I think, a good deal deeper into the human dilemma of the day than any of the formal philosophers of his time. Shaftesbury and Mandeville, for example, disagreed as to the motive power of the social machine; did benevolence or greed make it tick? But neither dreamed of repudiating the view that society at its best is a clockwork which absorbs and makes use of the various motives of men. While Locke was rendering Christianity reasonable in terms of a mechanical philosophy and while Berkeley was quietly gathering the spiritual principle into a defiant solipsism, Swift, instead of trying to reconcile the alternatives of spirit and matter or to choose between them, made it his concern to repudiate them both. He figures, then, as a man utterly deprived of those usual philosophical supports and props of belief with which the average man surrounds himself. Swift's pride is a particularly brilliant, because partly inadequate, substitute for a system; had it been more formalized, he would never have defined with such savage success his own prescriptions against scribbling. Standing apart from his society, and with special horror from those who had rebelled against it, Swift achieved at bitter expense an especially acute and individual insight into it. If his performance seems sometimes to partake of levitation or puppetry because he gets along with so much less positive, constructive belief than his contemporaries found decent, a modern eye may find in fact at least one measure of his achievement.

The cry of 'destructiveness' has long echoed about *A Tale of a Tub*; and though it may not be as damning as William Wotton and F. R. Leavis suppose, it is probably a valid cry. If there are positive teachings lurking in the book, one is hard put to know what they are. Certainly 'integrity' is no solution to the question of what Swift is inculcating. Integrity or moral realism is what Swift started with and never abandoned, even though it led him toward the most terrible of all conclusions, nihilism. Whether he ever actually formulated this conclusion may be debated; if he did not, only the hard and brilliant façade of his egotism saved him from it. For the evident tendency of his thought, which builds only to undermine and undermines in so many different directions, leaves as a shield against nihilism only that arrogance of temper which first led him toward it.

As to the precise nature of these temperamental impulses and their conditioning, one can do no more than speculate. Clearly, the frigid isolation of Swift's political and social thought corresponds in some measure to the alienation of his personal situation. Orphanage, genteel poverty, a temperamental horror of intimacy, the peculiar dilemmas of Anglo-Irish Protestantism, and the general debacle of enthusiasms political, literary and religious – all no doubt contributed. But these are general considerations. As for the precise determining qualities of Swift's individual mind, it must always be a curious, abstracted argument why the same vapor produces such peculiar effects upon different individuals; and perhaps no better answer can be found than a *Hiatus in MS*. In any event, the result can scarcely be mistaken. Neither in the individual nor in the group, neither in the 'common forms' nor out of them does Swift see any tolerable, let alone easy, way toward the good life.

Individual conscience is an engine of individual greed; systems and conquests are engines of collective greed; the way of the world is an engine of universal greed; and the most unexceptionable virtues are, as perverted by the inescapable corruptness of human nature, mere façades for filth, fraud and lust. The account of a clothes religion, which satirizes man as an empty, hollow exterior (in strict counterpoint to the Aeolists, who are despised as windy, shapeless enthusiasts), culminates in a series of ironic definitions:

To instance no more: is not religion a *cloak*; honesty a *pair of shoes*, worn out in the dirt, self-love a *surtout*; vanity a *shirt*; and conscience a *pair of breeches*, which, though a cover for lewdness as well as nastiness, is easily slipped down for the service of both? (I 47).

Although the ironies of this passage are many and complexly wrought, its decisive point seems directed against those who judge of men by their exterior – against the shallowness and emptiness of life as seen from the outside only. But this was in fact something of Swift's own position; he had, as we have seen, a profound sense that the deeper one looked into human nature the more corruption one was likely to uncover; and the greatest achievement of his ironic stoicism was the suggestion that men must be trained not to look beyond the surface of things, so that they might thereby attain to 'the sublime and refined point of felicity called the possession of being well deceived, the serene peaceful state of being a fool among knaves'.

Here, too, are ironies galore. By looking only at the surface of things one remains happy and a fool; by delving into the arcana one becomes miserable (for what one finds is ugly) and a knave (for obscure knowledge gives rise to flimflam systems). The structure of Swift's assertion here, as frequently elsewhere, involves an ascending rhetorical series culminating in a deliberate anticlimax, an act of destruction. Such is, for example, his metaphorical description of wisdom: it is

a *fox*, who after long hunting will at last cost you the
pains to dig out. 'Tis a *cheese*, which by how much the richer
has the thicker, the homelier and the coarser coat, and
whereof to a judicious palate the *maggots* are best. 'Tis a *sack-
posset*, wherein the deeper you go you will find it the sweeter.
Wisdom is a *hen*, whose cackling we must value and
consider because it is attended with an *egg*. But then, lastly,
'tis a *nut* which unless you choose with judgement may cost
you a tooth and pay you with nothing but a *worm* (I 40).

This comparative characterization may of course be taken in some degree seriously; but the homeliness of the imagery speaks another language. Maggots, worms and broken teeth are scarcely the appropriate rewards for a search after knowledge which is being wholeheartedly recommended. One of Swift's notes on a pretended gap in the manuscript speaks a much more direct language: 'Here is another defect in the manuscript, but I think the author did wisely and that the matter which thus strained his faculties was not worth a solution, and it were well if all metaphysical cobweb problems were not otherwise answered.' Dark authors are thus absurd on one side, as are superficial writers on the other; and in fact the two follies complement one another. A true 'modern' (that is, 'fool') pretends deep learning to conceal his ignorance of plain truths; and for the particular benefit of such our innocent author has prepared his *New Help of Smatterers; or, the Art of Being Deep-Learned and Shallow-Read*.

Satire of the credulous followed by satire of the skeptical; satire directed against the windy interiors and then against the hollow exteriors of men; satire directed against the machine and against the wind which fills it; satire so double-edged and double-directed leaves very little ground exempted from satire of one sort or another. Swift does not do anything so placid as teeter indecisively between two satiric points of view; he is the theater of a battle, the register of furiously conflicting tensions, where all thought and feeling is an area of dispute. The Toryism of Swift thus surpasses (or sinks beneath) the prudential principles of a Clarendon or a Harley. Swift is a psychological rather than a political Tory – a statement which takes us a good way toward the notion that the essence of his thinking was not Tory at all. At the very least, we may distinguish two sorts of Toryism, the one prudential, political, traditional, unprincipled and creative, the other emotional, psychological, individual, dogmatic and destructive.

The word 'Tory' and the usual concept of Toryism have oddly little to do with a point of view so austerely and complexly and self-defeatingly individual as Swift's. It is a paradox often remarked that the fury with which he undertook to bottle up every last outlet of individualism brought Swift to the very outposts of crankiness, eccentricity and overt insanity; his rage for order was such that it surpassed at once the limits of politics and later the limits of art, till it became unhesitatingly a question of his own individual existence. The psychological quality of Swift's Toryism derived from the fact that for him order was rage and torment, not an existing principle; and from this fact was determined the whole series of uneasy ambivalences (toward love and authority, toward mankind and himself, toward filth and cleanliness, toward past and present) which make up the fascination of his personality.

Generally speaking, the seventeenth century fell into psychology as into an ambush. Locke's experience summarized in capsule form that of the entire century. Setting out to dispute concerning a substantive matter, he and his friends quickly found themselves at a complete stand, unable to determine anything until they had come to an agreement concerning human understanding and the degree of certainty to which it could properly aspire. Swift fell into the same pit and never succeeded in getting out of it, perhaps because he never wanted to. But he made of it a kingdom of brilliant fantasy within which his own role, now as supreme monarch and now as tortured outcast, never ceased to be central and absorbing. Not only was his symbolic role within the fantasy strikingly dual, but so also was his personal role as creator of it. He was both the prisoner of his imagination and the jailer of it. His books served both to give Swift a revenge upon society and to ingratiate him with it. ('They may talk of the *you know what*,' he wrote to Stella, referring guardedly to *A Tale of a Tub*, 'but, gad, if it had not been for that, I should never have been able to get the access I have had.') His increasing use of symbols is itself a mark of this dualism; for the symbol, as allegory and object, looks two ways and exists in an essential tension even when, by a kind of stereoptical vision, object and idea seem to be fused. One's awareness of symbolic writing is never merely direct, and a particularly striking quality of Swift's symbolism is the duplicity of its effect. Among any group of readers there will always be some who find Swift hilarious and others who find only a deep sense of pain and misery. There will be some who giggle and some who wince. Neither of these responses is the proper one; neither is even preferable. Both are legitimate, and so intimately connected that they may exist within the same person almost at the same time. The comedy of the digression on madness is close to hysteria; as we laugh, we cringe. If one of the symbolic acts of *A Tale of a Tub* is the wallowing of a whale expending its wild, blind energies on a tub, another is what the physiologists in a significant secondary use of the word call 'teasing'. Part of Swift's humor is to cut and frazzle the reader's nerves by direct assault; jabber from Irenaus, pseudo-Rosicrucian interpretations and deliberate obscurities all serve to baffle and frustrate. Swift teases and irritates his reader, booby traps him with mock quotations and pretended subtleties, drops him into yawning chasms in the manuscript, and alters the character under which he himself writes with bewildering frequency. Having been provided by an obliging enemy with a set of annotations, he blandly annotates the notes and carries out a whole series of mystifying maneuvers with regard to the publication and authorship of the book. It is as if he were saying, '*I* am the plaything of the whale, passion, which I can divert only by using such foolishness as this – very well; but *you*, the reader, are *my* plaything, too.' The tub serves not only to divert but to annoy; and

though Swift's many attacks on his reader no doubt involve some
directly or indirectly satiric purposes, they also satisfy an impulse to
lacerate the reader's feelings, an impulse of which Swift's character is
never quite free and which reveals itself overtly in his more scabrous
verses.

Within *A Tale of a Tub* one mark of Swift's double attitude is his
double use of number and numerology. He mocks the rules of
mathematics for their pretended rigor and derides the 'mystic'
correspondences of numerology; for instance, one of the no less than
eleven treatises which his pseudo-author has in hand is a *Panegyrical
Essay upon the Number Three*. The number three, which perverse
ingenuity can demonstrate in so many insignificant places, thus
signifies for Swift the waste of spirit in brain-maggotry. But *A Tale
of a Tub* is itself written to an extraordinary degree in threes. There
are, for example, three sons, three varieties of critic, three engines for
achieving literary eminence, three characteristics of a critic, three
volumes to the proposed treatise on zeal, three distinct anima's or
winds to man, three classes of reader – not to mention the three fine
ladies, the three tiers to Peter's hat, and the three recommendations
as to numerology. Just as *Gulliver* plays with the quirks and oddities
of number while satirizing both arithmeticians and numerologists, so
A Tale of a Tub wavers between derision and fascination; and the
only outcome of this equivocation, which can at any time be turned
in either direction, is to put the reader in the position of a captive
mouse *vis-à-vis* a triumphant cat.

It is with regard to these latent aggressions against the reader that
the significant form of *A Tale of a Tub* comes most directly into
question. The story of Peter, Jack and Martin, which is a satire on
religious corruptions, dovetails perfectly well with the digressions,
which satirize corruptions in learning. Satire on the Aeolists complements satire on the formalists, and both satires illustrate corruptions in religion and learning. The various prefatory and introductory
materials illustrate the empty, pretentious devices of modern authorship; and the ancients-versus-moderns controversy casts a light on the
original simplicity and dignity of the institutions which modern folly
has corrupted. But the assaults upon the reader surpass or undermine
the limits of art; here the author emerges from the frame of his formal
presentation to agitate the reader directly. Esthetically speaking, the

effect is kinetic, not to say galvanic – and so, by some strict canons, improper. However this may be, it is certainly divisive. For the reader is not attacked as part of the satire, not lashed for partaking of the errors and follies being mocked in the body of the satiric work. The little tricks and games of esoteric interpretation and numerological obscurity will be puzzling and annoying to a reader almost precisely in the degree that he does *not* partake of 'modern' folly. In fact, Swift attacks the reader simply for being the reader; and *A Tale of a Tub* is undoubtedly flawed thereby, as a piece of formal art. But there is at least one variety of art other than formal art, and a spirit so complexly at war with itself as Swift's could find full expression only in that double-dealing which creates a formality chiefly to outrage it.

Houyhnhnm land is of course the *ultima Thule* of Swift's mental voyaging; and even here the savage debacle involves several elements in conflict: witness the animal imagery that Swift applies to the life of reason, the good life. An ironic purpose naturally governs, to a considerable extent, Swift's use of this imagery. As the lack of reason, he implies, will make beasts of men, so the presence of reason will make men of beasts. But the austere rule of reason itself has connotations and overtones not altogether grateful. The Houyhnhnms are not only superhuman in their repression of the soft emotions, in their reduction of reason to the direct, immediate perception of the unquestionable; they are also inhuman. The usual complaint against book four of *Gulliver* is that the satire here fails to be dramatically convincing, that we are not moved by the society of horses to that straightforward love of reason and hatred of unreason which seem to be the author's intent. Houyhnhnm and Yahoo revolt us, if not equally, at least in the same way; they are parodies of the human species, and not all Swift's skill in dramatic presentation can prevent the sledge-drawn horses, with their sober, pseudo-Stoic palavers against passion, from seeming grotesque. One may indeed feel that Swift not only could not but did not want to render the life of reason desirable in its own cold reasonable terms. The life of reason too is a form of assault by Swift on himself and his reader; the sacrifices it demands involve one ultimately in the surrender of humanity itself. Whether or not the author formulated this matter consciously, *Gulliver* implies in its conclusion a despairing suggestion that the life of reason must be lived down as well as up to. The sort of purity which is the norm of Swift's satire, its standard of rest and satisfaction, is not conceivable within a human frame; either angels or animals are its only conceivable habitation. That Swift chose animals to embody his conception of the good life suggests that his despair was trembling on the unrecognized verge of hatred. Perhaps this hatred is the ultimate fate of any man who persists, as long as Swift did, in manipulating the edged weapons of satire. But what force urges a man suffering from spiritual hemophilia to play so excitedly with edged weapons? It is, I think, a way of thinking and feeling about human nature which would prove this nature by the most perilous tests, which would exalt and liberate it even at the peril of destroying it. The motivation behind this frantic yet stunted and inverted idealism is perhaps a terror of being used, a desire to stand free of all the warm, ordinary human entanglements. The passion to test one's human existence by standing apart from all the comforts that make it human is, undoubtedly, Quixotic, as its contrary is merely Philistine. But though it does not provide any comfortable grounds of practical existence, the austere rage of Swift does mark out a way of thinking and feeling about one's existence which, even for those who do not themselves follow it, is strenuous, perilous and deeply influential.

For Swift himself the experiment was fatal, as everyone knows. The narrow isthmus of his arrogant character, a thin line of shifting sands between the two oceans of personal hysteria and impersonal mechanism, wavered at last and was overwhelmed. In his final terrible years Swift sat alone staring at a blank wall and muttering to himself over and over, 'I am what I am. I am what I am.'

What was he indeed? What is human character when it can no longer be distinguished from the socially conditioned reflex on the one hand or the sensually conditioned impulses of personal hysteria on the other? The form of Swift's passion was personal and fatal; its content has positive meaning for many – may, indeed, be seen as a constant preoccupation of the modern conscience. Whether for social, philosophical or temperamental reasons or for all at once, whether from choice or necessity, the exploration of the most dangerous freedoms of the self (those it wins at the expense of its own security within any single system of values) has been taken by a class of modern authors as their main interest. Whatever discoveries these authors are found to have made when we consider them as a group, the fact of their existence and their continuing activity has been a troubling and significant element in the literary atmosphere. The relevance of their preoccupations is by no means diminished today; rather the contrary. Of this author Swift serves as type and perhaps precursor; and *A Tale of a Tub*, which raised more monsters from the vasty deep than ever it diverted, stands at the head of a file of volumes profoundly expressive of an even more troubled 'modern' spirit than that which the *Tale* seems to take as its most hated target. Its form is open in several significant ways. The 'story' it starts to tell is never properly concluded, and even its limited structure as a fable is violated by a series of deliberate digressions. Its careering, egotistical author provides, in his intense self-exposure, only the rudiments of a structure. But on the thematic, as well as the abstract intellectual level, Swift's book lies wide open to a series of violent, self-destructive antitheses which are the real heart of its openness. The intensity of its nihilist feeling reminds us of Ibsen and his recurrent suicide fantasies; the intensity of its dramatic egotism recalls us to the world of Donne. This vision of the self as splintered but central, isolated but arrogant, is one in which satire, sinking into the gulf of its own disordered vision, comes to verge on pathology. (146–68)

Ronald Paulson

from 'The Quixote Theme', *Theme and Structure in Swift's Tale of a Tub* 1960

'God help us!' exclaimed Sancho, 'did I not tell your Grace to look well, that those were nothing but windmills, a fact which no one could fail to see unless he had other mills of the same sort in his head?'
Don Quixote

The Reordering of the Parodist

The basis for the *Tale*'s reordering of the opportunist chaos it imitates can be found in three areas of seventeenth-century literature. First, there are the works of the parodists who preceded Swift in the attempt to discredit the forms we have discussed. But, second, there are the writings parodied; for we shall see that the parodists draw our attention to the possible ways of achieving order in the anti-Ciceronian forms. Finally, there are the cases of which to say that Swift merely parodied is to oversimplify; these are models for his use of the eccentric, works which achieve order out of the materials of nominalist perception and suggest to us the theme such a process may embody. The *Tale* will thus be seen to represent a curious mixture of attack from without and imitation from within; even as it attacks it draws its sustenance from the enemy. In this section we shall discuss the attackers, and see to what extent the *Tale* belongs in the area of polemics.

During the Restoration a number of writers attacked the abuses we observed in the last chapter, among them men like John Eachard and Andrew Marvell of both Anglican and Puritan allegiance. The common ground for their different attacks is the mishandling of language, or the creation of a Quixotic reality which they feel it is their duty to see through. They represent a second strain of seventeenth-century literary thought which, beginning with Bacon and Hobbes, had been busy searching for the tangible and definite in the vague and rhetorical.[1] 'Wit', 'fancy' and 'imagination' had become words which evoked the Quixotic reality, as we can see in Locke's distinction between wit and judgement:

Wit [lies] most in the assemblage of ideas, and putting those together with quickness and variety, wherein can be found any resemblance or congruity, thereby to make up pleasant pictures, and agreeable visions in the fancy; judgement, on the contrary, lies quite on the other side, in separating carefully, one from another, ideas, wherein can be found the least difference; thereby to avoid being misled by similitude, and by affinity to take one thing for another (*An Essay Concerning Human Understanding*, 1690).

Wit is a combining and judgement a separating, a creative as opposed to a critical function. The beauty of metaphor, Locke adds, 'appears

1 For a discussion of this trend, see M. Price, *Swift's Rhetorical Art*, Yale University Press, 1953, pp. 1–14.

at first sight, and there is required no labour of thought to examine what truth or reason there is in it'.

In the seventeenth century a closer look was rendered necessary by two factors. One, we have seen, was the advocation of reform in language, a reaction against the excesses of both metaphysical wit and nonconformist zeal, which, in their different ways, emphasized *words* to such an extent that the reaction against them was itself compelled, in order to defeat them, to put a similar emphasis on words. The second factor is related to the nature of controversial writing in the period. When an answerer reproved or refuted a work he made the form of his rebuttal largely dependent on that work, following it argument for argument, sometimes page for page. Enough quotation had to be given from the work under attack to guide a reader.[1] With these treatises giving themselves up to the form of the catalogue, rather than allowing meaning to evolve a form of its own, it would appear that an anatomy had been produced to end all anatomies. But, in fact, the result sometimes only bore the appearance of an anatomy.

The method employed by Eachard was to pick up some words of the enemy – often submerged metaphors – and run away with them, thereby, first, showing their absurdity and, second, drawing from them his own meaning, which would at least appear to have been implicit in the enemy's original words. Then in the ensuing pages, while Eachard continues the ostensibly plodding pursuit of the enemy's argument, the metaphor he has unloosed is playing around it with its own sharp comment.

The critique in question is Eachard's *Some Observations upon the Answer* (1671) to his *Contempt of the Clergy*, which, significantly, dealt with the problem of language and meaning.[2] Having pointed out the deficiencies in the education and preaching of the clergy, he was accused by John Bramhall of breeding contempt for Anglican divines. This being the basis of argument, it is natural that he pounces

1 Cf. Price, op. cit., pp. 11–12, who attributes this to the need for holding the opponent down to his words, with the ideal form the dialogue. This practice of following the opponent's argument was not, of course, originated in the seventeenth century.

2 The book he answered was John Bramhall's *An Answer to a Letter of Enquiry into the Grounds and Occasions of the Contempt of the Clergy*, 1671.

upon Bramhall's use of language. Eachard begins his answer remarking, 'What service you or I should do to Church or State, by *cracking of nuts*, I do not understand.'[1] The italics announce that he has picked up some words of his opponent's, and he immediately adds, 'excepting the case of *chestnuts*, upon which, as it has been reported, the Kingdom of *Naples* has some mysterious dependence'. A few pages later he picks up the submerged metaphor again, interpreting it literally: 'e're he closes up his *Preface*, [Bramhall] sets my unwilling teeth to the difficult task of *cracking nuts*'. But just before this, he has turned an abstraction used by Bramhall into a sensory image which picks up another of Bramhall's submerged metaphors: 'he falls into such a commendation of me, for *joining the credit and the serviceableness of the clergy together*, as if he would have fed me with nothing but *sugar-sops* and *soft jellies*'.[2] This, followed directly by the reference to '*cracking nuts*', implies that the sugar-sops and soft jellies are to soften and weaken his teeth in order to catch him short with the nuts. Accordingly, Eachard succeeds in not only pointing out the casualness of his opponent's language but also in drawing from his metaphor a meaning of his own. The new implication can be either a logical conclusion the enemy had not foreseen when he set the metaphor going, or, since any metaphor allows a number of possible interpretations, the recognition of a different point of analogy.

The second function of Eachard's technique, then, is to impose his own form upon the form of his opponent, which he ostensibly follows. While along the surface he is laboriously meeting his opponent's arguments, one after the other, the nutcracking image is allowed to lead into the metaphor of dining, as we have seen, which blossoms luxuriantly when Eachard quotes Bramhall as inviting him '*very kindly to hear him preach ... one of the best of his sermons*'. He fears that Bramhall will tell him '*that his text is like a spiritual sack-*

1 Bramhall had remarked that 'if all were true, unless the author could probably think he might do some good service to the Church in this essay, he had better have been cracking of nuts all the while, they would not so much have hurt his teeth, as his teeth have hurt us'.

2 A little earlier he [Bramhall] had slipped into another submerged metaphor when he remarked that Eachard's book 'possibly ... hath been accounted none of the most unsavoury sauces to [the] late Christmas Cheer' of the unchurchly. As we see, Eachard joins the two metaphors.

posset', and he ends by pouring out a cascade of dining images, the effect of which is not simply to throw back at Bramhall with interest his metaphor, but rather to demonstrate the appropriateness of the metaphor to the kind of preaching they are discussing, where the congregation's senses are more aroused than its intelligence.

Meaning advances in a different way here than in an ordinary treatise. Eachard may take a particular point of his opponent's, like his employing Homer as an authority, and spend a long amusing digression playing on the fabulous nature of this Homer. The digression reflects contempt for the opponent's emphasis on Homer; but whereas in the original such a digression carries away the author's thought, in the parody it advances the satirist's theme. And this action is, of course, necessary, because these writers – whether directly like Eachard or indirectly like Marvell – are writing against abuses of language, and however much they parody their opponent, they must present an ideal of proper rhetoric themselves. Eachard's ideal is the preacher who 'has the command of true and useful *rhetoric*; discerning what words are most proper and intelligible'.

Marvell's *The Rehearsal Transprosed* (part 1, 1672, part 2, 1673) is important in this connexion because it carries the method we are examining further than Eachard's work does, and also because it takes a step away from dialectic toward dramatization. Whereas Eachard addresses himself to an 'Answerer', Marvell makes something of a character out of his anonymous opponent (Samuel Parker, Archdeacon of Canterbury), whom he calls Bayes after the playwright in *The Rehearsal Transprosed*.

First, as to the analysis of Bayes's language, Marvell's development of metaphor is far more elaborate than Eachard's. He quotes Bayes as saying of the Calvinists, 'There sprang up a mighty bramble on the south side the Lake Lemane, that (such is the rankness of the soil) spread and flourished with such a sudden growth, that partly by the industry of his agents abroad, and partly by its own indefatigable pains and pragmaticalness, it quite over-ran the whole Reformation.' Examining this metaphor, Marvell notices that the 'bramble' has 'agents abroad', and is itself an 'indefatigable bramble'. 'But straight our bramble is transformed to a man, and he "makes a chair of infallibility for himself" out of his own bramble timber: yet all this while we know not his name; one would suspect it might be a

Bishop Bramble.'[1] Having shown that the metaphor's denotative meaning is something not at all intended by its author, he develops its 'true' meaning. Bayes should have continued, he says, that

upon that bramble 'reasons grew as plentiful as blackberries', but both unwholesome, and they stained all the 'white aprons so' that there was no getting of it out. And then, to make a fuller description of the place, he should have added, that near to the city of roaring lions there was a lake, and that lake was all of brimstone, but stored with over-grown trouts, which trouts spawned Presbyterians, and those spawned the Millecantons of all other fanatics; that this shoal of Presbyterians landed at Geneva, and devoured all the bishops of Geneva's capons, which are of the greatest size of any in the reformed world. And ever since their mouths have been so in relish that the Presbyterians are in all parts the very cannibals of capons: insomuch, that if princes do not take care, the race of capons is in danger to be totally extinguished.

Marvell's imagination runs on and on, and it is a pity to stop here, but the point is that his metaphor is like a funnel, moving out in ever larger circles. He has accepted the active implications of 'bramble' and ignored the less pleasant ones which Bayes intended; thus, from a parasitical and prickly shrub the Calvinists become the active defenders of Protestantism and destroyers of Roman Catholics.

Marvell no longer even requires the opponent's words – instead he examines a cliché like 'to rise in the world', which expresses his view of Bayes's motive for writing his book. When Bayes is freed from 'the narrowness of the university', 'coming out of the confinement of the square-cap and the quadrangle into the open air', he begins to 'rise' – his body grows and, accepting another cliché

1 'Bramble' is a pun on Bramhall. Swift himself employs this exact method upon occasion, as in his essay on Dr Burnet: 'However, he "thanks God there are many among us who stand in the breach:" I believe they may; 'tis a breath of their own making, and they design to come forward, and storm and plunder, if they be not driven back' (A Preface to the B–p of S–r–m's Introduction to the Third Volume of the History of the Reformation of the Church of England, by Gregory Misosarum). The passage continues, taking Burnet's phrases one by one and analysing them. Price has discussed this process; see his Swift's Rhetorical Art, Yale University Press, 1953, pp. 36–56.

(heads swell with pride), his head swells 'like any bladder with wind and vapour'. His legs grow until he is so 'elevated' 'that he could not look down from top to toe but his eyes dazzled at the precipice of his stature'. Marvell exploits the similarity between *rising* 'in the world' and *rising* in spiritual ecstasy, until at last Bayes 'was seen in his prayers to be lifted up sometimes in the air, and once particularly so high that he cracked his skull against the chapel ceiling'.

As these examples suggest, Marvell also carries the unifying use of metaphor further than Eachard. One such metaphor finds its origin in Bayes's hatred of the printing press as a device for stirring up sedition. Marvell asks why Parker-Bayes has himself written so many books, considering this hatred. Lust, he concludes, is the answer: 'when a man's fancy is up, and his breeches are down;[1] when the mind and the body make contrary assignations, and he hath both a bookseller at once and a mistress to satisfy; like Archimedes, into the street he runs out naked with his invention'. The lust is, accordingly, for power and position, with a book the progeny; on the next page the metaphor is developed as a conflict of love and honor, and when passion for advancement joins the visual metaphor of growth and expansion we have followed, it turns out that, in terms of love, he is his own minion. Marvell builds to a dazzling climax.

For all this courtship had no other operation than to make him
still more in love with himself; and if he frequented their
[the ladies'] company, it was only to speculate his own baby
in their eyes. But being thus, without competitor or rival, the
darling of both sexes in the family and his own minion; he grew
beyond all measure elated, and that crack of his skull, as in broken
looking glasses, multiplied him in self-conceit and imagination.

Thus, the metaphor of love contributes to the metaphor of expansion, and expansion leads to the cracked skull when it is confined by natural limits. Then the crack in the skull leads to crack-in-mirror, and the mirror, representing vanity, when broken suggests madness; and madness is what follows in the next pages. Finally, the metaphor of love continues intermittently until it is implied that the affair has

---

1 Cf. 'a *pair of breeches*, which . . . is easily slipped down for the service of [nastiness and lewdness]'. The rhythm of the sentence suggests the passage which begins 'But when a man's fancy . . .'.

given Parker a venereal disease and that the book is an illegitimate child.

Another unifying element in Marvell's book is the figure of Bayes and the continued, if sketchy, filling in of his grotesque portrait. Not content merely to quote the opponent's solecisms, Marvell builds up the image of the corrupt imagination itself in the character he addresses. He names him Bayes, he explains, 'chiefly because Mr Bayes and he do very much symbolize [i.e. resemble each other], in their understandings, in their expressions, in their humor, in their contempt and quarrelling of all others, though of their own profession'. As we have seen, Bayes largely represents opportunism and casuistry. When asked the plot of his last play he answers, 'Faith, sir, the intrigo's now quite out of my head: but I have a new one in my pocket.' Bayes comes to Marvell as an example of the imagination run wild, with but a single assumption upon which all his creation is built: divert and hold the attention of the audience.[1] Thus, once Bayes is established as the opponent, and to some extent dramatized, he comes to *represent* the solecism, and any cliché becomes a manifestation of Bayes.

While the name 'Bayes' wears out its usefulness before Marvell has finished with it and his reiteration of 'Holla, Mr Bayes' becomes tiresome, it is nevertheless important to notice a line of descent for Swift's Grub Street Hack. For the Hack is a sort of Bayes, who is trying to create a diversion which, like Bayes's play, never really gets under way. Marvell's transprosing of Bayes is an intermediate step which may have suggested to Swift that the logical end was to let Bayes speak for himself.

What we have seen in writers like Eachard and Marvell is an awareness of language, a preoccupation with metaphor, and a sharp eye for cliché, which remorselessly sees through the shabby pretenses of language – through language as a cloak for nonmeaning or false meaning. Bayes best demonstrates the intention behind the practice of both Eachard and Marvell, which is either to absorb the enemy into a fiction of their own making or to create such a fiction around him like a cocoon; in either case the satirist has put him into a special

1 Parker, too, is made to appear an opportunist and a turncoat: Marvell claims that he was a Nonconformist before the Restoration, and thereafter a staunch Anglican.

world which does not work on his assumptions, in which his words and actions make him appear the fool. The preoccupation with language can be seen, in this light, as a way of taking a cornerstone from the enemy himself, and so implying that it is really his own world that is defeating him.

Putting the enemy in an alien context is, of course, the general method which characterizes Augustan satire, whether Roman or English. The enemy is made to appear an outsider, against all of *us*, and so we judge him by the standards of the *insiders*. But the particular techniques we have examined in Eachard and Marvell are Swift's most immediate source for the linguistic-type satire of *A Tale of a Tub*. That he was thoroughly familiar with the seventeenth-century polemicists in general and the parodists in particular is proved by the scores of specific echoes of their writings in the *Tale*. But Swift's indebtedness is quite balanced by the ways in which he differs from his predecessors. One difference, which we shall develop in the next section, is that in the *Tale* the pointing out of the error and the development of the metaphor have been eliminated together with the satirist, so that only the fiction remains. More important perhaps, the difference between the development of metaphor in Marvell and that which we shall trace in the *Tale* lies in the fact that Marvell's sounds more like the reiteration of a single point than the development of a theme. The metaphor that led up to Parker's rising to the ceiling and cracking his skull is carefully constructed; it says brilliantly that Parker is ambitious, proud and unaware of reality – but when this is said, we are left with nothing more than an *ad hominem* point scored. Thereafter, every time the metaphor is recovered a bell rings and Parker is reproached again; but no theme independent of the individual Parker is developed.

The Voice of the Hack

A way to approach the difference between these earlier satirists and Swift is to examine the tone of a style which is common to both and to see how differently Swift has utilized it. An example of this tone in the *Tale* is the familiar sentence from the digression on madness: 'Last week I saw a woman *flayed*, and you will hardly believe how much it altered her person for the worse.' If the first member shocks, we notice that the second implicates the reader, making an appeal to his imagination. By saying 'you will hardly believe' the speaker avoids having to describe a scene but implies that it is too vivid to be expressed. Such a phrase, pointing with wonder at the flayed woman, has an odd effect upon the reader, which I shall try to trace.

This tone is one aspect of a style which became prevalent after the Restoration, called by some raillery, by others banter.[1] If I prefer the term raillery it is because I think of it as implying monologue, while banter suggests dialogue or witty intercourse. Another reason is that the kind of argument found before the Restoration, in such writers as Nashe, Harvey and Milton, and that found after, in Marvell, Dryden and Eachard, share the noun raillery; but the verb of the first is *rail*, which is to utter abuse or invective, while the verb of the second is *rally*, which is to utter 'good humoured ridicule'.[2] A distinction may be noted if we compare a passage from a Restoration railer,

1 See H. MacDonald, 'Banter in English Controversial Prose after the Restoration', *Essays and Studies by Members of the English Association*, vol. 32, 1946, pp. 21–9. MacDonald cites a number of interesting examples, though he does not attempt to define the style. Ian Watt has an altogether different interpretation of 'banter' in 'The Ironic Tradition in Augustan Prose from Swift to Johnson', *Restoration and Augustan Prose*, William Andrews Clark Memorial Library, Los Angeles, 1956, p. 23.

2 I am using 'raillery' as I find it in the works discussed, not, for example, as Swift himself defines it, although his definition does give an indication of what I find. While he restricts 'raillery' to slight subjects, referring to it mainly in connexion with conversation or with poems he addresses to his friends, he defines it as 'something that at first appeared a reproach or reflection; but, by some turn of wit unexpected and surprising, ended always in a compliment . . .' ('Essay on Conversation').

Another possible source which may contribute to the tone of the Hack's style should be noticed. This is the tone of the cheerfully meretricious hack works like Dunton's *Voyage round the World*, which were doubtless the object of Swift's parody, but which tell us little about the operation of his satire. It will be sufficient to compare the tone (the subject matter is, of course, being parodied too) in passages like the Hack's claim that he is 'confident to have included and exhausted all that human imagination can *rise* or *fall* to' and Dunton's assurance that the reader will find in his work 'the whole description of, I *scorn* to say one *country*, one *age or one world*; but of all the habitable and uninhabitable creation'; or note another utterance of Dunton's that could have been the Hack's: 'Could you know all the good things in this book, without my telling it you, and so buy it, and be happy, I'd die before I'd give it all this commendation' (Cf. the Hack's preface).

Richard Bentley, on a long-dead monk, with one from Marvell's attack on Parker:

> That idiot of a monk has given us a book, which he calls
> the *Life of Aesop*, that, perhaps, cannot be matched in any
> language, for ignorance and nonsense.
> The whole *Posse Archidiaconatus* was raised to repress me, and
> great riding there was, and sending post every way to pick
> out the ablest ecclesiastical drolls to prepare an answer.[1]

Invective reveals too much emotion, too much personal commitment on the part of the speaker. If we are amused by the exaggeration it is at Bentley himself, the fussy pedant who uses words like 'ignorance and nonsense', creating with them a self-portrait. The tone of Marvell's passage is set by the inversion 'and great riding there was', which, while also a device of emphasis (the riding *was* prodigious), succeeds in giving the impression that this is not quite the real world. The words have an air of the superlative about them – they are the *most*: 'whole *Posse*' and 'ablest ... drolls'. Taking these adjectives with the almost gestural 'every way', we have one characteristic of the style in question: there is always something about a passage of raillery that makes the reader almost *see* an expansive gesture being made by the speaker. And this suggests a special relationship between speaker and reader, which we shall examine in due course. But put briefly, Marvell has stopped short a moment in his argument and sketched in a world where ecclesiastics form posses and run around looking for the drollest of their brethren. Presupposing the truth (that the church authorities had looked for a wit to answer him), he creates an alternative truth, a *different* reality. In Bentley's passage only the 'perhaps', a single qualification, suggests the beginning of a line of deviation from the real as Bentley saw it; Marvell has abandoned reality and has created a fiction about his problem. It is in this way that the Hack draws our attention to the picture of the dissection, setting it off from ordinary reality.

1 Richard Bentley, *A Dissertation upon the Epistles of Themistocles, Socrates, Euripides, etc. and the Fables of Aesop*, printed with William Wotton, *Reflections upon Ancient and Modern Learning*, 1705, p. 466; Marvell, *The Rehearsal Transprosed* in E. Thompson (ed.), *The Works of Andrew Marvell, Esq., Poetical, Controversial and Political*, 1776, vol. 2, p. 37.

The fiction is less a defining point of raillery than one of its characteristics. For the rhetorical implications of the method, Shaftesbury's
account of raillery in his 'Essay on the Freedom of Wit and Humour'
has not been bettered. One point he makes is that raillery is a disguise.

If men are forbid to speak their minds seriously on certain
subjects, they will do it ironically. If they are forbid to speak
at all upon such subjects, or if they find it really dangerous to
do so; they will then redouble their disguise, involve
themselves in mysteriousness, and talk so as hardly to be
understood, or at least not plainly interpreted, by those who
are disposed to do 'em mischief.[1]

That is, the relationship between speaker and reader is an intimate,
almost secret one; and this is why raillery is found in personal letters
and in the little talk of lovers. When it is published, as a book for the
public, the reader is given a flattering sense of being on the inside,
one of the initiate.

Shaftesbury says further, speaking of the familiarity implicit in
raillery, that it is 'that sort of freedom which is taken amongst
gentlemen and *friends*, who know one another perfectly well'. The
important word, 'freedom', implies a conversational style, but more
than that a style that is free, as one is in the company of friends, to
blossom suddenly into fancy or fantasy: into the new world we saw
Marvell or Eachard create. For example, Swift, in an early letter, tries
to explain away a reported interest in a girl of Leicester:

How all this suits with my behaviour to the woman in hand
you may easily imagine, when you know that there is
something in me which must be employed, and when I am
alone turns all, for want of practice, into speculation and
thought; insomuch that in these seven weeks I have been here,
I have writ, and burnt and writ again, upon almost all
manner of subjects, more perhaps than any man in England
(*Correspondence*, I 3–4).

Swift's case is that his advances to women are just symptoms of an
overabundance of energy, other symptoms of which are writing and

1 Anthony Ashley Cooper, 3rd Earl of Shaftesbury, *Characteristicks of Men,
Manners, Opinions, Times*, vol. 1, 1713, pp. 71–2.

speculating. He gives the impression of energy through the contrast of extravagant universals with particulars. 'The woman in hand', as related to his 'behaviour', is contrasted to 'all' – 'all this', 'something . . . which . . . turns all', 'all manner of subjects'. The sentence unfolds like a flower, ever moving outward in the direction of extravagance: from the specific woman to the generalization of his condition in terms of all England.

The line that separates Bentleyan abuse and raillery in Swift's letters can be seen in the following fragment, from the letter about the Leicester girl: 'the obloquy of a parcel of very wretched fools, which I solemnly pronounce the inhabitants of Leicester to be'. 'Solemnly pronounce' does the trick: it puts the frame of the speaker's own idiosyncrasy around the utterance and makes him complicitous; it shifts the argument in the direction of drama.

One other characteristic of raillery which should be mentioned, because of its appropriateness to the Hack, is the preposterous gesture at ordering words and ideas. The more ordered the expression the further it moves from the representation of concrete reality. 'I think you may henceforth reckon yourself easy, and have little [to] do besides serving God, your friends and yourself.' The complex relations of life are reduced to one of service, and experience is radically simplified by the contrasting hyperboles of 'easy' and the triad of services. Service itself is reduced to a triad of obligations.

In the *Tale* the tone we have examined colors almost every utterance of the Hack. 'I confess to have for a long time born a part in this general error; from which I should never have acquitted myself, but through the assistance of our noble *moderns*; whose most edifying volumes I turn indefatigably over night and day, for the improvement of my mind, and the good of my country'. This can be considered as exaggeration piled on by Swift to crush the speaker; I prefer to think of it as the Hack creating a picture of himself turning the pages of books without pause all day and all night. 'Confess' sets up the pose, or the imaginary scene; and the generalizing parallels attempt to equate the Hack's mind and his country.[1] Perhaps the

1 An example of this sort of attempt to order can be seen in a small stylistic quirk like the Hack's use of doublets: 'the sharp with the smooth, the light and the heavy, the round and the square'. In a single paragraph we find 'defects' divided into 'number and bulk', 'art to sodder and patch', 'flaws and im-

most noticeable characteristic of sentences like this in the *Tale* is the curious rising action, which ends in an almost visible gesture of the speaker.

The reason for having quoted from Swift's letters of the same period as the *Tale* is that they represent the intimate relationship in which raillery operates best. Something very odd happens, accordingly, when the style is given to the enemy Swift is exposing. As the example quoted from Marvell may have suggested, it is important to remember that he and Eachard use the extravagance of this style to play with their opponent. But Marvell still keeps a steady line between himself and Bayes. It is Marvell who rallies and who makes the images grow larger and larger, not Bayes. The devices we have examined are used by Eachard and Marvell to set off the special world in which the reader judges the enemy.

If this style is given to the opponent to speak it has the odd effect, first, of making him a sort of friend or confidant; here, where we have all the apparatus of runaway metaphors and violated language, the Hack's function becomes one of exposing *himself*. Second, the placing of this style on the figure of the Hack tends to make him more of a fiction; it creates a figure who is trying to reorder reality and who at every step points to his handiwork. What succeeds in keeping him a comic figure are these gestures of showing, unaccompanied by self-awareness. He is forever finding something out of place – like a picture crooked on a wall – which he tries to set straight, in the process knocking over something else.

Third, like raillery, irony also involves two audiences, a 'censor' and a friend; but the audience directly addressed is the 'censor' who must be fooled, while in raillery the intimate friend is directly addressed. This is the reason for the odd effect of the irony in the *Tale*, where the reader is to some extent both audience and accomplice.

Finally, because the guiding hand of the satirist is not so evident as in the work of Marvell and Eachard and because the gesturing Hack

---

perfections of nature', a science of 'widening and exposing' flaws, man's 'fortunes and dispositions', the '*films* and *images*' of the '*superficies* of things', 'the sower and the dregs' of nature, 'philosophy and reason' and 'the sublime and refined point of felicity'. These will be seen in chapter three [of *Theme and Structure in Swift's Tale of a Tub*] to be reflections of the idea that everything can be ordered by being reduced to *two*.

is all that is in sight, the reader feels himself to be in a world in which reality, rather than the satirist, is the Hack's opponent.

For example, when the Hack, after using a number of images in which the moderns are the light and the ancients darkness, says that moderns have 'eclipsed the weak and glimmering lights of the *ancients*', the word itself seems to assert its true meaning in this context of light and dark.[1] By 'eclipse' he means 'hide or extinguish' the luster of the ancients, to cancel them out; but in the context of the metaphor he has set going, an eclipse is 'the interposition of a dark celestial body between a luminous one and the eye'(Webster). Thus the darkness of the moderns conceals the light of the ancients. Then, a page or so later, he speaks of the '*save-all*', for want of which, if the *moderns* had not lent their assistance, we might yet have wandered *in the dark*'. A 'save-all,' as the footnote tells, holds candle ends so they may be burned to the last drop. In the accepted sense of the term used, the moderns are, accordingly, the butt ends of learning.

Such examples from the metaphor of light alone could go on and on; but in these cases something more is happening than simply the Hack's committing himself to a metaphor which becomes no longer relevant. The words in these passages are not doing exactly what he wants them to do. While he wants them to have a particular meaning of his own at this moment, they stubbornly retain the meaning they have always had. When meaning splits like this and there are two levels of awareness apparent, that of the speaker and that of the reader, language has reasserted its right as sign over the Hack's employment of it as symbol.

(35–52)

Hugh Kenner

from 'James Joyce: Comedian of the Inventory', *The Stoic Comedians* 1964

There are many ways of describing *A Tale of a Tub*; let us call it one thing more, a parody of the book as a book. For its method is to

1 Light is a typical image of the 'elect', we shall see in chapter three [of *Theme and Structure*]; the Hack's speaking to an 'elect' will be seen to be another reason for the intimate tone of his discourse.

emphasize to the point of grotesqueness exactly those features which distinguish the printed book *per se*, the printed book a technological artifact, from a human document. Human documents Swift is prepared to understand, though looking around him in 1704 or thereabouts, in the first dawn of the bookseller's paradise, he can discern precious few.

Between a human document and the thing that Gutenberg's monster typically disgorges, a distinction may be discovered which turns on the intimate nature of what the brain thinks and the hand writes. For Swift, a piece of writing is properly something that exists in a personal context, where one human being is seeking to gain the confidence and understanding of another. Pamphlets like *A Modest Proposal* or the *Argument against Abolishing Christianity* depend for their effect on our understanding and approving this fact: their supposed author reposes in a state of bland rapport with readers who will respond suitably to his insinuations and share his notions of rational conduct. Though the pamphlet is anonymous, its effect is not to efface the supposed author but to generalize him; he is the obedient humble servant of whatever reader is jackass enough to find him congenial. The rapport between them, while it depraves the rational intercourse of honest men, is still an intercourse between persons: as much so, Swift might add, as an act of sodomy. By contrast Swift finds in the typical contemporary printed book no trace of the inviolable human person. *A Tale of a Tub* is not at bottom a civil letter, as a pamphlet is essentially a letter. It is anonymous because it is written by nobody, by no person, but by the autonomous book-compiling machine itself; and it addresses itself, like a public speech from the scaffold, to the public at large and to posterity – that is, to no one. *A Tale of a Tub* is the first comic exploitation of that technological space which the words in a large printed book tend to inhabit. Commerce and capital had recently discovered that printing is not simply a way of disseminating manuscripts, but that a book is an artifact of a new kind. This discovery brought with it a host of technical gimmicks which Swift regards with fascinated disquiet. We have discovered in the same way that the motion picture is not simply a way of recording plays, but a different medium; and that television is not simply a way of disseminating motion pictures, but a different medium; and each of these discoveries has brought with it an embarrassing swarm of new techniques. So it was, in Swift's day, with the book: and *A Tale of a Tub* is the register of Gutenberg technology, discerned by a man who regarded each of the book-maker's devices as a monstrous affront to the personal intercourse which letters in a dialogue culture had served to promote.

The book as book entails, then, Introductions, Prefaces, Apologies and Dedications; Headings, Subheadings; Tables, Footnotes, Indices; even Pictures. The way in which some of these help mechanize the act of discourse is perfectly plain. Take the footnote, for instance.[1] The footnote's relation to the passage from which it depends is established wholly by visual and typographic means, and will typically defeat all efforts of the speaking voice to clarify it without visual aid. Parentheses, like commas, tell the voice what to do: an asterisk tells the voice that it can do nothing. You cannot read a passage of prose aloud, interpolating the footnotes, and make the subordination of the footnotes clear,[2] and keep the whole sounding natural. The language has forsaken a vocal milieu and a context of oral communication between persons, and commenced to take advantage of the expressive possibilities of technological space.

This ventriloqual gadget, the footnote, deserves some attention, partly because Swift became a great virtuoso on this new instrument, and Joyce later devoted a whole section of *Finnegans Wake* to ringing changes on the footnote and its cousin the marginalium. One would like to know when it was invented; it is as radical a discovery as the scissors or the rocking chair, and presumably as anonymous. The man who writes a marginal comment is conducting a dialogue with the text he is reading; but the man who composes a footnote, and sends it to the printer along with his text, has discovered among the devices of printed language something analogous with counterpoint: a way of speaking in two voices at once, or of ballasting or modifying or even bombarding with exceptions[3] his own discourse without interrupting it. It is a step in the direction of discontinuity: of

1 I do not mean the scholar's footnote which supplies a reference, but the footnote that supplements, qualifies, parallels, quips, digresses or elucidates.
2 And they are often less subordinated than counterpointed.
3 Some footnotes of course seem totally unrelated to the point in the text at which they are appended. They suggest an art form like the refrains in Yeats's late poems.

organizing blocks of discourse simultaneously in space rather than consecutively in time. We encounter its finest flower in the immense scheme of annotation to the final edition of the *Dunciad Variorum*, a project in which it is customary to discern Swift's hand. *The Dunciad*, like *A Tale of a Tub*, is not only a satire against the abuses of the Gutenberg era, but an exploitation of technical devices made available by that era. Because print enables us to distinguish verse from prose at once by eye, we may here observe, page by page, an Attic column of verse standing on a thick pedestal of miscellaneous learning. Or the verse plunges majestically forward amid a strangely orderly babel of commentaries, assailed at random by every fly in Grub Street. Very often the note is needed to complete a poetic effect; Mr Empson has analysed a famous instance of this. And Pope's intricate mosaic of allusions to other poems, it is pertinent to remark, depends for its witty precision on a prime assumption of the Dunces, namely that poetry is to be found exclusively in books, that the texts of past classics are as stable as mosaic tiles (having been quick-frozen by the printer), and that someone with fingernail scissors and a little bottle of paste can rearrange the general stock of literature to produce new beauties. The Dunces themselves, of course, do this all the time; Pope is always careful to imitate their every mannerism with insolent fidelity; and it is the easier to do because metrical varieties have become so standardized, like that standardization of machine-screw threads which today makes possible an international technology.

We called the footnote[1] a device for organizing units of discourse discontinuously in space rather than serially in time. The same is true of the Introductions, Dedications and Digressions with which the *Tale* is so lavishly equipped. They all of them instance and exploit the essential discontinuity of the book as book. The introductory matter expands to a heroic scale certain printers' conventions. A conventional heading in large capital letters suffices to legitimize the presence in a book of almost anything the author and bookseller choose: flattery of some patron, for instance, which we can incorporate into any book at all simply by heading it *Dedication*. Swift allows the eponymous author of the *Tale* to plume himself mightily on his own capacity for sheer miscellaneousness, and carries this theme into the

1 In the middle of the previous paragraph. Please pay attention.

text itself by the device of interpolating immense Digressions, each headed 'Digression' to prevent any earnest reader from supposing that he is losing the thread. The first section of the book proper (headed Section One: the Introduction) makes a great pother about the various conditions for the oral delivery of wisdom: from the pulpit, the stage itinerant, the scaffold and perhaps the bench; but nothing is clearer from the beginning of this book to the end than the fact that all conceivable modes of oral discourse are totally unrelated to it. The Digressions, indeed, treat not of speech or dialogue but of every aspect of bookmaking: notably indices, tables of contents, anthologies, compilations, the art of digression, the practice of criticism and the improvement of madness in the commonwealth.

(37–42)

The Poems

F. W. Bateson

'Swift's *Description of the Morning*', *English Poetry: A Critical Introduction* 1950

It is time Swift's status as a poet was reconsidered. Although his verse is uneven and often slipshod, at his best he seems to me one of the great English poets. I prefer him to Pope. Pope is a superb *talker* in verse, endlessly vivacious and amusing, but it is difficult to take him or his opinions very seriously. His pet theory of the Ruling Passion can only be described as half-baked. Swift, on the other hand, though he restricted himself to light verse, is fundamentally one of the world's most serious poets. Even his jokes have metaphysical implications. But to understand Swift he must be read in the social context of his own time.

The *Description of the Morning* was originally published in the ninth *Tatler* (28 April 1709), where it was preceded by a note by Steele, who explains that its realism is an attempt to avoid the usual neo-classic conventionalities (such as Dryden's description of night in *The Indian Emperor* which Rymer had recently extolled as the *ne plus ultra* of poetry):

Now hardly here and there a hackney coach
Appearing, showed the ruddy morn's approach.
Now Betty from her master's bed had flown,
And softly stole to discompose her own;
The slipshod 'prentice from his master's door
Had pared the dirt, and sprinkled round the floor.
Now Moll had whirled her mop with dexterous airs,
Prepared to scrub the entry and the stairs.
The youth with broomy stumps began to trace
The kennel-edge,[1] where wheels had worn the place.

1 The 'kennel' is the gutter in the middle of the street. The boy was hoping to find old nails.

The small-coal-man was heard with cadence deep,
Till drowned in shriller notes of chimney-sweep.
Duns at his lordship's gate began to meet;
And brick-dust Moll had screamed through half the street.
The turnkey now his flock returning sees,
Duly let out a-nights to steal for fees;
The watchful bailiffs take their silent stands,
And school-boys lag with satchels in their hands.
(*Poems*, I 124–5)

The opening couplets are a straightforward parody of the heroic
style. It is possible Swift had in mind a recent address to London in
Congreve's *Pindarique Ode ... On the Victorious Progress of Her
Majesty's Arms* (1706):

Rise, fair *Augusta*, lift thy head,
With golden tow'rs thy front adorn;
Come forth, as comes from *Tithon's* bed
With cheerful ray the ruddy morn.

But the parody is almost immediately abandoned for a catalogue of
the activities of a Saturday morning (the traditional 'scrubbing day')
in the West End of London. The clue to the poem's peculiar flavour –
the quality that Coleridge distinguished in Swift as *Anima Rabelaisii
habitans in sicco* (*Table Talk*, 15 June 1830) – is the juxtaposition of
what is morally neutral (the street cries, the charwoman, the boy
searching the gutter), or at most venial behaviour (the careless apprentice, the loitering schoolboy), with real social evils (the sexual im-
morality and financial irresponsibility of the upper class, the appalling
prison system). The implication is: 'This is life. Here you have a
corner of London at the beginning of the daily round. You recognize
the accuracy of the picture, don't you? A, B and C, men and women
with immortal souls, are each carrying out in an almost instinctive
way his or her particular function, side by side and yet completely
independent of each other. But some of these functions, which we all
take for granted, are criminal, aren't they? What sort of a society is
this in which you, gentle reader, are so deeply compromised?'
A paradox emerges. Like the Yahoos, these Londoners are human

beings and yet they are *not* human beings. The dissociated individual, mechanically pursuing his own professional function, irrespective of its social consequences, and oblivious of the activities of his neighbours, possesses none of the qualities that constitute real humanity. In the terminology of *The Battle of the Books*, he is a spider and not a bee.

The social order that Swift is attempting to discredit in this poem is the *laissez-faire* individualism of urban capitalism, and the moral that he is enforcing is the Christian one that we are members of one another. 'Only connect.' But behind the ethical humanism, giving it depth and force, is something more primitive – the countryman's sense of fact. It is this conviction of actuality that makes the poem refreshing instead of depressing. Bad though the state of the towns may be there is no need to despair, Swift implies, as long as it is possible to face the facts of the situation. The amoral urban automata, once seen in their true light, *must* become objects of contempt. There is also an implicit contrast between the uncreative activities of London – even the coalman and the charwoman, whose professions might be thought useful, are only engaged in moving carbon from one place to another – and the rural partnership of man with nature. 'The difference is, that, instead of dirt and poison, we have rather chosen to fill our hives with honey and wax, thus furnishing mankind with the two noblest of things, which are sweetness and light.' The tonic quality of Swift's poem derives from the *sanity* of the underlying philosophy of life. Because he was insane when he died, the nineteenth century dismissed everything that he wrote with which they did not agree as mad. Today it is the Victorian division of labour and the Victorian piling up of *things* that seem mad. Swift's special distinction is that he exposed *laissez-faire* capitalism, and all that it stands for, while it was still no bigger than a cloud the size of a man's hand.

To some extent Swift's satiric effectiveness derives from the attitude he adopts towards his readers. This is different from either Dryden's or Pope's, or indeed any of his contemporaries. As James Sutherland has pointed out in a useful pioneer survey (*A Preface to Eighteenth Century Poetry*, 1948) of the poet's audience in the eighteenth century, the reading public Swift was addressing was not primarily that of the upper classes of society:

It was his practice, we are told, to have two of his men-servants brought in to listen to his poems being read, 'which, if they did not comprehend, he would alter and amend, until they understood it perfectly well, and then would say, *This will do: for I write to the vulgar, more than to the learned*' [*Works*, 1762, vol. 1, 'To the Reader']. How well he succeeded may be seen on almost any page of his poetical works, where the idiomatic and familiar style carries his meaning easily and forcibly to the least learned reader. But here, as in some other matters, Swift was not wholly at one with his age.

Sutherland appears to impute eccentricity to Swift. In reality, in my opinion, he was not at one with his age only because he transcended it. The poems were, of course, read by the aristocracy. The parody in the opening lines of the *Description of the Morning* would only have been intelligible to the polite world. But Swift's uniqueness in his century lay in his ability to appeal to several social levels in one and the same work. It is this that sets him by Chaucer and Shakespeare.

Unlike Pope Swift's principal object as a satirist is not to get the reader 'on his side' against his enemies. The futility of such satire is the subject of his recurrent scorn. 'Satire is a sort of glass, wherein beholders do generally discover everybody's face but their own; which is the chief reason for that kind reception it meets in the world, and that so very few are offended with it'.[1] Swift's technique, on the contrary, is to insinuate himself into the enemy ranks disguised as a friend, and once he is there to spread all the alarm and despondency he can. 'I never wonder', he wrote in *Thoughts on Various Subjects*, 'to see men wicked, but I often wonder to see them not ashamed.' It was above all a sense of shame that he tried to inculcate in the capitalists of the middle class. In *A Modest Proposal for Preventing the Children of Ireland from being a Burden to their Parents or Country* (1729), perhaps the greatest of the prose ironies, the real object of Swift's attack is not, as is often asserted, the Irish policy of the Whig Government. The satire goes much deeper. It is an exposure of a whole social philosophy, of which the English economic discrimination against

1 *The Battle of the Books*, 'The Preface of the Author'. F. R. Leavis has a brilliant exposition of Swift's satiric methods, in *Determinations*, Chatto & Windus 1934, pp. 79-108.

Ireland was only one instance. As in the *Description of the Morning*, which can be considered an early experiment in the *genre* perfected in *A Modest Proposal*, it is again competitive capitalism that Swift is trying to discredit, but the mode of insinuation is more carefully chosen. The satire in the *Description* had camouflaged itself behind the parody of a recognized literary form. As such, however, it cannot have been likely to have attracted the attention of the City merchants, who were Philistines almost to a man. The trap had the wrong kind of bait. *A Modest Proposal*, on the other hand, talks the actual language of Cheapside and Threadneedle Street. It is to all appearances another essay in the 'political arithmetic' that was so popular in the City of London during the later seventeenth and early eighteenth centuries. The tone of voice, the method of argument, the statistical approach are exactly the kind of thing that the business world of the time had been accustomed to meet in the pamphlets of Sir William Petty, Charles Davenant and Daniel Defoe. Here was their old friend the Economic Man! The opening paragraphs have lulled any suspicions that Swift's authorship might have aroused, and the reader, who finds the Economic Man disposing of his surplus children to the butcher, is brought suddenly face to face with the contradiction between his own weekday and Sunday religions. It is the Augustan paradox, the familiar formula of the poetry of the squirearchy, but here it operates on a grander scale, charged with a higher intensity, than any of Swift's contemporaries were able to command.

(123–6)

Geoffrey Hill

from 'Jonathan Swift: The Poetry of "Reaction"', in B. Vickers (ed.), *The World of Jonathan Swift* 1968

The somewhat complex question of raillery as an eighteenth-century social and literary phenomenon has been the subject of much able and detailed discussion. In terms of pure theory it is possible to distinguish two major types: 'ironical praise that is really satire or reproof' and its opposite, 'something that at first appeared a reproach or reflection; but, by some turn of wit unexpected and surprising, ended always in a compliment, and to the advantage of the person it was addressed to'. Swift favoured, in principle, the second type and was particularly careful to make the distinction between constructive raillery and mere abuse:

So, the pert dunces of mankind
Whene're they would be thought refin'd,
Because the diff'rence lies abstruse
'Twixt raillery and gross abuse,
To show their parts, will scold and rail,
Like porters o'er a pot of ale.
(To Mr Delany, 1718; Poems, I 216)

In the light of these meticulous distinctions and the insistence on the social and ethical advantages of the art, one recognizes all the more sharply those occasions when it is bungled or simply set aside. When Swift was, at Market Hill, 'the neighbouring ladies', according to Faulkner, 'were no great understanders of raillery'. Market Hill was a rural estate and the implication here may be that country cousins are no match for urban wit. But it seems that these same urbanities frequently wore thin. Sheridan angered Delany and, in the end, lost Swift's friendship with raw remarks that were ill-taken. Participants in the humorous verse 'battles', which were a feature of the intellectual circle, not infrequently lost their tempers; Swift was at various times culprit, victim and peace-maker. His own poem The Journal, describing in terms of affectionate raillery the household activities of the Rochforts and their guests, led to his being critized for abusing the hospitality of friends. The casualty rate could, admittedly, have been higher; but the point would seem to be that notwithstanding the precise distinctions between fine raillery and coarse insult, mistakes were frequently made, even by such skilled practitioners. It may seem that infringements occurred through the necessity to turn in small tight circles of mutual exacerbation and the obligation to demonstrate superior skill. Despite accidents this high-strung technique had its value in a close community, permitting the reiteration of such real or imagined values as accuracy, tact and feeling. It offered a way of beating the bounds between the permissible and the unspeakable, of driving out the drones and instructing the rest. In a letter to William Pulteney of 7 March 1737 Swift acclaimed his recipient's 'more than an old Roman spirit' which had been 'the constant subject of discourse and of praise among the whole few of what unprostituted people have remain[ed] among us' (*Correspondence*, v 7). Swift had a tendency to count heads. 'Few' and 'unprostituted' is what the drama of unity required, in the teeth of human limitation, for the sake of the *manes*. He wrote to the Earl of Oxford, 3 July 1714:

For in your public capacity you have often angered me to the heart, but, as a private man, never once. So that if I only looked towards myself I could wish you a private man tomorrow (*Correspondence*, II 44–5)

In one sense this is telling praise; in another, it is a courteous and restrained lament for the failure to achieve unity of being. In one important respect, the mutual regard of two 'unprostituted' people is everything; but at the same time, given the ideal integrity of public life, it is not enough. Perhaps this is the value for Swift, emotionally and philosophically, of the defeated man and it may be the truly creative thing that he received from the ideas and example of Sir William Temple. Defeat restores unity of being, if only hermetically and in isolation. Although critics quite properly stress the manifest differences between the early Pindarics and the mature verse, it is possible to detect a thread of continuity, a line of development starting with the Pindaric celebration of the defeated man (Temple; Sancroft), continuing through the 1716 poem to Oxford, 'How blest is he, who for his country dies', and culminating in the comic exorcisms of Swift's own defeat. His political and ecclesiastical embarrassment, his 'exile', were factors to which he personally refused to succumb, but which, as a poet, he provoked into a series of difficult encounters. The situation of *An Apology to the Lady Carteret* (1725) and *Verses on the Death of Dr Swift* (1731) is defeat, either by bodily humiliation or the trivia of daily encounters or the triumph of Philistine life, but wit converts the necessitous failure into moral and rhetorical victory. The prime significance of Swift's 'sin of wit' is that it challenges and reverses in terms of metaphor the world's routine of power and, within safe parentheses, considers all alternatives including anarchy.

Swift's attitude towards the anarchic was significantly ambiguous.

In principle he abhorred all its aspects, from lexical and grammatical to social and political; pragmatically he played along with it to some extent; poetically he reacted to it with a kindling of creative delight. While, in the main, anarchy was a mob-attribute, it is open to suggestion that Swift also recognized a Jonsonian sense of disorder, an imbalance of humours in those who governed policy or money. Viewed in this light, great bad men like Marlborough or Walpole were a threat to the Body Politic. Although Swift, in common with other contemporaries, offered analyses of raillery and although a subsequent process of scholarly abstraction has tended to give such discussions an apparent universality in Augustan literary and social debate, his work is noteworthy for its so-called 'ungenerous' and 'inexcusable' attacks on Marlborough and somewhat lesser figures like Baron Cutts and Archbishop Hort, poems in which he abandons the salon of raillery for the pillory of invective. There seems little to distinguish the tone of *The Character of Sir Robert Walpole* or the anti-Marlborough piece *On the Death of a Late Famous General* from the kind of procedure that Swift, in *To Mr Delany*, purported to despise. It should be stressed that in considering the poems themselves, when one notes the distinction between raillery and invective one is describing the difference between two equal forces rather than between superior and inferior kinds. If *Verses on the Death of Dr Swift* is the apotheosis of raillery it is equally apparent that *The Legion Club* (1736) is Swift's masterpiece of invective:

> Keeper, show me where to fix
> On the puppy pair of *Dicks*;
> By their lanthorn jaws and leathern,
> You might swear they both are brethren:
> *Dick Fitz-Baker*, *Dick* the Player,
> Old acquaintance, are you there?
> Dear companions hug and kiss,
> Toast *old Glorious* in your piss.
> Tie them keeper in a tether,
> Let them stare and stink together;
> Both are apt to be unruly,
> Lash them daily, lash them duly . . .
> (*Poems*, III 835)

Invective is a touchy subject. Sir Harold Williams, to whose re-
searches all students of Swift are indebted, writes of *The Legion Club*
as an 'uncontrolled outburst', but it is difficult to see quite what he
means. In these lines Swift describes the vicious as being also, in a
sense, helpless. 'Stare' perfectly expresses fixated energy. 'Old
acquaintance' seems equally well judged: the two 'companions',
Richard Tighe and Richard Bettesworth were well-known opponents
of Swift, participants in lengthy feuds. In the poem he makes them
'old' in the sense that the devil is 'old' Nick; that is, their sinful
madness is inveterate. This is the fusion of familiar and formal in a
word. Or consider:

> Bless us, *Morgan*! Art thou there Man?
> Bless mine eyes! Art thou the Chairman?
> Chairman to yon damn'd Committee!
> Yet I look on thee with pity.
> (*Poems*, III 837)

Here an 'impossible' rhyme (there Man/Chairman) toys with the
'impossibility' of finding a decent man like Morgan in such a place,
while its thumping obviousness simultaneously confirms his presence.
The magisterial tone quite transcends the real source of Swift's outrage, a pot-and-kettle dispute between the Irish clergy and the
landowner-dominated Irish Parliament over the question of pasturage-
tithes. It is poetically convincing and technically invulnerable: not
an 'uncontrolled outburst' but in places a deft simulation of one.
Because it is so convincing it could even be said to react upon its
source. While admitting the parochial nature of the original feud,
one is prepared to accept that universal principles of human conduct –
justice, dignity and right dealing – are here involved and that Swift's
protest is uttered on behalf of common honesty and freedom.

Supposedly 'uncontrolled' outbursts also affect that most sensitive
area of Swiftian research, the so-called 'unprintable' poems. There is
a line of defence on these which laudably aims to explode the patho-
logical fallacy but requires careful qualification. It has been said that
Swift 'is hardly more scatological than others of his contemporaries'
and Professor Ehrenpreis has drawn attention to possible parallels in
Dryden's version of Juvenal's 'Tenth Satire', in a burlesque (dated

1702) of L'Estrange's *Quevedo's Visions* and in *Le Diable Boiteux* of Le Sage. Parts of Smollett's *Humphry Clinker* constitute admissible evidence. But when all has been allowed Swift still remains more comprehensively and concentratedly scatological than his English contemporaries. One cannot seriously compare such squibs as the anonymous *On a Fart Let in the House of Commons* with *Cassinus and Peter*, or *Strephon and Chloe* with the mild and modish pornography of Prior:

At last, I wish, said she, my dear –
(And whisper'd something in his ear)

'Whisper'd something' is truly symptomatic of the mode and perhaps helps to explain by contrast the nature of Swift's verse, which cuts through that barrier of shame and coquetry where it is only too easy to excite a snigger with gestures of mock reticence. The best of Swift's scatological poems can therefore be called 'harrowing' in the true sense of that word. It is open to argument that the best are those which are most susceptible to accusations, on the part of hostile critics, of violent morbid obsession. The range of these poems is extremely varied and Swift at his worst is quite capable of polite innuendo, superior to Prior in verbal *brio* but hardly superior in ethos.

It may be proper, as a preliminary step, to establish the robustness of Swift's scatological humour:

My Lord, on fire amidst the dames,
F[art]s like a laurel in the flames.
(*The Problem*, 1699; *Poems*, III 66)

Here it subsists in the comedy of 'on fire' and 'like a laurel', in the suggestion of genial heat and sparkling Olympian success. It occurs in later work such as *Strephon and Chloe* (1731):

He found her, while the scent increas'd,
As *mortal* as himself at least.
But, soon with like occasions prest,
He boldly sent his hand in quest,
(Inspir'd with courage from his bride,)
To reach the pot on t'other side.

And as he fill'd the reeking vase,
Let fly a rouzer in her face.
(*Poems*, x 589)

'He boldly sent his hand in quest' is the language of lyrical pornography applied to an unlyrical situation. The catharsis of the episode
has been well described by Maurice Johnson who speaks of 'the
surprise of the line in which that word [rouzer] appears, startling
the reader to laughter or at least to exclamation'. It would be difficult
to find a word that blends the outrageous and the festive more
effectively than this. Swift is capable of outrage at the world of
spontaneous reflexes but he is equally offended by the false notions of
'divinity' previously entertained by Strephon about women and by
Chloe about men; hence the real importance of the perception in
'*mortal*'. In a basic sense these anarchic explosions are more real than
the sublimities of attenuated fancy but they are still grotesque,
Swift suggests, when contrasted with the proper decencies and re-
straints of life:

On sense and wit your passion found,
By decency cemented round.
(*Poems*, II 593)

But the very fact that these basic functions do have this element of
truth in the situation, and come with a mixture of unexpectedness and
inevitability, produces something of the festive energy of farce. However deliberately the retrenching moralist may stand at guard (e.g.
the routine phraseology of the concluding lines) the poetic imagination still cherishes the creatures of its invention.

It would be a mistake to enter a plea for Swift's defence merely on
the evidence of 'healthy laughter', which is something of an escapist
term and fails to cover the dominant characteristics of Swift's major
scatological work. It could be said that the embarrassments of
Strephon and Chloe are trivial and susceptible to robust treatment but
that *The Lady's Dressing Room* (1730) and *A Beautiful Young Nymph
Going to Bed* (1731) reveal an appalled, and appalling, obsession with
filth and disease; that we are far from the delighted surprise of
'rouzer' in lines like these:

The basin takes whatever comes
The scrapings of her teeth and gums,
A nasty compound of all hues,
For here she spits, and here she spews.
(*The Lady's Dressing Room* Poems, II 527)

Although this may be basically comparable to passages in Dryden and
Le Sage, its emotional and verbal concentration is undeniably unique.
So far as accusations of simple 'bad taste' are concerned, there is no
great difficulty in showing that, in terms of the eighteenth-century
conditions of life, it would be virtually impossible to exceed plain
reality. Objections on this ground alone are like the tasteful reservations of Swift's aristocratic friends, such as the Earl of Orrery, who
saw, but didn't enjoy what they saw. On the other hand it is true
that the language of such poems may seem excessive when compared
with Swift's equally unflinching work in *A Modest Proposal*. There he
can cover the small circle of a mean intelligence (the 'persona') with
the ample radius of the intellect itself and make his tacit reservations
tense with humane implication. In *A Beautiful Young Nymph* it may
seem that the superior intelligence can assert itself only by extravagant
gestures of revulsion. Notwithstanding these objections, a modern
critic who appeals to the supposed imperative of compassion is
gesturing towards little more than a modern version of pastoral. To
fret at its absence from Swift is really to miss the point:

   The Nymph, tho' in this mangled plight,
Must ev'ry morn her limbs unite.
But how shall I describe her arts
To recollect the scatter'd parts?
Or show the anguish, toil and pain,
Of gath'ring up herself again?
The bashful Muse will never bear
In such a scene to interfere.
Corinna in the morning dizen'd,
Who sees, will spew; who smells, be poison'd.
(*A Beautiful Young Nymph* Poems, II 583)

The perfect dryness of 'recollect', the charged portentousness of
'dizen'd', inviting and awaiting the sharp crack of the final rhyme-

word, have complete control over the plangencies of 'anguish, toil and pain'. If one argues for compassion here it has to be admitted that it exists principally for the eye of the beholder; and this is not a currently acceptable form today, when pity is all for the object. One would also observe that if Swift's view of Corinna is scarcely charitable neither is it unfeeling.

Professor Ehrenpreis has convincingly answered a certain kind of objection to the emotional intensity of some of Swift's scatological verse by remarking: 'The complainants' case would be best proved if Swift were *not* intense on such subjects.' The accuracy of this as a general ethical observation can be sustained, even though the immediate defence-plea for Swift is damaged, by citing *A Panegyrick on the Dean, in the Person of a Lady in the North* (1730). This poem does not seem to be among those generally selected for attack, though it ought to be. Composed as a contribution to the mirth of the Achesons at Market Hill, it is cast in the form of an address of commendation to the Dean by Lady Acheson herself. One of its main themes is the erection of two latrines on the estate and the consequent partial reformation of manners:

> Yet, some devotion still remains
> Among our harmless Northern Swains;
> Whose off'rings plac't in golden ranks,
> Adorn our crystal river's banks:
> Nor seldom grace the flow'ry downs,
> With spiral tops and copple-crowns:
> Or gilding in a sunny morn
> The humble branches of a thorn.
> (*Poems*, III 896)

One could, in theory, defend *A Panegyrick* as being an elaborate but proper complaint about the recalcitrance of human behaviour: the 'swains', having been offered hygiene, still prefer their old casual filth. The poem, however, eludes this kind of defence. If it is set against *The Lady's Dressing Room* or *A Beautiful Young Nymph*, the intensity of the sensuous attack in those poems appears as a valid human reaction; one is convinced that the virtuosity of description is necessary to contain and express the range of Swift's feelings. *A Panegyrick*, on the other hand, is Swift's only scatological poem that seems in any sense coprophilous. It is, significantly enough, the one which most nearly approaches the conditions of *salon* verse. The poem's tonality suggests that Swift is writing, not out of fascinated disgust or angry contempt, but under the obligation to amuse: it is the very coolness of the verbal draughtsmanship, the detailing of the faecal coils, that is so chilling. The fact that Swift parodies the namby-pamby of fashionable pastoral is, I think, beside the point so far as the larger issues are concerned. *A Description of a City Shower* also parodies pastoral but this fact neither explains nor limits that poem's total effect. In *A Panegyrick* any plea of parody is really an alibi for the indulgence of a taste that is itself more dubious than 'straight' pastoral. It is a pity that terms like 'perfectly calculated' have become, out of context, mere laudatory commonplaces in criticisms of Swift. As a generalization this could apply to a great deal that he wrote; but between the perfect calculation of *A Description of a City Shower*, *Verses on the Death of Dr Swift* or *The Legion Club* and the perfect calculation of *A Panegyrick* there stretches a wide terrain of ethical and aesthetic distinction.

It is possible that 'perfectly calculated' could, in some instances, be better expressed as 'predetermined' or even 'academic'. The academic Swift is a significant figure, notably in *A Proposal for Correcting, Improving and Ascertaining the English Tongue*, an attempt to pre-determine the future shape of the language in accordance with his over-riding political convictions and apprehensions. Swift's linguistic attitude is a kind of Tory stoicism, a rather simpler form of resistance than that of the poems. Its limitations are perhaps best described by Dr Johnson, in the Preface to his *Dictionary*. Johnson remarks on the futility of trying to secure language from corruption and decay and of imagining that one has the 'power to change sublunary nature, and clear the world at once from folly, vanity and affectation'. One recalls Yeats's saying that Swift 'foresaw' democracy as 'the ruin to come'. If this is so, it only intensifies the creative paradox of his poetry whose energy seems at times to emerge from the destructive element itself. In his own copy of Dr Gibbs's paraphrase of the Psalms, Swift scribbled unflattering comments alongside examples of slovenly rhyming. Of 'more–pow'r' he commented 'Pronounce this like my Lady's woman'. Yet in Swift's own poetry this lexical and grammatical arrogance is transfigured, as in such a work as *The*

Humble Petition of Frances Harris (1701). Mrs Harris was one of Lady Berkeley's gentlewoman:

Yes, says the *Steward*, I remember when I was at my Lady
  Shrewsbury's,
Such a thing as this happen'd, just about the time of
  Gooseberries.

The *Devil* take me, said she (blessing herself), if I ever saw't!
So she roar'd like a *Bedlam*, as tho' I had call'd her all to naught;
(*Poems*, 1 71)

Some years later, in 1718, Swift wrote a further poem, *Mary the Cook-Maid's Letter to Dr Sheridan*, along similar lines of character and idiom. A number of his polemical pieces adopt, or affect, the form and phrasing of the popular street-ballads of the day: *Peace and Dunkirk: Being an Excellent New Song upon the Surrender of Dunkirk* (1712); *An Elegy upon the Much-Lamented Death of Mr Demar, the famous Rich Man* (1720); *An Excellent New Song Upon His Grace Our Good Lord Archbishop of Dublin* (1724); *Clever Tom Clinch Going to be Hang'd* (1726); *The Yahoo's Overthrow; or the Kevan Bayl's New Ballad . . . to the tune of 'Derry down'* (1734). The Bagford, Pepys and Roxburghe Collections contain possible precedents and analogues, such as the anonymous *South Sea Ballad* of 1720, which could be compared and contrasted with Swift's poem, *The Bubble*, of the same year. If we refer to the confrontation of two distinct kinds of poetic tradition and method, a popular and an aristocratic, and if we relate Swift's Pindaric 'aberration' to the kind of portentous sublimity advocated by Sir William Temple in his essay *Of Heroick Virtue* (1690) there will be a temptation to claim that a timely encounter with popular colloquial verse 'redeemed' Swift as a poet. But there is no simple and obvious way in which this could be affirmed. Some of Swift's poems may have achieved immediate popular success, but one still has reservations about calling him a 'popular' poet; he did not so much use as demonstrate the colloquial; the very kind of accuracy he achieved was the result of a certain aloofness. He was able to fix his perspectives:

And so say I told you so, and you may go tell my Master; what
  care I?

And I don't care who knows it, 'tis all one to *Mary*.
Everybody knows, that I love to tell truth and shame the Devil,
I am but a poor servant, but I think gentle folks should be civil. . . .
(*Mary the Cook-Maid's Letter*, 1718; *Poems*, III 986)

If one is conscious, throughout, of the dualistic nature of Swift's genius and achievement, it is not inappropriate that so much of his energy should have been expended upon, and re-charged from, the dualistic nature of Irish life and politics, or that one should be able to find both the cold disdain and the fervent identification of the poems co-existing in the style of the *Drapier's Letters*, whose effect on the Irish people is well described by Lecky:

He braced their energies; he breathed into them something of his own lofty and defiant spirit; he made them sensible at once of the wrongs they endured, of the rights they might claim, and of the forces they possessed.

Given the current English political attitude, to be in Ireland, the 'depending kingdom', as a member of the so-called governing class was to be in a 'situation' of considerable difficulty. Swift polemically rejected the situation as a principle in the fourth *Drapier's Letter* but encountered it daily as a fact. His sensitive reaction to this situation, both personal and national, resulted in a release of creative energy which could not have been produced by the application of principle alone. Swift had little sympathy with Shaftesbury; but the crowning paradox is that his own poetry is one of the most powerful expressions in eighteenth-century English literature, prior to Blake, of that kind of resistance which the Whig philosopher so eloquently described:

And thus the natural free spirits of ingenious men, if imprisoned and controlled, will find out other ways of motion to relieve themselves in their *constraint*. . . . 'Tis the persecuting spirit has raised the *bantering* one. . . . The greater the weight is, the bitterer will be the satire. The higher the slavery, the more exquisite the buffoonery.
(202–11)

Denis Donoghue

'The Sin of Wit', *Jonathan Swift: A Critical Introduction*   1969

When we say that Swift was an occasional poet and an amateur, we mean that he took his poetry with less gravity than his prose. But we mean a little more than that. There is more to his verse than 'simple topics told in rhyme'. It is true that many of his poems give the impression of being vacation exercises: he carried his verses lightly, and put them aside with equal nonchalance. The most useful service offered him by the very existence of poetry was that it helped him to deal with several modes of experience in a relatively un-demanding spirit. There are a few poems in which he is as severe as ever, full of indignation and rebuke, but these are exceptional occasions. Most of Swift's poems are more equable than his prose: they have the effect of releasing him, now and again, from his quarrel with the world. Even when the quarrel persists, it is free from the vexation of the prose. Indeed, there were many burdens which Swift could hardly have borne at all, but for the amateur nature of his poetry.

It is clear that many of the poems were written for fun. But fun, to Swift, was an athletic exercise to keep the mind in trim. A riddle, a lampoon, anything would serve. If he could turn a local irritation into verse, he could rid himself of the bitterness attending it: 'In a jest I spend my rage.' When Thomas Rundle was appointed Bishop of Derry in February 1735, Swift resented the appointment largely, it appears, because Rundle was sponsored by the Lord Chancellor. So he wrote a skit on the Bishop, and disposed of his resentment in sixty lines. A few months later he wrote a warm account of Rundle's merits in a letter to Pope. In turn, Pope exempted Rundle from the strictures of the *Epilogue to the Satires*.

In 1934 Yeats told Oliver Edwards that in poetry he took his later manner from Swift: and, for proof and illustration, he read the third stanza of the *Ode to the Honourable Sir William Temple* (*Poems*, 1 27):

But what does our proud ign'rance learning call,
   We odly *Plato's* paradox make good,
Our knowledge is but mere remembrance all,
   Remembrance is our treasure and our food;

Nature's fair table-book our tender souls
We scrawl all o'er with old and empty rules,
   Stale memorandums of the schools;
   For learning's mighty treasures look
     In that deep grave a book,
   Think she there does all her treasures hide,
And that her troubled ghost still haunts there since she dy'd;
Confine her walks to colleges and schools,
   Her priests, her train and followers show
   As if they all were spectres too,
   They purchase knowledge at the expence
   Of common breeding, common sense,
   And at once grow scholars and fools;
   Affect ill-manner'd pedantry,
Rudeness, ill-nature, incivility,
   And sick with dregs of knowledge grown,
   Which greedily they swallow down,
Still cast it up and nauseate company.

This comes from one of the earliest poems. We are accustomed to think of it as mere 'prentice work. But if we read the *Ode* again with Yeats in mind, we see that Swift is not shamed by that relation. There are many rough patches, but there are other places in which the poem has something of that vigour, that directness, which we admire in Yeats's later work. Yeats did not say what he admired in the *Ode*. When he quoted the same stanza again, in *On the Boiler*, he gave it without comment. But we may guess that what he admired was a certain tone; we hear it in the juxtaposition of 'common breeding, common sense'; before that, in the invocation to Learning's 'troubled ghost'; further back still, in the scrawling of Nature's table-book. If we think of this as a Yeatsian tone, we mark the strength of the tradition Yeats invoked: to a large extent it is Swift's tradition, tuned for a new context. The values to which Swift appeals in the *Ode* are Yeatsian values; Nature, civility, courtesy, a certain independence of spirit. The poem implies that they are still available, though they are increasingly under attack. Swift invokes these values, and the tradition of *sprezzatura* in which they are defined, but if necessary he will speak upon his own authority. One of the most compelling marks of his poetry is its commitment to one thing at a time. The poet does not claim to say everything at once, in one poem, one book, one word. He confronts every occasion as it arises. Much of nineteenth-century poetry is so grandiose in its intention that it is unwilling to say one thing at a time. Swift takes this limitation as a matter of course. To give one example: in September 1727, he was delayed for a week at Holyhead while coming back to Dublin. He was troubled about Stella, who was ill. During those days, while he had nothing better to do, he kept a diary and scribbled verses as they occurred to him. One of them begins:

Lo here I sit at holy head
With muddy ale and mouldy bread
All Christian vittals stink of fish
I'm where my enemies would wish.
(*Poems*, II 420)

It is easy to say that this is doggerel, but it is more important to recognize the continuity between Swift's doggerel and his finest work, that the imaginative resilience of the one depends upon the strength of the other, the readiness to speak out. There is something of this continuity in Joyce, too, a movement of feeling which joins *The Holy Office* to *Ulysses*. The sense of 'muddy ale and mouldy bread' animates the great occasions in *Gulliver's Travels*, *A Modest Proposal*, the *Description of the Morning*, and the other choice things. There are certain tones in poetry which depend upon that sense; as Yeats discovered when he wrote the occasional poems in *Responsibilities* and *The Green Helmet*.

Of course Swift did not strike this note as soon as he took to verse. Largely under the influence of Cowley, he stuck to the ode for his first poems and the ode proved an intractable form. He had very little feeling for it, and as long as he clung to it, he established only a fitful relation with his true concerns. To hear him going through the motions of an ode is to mark a certain ventriloquism in his style. Henri Focillon (in *The Life of Forms in Art*, 1948) speaks of a vocation of form corresponding to a vocation of mind. There is a technical destiny in these matters. The form of the ode was intractable to Swift because it had little to do with the chief qualities of his mind. The ode spreads itself over a long stanza, the lines unequal, the

rhythm resisting definition at any point. It delights in postponement.
If the lines are not to flag, they must aspire, and the poet must accept
the excelsior note and whatever it entails. It is hard to be your own
master in the ode: Swift is uncomfortable in this restriction, even
allowing for the splendid stanzas in the *Ode to Temple*. His mind
works best in the juxtaposition of small units, in balance and adjudica-
tion, where every change of direction is under minute control. He
does not like to wait to see what is going to develop. As a poet he
distrusts the vague, transitional moments, when a thing is neither
fully itself nor something else. He is restless with things that do not
maintain their own identity. In *The Day of Judgement* he speaks of
'the world's mad business', and to Swift the main forms of that
madness were abstraction, formlessness, bogus visions, clouds of
pride. Poems were worthwhile because they were receptacles of
sense, specific things, ways of getting things done. In *Verses on the
Death of Dr Swift* he praises Pope for putting an uncommon amount
of sense into his lines:

In Pope, I cannot read a line,
But with a sigh, I wish it mine:
When he can in one couplet fix
More sense than I can do in six.
(*Poems*, II 555)

'Fix' is a spatial term; a thing is fixed in position and related there to
other things. The relation is all the better if it is static, definitive; all
the worse if it is tentative, problematic; worse still, if it is arbitrary,
imposed by human will or whim. What Swift means by 'sense' is
clear enough; thoughts that have survived the trial of experience. It
is clearer still when he puts it beside a word like 'true'. In the
imitation of Horace's *Hoc erat in votis* he writes:

And let me in these shades compose
Something in verse as true as prose;
Remov'd from all th' ambitious scene,
  Nor puff'd by pride, nor sunk by spleen.
(*Poems*, I 199)

So the 'sin of wit' which he invoked in another poem means the
unpopular force of intelligence, truth, sense, the sharp edge of

discrimination. Swift is not interested in daring flights of fancy on which new meanings may be discovered. He distrusts every ambiguous cloud of significance. He is content with the old meanings and angry that they are denied: poetry is a way of maintaining their force. This is what he means by 'fixing' the sense.

Clearly, among the available literary forms, he needed the couplet. The couplet allowed him to direct a flow of energy through single meanings and finite relationships. This is a prior condition before there can be any general significance at all; general significance, to Swift, is merely the sum of specific acts of intelligence. The facility provided by the couplet is that it requires the deployment of specific meanings, moment by moment, every shot has to count. The result is that the double vocation of mind and form enabled him to hold at bay themes which, in the prose, threatened to run wild. In poems like *The Beasts' Confession* and *On Poetry: A Rhapsody* he curbs the same themes which, in prose, drive him to violence. The couplet gives him the assurance that control, embodied in a formal tradition, is still possible:

What reason can there be assign'd
For this perverseness in the mind?
Brutes find out where their talents lie:
A *bear* will not attempt to fly:
A founder'd *horse* will oft debate,
Before he tries a five-barr'd gate:
A *dog* by instinct turns aside,
Who sees the ditch too deep and wide.
But *Man* we find the only creature,
Who, led by *folly*, fights with *Nature*;
Who, when *she* loudly cries, *Forbear*,
With obstinacy fixes there;
And, where his *genius* least inclines,
Absurdly bends his whole designs.
(*Poems*, II 640-41)

If the tone is rueful, it is still safe. One reason for this urbanity, in a writer to whom urbanity comes hard, is that in English literature the tradition in which such comment is securely made is largely a verse tradition. The serious part of the tradition issues in the satires of Dryden and Pope; the burlesque part in Butler and John Philips. Swift could choose; the conventions were well established. In prose fiction the lines were not at all clear: it was much harder to conceive how the work might be done. The tradition of English verse satire, going back from Pope and Dryden through Donne, Raleigh and Greville to Lyndsay, the Scottish satirists and beyond, was a more complete accomplishment: it was in close relation to the great dramatic tragedies, for one thing. The satiric couplet in the early eighteenth century is the direct inheritor of this tradition; hence its vitality in the hands of Pope, Gay and Johnson. True, the tradition had changed between Raleigh and Pope: changed, and narrowed. Even in Pope there is little sense of the tragic dimension within which, in Raleigh, the individual reflection is made. The context of feeling in Pope is narrower than in Raleigh, mainly because the religious sense, the stress of that kind of implication, is weaker. There is nothing in Pope, or even in *The Vanity of Human Wishes*, to set beside Raleigh's *Even Such is Time*:

Even such is time, which takes in trust
Our youth, our joys, and all we have,
And pays us but with age and dust;
Who, in the dark and silent grave,
When we have wandered all our ways,
Shuts up the story of our days,
And from which earth and grave and dust,
The Lord shall raise me up, I trust.

By the time we reach Swift and Pope, this sense of age and dust has been replaced by a sense of social error and absurdity; if the cast is larger than ever, the screen is narrower than before. It is, in another form, the difference between the sermons of Donne and Swift; Donne in the sermons is a voice in the night, heavy with mortality; Swift's sermons are digests, the daily dozen of sensible exercises, 'what every Englishman should know'.

But Swift confronts the incorrigible themes, in the poems, with vigour and resource which are partly personal and partly traditional. The themes are those which irritate the prose: it is still the old, inescapable story – the vanity of human delusion, the decay of intelligence. The concern which reverberates through the poems is the fear that intelligence is beaten, that the enemies are already at the gate. The chief enemy is 'the slagheap of the unconscious', the realm of chaos and 'old night' invoked in Pope's *Dunciad*. Pope and Swift are determined to force things into the light of day. Swift goes even further than Pope in exposing whatever is dark or subliminal: so that even when he writes an occasional poem, he always keeps his mind focused on the object: to push things into the daylight of common sense, to force them into definition.

Already in Swift's day this seemed a last-minute attempt to hold the fort. One of the most remarkable developments in eighteenth-century literature is that within twenty-five years after the publication of *The Dunciad* the unconscious was considered the chief source of poetic vision. The slagheap became a mine. The crucial term in the story is imagination: in the first years of the eighteenth century it was still considered a wild and unreliable power. But by the middle of the century it had been promoted. Thomas Warton objects to Pope's poetry because it lives in sunlight, the world of the understanding, rather than the more subtle twilight of the imagination. Indeed, when Pope used images of darkness and night to represent the loss of clarity, form and intelligence, he stood on ground which was already shifting beneath his feet. Within a remarkably short time these images, despite the ridicule visited upon them in *Peri Bathous* and elsewhere, acquired a new and paradoxical 'radiance': the most profound visions were now available, it seemed, at night, and the moon took the place of the sun as the visionary power. The new text is Addison on the pleasures of the imagination. The suggestion is that the effect of the white light of reason is to enforce the separation of man from nature. The light of reconciliation is twilight, when the pleasures of imagination are available without rational effort. Along with this, there is a new assumption, that the crucial events take place within the mind; not outside. Admittedly, the materials, the sensations, come into our minds from outside, but as long as we agree with Locke that these sensations are the primary data, nothing in their origin is as important as their history within the individual mind. Psychology replaces politics (see E. L. Tuveson, *The Imagination as a Means of Grace*, 1960). It is easy to see why Swift would not speak the new language: to him, what happened inside the mind, in most cases, was delusion; the important events were public, social, political;

administrative acts performed to make the world a more tolerable place. Swift had the deepest suspicion of those who would have the great dramas enacted within the mind; much of his work is a demonstration of this absurdity. But he was the last great writer to maintain that position. The new feeling was expressed, at least in part, by Addison's insistence that many things which cannot pass the test of right reason are still eminently legitimate materials for poetry. Again, the new feeling took great stock in the notion of process. Since the chief value of life was to be found within the individual mind and was therefore a psychological matter, the whole process was considered crucial. Writers like Swift had little or no interest in process; they judged by results. But the new psychology fastens upon the individual psyche from the first arrival of a sensation and traces the graph of its history through all its stages. Swift regarded most of this history as trash and its devotees as fools: nothing was interesting until it revealed itself in form or until it could be forced into that degree of definition. The new law reads: anything on which the imagination can work is legitimate. As reason is supplanted by imagination, it becomes natural to rescue the unconscious from Pope's denunciation, because sensations and associations come vividly from that source. When this is done, the split between reason and imagination is complete. Reason is handed over to the scientists, the merchants and the philosophers. Imagination is retained and promoted as the strictly creative power, the only power which can see things in all their variety. In the middle years of the eighteenth century the notion of a direct engagement between man and Nature in a clear white light was considered too blunt, a harsh confrontation in which man's spirit was bound to suffer: besides, this had been tried. The new psychology invites man to much more diffuse experience, blurring the sharp edges: as, a century later, Mallarmé, appalled by the naked confrontation of man and sky, finds ease in a London fog. The price of this ease was high: one of the disadvantages of the new psychology was that it eventually drove the poet from society altogether. When Yeats pondered the fate of the *Tragic Generation*, he marked as one of the main causes of their catastrophe the morbid effort to create a new purity and beauty from 'images more and more separated from the general purposes of life'. These general purposes are the aims of man in society; to a writer like

Swift they are virtually the only important aims; or at least the only aims at once important and tangible. Pope and Swift spent their lives attending upon those aims; choosing, discriminating, adjusting. They worked on the assumption that if only the social purposes of man are clarified and tested, his private condition can be left to his own devices. The immediate necessity was to enlarge the domain of mind and intelligence. If something has to be rejected, well and good, let it be rejected; but keep the slagheap as small as possible.

We can consult these new assumptions in the aesthetic of darkness, the 'school of night' which urged that darkness is the true place of the sublime. Young's *Night Thoughts* is the first major poem in this tradition, Burke its most accomplished critical sponsor. These follow the new psychology. The old feeling is to be found mainly in Pope, Swift and Gay. When Gay writes *A Contemplation on Night* he tolerates night only by reminding himself that when it is night in one hemisphere it is day in the other. But even while rehearsing this pleasant truth, his images give him away: night is the place of 'gloom', he repeats 'the gloomy reign of night', the stars are the only proof that God's in His Heaven. The poem ends:

When the pure soul is from the body flown,
No more shall night's alternate reign be known:
The sun no more shall rolling light bestow,
But from th'Almighty streams of glory flow.
Oh, may some nobler thought my soul employ,
Than empty, transient, sublunary joy!
The stars shall drop, the sun shall lose his flame,
But thou, O God, for ever shine the same.

We can list the chief enemies of day and mind: the unconscious, sleep, dreams, visions of fancy, delusions of pride, the passions. Swift tried to rid himself of these and to perform the same service for the world. He seeks this object in many poems, including *On Dreams*:

Those dreams that on the silent night intrude,
And with false flitting shades our minds delude,
Jove never sends us downward from the skies,
Nor can they from infernal mansions rise;
But all are meer productions of the brain,
And fools consult interpreters in vain.

For, when in bed we rest our weary limbs,
The mind unburthen'd sports in various whims,
The busy head with mimic art runs o'er
The scenes and actions of the day before.

The drowsy tyrant, by his minions led,
To regal rage devotes some patriot's head.
With equal terrors, not with equal guilt,
The murd'rer dreams of all the blood he spilt.

The soldier smiling hears the widow's cries,
And stabs the son before the mother's eyes.
With like remorse his brother of the trade,
The butcher, feels the lamb beneath his blade.

The statesman rakes the town to find a plot,
And dreams of forfeitures by treason got.
Nor less Tom-Turd-Man of true statesman mold,
Collects the city filth in search of gold.

Orphans around his bed the lawyer sees,
And takes the plaintiff's and defendant's fees.
His fellow pick-purse, watching for a job,
Fancies his fingers in the cully's fob.

The kind physician grants the husband's prayers,
Or gives relief to long-expecting heirs.
The sleeping hangman ties the fatal noose,
Nor unsuccessful waits for dead men's shoes.

The grave divine with knotty points perplext,
As if he were awake, nods o'er his text:
While the sly mountebank attends his trade,
Harangues the rabble, and is better paid.

The hireling senator of modern days,
Bedaubs the guilty great with nauseous praise:
And *Dick* the Scavanger with equal grace,
Flirts from his cart the mud in Walpole's face.
(*Poems*, 11 363–4)

It is characteristic of Swift to put the blame on man himself; dreams
are not sent either from Heaven or from Hell, we ourselves manu-

facture them, they are functions of our own corruption. In *A Beautiful Young Nymph Going to Bed* there is the same suggestion, that dreams are in strict accord with the nature of the dreamer. Again in the early poem *To Mr Congreve* Swift writes:

Thus are the lives of fools a sort of dreams,
Rend'ring shades, things, and substances of names;
Such high companions may delusion keep,
Lords are a footboy's cronies in his sleep.
(*Poems*, 1 47–8)

So dreams delude our minds by setting before us our own memories, fancies and desires; an unwholesome compound from which we extract our visions. The only difference between the dream and the reality is that in the dream-world we pursue our evil desires with impunity: in society, at least up to now and for the moment, there are a few obstacles in our way. This tension between the real world, where our corruptions are at least held at bay, and the dream-world, in which we live as viciously as our desires, accounts for the weight of Swift's satire. The satire works by finding similarity beneath overt difference; as the dreams of soldiers and butchers are shown to be identical. It is the same force that presses together, in the one stanza, the physician and the hangman. But in this stanza the satire goes deeper still. 'The kind physician grants the husband's prayers'; plays God, granting and withholding. 'Or gives relief to long-expecting heirs'. This God conspires with the evil of men. If the physician's act is within the world of dreams, it is not clear that the husband's prayers for the death of his wife have even that much excuse; they are palpable facts, with which the diseased imagination plays. To find anything comparable in early eighteenth-century poetry we must go to Pope, to couplets like:

The hungry judges soon the sentence sign,
And wretches hang that jurymen may dine

– where the double hunger, a compounded outrage, is an effect on the same scale. Pope counts on the spread of words like 'appetite' and 'hunger' from the bodily to the ethical dimension; as Swift counts on the fact that sentences often find themselves reversed; if

the theologians say that man is made in the image of God, here is a
physician who can make God in the image of a diseased man. Swift
is demonstrating, in this remarkable poem, effects of adjustment and
juxtaposition which are possible only in the light of day and mind.
What is possible in dreams, he has already made clear. Over the course
of the next century poets invested a great deal of capital in dreams.
De Quincey proposes to help people to dream productively. 'Habitually to dream magnificently,' he says, 'a man must have a constitutional determination to reverie.' Thereafter, the main trouble is
that one's dream is constantly interrupted by social event. De
Quincey thinks this a disaster (see B. Dobrée (ed.), *Thomas De
Quincey*, 1965). The faculty of dreaming, he says, 'in alliance with
the mystery of darkness', is the 'one great tube through which man
communicates with the shadowy'. There, in one sentence, we have
Swift's defeat; for Swift regarded 'the shadowy' as a highly dubious
world, and all attempts to communicate with it as self-delusion.
Dreams represented a mode of life he detested and, against his best
official efforts, feared.

Swift's poem is an imitation of a very beautiful poem by Petronius,
'*Somnia quae mentes ludunt uolitantibus umbris*'. If we compare the
original with the imitation we can see the parts of the poem which
are entirely Swift's, and consider the pressure which incited them:

Somnia, quae mentes ludunt uolitantibus umbris,
non delubra deum nec ab aethere numina mittunt,
sed sibi quisque facit. Nam cum prostrata sopore
urget membra quies et mens sine pondere ludit,
quicquid luce fuit, tenebris agit. Oppida bello
qui quatit et flammis miserandas eruit urbes,
tela uidet uersasque acies et funera regum
atque exundantes perfuso sanguine campos.
Qui causas orare solent, legesque forumque
et pauidi cernunt inclusum chorte tribunal.

Condit auarus opes defossumque inuenit aurum;
uenator saltus canibus quatit; eripit undis
aut premit euersam periturus nauta puppem;
scribit amatori meretrix, dat adultera munus;

(et canis in somnis leporis uestigıa latrat).
In noctis spatium miserorum uulnera durant.[1]
(Petronius, *The Satyricon*)

Here there is no question of blame. Petronius' tone is sympathetic: whatever we do by day, we continue to do by night in our dreams, not because we are evil but because we are held in the grip of things. It is like Yeats's vision of necessity in *Purgatory*, where the Old Man is held in a chain of consequence which he cannot break. Petronius does not say, as Swift says by implication: 'Know thyself.' He is acknowledging the force of things, and the price our own nature has to pay. Swift cannot leave matters in this neutral realm; if he has a gift for rebuke and invective, he is driven to exercise it. 'A gift is an imperative.' So his poem is all blame. Memory of the things his characters have done is mixed with desire of things yet undone, the mixture an inventory of vice. In the stanza about the soldier the question of remorse is raised only to mark its absence. The soldier smiles when he hears the widow's cries, and to round out the symmetry of the occasion waits for the mother to see him before he stabs the son: there are possibilities here of a grisly decorum. The butcher's performance lacks an audience of this splendour, but he makes up for it by animating the preliminary gesture; nothing as detached as seeing his victim, he 'feels' him beneath the blade. By the time we reach this stage in the poem the participants have become emblematic figures, as in a grim tryptich or an allegory.

1 Dreams, | The fleeting shadow-play that mocks the mind, | Issue from no temples, | No heavenly power sends them – | Each man creates his own. | When prostrate limbs grow heavy | And the play of the mind is unchecked, | The mind enacts in darkness | The dramas of daylight. | The shatterer of cities in war, | Who fires unlucky towns, | Sees flying spears, broken ranks, the death of kings, | Plains awash with spilt blood. | The barrister pleads again in nightmare, | Sees the twelve tables, the court, the guarded bench. | The miser salts away his money | To find his gold dug up. | The hunter flushes the woodland with his hounds. | The sailor dreams he is doomed, | Drags out of the sea the upturned poop, | Or clings to it. | The mistress scribbles a note to her lover; | The guilty lover sends a gift ... | And the hound in his slumbers bays at the hare's tracks. | [The pangs of unhappiness last | Into the watches of the night.] Translation by J. P. Sullivan, *Petronius: The Satyricon and the Fragments*, Penguin Books, 1965, p. 174. [Ed.]

Clearly, there is a close relation between the insistence with which these emblem-figures are fixed in their settings and the vigour of the couplets themselves. The steady phalanx of Swift's couplets has the effect of ensuring that a certain perspective is maintained. Focillon has discussed two orders of shapes, two different relations between forms and their environments. In the first, the space which is liberally allowed to surround the form has the effect of keeping it intact and permanent. In the second, the forms enter into dynamic engagement with their environment to such an extent that the strict beginning and end of the forms are hidden. The first, Focillon calls the 'system of the series'; the second is the 'system of the labyrinth'. The system of the series is composed of 'discontinuous elements sharply outlined, strongly rhythmical, and defining a stable and symmetrical space that protects them against unforeseen accidents of metamorphosis'. The system of the labyrinth is a later exigency, where the labyrinth 'stretches itself out in a realm of glittering movement and colour' (*The Life of Forms in Art*). Swift's poem is a remarkably vivid example of the 'system of the series', where the elements, the couplets, are 'sharply outlined', holding a stable environment in place: the relation between these particular couplets and the forces pressing against them is so strong, so tense, that it indeed protects them 'against unforeseen accidents of metamorphosis'. Swift's equilibrium, indeed his sanity, depends upon the resilience with which this relation is maintained: if it were to shift, veering to a 'labyrinth', he would be defeated. His vocation for the enclosed couplet allows him to fix things in their places, with some confidence that they will stay there. In prose he was much more exposed. Wylie Sypher has remarked (in *Rococo to Cubism*, 1960) something along the same lines in Pope. Pope, he says, 'carefully sets all his scenes at a certain distance from his own feelings so that a sufficient interval is kept between himself and his poem, himself and his reader'. The focus 'does not shift'; but within the unchanging focus he can shift as much as he wants, varying the tone as much as he pleases because there is always that saving distance. To revert to Swift; it is a condition of his poetry that the reader is kept outside: he is never allowed to break in, or to secrete himself in the folds. What holds the reader's attention is the force with which Swift commands his own vision, his own perspective and the space that surrounds it.

We can see Swift trying to hold this perspective, and to command the surrounding space, in the 'boudoir' poems. If the note of these poems is strident, this is partly explained by his involvement in the relevant passions, and partly by the difficulty of holding the surrounding space in check.

A motto is given, by implication, in a passage from *The Lady's Dressing Room*:

The virtues we must not let pass,
Of *Celia's* magnifying glass.
When frighted *Strephon* cast his eye on't
It show'd the visage of a giant.
A glass that can to sight disclose,
The smallest worm in *Celia's* nose,
And faithfully direct her nail
To squeeze it out from head to tail;
For catch it nicely by the head,
It must come out alive or dead.
(*Poems*, II 527)

At this point poor Strephon has inspected the contents of Celia's bedroom; when he comes upon her glass and looks into it he sees the 'visage of a giant'. What stares back at him is his own terrified face, monstrously enlarged. But when Celia uses the glass to root out a worm in her nose, the glass is a commanding frame of reference; it holds its images within a determined frame and refuses to release them or – just as important – to allow anything else to enter. When the glass is in place, nothing can leave, nothing can enter, until the inspection is complete. This, however gruesome, is the technique of these poems. Nothing is allowed to leave, the tight form of the couplet encloses everything, the 'system of the series'. Nothing is allowed to enter, because it is prevented by the frame of the couplet as by the frame of the glass. The glass holds its image in this fixed position: it withdraws the image from its context only to fix it according to a more commanding perspective. The couplet withdraws an image from its context, that is, from all the things in its setting which might well modify our interpretation of it; and it puts the image in a setting of Swift's contrivance, where it will be subject to pressure of a much starker kind. This work is often done in Augustan literature by the great impersonal terms, wit, sense, nature and so forth. The object is to render impossible the formless or the labyrinthine sprawl, to hold everything at bay. If we add that the theme of these poems is, as I have suggested, the vanity of human delusion, we can see how that vanity is held or, in the best of these poems, transfixed.

In *The Progress of Love* the bashful Phillis, due to marry, runs away with the butler John, becomes a whore, contracts venereal disease. Swift's poem is a parody of the traditional romantic ballad: the falling in love, elopement, the maiden's letter to her father, the gay lover, pain, sadness and the tender death are held up against the facts. The 'system of the series' operates by crushing entire chapters of incident into a few couplets to dramatize the speed of Phillis's decay:

Fair maidens all attend the Muse
Who now the wandring pair pursues:
Away they rode in homely sort
Their journey long, their money short;
The loving couple well bemir'd,
The horse and both the riders tir'd:
Their vittels bad, their lodging worse,
Phil cry'd, and John began to curse;
Phil wish't, that she had strained a limb
When first she ventur'd out with him.
John wish'd, that he had broke a leg
When first for her he quitted Peg.

(*Poems* 1 224)

It is a technique of speed; incidents are given so swiftly that the faintest suggestion of pathos is swept aside. Where a sentimental novelist would spend several chapters describing how John lost his job and Phillis, to support them, had to sell herself on the streets and there picked up the disease, Swift tosses these chapters into a few lines:

How oft she broke her marriage vows
In kindness to maintain her spouse;
Till swains unwholesome spoiled the trade,

For now the surgeon must be paid;
To whom those perquisites are gone
In Christian justice due to John.
(*Poems*, I 125)

So he commands the space in which his couplets are set by fending off the conventional response to romantic ballads. It is entirely in keeping, for instance, that he does not even let Phillis die: the last lines of the poem leave her and John transfixed, running a public house in Staines, where even the rhymes tell against them:

They keep at Staines the Old Blue Boar,
Are cat and dog, and rogue and whore.
(*Poems*, I 125)

Normally, when Swift holds up a magnifying glass against a situation, it is to look at it more closely than convention requires or allows. Often this takes the form of reading literally what is meant figuratively: in *The Progress of Beauty* he makes fun of beauty by taking literally the poetic comparison between a beautiful face and the moon. As the moon wanes, Celia declines into a whore. If you insist upon living by sentimental analogies, you must pay Swift's price, their consequence. He compares a woman's face to a piece of china-ware, because both can be repaired by the application of white lead. But the basic technique is an elaborate parody of the philosophical discussion of form and matter:

Matter, as wise logicians say,
Cannot without a form subsist,
And form, say I, as well as they,
Must fail if matter brings no grist.
(*Poems*, I 228)

If the diseased Celia loses her nose and her teeth, the form is ruined, and the best she can do is to make sure to appear, like the stars, only at a distance and by night:

Two balls of glass may serve for eyes,
White lead can plaister up a cleft,
But these alas, are poor supplies
If neither cheeks, nor lips be left.
(*Poems*, I 229)

The procedure here is to 'translate downwards'. Treat the soul as if it were body, then treat the body as the mere sum of its parts; work up the picture of an ideal body as a structure of replaceable parts, so that when one part wears out by disease you can replace it. Then advert to the fact that this, alas, is impossible. So the only recourse is to discard the worn-out body. This is hard on women, but they have only themselves to blame. As for their men; they can only pray to get a new woman every month:

Ye pow'rs who over love preside,
Since mortal beauties drop so soon,
If you would have us well supply'd,
Send us new nymphs with each new moon.
(*Poems*, I 228)

This is eminently Swiftian; to treat the organic as if it were mechanical. He does it again, more systematically, in *A Beautiful Young Nymph Going to Bed*. Corinna is a machine, her bedroom a factory; when she goes to bed, the factory is shut down. It is essential to this device that all the moving parts of the body are detachable:

Then, seated on a three-legg'd chair,
Takes off her artificial hair:
Now, picking out a crystal eye,
She wipes it clean, and lays it by.
Her eye-brows from a mouse's hide,
Stuck on with art on either side,
Pulls off with care, and first displays 'em,
Then in a play-book smoothly lays 'em.
Now dextrously her plumpers draws,
That serve to fill her hollow jaws.
Untwists a wire; and from her gums
A set of teeth completely comes.
Pulls out the rags contriv'd to prop
Her flabby dugs and down they drop.
(*Poems*, II 581-2)

In the morning Corinna finds the machine destroyed; the crystal eye is gone, a rat has stolen the plaster, all the other parts are in a mess.

But she is a resourceful mechanic, and the merit of mechanical things is that they can be replaced:

The nymph, tho' in this mangled plight,
Must ev'ry morn her limbs unite.
(*Poems*, II 583)

How she does this, Swift does not say. Or rather, he implies that the Muse is too 'bashful' to look very close; the Muse speaks a different idiom. The poem ends with the factory still in chaos, but Corinna is about to put herself together again. Lovers should not investigate factories. As Swift says in *Strephon and Chloe*:

Why is a handsome wife ador'd
By ev'ry coxcomb, but her Lord?
From yonder puppet-man inquire,
Who wisely hides his wood and wire;
Shows *Sheba's* Queen completely drest,
And *Solomon* in royal vest;
But, view them litter'd on the floor,
Or strung on pegs behind the door;
Punch is exactly of a piece
With *Lorraine's* Duke, and Prince of *Greece*.
(*Poems*, II 592)

This is Swift's country by general assent, but he was not the first to discover it. Close at hand, it figures largely in Rochester's poems, especially in *A Letter from Artemisa in the Town, to Chloe, in the Country*. Artemisa is telling her country cousin the ways of men in the city. Anticipating a famous sentiment in Swift, she says:

They little guess, who at our arts are grieved,
The perfect joy of being well deceiv'd.

If 'wonder', which Swift calls delusion, is to be preserved, the lover must fend off 'clear knowledge':

Woman, who is an arrant bird of night,
Bold in the dusk, before a fool's dull sight,
Must fly, when reason brings the glaring light.
(Rochester, *Poems*, 1926, p. 29)

The glaring light is also Swift's recourse, to protect himself from his own passions, from the unconscious, and now the human rage for delusion. But it is a severe test. In several poems Swift shows us the lover who insists upon the truth of things and goes in search of it; but invariably he is blinded by what he sees, and, unless he is already overwhelmed, settles for the perpetual possession of being well deceived. The motto of these poems is: live with illusion, but know that you are being deceived; beguile yourself with the image before you, but know that it is a pleasant fiction. In *The Lady's Dressing Room* Strephon steals into Celia's bedroom while she is out. He is determined to seek the truth. Swift warns us, by a pun on Milton's lines in *Paradise Lost*, that we would be wiser to leave uninspected the 'secrets of the hoary deep'. As the culmination of Strephon's vision, there is the discovery that Celia excretes. Strephon's folly is a new original sin, an insistence upon man's right to go 'to the end of the line', disobeying God, nature and common sense. Strephon's sin is the presumption of knowledge: he insists upon penetrating to the truth of Celia, and his only reward is the acquisition of a 'foul imagination'. The chief characteristic of this imagination is that it translates Celia 'downward': she is equated with her stink, and in that respect she becomes Everywoman. Celia's bodily nature is 'original' in the sense in which Strephon's sin is original. Swift says:

But Vengeance, Goddess never sleeping
Soon punish'd Strephon for his peeping;
His foul imagination links
Each dame he sees with all her stinks . . . .
(*Poems*, II 529)

But it is Strephon's 'vicious fancy' which generalizes in this way. The poem ends with the return of the prudent narrator, apostle of the reasonable middle-way. This man lives with the public show of things, and he never questions further. If Celia looks like a goddess, well and good, enough is enough; celebrate her as if she were a goddess. Common sense is the philosophy of 'as if', maintained with prudence. If we do this, we easily get over the problem of Celia's 'ointments, daubs, and paints and creams', these are merely her votive accompaniments. Strephon's foul imagination cannot see these things without blaspheming; foulness is the price he pays for the truth. If he could bring himself to rest in the appearance of things, Swift says:

He soon would learn to think like me,
And bless his ravisht sight to see
Such order from confusion sprung,
Such gaudy tulips rais'd from dung.
(*Poems*, II 530)

Middleton Murry has argued that this last part of the poem is an attempt to take the harm out of the earlier, excremental part. It has the air of being tacked on as an afterthought. *The Lady's Dressing Room* is yet another version of Swift's invariable theme, the question of form and matter, spirit and body. In other places Swift tends to show that spirit is 'nothing more than' body. Here he says: accept the fact that the spirit of beauty is implicated in the matter of body; accept it, live with it, get used to it and live with corresponding prudence. But this is just another way of saying that we must in this case 'sublimate', cling to the pleasing delusion if we are not to go mad, like Strephon, with our foul imaginations.

The story is complicated in *Strephon and Chloe*, a parody of those fables in which a goddess, like Thetis, comes to earth and marries a man. Chloe, seemingly a goddess in human form, marries Strephon but on her wedding night reveals herself just as mortal as he. Their love duet becomes a collusion of obscenities. Swift's feeling is not so much horror at the 'excremental vision'; but rather, hatred of everything in life that depends upon the absurd delusions of pride and pretence. Often the pride is spiritual or even aesthetic; hence the parody of the Grand Style with its world of 'fine ideas'. The implication is that the only way to hold ourselves safe is by ensuring that our passions are subject to the test of common sense. To achieve this reduction Swift is willing to answer one extremity by another. This complicates the argument of *The Lady's Dressing Room*, where we are admonished to rest in beguiling appearance. Now we are to seek our safety by modifying our passions: for this urgent purpose Swift is willing to confront the facts. The narrator tells Strephon that if he had been fortunate enough to see the excremental truth of Chloe before he was too deeply sunk in passion, he would now be easy in heart:

Your fancy then had always dwelt
On what you saw, and what you smelt;
Would still the same ideas give ye,
As when you spied her on the privy.
And, spite of Chloe's charms divine,
Your heart had been as whole as mine.
(*Poems*, II 591)

This implies that even Strephon's foul imagination might be a small price to pay for ease of heart and indifference. Meanwhile the advice is: prudence and limitation:

On sense and wit your passion found,
By decency cemented round;
Let prudence with good nature strive,
To keep esteem and love alive.
Then come old age whene'er it will,
Your friendship shall continue still:
And thus a mutual gentle fire,
Shall never but with life expire.
(*Poems*, II 593)

It is interesting that Swift does not subvert either the emotion of love or the institution of marriage; only insisting that both be pursued in reasonable terms. Love is a function of friendship, and passion rises no higher than 'a mutual gentle fire'. In *The Phoenix and Turtle* Shakespeare speaks of the lovers' passion as a 'mutual flame'; Swift's flame is still mutual but it is to burn gently. The tone of the poem is rueful. Swift is rebuking women for ignoring, after marriage, the considerations by which the marriage was achieved:

They take possession of the crown,
And then throw all their weapons down;
Though by the politicians scheme
Who'er arrives at pow'r supreme,
Those arts by which at first they gain it,
They still must practise to maintain it.
(*Poems*, II 592)

The reference is to Marvell's *Horatian Ode upon Cromwell's Return from Ireland*; to the last stanza, where Marvell advises Cromwell to press on, and now that he has achieved power, to maintain it by the same arts. Swift is bringing to the situation of love and marriage the same considerations, and the same attitudes, which Marvell exhibits toward Cromwell; as if to say: whatever moral reservations I might have about your actions up to this point, I must concede that you have been successful; so, proceed, this must be done and there is nothing else to do. The tone common to Swift and Marvell arises from the force of fact, judiciously acknowledged. Norman O. Brown has argued that in *Strephon and Chloe* sublimation and awareness of the excremental functions are presented as mutually exclusive; the conclusion being that sublimation must be cultivated even at the cost of repression. But this assumes that Swift is dealing with a force of passion which is constant. In fact, Swift urges Strephon to keep the horror to a minimum by cutting back the passion, to begin with: start by looking hard and long at the facts of the case, this will have the effect of curbing your passion. Then if you wish, proceed. You do so with impunity, because the force of your passion is now small, there is little to repress. This is in line with Swift's prayer for Stella, that she be granted happiness by the reduction of her desires. It follows naturally from his assumption that happiness, a ratio between one's desires and one's possessions, can be preserved either by increasing the possessions or by reducing the desires.

This interpretation is supported by *Cassinus and Peter*. Strephon's error consisted in his failure to curb his passion when he had a chance; a sharp vision of the facts would have done the trick. But Strephon did not take this opportunity. In the present poem Cassinus has made the same mistake; now it is too late. He has loved the illusion of Celia. Now when the facts collide with his passion, they turn its force into disgust, hatred, foul imagination. Hating Celia, Cassinus hates all women and therefore life itself. So he is the type of Swift's victims. In these poems lovers who did not take the first opportunity of modifying their passions are for ever lost, and they must pay the price in universal disgust. Cassinus is driven mad by his vision of omnivorous excrement. Even now, mad, he thinks that Celia's excreting is a unique sin against her race and sex. He can hardly bring himself to tell Peter his frightful secret, and he warns him never to tell anyone else:

To force it out my heart must rend;
Yet, when conjur'd by such a friend –
Think, *Peter,* how my soul is rack'd.
These eyes, these eyes beheld the fact.
Now bend thine ear; since out it must:
But, when thou seest me laid in dust,
The secret thou shalt ne'er impart;
Not to the nymph that keeps thy heart;
(How would her virgin soul bemoan
A crime to all her sex unknown!)
Nor whisper to the tattling reeds,
The blackest of all female deeds.
(*Poems,* II 596)

Brown (*Life Against Death,* 1959) thinks that this poem shatters the
solution reached in *Strephon and Chloe*; the life of civilized sublimation is destroyed because the excremental vision cannot be repressed.
But this would be so only if we were to identify Cassinus with
Swift himself. This is out of the question. For one thing, it would
mean forgetting Peter. In the first lines Cassinus and Peter are 'lovers
both'. But Peter is a sensible fellow, he never runs to extremes.
When he visits Cassinus and finds him in distraction, he cannot understand what has happened. When Cassinus says 'Celia', Peter can only
think that she has been killed, or she has 'played the whore' or caught
the pox. These are the thoughts of a solid man. This, Swift implies,
is the way to take one's passions, with rough common sense.
Poor Cassinus is an idealist, a naïf, compounding fictions and giving
them names. No wonder he goes mad. I am suggesting, of course,
that this tragical elegy is richly comic: the comedy is 'black', but
it does not require us to assume that Cassinus is Swift or that the
poem is Swift's last letter to the world. That passion can be kept
on a close rein is Peter's message; that we go mad unless we
keep it so is the point of Cassinus. But the poem gives us both
idioms.

These poems are not, in fact, obsessed; their 'excremental vision'
is held in check by other forces. Swift is merely pursuing the logic of
his terms: soul and body, soul in sin, body in disease. If the motto
of Swift's prose is: negate; the motto of the poems is: modify your

desires and passions. Better still if we can substitute friendship for love. In *Cadenus and Vanessa* Swift says:

But friendship in its greatest height,
A constant, rational delight,
  On virtue's basis fix'd to last,
When love's allurements long are past;
Which gently warms, but cannot burn;
He gladly offers in return.
(*Poems*, II 711)

If friendship is safer than love, this underlines the general advice to live by modest desires; it is given in several poems, particularly in *Desire and Possession*. Reduce desire: then hold what remains with all the resources of perspective and force. If something appears intractable, translate it downward; if it is organic, treat it as if it were mechanical. If it is human, be on the watch for animal imagery which will intimidate it, thereby releasing you. It is not enough to hold the object; you must command the space surrounding it and live by that command.

These are the chief terms of Swift's poetry. Clearly, they are strong enough and flexible enough to sustain many kinds of poem. But if we think of them in loose association, they point toward the poetry of invective. The greatest example is *The Legion Club*.

The poem is an attack upon the Members of the Irish House of Commons after they had voted to deprive the clergy of certain tithes legally due. But although it has an object and a local occasion, it is invective in the further sense that it develops energy and momentum from its own resources, once it has started. Kenneth Burke has discussed invective as a kind of Pure Poetry, which needs little external stimulus to keep it going. Once started, it can work up a fine head of steam with only occasional assistance from its object. It is like the *encomium*, the essay in pure praise, panegyric turned upside-down. It may be argued that Swift was happy in this form because he delighted in carrying things to the end of the line, exploiting purely internal resources far beyond the requirement of the occasion. This would account for his most extreme riddles and puns and, in this poem, for the virtuosity of the rhymes. The poem is called *The Legion Club* because of the answer of the unclean spirit in *Mark* (v9): 'My name is Legion; for we are many.' This prompts Swift to develop the notion that the Members are all mad, that the house is Bedlam, that when they speak they rave. Or, again, that the house is hell, full of evil shadows and spirits. Or a cage for weird animals. Each of these visions is driven by energy which is engendered as one line is generated from another; nothing else is required. In one stanza he dreams of destroying the House, with the Devil's aid, on the understanding that God often uses the Devil as His scourge. But then he thinks of letting the house stand, and using it as a lunatic asylum:

Since the house is like to last,
Let a royal grant be pass'd,
That the club have right to dwell
Each within his proper cell;
With a passage left to creep in,
And a hole above for peeping.
  Let them, when they once get in
Sell the nation for a pin;
While they sit a picking straws
Let them rave of making laws;
While they never hold their tongue,
Let them dabble in their dung;
Let them form a grand committee,
How to plague and starve the City;
Let them stare and storm and frown,
When they see a clergy-gown.
Let them, 'ere they crack a louse,
Call for th' orders of the house.
(*Poems*, III 830–31)

It could go on indefinitely. The chief effect of the couplets is to ensure that they command whatever they touch. Often this is a matter of bringing images into startling relationships, by fiat and insistence. The relation between 'picking straws' and 'making laws' is a brilliant parody of choice and chance, achieved with the connivance of an accommodating language. The same feature in the language makes it possible for Swift to suggest the quality of speeches in the House of Commons by adding an appropriate accompaniment:

While they never hold their tongue,
Let them dabble in their dung.

This is, presumably, what Swift meant when he referred to 'my own hum'rous biting way', in the *Verses on the Death of Dr Swift*. In the poem *To Mr Delany* he distinguishes between raillery and abuse, and he attaches the adjective 'obliging' to the nouns 'ridicule' and 'jest'. The distinctions are never clear. In prose, Swift recommended Voiture; in verse, Delany – at least on this occasion. We may accept his terms; raillery, jest, with the addition of invective. There is also humour, which he described in the same poem:

Humour is odd, grotesque, and wild,
Onely by affectation spoild. . . .

This is clearly Swift's possession in such poems as *The Legion Club*. Rochester seems to have thought of it as 'pointed satire'. Under whatever name, it is an achievement of style.

I should not imply that Swift's poems are all in these keys. He had his light moments, when the easy occasion called for the other kind of wit; as in *Petition of Mrs Frances Harris*. Indeed, to go through Swift's entire poetry is to be astonished by its variety, the range of feeling invoked. We often think that of all the different kinds of poetry, he wrote only two or three; but we forget the occasions when the writing of a poem served him instead of a letter, a pun, a conversation, a journey, a postcard or a public speech:

By faction tir'd, with grief he waits a while,
His great contending friends to reconcile.
Performs what friendship, justice, truth require:
What could he more, but decently retire?
(*Poems*, 1 196)

If we did not know, it would be hard to ascribe that to Swift, at least with any conviction. The tone seems more delicate, more charitable, more Johnsonian than our standard impression of him. He wrote the poem, *The Author upon Himself*, in the summer of 1714 distressed by the growing bitterness between his great contending, friends Oxford and Bolingbroke. We must allow for this tone; we find it again in the birthday poems to Stella.

Indeed, Swift's finest poems are remarkable achievements of style: his handling of tone, for instance, is never random or awkward. The *Satirical Elegy on the Death of a Late Famous General* is a case in point. Marlborough died on 16 June 1722 but his defeat was already achieved on 30 December 1711, when he was deprived of all appointments, an event celebrated in Swift's *The Fable of Midas*. The Elegy reads:

His Grace! impossible! what dead!
Of old age too, and in his bed!
And could that mighty warrior fall?
And so inglorious, after all!
Well, since he's gone, no matter how,
The last loud trump must wake him now:
And, trust me, as the noise grows stronger,
He'd wish to sleep a little longer.
And could he be indeed so old
As by the news-papers we're told?
Threescore, I think, is pretty high;
'Twas time in conscience he should die.
This world he cumber'd long enough;
He burnt his candle to the snuff;
And that's the reason, some folks think,
He left behind *so great a stink*.
Behold his funeral appears,
Nor widow's sighs, nor orphan's tears,
Wont at such times each heart to pierce,
Attend the progress of his herse.
But what of that, his friends may say,
He had those honours in his day.
True to his profit and his pride,
He made them weep before he dy'd.
Come hither, all ye empty things,
Ye bubbles rais'd by breath of Kings;
Who float upon the tide of state,
Come hither, and behold your fate.

Let pride be taught by this rebuke,
How very mean a thing's a Duke;
From all his ill-got honours flung,
Turn'd to that dirt from whence he sprung.
(*Poems*, I 296–7)

The elegiac genre is mocked, its skeleton retained for that purpose.
The form of the poem enacts the burial arrangements as if to make
the reported death doubly sure. Marlborough is to be put into the
grave, the 'dirt from whence he sprung', because this is required by
decency. The poem begins in astonishment; registering the receipt of
news by one who is merely surprised to hear it. This note marks one
limit beyond which the feeling will not go, and it implies other
limits in other directions. The individual stages in the development of
the poem are therefore the occasions on which the surprise is, in one
degree or another, assimilated: 'Well, since he's gone, no matter
how. . . .' The event is treated as news, so that no other treatment
may be allowed. Just as the body is to be put into the grave, the
discourse is also to be reduced from the first note of astonishment.
Swift's way is to use the conventional figures – the candle of life,
the trump of doom, the procession of weeping mourners – but to
pursue them beyond the limit of decorum until their conventional
glories drop away; then, in their literal state, they collapse. He holds
these poor figures aloft until the venal attributes which they conceal
have time and force to drag them down; the stink of the snuffed
candle, the trump which cannot be ignored, the widows and orphans
who wept while Marlborough was alive. Pope's version is quite
different in its significance:

Behold him loaded with unreverend years
Bath'd in unmeaning unrepentant tears
Dead, by regardless vet'rans born on high
Dry pomps and obsequies without a sigh.
(*A Character*)

Roland Barthes has remarked that in the ages which he calls classical,
the language was a common property and 'thought alone bore the
weight of being different'. To Pope and Swift language is a system
of signs embodying relations; exercises of the system may be different

in detail because they are the same at large. All poetic couplets are
the same in one respect; hence their difference in every other respect.
In the Marlborough poems the weight of being different is a matter
of tone. Pope's magnificence is the force of solemnity which refuses,
even on this occasion, to sink beneath itself: the values which sustain
the solemnity have been humiliated in Marlborough's life, so they
are potent in absence and denial, 'unreverend', 'unmeaning', 'unrepentant' and 'obsequies without a sigh'. Swift begins the corresponding part as if solemnity might be in question: 'Behold his
funeral appears . . .'; again, absence is the sign. Pursuing this line, he
makes an abrupt change to the colloquial: 'But what of that, his
friends may say'; until the General is condemned by his wretched
advocates. The solemn note is admitted, only to enrich the mockery.
In Swift and Pope we are to watch an action: 'Behold'. But in Pope
we are to mark its moral solemnity; in Swift we are to attend an
event corresponding to the mean accountancy by which it is
described. 'True to his profit and his pride'; the two are one, as the
language allows. This is Swift's method, when he attacks someone
who is omnivorous and impartial in vice. In the *Short Character of the
Earl of Wharton* he adverts to politics, religion and lechery, but only
to say that in this case they are all one; there is no point in differen-
tiating where the acts are indistinguishable:

He is a Presbyterian in politics, and an atheist in religion;
but he chooses at present to whore with a Papist
(*Prose Writings*, III 179)

In the satirical elegy the definitive gesture comes at the end, heaving
the body into the grave. Alluding to the events of 1711, Swift
pursues the figure ('From all his ill-got honours flung') until life itself
is seen as one of the ill-got honours; as Marlborough rightly lost his
offices, so now he has rightly lost his life. Belatedly, justice is done:
'Turn'd to that dirt from whence he sprung'. 'Sprung' and 'dung'
make one of Swift's favourite rhymes; 'sprung' and 'flung', another.
Grim propriety is ensured when the body cannot be distinguished
from its origin. The relief is audible when mighty things are brought
low. 'Come hither, all ye empty things': meaning the readers, too,
if we are tempted to high vice, and in any event all the little Marl-
boroughs who have not yet been caught. The last lines are an *exem-*

plum, a demonstration of a process in the world at large, Marlborough's inglorious death the proof of the case. The act of Fate is given in the last two lines as a process at once majestic and impersonal; personal only by analogy. Most of the action is done by 'flung' and 'turn'd': they are poised together for precisely this reason. Syntax is working here to ensure that one part of the action is immediately followed by another: flung from his honours, Marlborough is then flung further, beyond all considerations of this transitory kind, into death and corruption. The turning, the transformation into dirt, is already accomplished, as if the spectators' outraged feeling could not wait.

(188–221)

William Empson

from 'Alice in Wonderland', *Some Versions of Pastoral* 1935

But talking animals in children's books had been turned to didactic purposes ever since Aesop; the schoolmastering tone in which the animals talk nonsense to Alice is partly a parody of this – they are really childish but try not to look it. On the other hand, this tone is so supported by the way they can order her about, the firm and surprising way their minds work, the abstract topics they work on, the useless rules they accept with so much conviction, that we take them as real grown-ups contrasted with unsophisticated childhood. 'The grown-up world is as odd as the child-world, and both are a dream.' This ambivalence seems to correspond to Dodgson's own attitude to children; he, like Alice, wanted to get the advantages of being childish and grown-up at once. In real life this seems to have at least occasional disadvantages both ways; one remembers the little girl who screamed and demanded to be taken from the lunch-table because she knew she couldn't solve his puzzles (not, apparently, a usual, but one would think a natural reaction to his mode of approach) – she clearly thought him too grown-up; whereas in the scenes of jealousy with his little girls' parents the grown-ups must have thought him quite enough of a child. He made a success of the process, and it seems clear that it did none of the little girls any harm, but one cannot help cocking one's eye at it as a way of life.

The changes of size are more complex. In Gulliver they are the impersonal eye; to change size and nothing else makes you feel 'this makes one see things as they are in themselves'. It excites wonder but of a scientific sort. Swift used it for satire on science or from a horrified interest in it, and to give a sort of scientific authority to his deductions, that men seen as small are spiritually petty and seen as large physically loathsome. And it is the small observer, like the child, who does least to alter what he sees and therefore sees most truly.

(267)

Arthur E. Case

'Personal and Political Satire in *Gulliver's Travels*' 1945

No one who reads a modern annotated edition of *Gulliver's Travels* can fail to observe the abundance of the commentary upon the first and third voyages and the comparative scarcity of it in connexion with the second and fourth. The reason for this, of course, is that the first and third voyages are primarily satiric in tone, with frequent references to contemporary persons and events in Western Europe. On the other hand, since Brobdingnag and Houyhnhnmland are in differing degrees Utopian commonwealths, Swift has no desire to identify their ruling classes with those of his own country. There are a few scattered exceptions which are worth remark. The maids of honor at the court of George I regarded the account of their Brobdingnagian counterparts (XI 118) as a direct insult. King George himself is ridiculed as a foreigner in a not too cautious passage in the second chapter of the same voyage (X1 95), and again in the fourth voyage as one of the beggarly German princes who hire out troops (X1 247). And in the descriptions of Europe which Gulliver gives to the King of Brobdingnag and to his master Houyhnhnm there are, in the midst of much general satire, a few attacks on identifiable individuals.

Most of these references, however, seem to be incidental and opportunistic. It is not strange, perhaps, that the personal attacks in the two primarily satiric voyages have generally been held to be equally planless – a sort of literary Donnybrook Fair, in which Swift followed the good old Irish maxim, 'Whenever you see a head, hit it!' Consequently no one has been greatly disturbed by allegorical interpretations of the first voyage which identify Gulliver now as Oxford, now as Bolingbroke, and now as Swift himself. As the careers of both of the first two politicians undoubtedly contribute incidents to Gulliver's career, the burden of proof lies on the shoulders of anyone who argues that the political allegory is consistent.

Consistency can be obtained, however, by supposing that Gulliver's career in Lilliput represents the joint political fortunes of Oxford and Bolingbroke during the latter half of Queen Anne's reign, when the two men shared the leadership of the Tory party. This device permits Swift to make use of the most dramatic incidents from the life of each man, and at the same time to avoid too close a parallel with the life of either.

The allegory is exactly coincidental with Gulliver's residence in Lilliput and Blefuscu. It begins with the hero's shipwreck and captivity, which correspond to the temporary fall from power of Oxford and Bolingbroke (then Robert Harley and Henry St John) in 1708, when the Whigs, led by Godolphin and Marlborough, secured control of the Cabinet and the House of Commons. These events take place in the first chapter of the voyage, in which the nature of the allegory is not yet so clearly apparent. Looking back from later chapters, however, it is possible to extract a number of probable allusions to events of the years 1708–10. Gulliver is pictured as having been caught off guard; as contemplating violence against his enemies, then as deciding upon submission as the more prudent course, and later as regarding this submission as a tacit promise binding him in honor not to injure his captors even when it lies within his power to do so. It is hardly necessary to point out the parallel between this conduct and that of the Tory leaders toward the Whigs.

In the second chapter we are introduced to the Emperor and to another simplification of history. Swift is telling a story which began in the reign of Anne and ended in that of George I. To supply Lilliput with an Empress and an Emperor reigning successively would have been to make the author's meaning dangerously plain: it was safer to make them husband and wife. For the same reason the Emperor was described as being almost the exact antithesis of George:

He is taller by almost the breadth of my nail, than any of his court, which alone is enough to strike an awe into the beholders. His features are strong and masculine, with an Austrian lip and arched nose, his complexion olive, his countenance erect, his body and limbs well proportioned, all his motions graceful, and his deportment majestic. He was then past his prime, being twenty-eight years and three-quarters old, of which he had reigned about seven, in great felicity, and generally victorious. ... His dress was very plain and simple, and the fashion of it between the Asiatic and European; but he had on his head a light helmet of gold, adorned with jewels, and a plume on the

crest. He held his sword drawn in his hand, to defend himself,
if I should happen to break loose; it was almost three inches
long, the hilt and scabbard were gold enriched with diamonds.
His voice was shrill, but very clear and articulate, and I could
distinctly hear it when I stood up (XI 30-31).

When one recalls George's thick and ungainly form, his bad taste
in dress, and his guttural and unintelligible pronunciation of the
little English he knew, it becomes clear that Swift is employing with
unusual effectiveness the same technique that Pope was to use a few
years later when he caricatured George II in the *Epistle to Augustus.*
'Praise undeserved is scandal in disguise.'

The most important event in the second chapter is the making of
the inventory of Gulliver's possessions by a committee appointed by
the Emperor. This, probably, stands for the investigation, by a committee of Whig lords, of one William Gregg, a clerk in Harley's
office who had been guilty of treasonable correspondence with
France. No evidence was found to implicate Harley in the affair, and
he, of course, strenuously protested his innocence and his loyalty.
This is reflected in a sentence describing what took place at the reading
of the inventory. 'In the mean time [the Emperor] ordered three
thousand of his choicest troops (who then attended him) to surround
me at a distance, with their bows and arrows just ready to discharge:
but I did not observe it, for my eyes were wholly fixed upon his
Majesty' (XI 36).

With the third chapter events begin to move more rapidly.
Gulliver's gentleness and good behavior impress the Emperor and the
populace favorably, and he becomes more and more importunate for
his release. This is opposed only by Skyresh Bolgolam, a cabinet
minister who, when finally overborne by the other authorities,
manages at least to provide that Gulliver's liberty shall be hedged
about with restrictions. This corresponds to a series of political
developments which culminated early in 1711. The Tories gradually
won their way back into public favor: the Queen had always been
inclined toward them. The identity of Skyresh Bolgolam has been a
matter of dispute. William Cooke Taylor thought he might be the
Duke of Argyle, whom Swift had offended by his attacks on the
Scotch. Sir Charles Firth pointed out that Bolgolam was described as

being 'of a morose and sour complexion,' and proposed the name of the Earl of Nottingham, because there was mutual enmity between Swift and the Earl. Swift had, indeed, been the instrument of fixing upon the Earl the sobriquet of 'Dismal'. Both these identifications rest, however, upon the supposition that Gulliver is Swift, and both men had good reason for hating the author, whereas Gulliver protests (x142) that Bolgolam's hatred arose 'without any provocation'. Now Nottingham was also an enemy of Harley, on no better ground than that the latter had succeeded him in office in 1704. Moreover, while the Earl never proposed anything resembling a set of conditions on which Swift might be allowed liberty, he did, in 1711, execute a political maneuver which could easily have been interpreted in these terms with regard to Harley. On the latter's rise to power as Chancellor of the Exchequer (in effect Prime Minister) Nottingham proposed in the House of Lords an amendment to the royal address which stipulated that no peace with France should be made which left Spain and the Indies in the possession of the House of Bourbon. This was an open attempt to restrict the powers of the new Tory administration, and to embarrass them by the implication that they could not be trusted to safeguard the interests of England. Harley and St John felt it prudent not to oppose this amendment, and it was consequently carried. This is expressed allegorically by Gulliver's remark, 'I swore and subscribed to these articles with great cheerfulness and content, although some of them were not so honourable as I could have wished; which proceeded wholly from the malice of *Skyresh Bolgolam* the High Admiral . . .' (x144).

The articles to which Gulliver swore are not all of the same kind. Most of them are amusing provisions arising out of the difference in size between him and the Lilliputians. But two are connected with the underlying narrative. The first provides that Gulliver shall not leave Lilliput without the Emperor's license given under the great seal. The sixth requires Gulliver to be the Emperor's ally against Blefuscu, and to do his utmost to destroy the enemy's fleet. The true significance of these stipulations does not appear until much later.

The fourth chapter is explanatory and preparatory. Swift takes an opportunity, in describing Gulliver's visit to the palace, to emphasize the Queen's complaisance toward Gulliver, or, in other words, Queen Anne's inclination toward the Tories. The chief interest of the chapter, however, lies in the detailed account of the political situation in Lilliput and the events which led up to it. There is no special significance in the fact that the narrator is Reldresal, whose identity and relationship to the allegory do not become clear until the seventh chapter. He first explains the party system, admitting that the High-Heels (Tories) exceed in number his own party, the Low-Heels (Whigs), though the latter, through the Emperor's favor, are in power: he also admits a fear that the heir to the crown (the Prince of Wales, later George II) is partial to the High-Heels, though he tries to retain the friendship of both sides. Reldresal also expounds the religious differences of the day under the guise of the dispute between the Big-Endians and the Small-Endians (Roman Catholics and Protestants). The trouble began, he relates, with the reigning Emperor's great-grandfather, who, when his son was a boy, published an edict commanding his subjects to break their eggs at the smaller end because his son had cut his fingers in breaking an egg at the larger end, according to primitive custom. The great-grandfather is Henry VIII; the son, presumably, Elizabeth, who was declared illegitimate by the Pope; the edict, Henry's proclamation of himself as head of the national church. The choice of the symbol of the egg may have been guided by a desire to refer to the Eucharist, the nature of which was the chief theological point at issue in the great schism. Reldresal reviews the controversy, in the course of which 'one Emperor [Charles I] lost his life, and another [James II] his crown'. This all leads naturally to an explanation of international relations with Blefuscu (France), which is represented as harboring and encouraging Big-Endian exiles who have fled thither after unsuccessful rebellions. This is as close as Swift comes to a reference to the Jacobite movement, but it was close enough to leave contemporary readers in no doubt as to his meaning. Finally, the War of the Spanish Succession is described as 'a bloody war [that] has been carryed on between the two Empires for six and thirty moons with various success'. Swift, as a Tory, has no desire to exalt the Duke of Marlborough, or to make it appear that England, in 1711, was clearly superior to France in arms: consequently Reldresal's account ends upon this note, with the further addition that Lilliput is in imminent danger from attack by Blefuscu, and that the Emperor relies upon Gulliver (the Tory administration) to save the country.

The fifth chapter brings the crisis. For dramatic purposes Swift condenses into a short space of time happenings which historically took up more than two years. The first concern of Harley and St John, on obtaining power, was peace with France. The war had become increasingly a Whig war, from which Marlborough gained military prestige and the commercial interests foresaw the destruction of France's international trade, to their own profit. The Tories, on the other hand, did not anticipate any advantages from a continuation of hostilities, which they believed could not be carried to the point of a decisive English victory. They could not negotiate openly with France, however, because the war was still generally popular, and the Whigs might raise the cry (as they did later) that the Tories were robbing England of the fruits of victory by granting the enemy easy terms. But secret negotiations also involved difficulties. England was bound by treaties not to make peace without the consent of her allies, and the ministry had no right, under English law, to enter into discussions of the peace terms without special royal authority granted under the great seal. Despite all this the administration did begin negotiations in secret, justifying this action on the ground that peace was necessary for the welfare of England. Eventually, in 1713, both countries signed a treaty at Utrecht, by the terms of which France gained more than the military situation warranted, but did agree, among other things, to dismantle the port of Dunkirk, one of the chief threats to English naval supremacy.

Swift's symbolical representation of these events is masterly. He avoids any celebration of Marlborough's military genius by making the victory over Blefuscu a naval triumph, standing for the demolition of the defenses of Dunkirk. The Whig desire for a crushing defeat of France is pictured as a malicious and despotic wish of the Emperor to humiliate and tyrannize over 'a free and brave people'. The collusion of the Tories with the French, as charged by their opponents, is explained and defended as common politeness on Gulliver's part toward the diplomatic representatives of a foreign power.

The chapter concludes with an episode which seems unconnected with what has preceded it. When one understands its real meaning, however, the chapter becomes the most completely unified in the voyage. The story of the fire in the royal palace is Swift's defense of the Tories' illegal negotiation of the peace. What Swift wanted was an instance of an emergency met by an act technically illegal, but clearly justifiable because of the dangerous circumstances. Gulliver's method of extinguishing the fire answered the purpose admirably. Critics of Swift have often complained that the allegory is needlessly gross, but this is unfair. There was more than one reason for Harley's fall from power. Almost from the time of his accession to the chancellorship he had begun to lose the personal, though not the political favor of the Queen. He had a weakness for the bottle, and pride of place combined with a contempt for Anne's intellect led him on more than one occasion to appear drunk in her presence and to use language which she felt was an affront to her dignity. Swift was aware of all this. While he was in Yorkshire in the dark days of the early summer of 1714, Erasmus Lewis had written to him from London:

I have yours of the 25th. You judge very right; it is not the going out, but the manner, that enrages me. The Queen has told all the Lords the reasons of her parting with [Harley, now Earl of Oxford], viz. that he neglected all business; that he was seldom to be understood; that when he did explain himself, she could not depend upon the truth of what he said; that he never came to her at the time she appointed; that he often came drunk; that lastly, to crown all, he behaved himself toward her with ill manner, indecency and disrespect. *Pudet haec opprobria nobis*, etc. (*Correspondence*, II 86).

The brilliance of Swift's symbolism is now clear. In a single action he embodied both the political and the personal charges against Oxford. Gulliver saved the palace, though his conduct was both illegal and indecent: Oxford saved the state, in return for which incidental illegalities and indecencies should have been overlooked. But prudery was stronger than gratitude. 'I was privately assured,' says Gulliver, 'the Empress conceiving the greatest abhorrence of what I had done, removed to the most distant side of the court, firmly resolved that those buildings should never be repaired for her use; and in the presence of her chief confidents, could not forbear vowing revenge' (XI 56). In plain terms, Queen Anne dispensed with Oxford's services and vowed never to make use of them again.

Paraphrase

At this point Swift, to heighten suspense, interpolates a chapter on general conditions of life in Lilliput, which, while it contains a number of isolated satiric references, does not advance the main plot. This is resumed at the beginning of the seventh chapter with the secret visit to Gulliver of 'a considerable person at court to whom [Gulliver] had been very serviceable at a time when he lay under the highest displeasure of his Imperial Majesty'. The considerable person was no less than the Duke of Marlborough. Early in 1715 Bolingbroke heard rumors that the victorious Whigs intended to impeach him, together with Oxford and other Tory leaders, of high treason. Relying on old friendship he inquired about the truth of these rumors from Marlborough, who, seeing an opportunity to get revenge for his dismissal four years earlier, so played upon Bolingbroke's fears that he fled to France. It is upon Bolingbroke's adventures that the story of Gulliver in Lilliput is based from this point onward, since Oxford, with more courage, remained to stand his trial and to be freed.

The tale of what was in store for Bolingbroke, as translated into Lilliputian terms, was sufficiently disquieting. Gulliver's enemies are listed as Skyresh Bolgolam; Flimnap, the High Treasurer; Limtoc, the General; Lalcon, the Chamberlain; and Balmuff, the Grand Justiciary. These represent Whigs or independent Tories who displayed their hostility to the Oxford-Bolingbroke administration either by speaking against it in Parliament or by acting as members of the Committee of Secrecy which, early in 1715, investigated the conduct of the ministry in the negotiation of the peace. Bolgolam has already been identified as the Earl of Nottingham, whose hatred of Oxford has been explained. Flimnap was Robert Walpole, the rising leader of the Whigs and chairman of the Committee of Secrecy. Limtoc the General, Lalcon the Chamberlain, and Balmuff the Grand Justiciary were, respectively, General Stanhope, Secretary of State for War; the Duke of Devonshire, Lord Steward; and Lord Cowper, Lord Chancellor. The second of these identifications is a little doubtful because there was in the British cabinet an official entitled Lord Chamberlain, but in 1715 this minister was the Duke of Shrewsbury, a mild man who took no active part in the attack on the defeated ministry.

All of the four articles of impeachment are counterparts of actual charges made against Oxford and Bolingbroke. The first accuses Gulliver of illegally extinguishing the fire in the palace (the ministry's technically unlawful negotiation of the Peace of Utrecht). The second dwells on Gulliver's refusal to subjugate Blefuscu completely (the granting of easy terms of peace to France). The third attacks the friendliness of Gulliver and the Blefuscudian ambassadors (the secret understanding between the Tory administration and the French diplomats). The fourth asserts that Gulliver intends to visit Blefuscu with only verbal license from the Emperor (a repetition of the first charge, with special reference to the failure of Oxford to procure a license under the great seal to negotiate the peace). The second and fourth articles contain allusions to the sixth and first provisions, respectively, of the agreement by which Gulliver was set at liberty.

The report of the council at which Gulliver's fate was debated is mordantly ironic. His bitterest enemies demand that he be put to a painful and ignominious death. The Emperor is more merciful, remembering Gulliver's former services: and Reldresal, Principal Secretary of State for Private Affairs and Gulliver's 'true friend', proposes and eventually carries a more 'lenient' motion. Gulliver is merely to be blinded, after which, if the council finds it expedient, he may easily be starved to death. Blinding is the equivalent of barring Oxford and Bolingbroke from political activity for the remainder of their lives. Reldresal's pretended friendship is a reference to the behavior of Charles, Viscount Townshend, Secretary of State in the Whig cabinet, whom the Tory leaders at first regarded as a friend at court after their fall, but whose sincerity they came to distrust. The 'mercy' of the Emperor is a fling at the execution of a number of the leaders of the rebellion of 1715 shortly after the House of Lords, in an address to George I, had praised his 'endearing tenderness and clemency'. Gulliver's reaction to this clemency is illuminating in its indication of the attitude of Oxford and Bolingbroke toward the Hanoverian dynasty as Swift wished it to be understood:

And as to myself, I must confess, having never been designed for a courtier either by my birth or education, I was so ill a judge of things, that I could not discover the lenity and favour of this sentence, but conceived it (perhaps erroneously) rather to be rigorous than gentle. I sometimes thought of standing my trial, for although I could not deny the facts alleged in the several articles, yet I hoped they would admit of some extenuations. But having in my life perused many state-trials, which I ever observed to terminate as the judges thought fit to direct, I durst not rely on so dangerous a decision, in so critical a juncture, and against such powerful enemies. Once I was strongly bent upon resistance, for while I had liberty, the whole strength of that empire could hardly subdue me, and I might easily with stones pelt the metropolis to pieces; but I soon rejected that project with horror, by remembering the oath I had made to the emperor, the favours I received from him, and the high title of *Nardac* he conferred upon me. Neither had I so soon learned the gratitude of courtiers, to persuade myself that his Majesty's present severities acquitted me of all past obligations (XI 72–3).

Little more of the allegory remains to be unraveled. Gulliver prudently and secretly seeks the protection of the Emperor of Blefuscu, as Bolingbroke fled to France. Like Bolingbroke, too, Gulliver ignores a proclamation threatening to stigmatize him as a traitor unless he returns to stand trial for his alleged crimes. Here Swift breaks off: it would hardly have been politic to discuss the period during which Bolingbroke was openly Secretary of State to the Pretender. The account of Gulliver's return to Europe is, like that of his arrival in Lilliput, a narrative to be taken at its face value.

The strongest arguments in favor of this interpretation of the *Voyage to Lilliput* are its consistency and the exactness with which it follows the chronology of the events which it symbolizes. Single incidents are often open to more than one explanation: a series carries conviction in proportion to its length. There are, of course, a few cases in which Swift takes slight and unimportant liberties with chronology for the sake of simplicity. For example, he represents Gulliver as being ennobled after the capture of the fleet, whereas Oxford and Bolingbroke received their titles not after the signing of the Peace of Utrecht, but while it was still being secretly negotiated. Similarly Flimnap is represented from the beginning of the story as Prime Minister and Gulliver's most potent enemy, though Walpole did not become head of the government until 1720. Swift is careful, however, not to attribute to Walpole any act of hostility to the Tory administration for which he was not responsible.

Swift also introduces incidental satiric touches as opportunity offers wherever the events or conditions have no temporal connexion with the main plot. This is especially true in the sixth chapter, where, among other things, there are references to the trial of Bishop Atterbury in 1722 and 1723 (in the use of the informers Clustril and Drunlo by Flimnap, standing for Walpole's employment of the spies Pancier and Neynoe), and a gratuitous gibe, in the final paragraph, at the notorious infidelities of Walpole's wife.

The political allegory of the first voyage is primarily concerned with the defense of the conduct of the Oxford-Bolingbroke ministry, and incidentally with an attack upon the Whigs. In the third voyage the emphasis is exactly reversed. It is important to realize from the beginning that the chief purpose of the allegory is *not*, as has so often been asserted, to attack the new science, but to attack learned folly, or 'pedantry', to use the word in its eighteenth-century meaning, and especially innovations and innovators in general. The focus of this attack is the Whig ministry under George I, which is accused of experimentation in the field of government, and of fostering experimenters in many other fields. Whiggery, to Swift, is the negation of that certainty which results from adherence to tried and approved procedures. In the light of this interpretation of Swift's design it becomes evident that the third voyage is much more unified in purpose than has commonly been supposed. A very large preponderance of its specific references to contemporary persons and events is contained in the first four chapters. The key to the satire is the identification of Laputa, the flying island, which has been variously interpreted as the English court under George I, and as the whole of England. The former interpretation was the normal one until about half a century ago. Swift's own verse (in his poem *The Life and Character of Dr Swift*) lends authority to this earlier view, for the supposed detractor of the Dean who there catalogues Swift's writings lists among them.

... *Libels* yet conceal'd from sight,
Against the *Court* to show his *spite*.
Perhaps his *Travels, Part the Third*;

A lie at every *second* word;
Offensive to a *loyal ear* —
(*Poems*, II 550)

In 1896, however, G. A. Aitken published in an appendix to an
edition of *Gulliver's Travels* four previously unprinted paragraphs
contained in the manuscript emendations in the Ford copy of the
first edition. Three years later these paragraphs, which described the
rebellion of Lindalino against Laputa, were restored to their proper
place in the third chapter of the third voyage by G. R. Dennis, who
edited the *Travels* for the Temple Scott edition. The effect of the
new passage on the interpretation of the voyage was remarkable.
There could be little doubt that it was an allegorical description of
the controversy over Wood's halfpence, with which Swift had dealt
so brilliantly in the *Drapier's Letters* only two years before *Gulliver's
Travels* was published. And since Lindalino obviously stood for
Dublin, it is hardly surprising that Laputa should have been taken for
England as a whole, hovering over all of Ireland, or Balnibarbi. In
1919 Sir Charles Firth not only endorsed this view, but extended it
to the interpretation of other parts of the third voyage, and even
allowed it to color his ideas of the fourth. In particular he suggested
that Munodi was Viscount Midleton, Chancellor of Ireland from
1714 to 1725, and that Balnibarbi in the impoverished state described
in the third chapter represented Ireland under English domination.
This theory, of course, necessitates a belief that Swift changed the
meaning of his symbols from time to time: for example, Lagado is
in Balnibarbi, but the Grand Academy of Lagado is generally identified as the Royal Society of London; therefore Balnibarbi, of which
Lagado is the metropolis, must sometimes stand for Ireland, and
sometimes for England or for the British Isles as a whole. Other
inconsistencies involved in Sir Charles's theory suggest themselves on
further examination. From the beginning of the voyage Swift makes
a good deal of the minuteness of Laputa and the relatively great
extent of the land of Balnibarbi which it dominates. Moreover,
Laputa is inhabited only by a small number of courtiers and their
hangers-on (chiefly scientific and musical); it is not self-supporting,
but is dependent upon sustenance drawn from below; it travels
about by a series of oblique motions which probably symbolizes the

indirect and erratic course of Whig policy under the ministerial clique headed by Walpole. Lagado, the metropolis of the kingdom, which certainly stands for London, is below and subject to Laputa. Lindalino, or Dublin, is described as the second city of the kingdom – an accurate description if the kingdom is the whole British Isles, but not if it is Ireland alone. Moreover, the general account of the King's methods of suppressing insurrections which precedes the story of Lindalino's revolt is accurate only if Balnibarbi includes Great Britain.

The King would be the most absolute Prince in the Universe, if he could but prevail on a ministry to join with him; but these having their estates below on the continent, and considering that the office of a favourite hath a very uncertain tenure, would never consent to the enslaving their country ... nor dare his ministers advise him to an action, which as it would render them odious to the people, so it would be a great damage to their own estates, which lie all below, for the Island is the King's demesne (XI 171).

It is hardly necessary to point out that few of George I's ministry held any significant amount of Irish land, and that none of them displayed any fear of Irish public opinion.

If the older theory, which identified Balnibarbi as England and Laputa as the Court, is reconsidered, it will be seen that one slight emendation will bring it into conformity with the account of the revolt of Lindalino. If the continent of Balnibarbi represents all of the British Isles, the inconsistencies in the allegory disappear. There can be no serious doubt that Swift, in this restored passage of *Gulliver's Travels*, is using the affair of Wood's halfpence again, but this time it is for a different purpose. In 1724, addressing Irishmen through the *Drapier's Letters*, he was trying to arouse national feeling and to make the issue one of Ireland against England. In 1726, in a more general work, addressed to the English more than to any other nation, he made the issue one of tyranny over the subject by a would-be absolute monarch. When this is once understood it is not difficult to find plausible counterparts in history for the various details of the description of the Laputian method of suppressing insurrections.

The three ways of punishing a recalcitrant city (interposing the island between the city and the sun; pelting the city with rocks; and completely crushing it by dropping the island down upon it) represent three degrees of severity in actual practice, perhaps threats, accompanied by withdrawal of court patronage, moderate civil repressive action and military invasion. The reason given for the King's disinclination to proceed to the last degree of severity is that this might endanger the adamantine bottom of the island, which appears to stand either for the monarchy or for the British constitution. It should be remembered that Swift believed in the theory of government which divided the power among the three estates of the realm, and which relied on a balance among them. Any estate which arrogated to itself an undue share of power was held to endanger the whole structure of the government.

The chief defenses of any city against oppression by the King and his court are thus expressed allegorically:

... if the town intended to be destroyed should have in it any tall rocks, as it generally falls out in the larger cities, a situation probably chosen at first with a view to prevent such a catastrophe; or if it abound in high spires or pillars of stone, a sudden fall might endanger the bottom or under surface of the island ... (XI 171).

Of the three defenses, the 'high spires' seem least ambiguous: almost certainly these represent churches or churchmen — possibly the ecclesiastical interest generally, which rallied almost unanimously to the Irish cause. The 'tall rocks' seem to differ from the 'pillars of stone' chiefly in being natural rather than creations of man, which suggests that the rocks may represent either the hereditary nobility, who constituted the second estate of the realm, or the higher ecclesiastical authorities, representing a divine rather than a man-made institution. Similarly the 'pillars of stone' may be either self-made citizens of power and importance, or certain man-made legal institutions. In the story of the revolt of Lindalino the strong pointed rock in the middle of the city is almost certainly the combined power of the Irish Church, centered in St Patrick's Cathedral; and the 'four large towers' presumably stand for the four most important local governmental agencies of Ireland – the Privy Council, the Grand Jury and the two houses of the Irish Parliament. The 'vast quantity of the most combustible fuel' collected by the inhabitants probably stands for the multitude of incendiary pamphlets written against Wood's halfpence by Swift and others. Finally, the unsuccessful experiment made by one of the King's officers, who let down a piece of adamant from Laputa and found it so strongly drawn toward the towers and the rock that he could hardly draw it back, presumably represents the bold resistance of the Irish civil and ecclesiastical institutions to the King's measures.

That this incident could have been omitted from the text of *Gulliver's Travels* without causing an apparent break in the continuity of the story is characteristic of the structure of the third voyage, which differs markedly from that of the first. In his account of Lilliput Swift provided a climactic plot, based upon the fortunes of a particular Tory administration. In the third voyage no such plot is practicable: the history of Walpole's administration had not reached a climax in 1726, and Swift would not have wished to tell a story which could only have emphasized the success of his enemies. He therefore chose to attack the Whigs not by dramatic narrative, but by satiric portraiture. There is, consequently, no chronological scheme for the third voyage, which is a picture of conditions rather than of acts.

As in the first voyage, Swift is chary of drawing too obvious a portrait of George I. Not much is said of the physical appearance of the King of Laputa; there are, however, several references which intelligent contemporaries must have interpreted without difficulty. One is the parenthetical remark (XI 160) about the King's 'being distinguished above all his predecessors for his hospitality to strangers' – a palpable hit at George's extensive appointments of Hanoverians to posts of profit in England. The last paragraph of the third chapter is still more open satire – almost dangerously open. 'By a fundamental law of this realm,' Gulliver observes, 'neither the King nor either of his two elder sons are permitted to leave the Island, nor the Queen till she is past childbearing.' No Englishman could have failed to be reminded by this sentence that the Act of Settlement had originally forbidden the departure of the sovereign from England without the express consent of Parliament, and that George I, whose journeys to his beloved Hanover aroused the general resentment of his English subjects, had persuaded Parliament to repeal this provision of the Act in 1716. George's delight in music is parodied by the description of the Laputian King's fondness for the art. Here, however, and even more in the case of the King's supposed personal interest in science, Swift modifies the actual facts for the sake of his thesis. Under the reign of Anne men of letters had received a considerable amount of royal patronage, especially during the administration of Oxford. Under the reign of George I it seemed, especially to Tory wits who had been deprived of their posts of profit, that the pendulum had swung away from the profession of literature in the direction of musicians and experimental scientists. Patronage being, at least in theory, a personal prerogative of the King, Swift in his allegory attributed the shift in patronage to the King's inclinations. How far this shift was a fact, and, if a fact, how far it was due to conscious intention on the part of the government, are matters of secondary importance to the present inquiry. It may be said, however, that while Whig writers received some government patronage during the administration of Oxford (largely because of Swift's insistence), Tory writers got very little after the Whigs came into power in 1714. Moreover, a great wave of invention and commercial exploitation of inventions coincided with the opening years of George I's reign, and scientists, notably the astronomers Newton and Flamsteed, were given generous encouragement.

The Prince of Wales, whom Swift had once portrayed as the heir to the Lilliputian crown, with one high and one low heel, is in the third voyage aligned more definitely and sympathetically with the Tories. He is described as 'a great Lord at court, nearly related to the King, and for that reason alone used with respect' (xi 173). The hostility between the Prince and his father, and his consequent unpopularity in the King's court, were, of course, common knowledge. Swift represents the Prince as one who 'had great natural and acquired parts, adorned with integrity and honour, but so ill an ear for music, that his detractors reported he had been often known to beat time in the wrong place; neither could his tutors without extreme difficulty teach him to demonstrate the most easy proposition in the mathematics' (xi 173). It is undoubtedly true that Prince George had a supreme contempt for academic learning, and while he probably had a better knowledge of music than Swift ascribes to him here, his interest in the art fell far below his father's: his patronage of Buononcini seems to have been motivated by a desire to annoy George I by support of a supposed rival to Handel, whom the King delighted to honor.

"The Prince of Laputa is not only uninterested in the subjects which engross the attention of his father's court: he is positively interested in all the other things which they neglect. Here again Swift contrasts the theoretical Whig King with the practical Tory Prince. Alone among the Laputians the latter is anxious to learn from Gulliver the laws and customs of other countries. Alone among Laputians of rank he dispenses with the services of a flapper. He makes 'very wise observations' on everything Gulliver tells him, and is loath to allow the traveler to depart, although helpful and generous when Gulliver persists in his intention. Swift makes clear the Tory hopes of the early 1720s – that Prince George on his accession to the throne might call the old Tory administration to power – through the Laputian Prince's recommendation of Gulliver to a friend of his in Lagado, the lord Munodi, who has been variously identified with Bolingbroke and Lord Midleton, but never, apparently, with Oxford, whom he actually represents. The evidence for this identification is plentiful. Munodi is described as a former governor of Lagado, which must be translated either as Lord Mayor of London or Prime Minister of England. As Swift displays no interest in the municipal government of London, the second alternative is much more probable. Munodi is represented as having been discharged from office for inefficiency by a cabal of ministers – a close parallel with Oxford's dismissal from his post in 1714 and his trial on the charge of treason between 1715 and 1717. It will be recalled that when the accusation against Oxford was finally dropped in 1717 he returned from politics to the quiet existence of a country gentleman on his estates in Herefordshire. This retirement is reflected not only in Munodi's having withdrawn from public life, but in his name, which seems to be a contraction of 'mundum odi' – 'I hate the world.'

Munodi's story is a thinly veiled allegory of the results to be expected from flighty experimental Whig government as opposed to sound conservative Tory government. Balnibarbi, the inhabitants of which are occupied with financial speculation and with the exploitation of chimerical 'projects', both in the city and in the country, is a symbol of the British Isles under George I and the Whigs: Munodi's private estate, managed in 'the good old way', to the evident profit of its owner and the pleasure of its citizenry, represents the way of the Tory remnant, sneered at by the adherents of the newer way as reactionary. The triumph of the innovators is attributed to the conversion of weak-minded members of the governing class by the court circle in Laputa, with the result that their principles have been imported into the management of the subject continent, and a center of the new experimental culture has even been founded in Lagado. The Grand Academy no doubt stands in part for the Royal Society, and the fact that Swift in his allegory lays its creation at the door of the court is significant as indicating the center of his interest, since the Royal Society, while it had received encouragement from the court of Charles II at the time of its foundation in 1660, certainly had more influence on the court of George I than the court had upon it.

The last detail in the history of Munodi is of particular interest, since its true significance seems never to have been pointed out by any commentator upon the *Travels*, though it must have been apparent to many of Swift's contemporaries. There was one act of Oxford's administration which laid him open to criticism as an experimenter in governmental economics – an experimenter more speculative and unsound than any Whig. The act was the sponsoring of the South Sea Company. This device for refunding the public debt of England had been urged upon Oxford by Defoe, who had finally persuaded his superior to give the company a charter in 1712, and to arrange for the exchange of governmental obligations for South Sea stock. The public was encouraged to make the exchange on the ground that the new investment was quite as safe as the old and much more profitable. The details of the great speculation and of the ultimate crash of 1720 – the 'South Sea year' – need not be rehearsed in detail. The crash brought with it much criticism of Oxford, and many demands that he emerge from retirement to assist in clearing up the mess for which he was responsible. Swift does what he can to rehabilitate Oxford's reputation as an economist through the allegory of the mill, near the end of the fourth chapter. Gulliver relates that there had been on Munodi's estate (England under Oxford's administration) an old mill (the old English fiscal system), turned by the current of a large river (England's income from agriculture and trade), and sufficient not only for Munodi's family (the British empire), but also for a great number of his tenants (England's allies in the War of the Spanish Succession). A club of projectors (Defoe and his abettors) proposed to destroy the old mill and substitute a new one much farther away (the South Sea Company), requiring artificial means (stockjobbing) to pump up water for its operation, on the plea that water agitated by wind and air upon a height (money put into active circulation by speculation) would turn the mill with half the current of a river whose course was more upon the level (would provide sufficient government revenues with the use of half the capital required by the old fiscal policy). Munodi, 'being then not very well with the Court' (Anne had shown her displeasure at Oxford's personal behavior toward her as early as 1712), and being pressed by many of his friends, complied with the proposal. It is hardly necessary to labor the significance of the rest of the allegory. 'After employing an hundred men for two years, the work miscarried, the projectors went off, laying the blame entirely upon him, railing at him ever since, and putting others upon the same experiment, with equal assurance of success, as well as equal disappointment.'

The fifth and sixth chapters of the third voyage are concerned with the Grand Academy of Lagado, generally held to stand for the Royal Society of London. That the Society was in Swift's mind cannot be doubted, but that it is the primary object of the satire in these chapters is a conclusion that deserves examination, at least. The first discrepancy in the account has to do with the physical appearance of the Academy's buildings. 'This Academy', says Gulliver, 'is not an entire single building, but a continuation of several houses on both sides of a street; which growing waste, was purchased and applyed to that use' (xi 179). The description does not fit the buildings of the real Society, which in 1710 had moved its Museum from Arundel House to a building in Crane Court, Fleet Street, quite unlike the structure pictured by Gulliver. In the light of the emphasis placed on the Academy's school of political projectors it is not impossible that the description should be applied rather to the rapidly expanding governmental buildings on both sides of Whitehall.

Far more interesting than the outward appearance of the Academy is the nature of the activities carried on within. Many of the Royal Society's experiments were in the realm of pure science, and were conducted for no immediately practical end. In the Academy the large majority of the projects are designed to bring about supposed improvements in commerce, medicine, or some other field of importance in daily life: what is ridiculous is that the methods, rather than the purposes of the inventors, are chimerical. Another important fact is the insistence upon the word 'projectors' in the title of the Academy: it is printed in capitals, and it occurs, together with the word 'projects', again and again in this section of the voyage. These words were not very frequently applied to members of the Royal Society and their exercises in the seventeenth and eighteenth centuries: the usual terms of contempt were 'virtuosi' and 'experiments'. 'Projector' was, however, a word all too familiar to Englishmen of the second decade of the eighteenth century. To them it signified a man who promoted a get-rich-quick scheme, plausible but impracticable, for the carrying out of which he levied upon the public. This latter habit seems to be alluded to twice in the fifth chapter: first, when Gulliver remarks that it is customary for the projectors to beg money from all who visit them (XI 179) and, secondly, when the inventor of the frame for writing books suggests that his operations 'might be still improved, and much expedited, if the public would raise a fund for making and employing five hundred such frames in *Lagado*' (XI 184). Speculative schemes actually floated during the first six years of the reign of George I, and especially in 1720 – the 'South Sea year' – were in some instances almost as illusory as those described by Swift, and may even have suggested a few of them. Companies advertising for subscriptions included one for extracting silver from lead, and others for making bays in Colchester and elsewhere, for manuring farm lands, for a more inoffensive method of emptying and cleansing 'necessary houses', for bringing live sea-fish to London in specially built tank-vessels, for making salt water fresh, for planting mulberry trees and raising silk-worms in Chelsea Park, for fishing for wrecks along the Irish coast, for a wheel for perpetual motion, and, finally, for 'an undertaking which shall in due course be revealed'. An anonymous wag advertised for subscriptions to a company for melting down sawdust and chips and casting them into clean deal boards without cracks or knots: another group, having obtained several hundred subscriptions to a scheme almost equally vague, publicly announced that the venture had been a hoax intended to make the public more cautious, and returned the subscription money.

The school for political projectors clearly has no connexion with the Royal Society: it is a satiric attack on corruption and stupidity in government, with a section at the end based upon what Swift regarded as the biased and unjust prosecution of Bishop Atterbury, in 1723, for complicity in the Jacobite plot. The paragraph on copromancy (XI 190) arises from the putting in evidence at the trial of the Bishop of correspondence found in his close-stool. The discussion of secret codes which follows has to do with the charge that the Bishop and his correspondents used the name of the Bishop's lame dog Harlequin as a symbol for the Pretender: hence the inclusion by Swift in his burlesque secret code of '*a lame dog, an invader*'. This code, incidentally, was one of the few passages which Motte altered out of an apparent fear that the satire was too obvious and too dangerous. His emendations, aside from a slight rearrangement, consisted of the omission of four code pairs and the alteration of another. The phrases omitted were: 'a close-stool a privy council, a flock of geese a senate . . . a codshead a — . . . a gibbet a secretary of state': the alteration consisted of the weakening of 'a buzzard a prime minister' to '*a buzzard a great statesman*'. Presumably the blank after 'codshead' was to be filled in by the reader with 'king'. It is not difficult to understand why Motte, in 1726, preferred not to print this part of the manuscript as it stood.

The last type of code discussed is the anagram, a device which was also alleged to be used by the Jacobites. Swift's Tribnian experts, analysing the sentence, '*Our Brother Tom has just got the piles*', produce the message, '*Resist; a plot is brought home, The Tour.*' It is not an accident that while the '*a*' in this message is a lower-case letter, the 'T' of 'The' is a capital. 'The Tour' is a signature. During part of his exile in France Bolingbroke requested his friends to address him as M. La Tour. A grammarian would point out that 'la tour' is a tower: a tour is 'le tour': but Swift apparently did not regard this as a serious objection. Perhaps, too, he did not wish to abandon what he felt was a very appropriate anagram.

The remainder of the third voyage contains only scattering references to specific events or persons contemporary with Swift. In the seventh chapter it is sufficiently clear that the 'modern representative' of assemblies, which compares so unfavorably with the Senate of ancient Rome, is the British Parliament. In the next chapter the nameless ghost in Glubbdubdrib who informs Gulliver about the confounding of the commentators on Homer and Aristotle may be Sir William Temple, whose views on classical scholarship Swift had espoused so warmly in *The Battle of the Books*, but there is not enough evidence to confirm this surmise. In the following paragraph Aristotle decries the theory of gravitation propounded by Sir Isaac Newton, one of Swift's enemies. Shortly afterward occurs one of the most mysterious references in the entire *Travels*. In the midst of a series of general exposures of the true genealogies and histories of 'great families' Gulliver observes that he learned in Glubbdubdrib 'whence it came what Polydore Virgil says of a certain great house, *'nec vir fortis, nec foemina casta'*'. A careful search of the works of Polydore Virgil has not brought this phrase to light: on the other hand, it is the exact converse of a much-quoted sentence, famous in that day, from the epitaph on the tomb of Margaret Cavendish, Duchess of Newcastle, born Margaret Lucas: 'All the brothers were valiant, and all the sisters virtuous.' (Addison quoted the phrase in the *Spectator*, 23 June 1711.) As Swift seems to have had no personal animus against the Lucases, and as that family, more than most, deserved the monumental flattery, it is possible that Swift merely borrowed and twisted an effective phrase to enforce a general satire on the nobility.

One last passage in the eighth chapter contains enough specific detail to suggest a reference to an individual. This is the paragraph which reads:

Among others there was one person whose case appeared a little singular. He had a youth about eighteen years old standing by his side. He told me he had for many years been commander of a ship, and in the sea fight at *Actium*, had the good fortune to break through the enemy's great line of battle, sink three of their capital ships, and take a fourth, which was the sole cause of Anthony's flight, and of the victory that ensued; that the youth standing by him, his only son, was killed in the action. He added, that upon the confidence of some merit, the war being at an end, he went to Rome, and solicited at the Court of Augustus to be preferred

to a greater ship, whose commander had been killed; but
without any regard to his pretensions, it was given to a youth
who had never seen the sea, the son of [a] Libertina, who waited
on one of the Emperor's mistresses. Returning back to his own
vessel, he was charged with neglect of duty, and the ship was
given to a favourite page of Publicola the Vice-Admiral;
whereupon he retired to a poor farm, at a great distance from
Rome, and there ended his life. I was so curious to know the
truth of this story, that I desired Agrippa might be called, who
was Admiral in that fight. He appeared and confirmed the
whole account, but with much more advantage to the
captain, whose modesty had extenuated or concealed a great
part of his merit (XI 201).

The general purport of the third voyage suggests that this is an
allegorical account of an individual instance of Whig ingratitude
toward a Tory. The two most eminent Tory 'martyrs' of the day
were General Webb, whose exploits had been slighted by Marlborough, and Charles Mordaunt, third Earl of Peterborough. The
latter military leader, a personal friend of Swift's, had fought both
on land and at sea during the War of the Spanish Succession, but after
some brilliant successes in the Peninsular campaign of 1706 he disagreed with the other leaders of the Allies, and was eventually
recalled to England. In 1707, on the way to Genoa, his ship was
attacked by the enemy; he escaped, but a convoying ship under the
command of his son was badly damaged, and the son received grave
wounds which may have contributed to his death some time later.
Peterborough's removal from command, and his failure to secure
reinstatement, were at least partly due to the enmity of the young
Emperor Charles, who succeeded him in the direction of the Peninsular campaign. Swift, in *The Conduct of the Allies*, had already taken
up the cudgels for Peterborough, though without naming him
explicitly,

. . . there [in Spain] we drove on the war at a prodigious
disadvantage . . . and by a most corrupt management, the only
general who, by a course of conduct and fortune almost
miraculous, had nearly put us into possession of the kingdom,

was left wholly unsupported, exposed to the envy of his rivals, disappointed by the caprices of a young unexperienced prince, under the guidance of a rapacious German ministry, and at last called home in discontent (VI 21).

The young unexperienced prince was, of course, the Emperor Charles. It seems not unlikely that he was the 'youth who had never seen the sea', who displaced the Roman hero of Gulliver's tale. The identity of the 'favourite page of Publicola' does not appear.

Perhaps the most striking feature of this explanation of the personal and political allegory is that it leaves no room for an autobiographical interpretation of *Gulliver's Travels*. The various passages upon which this interpretation has rested are seen to be susceptible of other meanings more significant in themselves, and more consistent with each other and with the intent of the book. If this view is correct, Swift, so often conceived as the complete egoist, did not regard his own fortunes and misfortunes as being of equal importance with the affairs of public figures such as Oxford, Bolingbroke and Peterborough. This is confirmed by his correspondence. Swift evidently felt that both Whigs and Tories were ungrateful to him, but his services to the Whigs were, as far as we know, relatively slight. His pamphleteering for the Tories, on the other hand, was of inestimable value, yet for years Oxford slighted him in favor of less deserving men, and finally obtained for him a post which he regarded as little else than exile, and which he accepted in a mood of bitterness. On 16 April 1713, he wrote to Stella:

Mr Lewis tells me that D. Ormd has been today with Qu[een] and she was content that Dr Stearn should be Bp of Dromore and I Dean of St Patrick's, but then out came Ld Tr, [and said] he would not be satisfied, but that I must be Prebend of Windsor, thus he perplexes things – I expect neither; but I confess, as much as I love England, I am so angry at this Treatm[en]t, that if I had my choice I would rather have St Patrick's (*Journal*, II 662).

That this was no passing mood is shown by his letter of 13 July 1714, written from Letcombe to John Arbuthnot when it was evident that the Tory ministry had run its race:

Dear — I wonder how you came to mention that business to
Lady M[asham], if I guess right, that the business is the
Histor[ian]'s Place. It is in the D[uke] of Shr[ewsbury]'s gift, and
he sent L[or]d Bol[ingbroke] word that though he was under
some engagement, he would get it me. Since which time I
never mentioned it, though I had a memorial some months
in my pocket, which I believe you saw, but I would never give
it Lady M[asham] because things were embroiled with her.
I would not give two pence to have it for the value of it, but
I have been told by L[or]d P[eterborough] L[a]dy M[asham]
and you, that the Qu[een] has a concern for her History, &c.,
and I was ready to undertake it. I thought L[or]d Bol[ingbroke]
would have done such a trifle, but I shall not concern myself,
and I should be sorry the Qu[een] should be asked for it
otherwise than as what would be for her honour and reputation
with posterity, etc. Pray, how long do you think I should be
suffered to hold that post in the next reign? I have enclosed
you the original memorial as I intended it; and if L[or]d
Bol[ingbroke] thinks it of any moment, let him do it, but do
not give him the memorial unless he be perfectly willing. For
I insist again upon it, that I am not asking a favour, and there
is an end of that matter, only one word more, that I would
not accept it if offered, only that it would give me an
opportunity of seeing those I esteem and love the little time
they will be in power. . . . I must repeat it again, that if
L[or]d Bol[ingbroke] be not full as ready to give this
memorial enclosed, as you are to desire him, let it drop, for in
the present view of things, I am perfectly indifferent, for I
think every reason for my leaving you is manifestly doubled
within these six weeks, by your own account as well as that of
others. Besides I take it perfectly ill that the Dragon, who
promised me so solemnly last year to make me easy in my
debts, has never done the least thing to it. So that I can safely
say I never received a penny from a minister in my life. And
though I scorn to complain, yet to you I will speak it, that
I am very uneasy that I am likely to lose near 300 pounds,
beside the heavy debts I lie under at a season of my life when
I hoped to have no cares of that sort (*Correspondence*, II 62–3).

In the face of this ingratitude to himself, which he so clearly recognized, Swift nevertheless remained loyal to the defeated leaders, offering to accompany Oxford into retirement, and steadfastly defending both Oxford and Bolingbroke while they lay under charges of treason, even after Bolingbroke fled to France and joined the Pretender. All this was done, as Swift's letters show, in the face of a conviction that he himself could gain nothing from his friendship save, perhaps, a reputation of being himself a Jacobite traitor. Is it too difficult to suppose that he did this because of a sincere belief that the Tories' ingratitude to him was outweighed by their devotion to what were, in Swift's mind, the right principles of government? (69–96)

George Orwell

'Politics v. Literature: An Examination of *Gulliver's Travels*' 1946 (reprinted in Sonia Orwell and Ian Angus (eds.), *The Collected Essays, Journalism and Letters of George Orwell*, vol. 4, 1968)

In *Gulliver's Travels* humanity is attacked, or criticized, from at least three different angles, and the implied character of Gulliver himself necessarily changes somewhat in the process. In Part I he is the typical eighteenth-century voyager, bold, practical and unromantic, his homely outlook skilfully impressed on the reader by the biographical details at the beginning, by his age (he is a man of forty, with two children, when his adventures start), and by the inventory of the things in his pockets, especially his spectacles, which make several appearances. In Part II he has in general the same character, but at moments when the story demands it he has a tendency to develop into an imbecile who is capable of boasting of 'our noble country, the mistress of arts and arms, the scourge of France' etc. etc., and at the same time of betraying every available scandalous fact about the country which he professes to love. In Part III he is much as he was in Part I, though, as he is consorting chiefly with courtiers and men of learning, one has the impression that he has risen in the social scale. In Part IV he conceives a horror of the human race which is not apparent, or only intermittently apparent, in the earlier books, and changes into a sort of unreligious anchorite whose one desire is to live in some desolate spot where he can devote himself to meditating on the goodness of the Houyhnhnms. However, these inconsistencies are forced upon Swift by the fact that Gulliver is there chiefly to provide a contrast. It is necessary, for instance, that he should appear sensible in Part I and at least intermittently silly in Part II, because in both books the essential manoeuvre is the same, i.e. to make the human being look ridiculous by imagining him as a creature six inches high. Whenever Gulliver is not acting as a stooge there is a sort of continuity in his character, which comes out especially in his resourcefulness and his observation of physical detail. He is much the same kind of person, with the same prose style, when he bears off the warships of Blefuscu, when he rips open the belly of the monstrous rat, and when he sails away upon the ocean in his frail coracle made from the skins of Yahoos. Moreover, it is difficult not to feel that in his shrewder moments Gulliver is simply Swift himself, and there is at least one incident in which Swift seems to be venting his private grievance against contemporary society. It will be remembered that when the Emperor of Lilliput's palace catches fire, Gulliver puts it out by urinating on it. Instead of being congratulated on his presence of mind, he finds that he has committed a capital offence by making water in the precincts of the palace, and

I was privately assured, that the Empress, conceiving the greatest abhorrence of what I had done, removed to the most distant side of the court, firmly resolved that those buildings should never be repaired for her use; and, in the presence of her chief confidents, could not forbear vowing revenge (XI 56).

According to Professor G. M. Trevelyan (*England under Queen Anne*), part of the reason for Swift's failure to get preferment was that the Queen was scandalized by *A Tale of a Tub* – a pamphlet in which Swift probably felt that he had done a great service to the English Crown, since it scarifies the Dissenters and still more the Catholics while leaving the Established Church alone. In any case no one would deny that *Gulliver's Travels* is a rancorous as well as a pessimistic book, and that especially in Parts I and III it often descends into political partisanship of a narrow kind. Pettiness and magnanimity, republicanism and authoritarianism, love of reason and lack of curiosity, are all mixed up in it. The hatred of the human body with which Swift is especially associated is only dominant in Part IV, but somehow this new preoccupation does not come as a surprise. One feels that all these adventures, and all these changes of mood, could have happened to the same person, and the interconnexion between Swift's political loyalties and his ultimate despair is one of the most interesting features of the book.

Politically, Swift was one of those people who are driven into a sort of perverse Toryism by the follies of the progressive party of the moment. Part I of *Gulliver's Travels*, ostensibly a satire on human greatness, can be seen, if one looks a little deeper, to be simply an attack on England, on the dominant Whig Party and on the war with France, which – however bad the motives of the Allies may have been – did save Europe from being tyrannized over by a single reactionary power. Swift was not a Jacobite nor strictly speaking a Tory, and his declared aim in the war was merely a moderate peace treaty and not the outright defeat of England. Nevertheless there is a tinge of quislingism in his attitude, which comes out in the ending of Part I and slightly interferes with the allegory. When Gulliver flees from Lilliput (England) to Blefuscu (France) the assumption that a human being six inches high is inherently contemptible seems to be dropped. Whereas the people of Lilliput have behaved towards Gulliver with the utmost treachery and meanness, those of Blefuscu behave generously and straightforwardly, and indeed this section of the book ends on a different note from the all-round disillusionment of the earlier chapters. Evidently Swift's animus is, in the first place, against *England*. It is 'your natives' (i.e. Gulliver's fellow countrymen) whom the King of Brobdingnag considers to be 'the most pernicious race of little odious vermin that nature ever suffered to crawl upon the surface of the earth', and the long passage at the end, denouncing colonization and foreign conquest, is plainly aimed at England, although the contrary is elaborately stated. The Dutch, England's allies and target of one of Swift's most famous pamphlets, are also more or less wantonly attacked in Part III. There is even what sounds like a personal note in the passage in which Gulliver records his satisfaction that the various countries he has discovered cannot be made colonies of the British Crown:

The *Houyhnhnms,* indeed, appear not to be so well prepared
for war, a science to which they are perfect strangers, and
especially against missive weapons. However, supposing myself
to be a Minister of State, I could never give my advice for
invading them. ... Imagine twenty thousand of them
breaking into the midst of a *European* army, confounding
the ranks, overturning the carriages, battering the warriors'
faces into mummy, by terrible yerks from their hinder hoofs. ...
(XI 293).

Considering that Swift does not waste words, that phrase, 'battering
the warriors' faces into mummy', probably indicates a secret wish
to see the invincible armies of the Duke of Marlborough treated in a
like manner. There are similar touches elsewhere. Even the country
mentioned in Part III, where 'the bulk of the people consist, in a
manner, wholly of discoverers, witnesses, informers, accusers, prosecutors, evidences, swearers, together with their several subservient
and subaltern instruments, all under the colours, the conduct and pay
of Ministers of State', is called Langdon, which is within one letter
of being an anagram of England. (As the early editions of the book
contain misprints, it may perhaps have been intended as a complete
anagram.) Swift's *physical* repulsion from humanity is certainly real
enough, but one has the feeling that his debunking of human grandeur, his diatribes against lords, politicians, court favourites, etc. have
mainly a local application and spring from the fact that he belonged
to the unsuccessful party. He denounces injustice and oppression, but
he gives no evidence of liking democracy. In spite of his enormously
greater powers, his implied position is very similar to that of the
innumerable silly–clever Conservatives of our own day – people like
Sir Alan Herbert, Professor G. M. Young, Lord Elton, the Tory
Reform Committee or the long line of Catholic apologists from
W. H. Mallock onwards: people who specialize in cracking neat
jokes at the expense of whatever is 'modern' and 'progressive', and
whose opinions are often all the more extreme because they know
that they cannot influence the actual drift of events. After all, such a

pamphlet as *An Argument to Prove that the Abolishing of Christianity* etc. is very like 'Timothy Shy' having a bit of clean fun with the Brains Trust, or Father Ronald Knox exposing the errors of Bertrand Russell. And the ease with which Swift has been forgiven – and forgiven, sometimes, by devout believers – for the blasphemies of *A Tale of a Tub* demonstrates clearly enough the feebleness of religious sentiments as compared with political ones.

However, the reactionary cast of Swift's mind does not show itself chiefly in his political affiliations. The important thing is his attitude towards science, and, more broadly, towards intellectual curiosity. The famous Academy of Lagado, described in Part III of *Gulliver's Travels*, is no doubt a justified satire on most of the so-called scientists of Swift's own day. Significantly, the people at work in it are described as 'projectors', that is, people not engaged in disinterested research but merely on the look-out for gadgets which will save labour and bring in money. But there is no sign – indeed, all through the book there are many signs to the contrary – that 'pure' science would have struck Swift as a worthwhile activity. The more serious kind of scientist has already had a kick in the pants in Part II, when the 'scholars' patronized by the King of Brobdingnag try to account for Gulliver's small stature:

After much debate, they concluded unanimously that I was only *Relplum Scalcath*, which is interpreted literally, *Lusus Naturae*; a determination exactly agreeable to the modern philosophy of Europe, whose professors, disdaining the old evasion of *occult causes*, whereby the followers of *Aristotle* endeavour in vain to disguise their ignorance, have invented this wonderful solution of all difficulties, to the unspeakable advancement of human knowledge (XI 104).

If this stood by itself one might assume that Swift is merely the enemy of *sham* science. In a number of places, however, he goes out of his way to proclaim the uselessness of all learning or speculation not directed towards some practical end:

The learning of (the Brobdingnagians) is very defective, consisting only in morality, history, poetry and mathematics, wherein they must be allowed to excel. But, the last of these is wholly applied to what may be useful in life, to the improvement of agriculture, and all mechanical arts; so that among us it would be little esteemed. And as to ideas, entities, abstractions and transcendentals, I could never drive the least conception into their heads (XI 136).

The Houyhnhnms, Swift's ideal beings, are backward even in a mechanical sense. They are unacquainted with metals, have never heard of boats, do not, properly speaking, practise agriculture (we are told that the oats which they live upon 'grow naturally'), and appear not to have invented wheels.[1] They have no alphabet, and evidently have not much curiosity about the physical world. They do not believe that any inhabited country exists beside their own, and though they understand the motions of the sun and moon, and the nature of eclipses, 'this is the utmost progress of their *astronomy*'. By contrast, the philosophers of the flying island of Laputa are so continuously absorbed in mathematical speculations that before speaking to them one has to attract their attention by flapping them on the ear with a bladder. They have catalogued ten thousand fixed stars, have settled the periods of ninety-three comets, and have discovered, in advance of the astronomers of Europe, that Mars has two moons – all of which information Swift evidently regards as ridiculous, useless and uninteresting. As one might expect, he believes that the scientist's place, if he has a place, is in the laboratory, and that scientific knowledge has no bearing on political matters:

What I . . . thought altogether unaccountable, was the strong disposition I observed in them towards news and politics, perpetually inquiring into public affairs, giving their judgements in matters of state, and passionately disputing every inch of a party opinion. I have, indeed, observed the same disposition among most of the mathematicians I have known in Europe, though I could never discover the least analogy between the two sciences; unless those people suppose, that, because the smallest circle has as many degrees as the

1 Houyhnhnms too old to walk are described as being carried in 'sledges' or in 'a kind of vehicle, drawn like a sledge'. Presumably these had no wheels.

largest, therefore the regulation and management of the
World require no more abilities, than the handling and
turning of a globe (XI 164).

Is there not something familiar in that phrase 'I could never discover
the least analogy between the two sciences'? It has precisely the note
of the popular Catholic apologists who profess to be astonished when
a scientist utters an opinion on such questions as the existence of God
or the immortality of the soul. The scientist, we are told, is an expert
only in one restricted field: why should his opinions be of value in
any other? The implication is that theology is just as much an exact
science as, for instance, chemistry, and that the priest is also an expert
whose conclusions on certain subjects must be accepted. Swift in
effect makes the same claim for the politician, but he goes one better
in that he will not allow the scientist – either the 'pure' scientist or
the *ad hoc* investigator – to be a useful person in his own line. Even if
he had not written Part III of *Gulliver's Travels*, one could infer from
the rest of the book that, like Tolstoy and like Blake, he hates the
very idea of studying the processes of nature. The 'reason' which
he so admires in the Houyhnhnms does not primarily mean the
power of drawing logical inferences from observed facts. Although
he never defines it, it appears in most contexts to mean either common sense, i.e. acceptance of the obvious and contempt for quibbles
and abstractions, or absence of passion and superstition. In general
he assumes that we know all that we need to know already, and
merely use our knowledge incorrectly. Medicine, for instance, is a
useless science, because if we lived in a more natural way, there would
be no diseases. Swift, however, is not a simple-lifer or an admirer of
the noble savage. He is in favour of civilization and the arts of
civilization. Not only does he see the value of good manners, good
conversation, and even learning of a literary and historical kind, he
also sees that agriculture, navigation and architecture need to be
studied and could with advantage be improved. But his implied aim
is a static, incurious civilization – the world of his own day, a little
cleaner, a little saner, with no radical change and no poking into the
unknowable. More than one would expect in anyone so free from
accepted fallacies, he reveres the past, especially classical antiquity,
and believes that modern man has degenerated sharply during the

past hundred years.[1] In the island of sorcerers, where the spirits of the dead can be called up at will:

I desired that the Senate of Rome might appear before me in one large chamber, and a modern representative in counterview, in another. The first seemed to be an assembly of heroes and demi-gods, the other a knot of pedlars, pick-pockets, highwaymen and bullies (XI 195–6).

Although Swift uses this section of Part III to attack the truthfulness of recorded history, his critical spirit deserts him as soon as he is dealing with Greeks and Romans. He remarks, of course, upon the corruption of Imperial Rome, but he has an almost unreasoning admiration for some of the leading figures of the ancient world:

I was struck with [a] profound veneration at the sight of Brutus, and could easily discover the most consummate virtue, the greatest intrepidity and firmness of mind, the truest love of his country, and general benevolence for mankind, in every lineament of his countenance. . . . I had the honour to have much conversation with Brutus, and was told, that his ancestor Junius, Socrates, Epaminondas, Cato the younger, Sir Thomas More and himself, were perpetually together: a sextumvirate, to which all the ages of the world cannot add a seventh (XI 196).

It will be noticed that of these six people only one is a Christian. This is an important point. If one adds together Swift's pessimism, his reverence for the past, his incuriosity and his horror of the human body, one arrives at an attitude common among religious reaction-aries – that is, people who defend an unjust order of society by claiming that this world cannot be substantially improved and only the 'next world' matters. However, Swift shows no sign of having any religious beliefs, at least in any ordinary sense of the words. He does not appear to believe seriously in life after death, and his idea

---

1 The physical decadence which Swift claims to have observed may have been a reality at that date. He attributes it to syphilis, which was a new disease in Europe and may have been more virulent than it is now. Distilled liquors, also, were a novelty in the seventeenth century and must have led at first to a great increase in drunkenness.

of goodness is bound up with republicanism, love of liberty, courage, 'benevolence' (meaning in effect public spirit), 'reason' and other pagan qualities. This reminds one that there is another strain in Swift, not quite congruous with his disbelief in progress and his general hatred of humanity.

To begin with, he has moments when he is 'constructive' and even 'advanced'. To be occasionally inconsistent is almost a mark of vitality in Utopia books, and Swift sometimes inserts a word of praise into a passage that ought to be purely satirical. Thus, his ideas about the education of the young are fathered on to the Lilliputians, who have much the same views on this subject as the Houyhnhnms. The Lilliputians also have various social and legal institutions (for instance, there are old age pensions, and people are rewarded for keeping the law as well as punished for breaking it) which Swift would have liked to see prevailing in his own country. In the middle of this passage Swift remembers his satirical intention and adds, 'In relating these and the following laws, I would only be understood to mean the original institutions, and not the most scandalous corruptions into which these people are fallen by the degenerate nature of Man': but as Lilliput is supposed to represent England, and the laws he is speaking of have never had their parallel in England, it is clear that the impulse to make constructive suggestions has been too much for him. But Swift's greatest contribution to political thought, in the narrower sense of the words, is his attack, especially in Part III, on what would now be called totalitarianism. He has an extraordinarily clear prevision of the spy-haunted 'police state', with its endless heresy-hunts and treason trials, all really designed to neutralize popular discontent by changing it into war hysteria. And one must remember that Swift is here inferring the whole from a quite small part, for the feeble governments of his own day did not give him illustrations ready-made. For example, there is the professor at the School of Political Projectors who 'showed me a large paper of instructions for discovering plots and conspiracies', and who claimed that one can find people's secret thoughts by examining their excrement:

Because men are never so serious, thoughtful and intent, as when they are at stool, which he found by frequent experiment:

for in such conjunctures, when he used merely as a trial to
consider what was the best way of murdering the King, his
ordure would have a tincture of green; but quite different
when he thought only of raising an insurrection, or burning
the metropolis (XI 190).

The professor and his theory are said to have been suggested to
Swift by the – from our point of view – not particularly astonishing
or disgusting fact that in a recent State trial some letters found in
somebody's privy had been put in evidence. Later in the same chapter
we seem to be positively in the middle of the Russian purges:

In the Kingdom of Tribnia, by the natives called Langdon ...
the bulk of the people consist, in a manner, wholly of
discoverers, witnesses, informers, accusers, prosecutors,
evidences, swearers. ... It is first agreed, and settled among
them, what suspected persons shall be accused of a plot: then,
effectual care is taken to secure all their letters and papers, and
put the owners in chains. These papers are delivered to a sett
of artists, very dexterous in finding out the mysterious
meanings of words, syllables and letters. ... Where this method
fails, they have two others more effectual, which the learned
among them call *Acrostics* and *Anagrams*. *First*, they can
decipher all initial letters into political meanings: thus, N shall
signify a plot, B a regiment of horse, L a fleet at sea; or,
secondly, by transposing the letters of the alphabet in any
suspected paper, they can lay open the deepest designs of a
discontented party. So, for example, if I should say in a
letter to a friend, *Our Brother Tom has just got the piles*, a skilful
decipherer would discover that the same letters, which
compose that sentence, may be analysed in the following words:
Resist; a plot is brought home, The Tour. And this is the
anagrammatic method (XI 191-2).

Other professors at the same school invent simplified languages,
write books by machinery, educate their pupils by inscribing the
lessons on a wafer and causing them to swallow it, or propose to
abolish individuality altogether by cutting off part of the brain of

one man and grafting it on to the head of another. There is something
queerly familiar in the atmosphere of these chapters, because, mixed
up with much fooling, there is a perception that one of the aims of
totalitarianism is not merely to make sure that people will think the
right thoughts, but actually to make them *less conscious*. Then,
again, Swift's account of the Leader who is usually to be found ruling
over a tribe of Yahoos, and of the 'favourite' who acts first as a dirty-
worker and later as a scapegoat, fits remarkably well into the pattern
of our own times. But are we to infer from all this that Swift was
first and foremost an enemy of tyranny and a champion of the free
intelligence? No: his own views, so far as one can discern them, are
not markedly liberal. No doubt he hates lords, kings, bishops,
generals, ladies of fashion, orders, titles and flummery generally, but
he does not seem to think better of the common people than of their
rulers, or to be in favour of increased social equality, or to be enthusiastic about representative institutions. The Houyhnhnms are organized upon a sort of caste system which is racial in character, the
horses which do the menial work being of different colours from their
masters and not interbreeding with them. The educational system
which Swift admires in the Lilliputians takes hereditary class distinctions for granted, and the children of the poorest class do not go to
school, because 'their business being only to till and cultivate the
earth ... therefore their education is of little consequence to the
public'. Nor does he seem to have been strongly in favour of freedom
of speech and the press, in spite of the toleration which his own
writings enjoyed. The King of Brobdingnag is astonished at the
multiplicity of religious and political sects in England, and considers
that those who hold 'opinions prejudicial to the public' (in the context
this seems to mean simply heretical opinions), though they need not
be obliged to change them, ought to be obliged to conceal them: for
'as it was tyranny in any government to require the first, so it was
weakness not to enforce the second'. There is a subtler indication of
Swift's own attitude in the manner in which Gulliver leaves the land
of the Houyhnhnms. Intermittently, at least, Swift was a kind of
anarchist, and Part IV of *Gulliver's Travels* is a picture of an anarchistic society, not governed by law in the ordinary sense, but by the
dictates of 'Reason', which are voluntarily accepted by everyone.
The General Assembly of the Houyhnhnms 'exhorts' Gulliver's

master to get rid of him, and his neighbours put pressure on him to
make him comply. Two reasons are given. One is that the presence
of this unusual Yahoo may unsettle the rest of the tribe, and the other
is that a friendly relationship between a Houyhnhnm and a Yahoo
is 'not agreeable to reason or nature, or a thing ever heard of before
among them'. Gulliver's master is somewhat unwilling to obey, but
the 'exhortation' (a Houyhnhnm, we are told, is never *compelled* to
do anything, he is merely 'exhorted' or 'advised') cannot be dis-
regarded. This illustrates very well the totalitarian tendency which is
implicit in the anarchist or pacifist vision of society. In a society in
which there is no law, and in theory no compulsion, the only arbiter
of behaviour is public opinion. But public opinion, because of the
tremendous urge to conformity in gregarious animals, is less tolerant
than any system of law. When human beings are governed by 'thou
shalt not', the individual can practise a certain amount of eccentricity:
when they are supposedly governed by 'love' or 'reason', he is
under continuous pressure to make him behave and think in exactly
the same way as everyone else. The Houyhnhnms, we are told, were
unanimous on almost all subjects. The only question they ever *discussed* was how to deal with the Yahoos. Otherwise there was no
room for disagreement among them, because the truth is always
either self-evident, or else it is undiscoverable and unimportant. They
had apparently no word for 'opinion' in their language, and in their
conversations there was no 'difference of sentiments'. They had
reached, in fact, the highest stage of totalitarian organization, the
stage when conformity has become so general that there is no need
for a police force. Swift approves of this kind of thing because
among his many gifts neither curiosity nor good nature was included.
Disagreement would always seem to him sheer perversity. 'Reason',
among the Houyhnhnms, he says, 'is not a point problematical, as
with us, where men can argue with plausibility on both sides of a
question; but strikes you with immediate conviction; as it must
needs do, where it is not mingled, obscured or discoloured by passion
and interest.' In other words, we know everything already, so why
should dissident opinions be tolerated? The totalitarian society of the
Houyhnhnms, where there can be no freedom and no development,
follows naturally from this.

We are right to think of Swift as a rebel and iconoclast, but except in certain secondary matters, such as his insistence that women should receive the same education as men, he cannot be labelled 'left'. He is a Tory anarchist, despising authority while disbelieving in liberty, and preserving the aristocratic outlook while seeing clearly that the existing aristocracy is degenerate and contemptible. When Swift utters one of his characteristic diatribes against the rich and powerful, one must probably, as I said earlier, write off something for the fact that he himself belonged to the less successful party, and was personally disappointed. The 'outs', for obvious reasons, are always more radical than the 'ins'.[1] But the most essential thing in Swift is his inability to believe that life – ordinary life on the solid earth, and not some rationalized, deodorized version of it – could be made worth living. Of course, no honest person claims that happiness is *now* a normal condition among adult human beings; but perhaps it *could* be made normal, and it is upon this question that all serious political controversy really turns. Swift has much in common – more, I believe, than has been noticed – with Tolstoy, another disbeliever in the possibility of happiness. In both men you have the same anarchistic outlook covering an authoritarian cast of mind; in both a similar hostility to science, the same impatience with opponents, the same inability to see the importance of any question not interesting to themselves; and in both cases a sort of horror of the actual process of life, though in Tolstoy's case it was arrived at later and in a different way. The sexual unhappiness of the two men was not of the same kind, but there was this in common, that in both of them a sincere loathing was mixed up with a morbid fascination. Tolstoy was a reformed rake who ended by preaching complete celibacy, while continuing to practise the opposite into extreme old

---

1 At the end of the book, as typical specimens of human folly and viciousness, Swift names 'a lawyer, a pickpocket, a colonel, a fool, a lord, a gamester, a politician, a whore-master, a physician, an evidence, a suborner, an attorney, a traitor, or the like'. One sees here the irresponsible violence of the powerless. The list lumps together those who break the conventional code, and those who keep it. For instance, if you automatically condemn a colonel, as such, on what grounds do you condemn a traitor? Or again, if you want to suppress pickpockets, you must have laws, which means that you must have lawyers. But the whole closing passage, in which the hatred is so authentic, and the reason given for it so inadequate, is somehow unconvincing. One has the feeling that personal animosity is at work.

age. Swift was presumably impotent, and had an exaggerated horror of human dung: he also thought about it incessantly, as is evident throughout this works. Such people are not likely to enjoy even the small amount of happiness that falls to most human beings, and, from obvious motives, are not likely to admit that earthly life is capable of much improvement. Their incuriosity, and hence their intolerance, spring from the same root.

Swift's disgust, rancour and pessimism would make sense against the background of a 'next world' to which this one is the prelude. As he does not appear to believe seriously in any such thing, it becomes necessary to construct a paradise supposedly existing on the surface of the earth, but something quite different from anything we know, with all that he disapproves of – lies, folly, change, enthusiasm, pleasure, love and dirt – eliminated from it. As his ideal being he chooses the horse, an animal whose excrement is not offensive. The Houyhnhnms are dreary beasts – this is so generally admitted that the point is not worth labouring. Swift's genius can make them credible, but there can have been very few readers in whom they have excited any feeling beyond dislike. And this is not from wounded vanity at seeing animals preferred to men; for, of the two, the Houyhnhnms are much liker to human beings than are the Yahoos, and Gulliver's horror of the Yahoos, together with his recognition that they are the same kind of creature as himself, contains a logical absurdity. This horror comes upon him at his very first sight of them. 'I never beheld,' he says, 'in all my travels, so disagreeable an animal, nor one against which I naturally conceived so strong an antipathy.' But in comparison with what are the Yahoos disgusting? Not with the Houyhnhnms, because at this time Gulliver has not seen a Houyhnhnm. It can only be in comparison with himself, i.e. with a human being. Later, however, we are to be told that the Yahoos *are* human beings, and human society becomes insupportable to Gulliver because all men are Yahoos. In that case why did he not conceive his disgust of humanity earlier? In effect we are told that the Yahoos are fantastically different from men, and yet are the same. Swift has over-reached himself in his fury, and is shouting at his fellow creatures: 'You are filthier than you are!' However, it is impossible to feel much sympathy with the Yahoos, and it is not because they oppress the Yahoos that the Houyhnhnms are unattractive. They are unattractive because the 'reason' by which they are governed is really a desire for death. They are exempt from love, friendship, curiosity, fear, sorrow and – except in their feelings towards the Yahoos, who occupy rather the same place in their community as the Jews in Nazi Germany – anger and hatred. 'They have no fondness for their colts or foles, but the care they take, in educating them, proceeds entirely from the dictates of *reason*.' They lay store by 'friendship' and 'benevolence', but 'these are not confined to particular objects, but universal to the whole race'. They also value conversation, but in their conversations there are no differences of opinion, and 'nothing passed but what was useful, expressed in the fewest and most significant words'. They practise strict birth control, each couple producing two offspring and thereafter abstaining from sexual intercourse. Their marriages are arranged for them by their elders, on eugenic principles, and their language contains no word for 'love', in the sexual sense. When somebody dies they carry on exactly as before, without feeling any grief. It will be seen that their aim is to be as like a corpse as is possible while retaining physical life. One or two of their characteristics, it is true, do not seem to be strictly 'reasonable' in their own usage of the word. Thus, they place a great value not only on physical hardihood but on athleticism, and they are devoted to poetry. But these exceptions may be less arbitrary than they seem. Swift probably emphasizes the physical strength of the Houyhnhnms in order to make clear that they could never be conquered by the hated human race, while a taste for poetry may figure among their qualities because poetry appeared to Swift as the antithesis of science, from his point of view the most useless of all pursuits. In Part III he names 'imagination, fancy and invention' as desirable faculties in which the Laputan mathematicians (in spite of their love of music) were wholly lacking. One must remember that although Swift was an admirable writer of comic verse, the kind of poetry he thought valuable would probably be didactic poetry. The poetry of the Houyhnhnms, he says:

must be allowed to excel (that of) all other mortals; wherein
the justness of their similes, and the minuteness, as well as
exactness, of their descriptions, are, indeed, inimitable. Their

verses abound very much in both of these; and usually contain
either some exalted notions of friendship and benevolence, or
the praises of those who were victors in races, and other
bodily exercises (XI 273-4).

Alas, not even the genius of Swift was equal to producing a specimen
by which we could judge the poetry of the Houyhnhnms. But it
sounds as though it were chilly stuff (in heroic couplets, presumably),
and not seriously in conflict with the principles of 'reason'.

Happiness is notoriously difficult to describe, and pictures of a just
and well-ordered society are seldom either attractive or convincing.
Most creators of 'favourable' Utopias, however, are concerned to
show what life could be like if it were lived more fully. Swift
advocates a simple refusal of life, justifying this by the claim that
'reason' consists in thwarting your instincts. The Houyhnhnms,
creatures without a history, continue for generation after generation
to live prudently, maintaining their population at exactly the same
level, avoiding all passion, suffering from no diseases, meeting death
indifferently, training up their young in the same principles – and all
for what? In order that the same process may continue indefinitely.
The notions that life here and now is worth living, or that it could be
made worth living, or that it must be sacrificed for some future good,
are all absent. The dreary world of the Houyhnhnms was about as
good a Utopia as Swift could construct, granting that he neither
believed in a 'next world' nor could get any pleasure out of certain
normal activities. But it is not really set up as something desirable in
itself, but as the justification for another attack on humanity. The aim,
as usual, is to humiliate Man by reminding him that he is weak
and ridiculous, and above all that he stinks; and the ultimate motive
probably, is a kind of envy, the envy of the ghost for the living, of the
man who knows he cannot be happy for the others who – so he fears
– may be a little happier than himself. The political expression of
such an outlook must be either reactionary or nihilistic, because the
person who holds it will want to prevent society from developing
in some direction in which his pessimism may be cheated. One can
do this either by blowing everything to pieces, or by averting social
change. Swift ultimately blew everything to pieces in the only way
that was feasible before the atomic bomb – that is, he went mad –

but, as I have tried to show, his political aims were on the whole reactionary ones.

From what I have written it may have seemed that I am *against* Swift, and that my object is to refute him and even to belittle him. In a political and moral sense I am against him, so far as I understand him. Yet curiously enough he is one of the writers I admire with least reserve, and *Gulliver's Travels*, in particular, is a book which it seems impossible for me to grow tired of. I read it first when I was eight – one day short of eight, to be exact, for I stole and furtively read the copy which was to be given me next day on my eighth birthday – and I have certainly not read it less than half a dozen times since. Its fascination seems inexhaustible. If I had to make a list of six books which were to be preserved when all others were destroyed, I would certainly put *Gulliver's Travels* among them. This raises the question: what is the relationship between agreement with a writer's opinions, and enjoyment of his work?

If one is capable of intellectual detachment, one can *perceive* merit in a writer whom one deeply disagrees with, but *enjoyment* is a different matter. Supposing that there is such a thing as good or bad art, then the goodness or badness must reside in the work of art itself – not independently of the observer, indeed, but independently of the mood of the observer. In one sense, therefore, it cannot be true that a poem is good on Monday and bad on Tuesday. But if one judges the poem by the appreciation it arouses, then it can certainly be true, because appreciation, or enjoyment, is a subjective condition which cannot be commanded. For a great deal of his waking life, even the most cultivated person has no aesthetic feelings whatever, and the power to have aesthetic feelings is very easily destroyed. When you are frightened, or hungry, or are suffering from toothache or seasickness, *King Lear* is no better from your point of view than *Peter Pan*. You may know in an intellectual sense that it is better, but that is simply a fact which you remember: you will not *feel* the merit of *King Lear* until you are normal again. And aesthetic judgement can be upset just as disastrously – more disastrously, because the cause is less readily recognized – by political or moral disagreement. If a book angers, wounds or alarms you, then you will not enjoy it, whatever its merits may be. If it seems to you a really pernicious book, likely to influence other people in some undesirable way, then you will probably construct an aesthetic theory to show that it *has* no merits. Current literary criticism consists quite largely of this kind of dodging to and fro between two sets of standards. And yet the opposite process can also happen: enjoyment can overwhelm disapproval, even though one clearly recognizes that one is enjoying something inimical. Swift, whose world-view is so peculiarly unacceptable, but who is nevertheless an extremely popular writer, is a good instance of this. Why is it that we don't mind being called Yahoos, although firmly convinced that we are *not* Yahoos?

It is not enough to make the usual answer that of course Swift was wrong, in fact he was insane, but he was 'a good writer'. It is true that the literary quality of a book is to some small extent separable from its subject-matter. Some people have a native gift for using words, as some people have a naturally 'good eye' at games. It is largely a question of timing and of instinctively knowing how much emphasis to use. As an example near at hand, look back at the passage I quoted earlier, starting 'In the Kingdom of Tribnia, by the natives called Langdon'. It derives much of its force from the final sentence: 'And this is the anagrammatic method.' Strictly speaking this sentence is unnecessary, for we have already seen the anagram deciphered, but the mock-solemn repetition, in which one seems to hear Swift's own voice uttering the words, drives home the idiocy of the activities described, like the final tap to a nail. But not all the power and simplicity of Swift's prose, nor the imaginative effort that has been able to make not one but a whole series of impossible worlds more credible than the majority of history books – none of this would enable us to enjoy Swift if his world-view were truly wounding or shocking. Millions of people, in many countries, must have enjoyed *Gulliver's Travels* while more or less seeing its anti-human implications: and even the child who accepts Parts I and II as a simple story gets a sense of absurdity from thinking of human beings six inches high. The explanation must be that Swift's world-view is felt to be *not* altogether false – or it would probably be more accurate to say, not false all the time. Swift is a diseased writer. He remains permanently in a depressed mood which in most people is only intermittent, rather as though someone suffering from jaundice or the after-effects of influenza should have the energy to write books. But we all know that mood, and something in us responds to the expression of it. Take, for instance, one of his most characteristic works, *The Lady's Dressing Room*: one might add the kindred poem, *Upon a Beautiful Young Nymph Going to Bed*. Which is truer, the viewpoint expressed in these poems, or the viewpoint implied in Blake's phrase, 'The naked female human form divine'? No doubt Blake is nearer the truth, and yet who can fail to feel a sort of pleasure in seeing that fraud, feminine delicacy, exploded for once? Swift falsifies his picture of the whole world by refusing to see anything in human life except dirt, folly and wickedness, but the part which he abstracts from the whole does exist, and it is something which we all know about while shrinking from mentioning it. Part of our minds – in any normal person it is the dominant part – believes that man is a noble animal and life is worth living: but there is also a sort of inner self which at least intermittently stands aghast at the horror of existence. In the queerest way, pleasure and disgust are linked together. The human body is beautiful: it is also repulsive and ridiculous, a fact which can be verified at any swimming pool. The sexual organs are objects of desire and also of loathing, so much so that in many languages, if not in all languages, their names are used as words of abuse. Meat is delicious, but a butcher's shop makes one feel sick: and indeed all our food springs ultimately from dung and dead bodies, the two things which of all others seem to us the most horrible. A child, when it is past the infantile stage but still looking at the world with fresh eyes, is moved by horror almost as often as by wonder – horror of snot and spittle, of the dogs' excrement on the pavement, the dying toad full of maggots, the sweaty smell of grown-ups, the hideousness of old men, with their bald heads and bulbous noses. In his endless harping on disease, dirt and deformity, Swift is not actually inventing anything, he is merely leaving something out. Human behaviour, too, especially in politics, is as he describes it, although it contains other more important factors which he refuses to admit. So far as we can see, both horror and pain are necessary to the continuance of life on this planet, and it is therefore open to pessimists like Swift to say: 'If horror and pain must always be with us, how can life be significantly improved?' His attitude is in effect the Christian attitude, minus the bribe of a 'next world' – which, however, probably has less hold upon the minds of believers than the conviction that this world is a vale of tears and the grave is a place of rest. It is, I am certain, a wrong attitude, and one which could have harmful effects upon behaviour; but something in us responds to it, as it responds to the gloomy words of the burial service and the sweetish smell of corpses in a country church.

It is often argued, at least by people who admit the importance of subject-matter, that a book cannot be 'good' if it expresses a palpably false view of life. We are told that in our own age, for instance, any book that has genuine literary merit will also be more or less 'progressive' in tendency. This ignores the fact that throughout history a similar struggle between progress and reaction has been raging, and that the best books of any one age have always been written from several different viewpoints, some of them palpably more false than others. In so far as a writer is a propagandist, the most one can ask of him is that he shall genuinely believe in what he is saying, and that it shall not be something blazingly silly. Today, for example, one can imagine a good book being written by a Catholic, a Communist, a Fascist, a Pacifist, an Anarchist, perhaps by an old-style Liberal or an ordinary Conservative: one cannot imagine a good book being written by a spiritualist, a Buchmanite or a member of the Ku-Klux-Klan. The views that a writer holds must be compatible with sanity, in the medical sense, and with the power of continuous thought: beyond that what we ask of him is talent, which is probably another name for conviction. Swift did not possess ordinary wisdom, but he did possess a terrible intensity of vision, capable of picking out a single hidden truth and then magnifying it and distorting it. The durability of *Gulliver's Travels* goes to show that, if the force of belief is behind it, a world-view which only just passes the test of sanity is sufficient to produce a great work of art.
(205–23)

Kenneth Burke

from *A Rhetoric of Motives* 1950

[On Kafka] Another respect in which the paradoxes of the absurd can be derived dialectically involves the grammatical resource whereby the sacred and the obscene become interchangeable, since each is a kind of 'untouchability'. The ritual uncleanness of the lowest Hindu class was but the counterpart of the 'absolute dignity' possessed by superior classes. And looking too hastily, we may tend to see a mere evidence of 'irrationality' in the 'ambivalence' whereby the Latins could apply to criminals their word for 'sacred' (a relation also involved in the outlaw's right of sanctuary at the altar). When K. asks a school-teacher about the castle, the teacher in embarrassment calls attention to the fact that there are children present, speaking to him in French (as the language of 'social distinction' in which one can also speak of subjects socially forbidden). The incident foreshadows in quality the letter in which the official Soltini makes filthy proposals to Amalia. Such 'irrational ambivalence' need not be derived from a source essentially absurd. It can be explained grammatically as the dramatic expression of a normal relation between species and genus. For if both the holy and the obscene are *set apart* from other classes of things or persons, this *exceptional* quality is something they share in common, *generically*, though each manifests its own *specific* variants of this common element.

The forbidden (of either holy or obscene sorts) can become identified with the magic experiences of infancy, the tabus of the excremental, which are established along with the first steps in language, and fade into the prelinguistic stage of experience. Thus, ironically, the very 'seat of highest dignity' can become furtively one with the connotations of the human posterior, in a rhetorical identification between high and low, since both can represent the principle of the tabu. A friend said: 'When I was young, I thought that a king's "royal highness" was his behind, and that his subjects were required to show it great deference. I could not have told you what the principle of hierarchy is, but in this error I showed that I had got to the very foundations of it.'

Gulliver's Travels has many episodes which, in Swift's morbidly playful way, exemplify the symbolic connexion between the 'sacred' taboos of royalty and the 'obscene' taboos of the fecal. Most notably the identification figures roundabout, in satiric denial, near the beginning of chapter 6, in the *Voyage to Brobdingnag*. Here Gulliver recounts:

I desired the Queen's woman to save for me the combings of her Majesty's hair, whereof in time I got a good quantity, and consulting with my friend the cabinet-maker, who had received general orders to do little jobs for me, I directed him to make two chair frames, no larger than those I had in my box, and then to bore little holes with a fine awl round those parts where I designed the backs and seats; through these holes I wove the strongest hairs I could pick out, just after the manner of cane chairs in England. When they were finished, I made a present of them to her Majesty, who kept them in her cabinet, and used to show them for curiosities, as indeed they were the wonder of every one that beheld them. The Queen would have me sit upon one of these chairs, but I absolutely refused to obey her, protesting I would rather die a thousand deaths than place a dishonourable part of my body on those precious hairs that once adorned her Majesty's head (XI 124-5).

Immediately after, there is another identification, though of a nature that could be detected only by internal analysis of Swift's vocabulary. Gulliver speaks of his 'mechanical genius'. And for the overtones of the word 'mechanical' in Swiftian satire, the reader is referred to the grotesquely gnarled adumbrations of psychoanalysis in Swift's essay on *The Mechanical Operation of the Spirit*, where he attacks idealistic enthusiasm by deriving it from sources connected with the privy parts.
(256-7)

R. S. Crane

'The Houyhnhnms, the Yahoos and the History of Ideas', *The Idea of the Humanities, and other Essays* 1959 (reprinted 1967)

I shall be concerned in this essay with two ways of using the history of ideas – or, in the case of the first of them, as I shall argue, misusing it – in the historical interpretation of literary works. The particular issue I have in mind is forced on one in an unusually clear-cut manner, I think, by what has been said of the *Voyage to the Country of the Houyhnhnms* in the criticism of the past few decades; and for this reason, and also because I wish to add a theory of my own about

Swift's satirical argument in that work to the theories now current, I base the discussion that follows almost exclusively on it.

With a very few exceptions (the latest being George Sherburn)[1] since the 1920s, and especially since the later 1930s, writers on the fourth voyage have been mainly dominated by a single preoccupation.[2] They have sought to correct the misunderstanding of Swift's purpose in the voyage which had vitiated, in their opinion, most earlier criticism of it and, in particular, to defend Swift from the charge of all-out misanthropy that had been leveled against him so often in the past – by Thackeray, for example, but many others also – on the strength of Gulliver's wholesale identification of men with the Yahoos and his unqualified worship of the Houyhnhnms.

It is easy to see what this task would require them to do. It would require them to show that what Gulliver is made to say about human nature in the voyage, which is certainly misanthropic enough, and what Swift wanted his readers to believe about human nature are, in

1 See his 'Errors Concerning the Houyhnhnms', *Modern Philology*, vol. 56, 1958, pp. 92–7. To this may now be added E. Rosenheim, Jr, 'The Fifth Voyage of Lemuel Gulliver: A Footnote', *Modern Philology*, vol. 60, 1962, pp. 103–19, and his *Swift and the Satirist's Art*, University of Chicago Press, 1963, *passim*.

2 The list of writings that reflect this preoccupation is now a fairly long one; in the present essay I have had in view chiefly the following: E. Bernbaum, 'The Significance of *Gulliver's Travels*', in his edition of that work (New York, 1920); T. O. Wedel, 'On the Philosophical Background of *Gulliver's Travels*', *Studies in Philology*, vol. 23, 1926, pp. 434–50; J. F. Ross, 'The Final Comedy of Lemuel Gulliver', in *Studies in the Comic*, University of California Publications in English, vol. 8, no. 2, 1941, pp. 175–96; R. B. Heilman, Introduction to his edition of *Gulliver's Travels*, Modern Library, 1950, especially pp. xii–xxii; E. Tuveson, 'Swift: The Dean as Satirist', *University of Toronto Quarterly*, vol. 22, 1953, pp. 368–75; R. M. Frye, 'Swift's Yahoo and the Christian Symbols for Sin', *Journal of the History of Ideas*, vol. 15, 1953, pp. 201–15; W. A. Murray's supplementary note to Frye, ibid., pp. 596–601; S. H. Monk, 'The Pride of Lemuel Gulliver', *Sewanee Review*, vol. 63, 1955, pp. 48–7; I. Ehrenpreis, 'The Origins of *Gulliver's Travels*', *PMLA* (*Publications of the Modern Language Association of America*), vol. 72, 1957, pp. 880–99 (reprinted with some revisions in his *The Personality of Jonathan Swift*, Methuen, 1958); Kathleen Williams, *Jonathan Swift and the Age of Compromise*, University of Kansas Press, 1958; C. Winton, 'Conversion on the Road to Houyhnhnmland', *Sewanee Review*, vol. 68, 1960, pp. 20–23; M. Kallich, 'Three Ways of Looking at a Horse. Jonathan Swift's *Voyage to the Houyhnhnms* Again', *Criticism*, vol. 2, 1960, pp. 107–24.

certain crucial respects at any rate, two different and incompatible things. It would require them, that is, to draw a clear line between what is both Swift and Gulliver and what is only Gulliver in a text in which Gulliver alone is allowed to speak to us.

The resulting new interpretations have differed considerably in emphasis and detail from critic to critic, but they have been generally in accord on the following propositions: the attitudes of Swift and his hero do indeed coincide up to a certain point, it being true for Swift no less than for Gulliver that men in the mass are terrifyingly close to the Yahoos in disposition and behavior, and true for both of them also that the Houyhnhnms are in some of their qualities – their abhorrence of falsehood, for instance – proper models for human emulation. That, however, is about as far as the agreement goes: it is to Gulliver alone and not to Swift that we must impute the radical pessimism of the final chapters – it is he and not Swift who reduces men literally to Yahoos; it is he and not Swift who despairs of men because they cannot or will not lead the wholly rational life of the Houyhnhnms. Gulliver, in other words, is only in part a reliable spokesman of his creator's satire; he is also, and decisively at the end, one of the targets of that satire – a character designed to convince us, through his obviously infatuated actions, of the absurdity both of any view of man's nature that denies the capacity of at least some men for rational and virtuous conduct, however limited this capacity may be, and of any view of the best existence for man that makes it consist in taking 'reason alone' as a guide. What, in short, Swift offers us, as the ultimate moral of the voyage, is a compromise between these extremist opinions of Gulliver: human nature, he is saying, is bad enough, but it is not altogether hopeless; reason is a good thing, but a life of pure reason is no desirable end for man.

Now it is evident that however appealing this interpretation may be to those who want to think well of Swift and to rescue him from his nineteenth-century maligners, it is not a merely obvious exegesis of the *Voyage to the Country of the Houyhnhnms*, or one that most common readers, past or present, have spontaneously arrived at. It is not an exegesis, either, that goes at all comfortably with that famous letter of Swift's in 1725 in which he told Pope that his chief aim was 'to vex the world rather than divert it' and that he never would have peace of mind until 'all honest men' were of his opinion. For there is nothing particularly vexing in the at least partly reassuring moral now being attributed to the voyage or anything which 'honest men' in 1726 would have had much hesitation in accepting. And again, although we must surely agree that there is a significant difference between Gulliver and Swift, why must we suppose that the difference has to be one of basic doctrine? Why could it not be simply the difference between a person who has just discovered a deeply disturbing truth about man and is consequently, like Socrates' prisoner in the myth of the cave, considerably upset and one who, like Socrates himself, has known this truth all along and can therefore write of his hero's discovery of it calmly and with humor?

I introduce these points here not as decisive objections to the new interpretation but rather as signs that it is not the kind of interpretation which (in Johnson's phrase), upon its first production, must be acknowledged to be just. Confirmatory arguments are plainly needed; and a consideration of the arguments that have in fact been offered in support of it will bring us rather quickly to the special problem I wish to discuss.

A good deal has been made, to begin with, of what are thought to be clear indications in the voyage itself that Swift wanted his readers to take a much more critical view than Gulliver does of 'the virtues and ideas of those exalted Houhynhnms' and a much less negative view of human possibilities. If he had designed the Houyhnhnms to be for us what they are for Gulliver, namely, the 'perfection of nature' and hence an acceptable standard for judging of man, he would surely, it is argued, have endowed them with more humanly engaging qualities than they have; he would surely not have created them as the 'remote, unsympathetic, and in the end profoundly unsatisfying' creatures so many of his readers nowadays find them to be. We must therefore see in Gulliver's worship of the rational horses a plain evidence of the extremist error into which he has fallen. And similarly, if Swift had expected us to go the whole way with Gulliver in his identification of men with the Yahoos, he would hardly have depicted the human characters in his story – especially the admirable Portuguese captain, Don Pedro de Mendez, and his crew – in the conspicuously favorable light in which they appear to us. They are bound to strike us as notable exceptions to the despairing estimate of 'human kind' to which Gulliver has been led by his Houyhnhnm master; and we can only conclude that Gulliver's failure to look upon them as other than Yahoos, whom at best he can only 'tolerate', is meant as still another sign to us of the false extremism of his attitude.

All this looks at first sight convincing – until we begin to think of other possible intentions that Swift might have had in the voyage with which these signs would be equally compatible. Suppose that his primary purpose was indeed to 'vex the world' by administering as severe a shock as he could to the cherished belief that man is *par excellence* a 'rational creature,' and suppose that he chose to do this, in part at least, by forcing his readers to dwell on the unbridgeable gap between what is involved in being a truly 'rational creature' and what not only the worse but also the better sort of men actually are. It is plain what he would have had to do in working out such a design. He would have had to give to his wholly rational beings precisely those 'unhuman' characteristics that have been noted, to their disadvantage, in the Houyhnhnms; to have made them creatures such as we would normally like or sympathize with would have been to destroy their value as a transcendent standard of comparison. And it would have been no less essential to introduce characters, like Don Pedro, or, for that matter, Gulliver himself, who, in terms of ordinary human judgements, would impress us as unmistakably good; otherwise he would have exempted too many of his readers from the shock to their pride in being men which, on this hypothesis, he was trying to produce. He would have had to do, in short, all those things in the voyage that have been taken as indications of a purpose very different from the one I am now supposing, and much less misanthropic. Clearly, then, some other kind of proof is needed than these ambiguous internal signs before the current view of Swift's meaning can be thought of as more than one possibility among other competing ones.

A good many defenders of this view, especially during the past decade, have attempted to supply such proof by relating the voyage to its presumed background in the intellectual and religious concerns of Swift and his age; and it is their manner of doing this – of using hypotheses based on the history of ideas in the determination of their author's meaning–that I want to examine in what immediately follows.

They have been fairly well agreed on these three points: in the first place, that Swift's main design in the voyage was to uphold what they describe as the traditional and orthodox conception of human nature, classical and Christian alike, that 'recognizes in man an inseparable complex of good and evil', reason and passion, spiritual soul and animal body; secondly, that he conceived the Houyhnhnms and the Yahoos, primarily at least, as allegorical embodiments of these two parts of man's constitution taken in abstraction the one from the other; and thirdly, that he developed his defense of the orthodox view by directing his satire against those contemporary doctrines, on the one hand, that tended to exalt the Houyhnhnm side of man in forgetfulness of how Yahoo-like man really is, and those doctrines, on the other hand, that tended to see man only as a Yahoo in forgetfulness of his Houyhnhnm possibilities, limited though these are. All this has been more or less common doctrine among critics of the voyage at least since Ernest Bernbaum in 1920; there has been rather less agreement on the identity of the contemporary movements of ideas which Swift had in view as objects of attack. It was usual in the earlier phases of the discussion to say simply, as Bernbaum does, that he was thinking, at the one extreme, of the 'sentimental optimism' of writers like Shaftesbury and, at the other, of the pessimism or cynicism of writers like Hobbes and Mandeville. Since then, however, other identifications have been added to the list, as relevant especially to his conception of the Houyhnhnms; we have been told, thus, that he 'obviously' intended to embody in the principles and mode of life of these creatures, along with certain admittedly admirable qualities, the rationalistic errors of the neo-Stoics, the Cartesians and the deists – some or all of these, depending upon the critic.

Now if we could feel sure that what was in Swift's mind when he conceived the fourth voyage is even approximately represented by these statements, we should have little reason for not going along with the interpretation of his design they have been used to support. For if he was indeed engaged in vindicating the 'Christian humanist' view of human nature against those contemporary extremists who made either too much or too little of man's capacity for reason and virtue, the current view of Gulliver as partly a vehicle and partly an object of the satire is surely correct. Everything depends, therefore, on how much relevance to what he was trying to do in the voyage this particular historical hypothesis can be shown to have.

Its proponents have offered it as relevant beyond reasonable doubt; which suggests to me that some special assumptions about the application of intellectual history to the exegesis of literary works must be involved here. For they would find it difficult, I think, to justify their confidence in terms merely of the ordinary canons of proof in this as well as other historical fields.

They can indeed show that the hypothesis is a possible one, in the sense that it is consistent with some of the things we know about Swift apart from the voyage. We know that he was a humanistically educated Anglican divine, with traditionalist inclinations in many matters; that he looked upon man's nature as deeply corrupted by the Fall but thought that self-love and the passions could be made, with the help of religion, to yield a positive though limited kind of virtue; that he held reason in high esteem as a God-given possession of man but distrusted any exclusive reliance on it in practice or belief, ridiculing the Stoics and Cartesians and making war on the deists; and that he tended, especially in his political writings, to find the useful truth in a medium between extremes. A man of whom these things can be said might very well have conceived the *Voyage to the Country of the Houyhnhnms* in the terms in which, on the present theory, Swift is supposed to have conceived it. And beyond this, it is possible to point to various characteristics in the voyage itself which, *if* the hypothesis is correct, can be interpreted as likely consequences of it. *If* Swift had in fact intended to symbolize, in the sustained opposition of Houyhnhnms and Yahoos, the deep division and conflict within man between his rational and his animal natures, he would undoubtedly have depicted these two sets of creatures, in essentials at least, much as they are depicted in the text (although this would hardly account for his choice of horses as symbols of rationality). So, too, with the supposition that we were meant to see in the Houyhnhnms, among other things, a powerful reminder of how inadequate and dangerous, for weak and sinful human nature, is any such one-sided exaltation of reason as was being inculcated at the time by the deists, the neo-Stoics and the Cartesians: it would not be surprising, if that were actually Swift's intention, to find Gulliver saying of 'those exalted quadrupeds', as he does, that they consider 'reason alone sufficient to govern a rational creature', that they neither affirm nor deny anything of which they are not certain, and that they keep their passions under firm control, practice 'universal friendship and benevolence', and are immune to fear of death and grief for the death of others.

Now all this is to the good, to the extent at least that without such considerations as these about both Swift and the fourth voyage there would be no reason for entertaining the hypothesis at all. But can we say anything more than this – so long, that is, as we judge the question by the ordinary standards of historical criticism? In other words, do the considerations I have just summarized tend in any decisive way to establish the hypothesis as fact? The answer must surely be that they do not, and for the simple reason that they are all merely positive and favoring considerations, such as can almost always be adduced in support of almost any hypothesis in scholarship or common life, however irrelevant or false it may turn out to be. It is a basic maxim of scholarly criticism, therefore, that the probability of a given hypothesis is proportionate not to our ability to substantiate it by confirmatory evidence (although there obviously must be confirmatory evidence) but to our inability – after serious trial – to rule it out in favor of some other hypothesis that would explain more completely and simply the particulars it is concerned with. We have to start, in short, with the assumption that our hypothesis may very well be false and then permit ourselves to look upon it as fact only when, having impartially considered all the counter-possibilities we can think of, we find disbelief in it more difficult to maintain than belief. This is a rule which few of us consistently live up to (otherwise we would not publish as much as we do); but there are varying degrees of departure from it; and I can see few signs that its requirements are even approximated in the current historical discussions of the fourth voyage. It would be a different matter if these critics had been able to show statements by Swift himself about *Gulliver's Travels* that defy reasonable interpretation except as references to the particular issues and doctrines which the hypothesis supposes were in his mind when he wrote the voyage. But they have not succeeded in doing this; and they have given no attention at all to the possibility that there were other traditions of thought about human nature in Swift's time (I can think of one such, as will appear later) with which he can be shown to have been familiar – traditions which they ought to have considered and then, if possible, excluded as irrelevant before their hypothesis can be said, on ordinary scholarly grounds, to be confirmed.

What then are the special assumptions about interpretative method on which, in view of all this, their confidence must be presumed to rest? Their problem has naturally led them, as it would any historian, to make propositions about Swift's thought apart from *Gulliver* and about the thought of Swift's age: what is distinctive is the character of these propositions and the use they are put to in the interpretation of the voyage. In the eyes of the ordinary historian of ideas inquiring into the intellectual antecedents and constituents of this work, the thought of Swift as expressed in his other writings is simply an aggregate of particular statements and arguments, some of which may well turn out to be relevant to an understanding of its meaning; for any of them, however, this is merely a possibility to be tested, not a presumption to be argued from. It is the same, too, with the thought of Swift's age: this, again, in the eyes of the ordinary historian, is nothing more determinate than the sum of things that were being written in the later seventeenth and early eighteenth centuries, from varying points of view and in varying traditions of analysis, on the general theme of human nature. Some of these, once more, may well be relevant to the argument developed in the voyage, but the historian can know what they are only after an unprejudiced inquiry that presupposes no prior limitation of the ideas Swift might have been influenced by or have felt impelled to attack in constructing it. For the ordinary historian, in short, the fact that the *Voyage to the Country of the Houyhnhnms* was written by Swift at a particular moment in the general history of thought about man has only this methodological significance: that it defines the region which he may most hopefully look for the intellectual stimuli and materials that helped to shape the voyage; it gives him, so to speak, his working reading list; it can never tell him – only an independent analysis of the voyage can do that – how to use the list.

That the critics we are concerned with have taken a different view of the matter from this is suggested by the title of the book in which the current historical theory of Swift's intentions in the voyage is argued most fully and ingeniously – Kathleen Williams's *Jonathan Swift and the Age of Compromise*. For to think of a period in intellectual history in this way – as the age *of* something or other, where the something or other is designated by an abstract term like 'compromise' – is obviously no longer to consider it as an indefinite aggregate of happenings; it is to consider it rather as a definite system of happenings; something like the plot of a novel in which a great many diverse characters and episodes are unified, more or less completely, by a principal action or theme. It is to assume, moreover, not only that the historian can determine what was the central problem, the basic conflict or tension, the dominant world view of a century or generation, either in general or in some particular department of thought, but that he can legitimately use his formula for this as a confirmatory premise in arguing the meanings and causes of individual works produced in that age. It is to suppose that there is a kind of probative force in his preferred formula for the period which can confer *a priori* a privileged if not unique relevance upon one particular hypothesis about a given work of that period as against other hypotheses that are less easily brought under the terms of the formula, so that little more is required by way of further proof than a demonstration, which is never hard to give, that the work makes sense when it is 'read' as the hypothesis dictates.

These are, I think, the basic assumptions which underlie most of the recent historical discussions of the fourth voyage and which go far toward explaining the confidence their authors have felt in the correctness of their conclusions. It would be hard, otherwise, to understand why they should think it important to introduce propositions about what was central and unifying in the moral thought of Swift's age; the reason must be that they have hoped, by so doing, to establish some kind of antecedent limitation on the intentions he could be expected to have had in writing the voyage. And that, indeed, is the almost unavoidable effect of the argument for any reader who closes his mind, momentarily, to the nature of the presuppositions on which it rests. For suppose we agree with these critics that the dominant and most significant issue in the moral speculation of the later seventeenth and early eighteenth centuries was a conflict between the three fundamentally different views of man's nature represented by the orthodox 'classical-Christian' dualism in the middle and, at opposite extremes, the newer doctrines of the rationalists and benevolists on the one side and of the materialists and cynics on the other. Since this is presented as an exhaustive scheme of classification, it will be easy for us to believe that the view of man asserted in the voyage must have been one of these three. And then suppose we agree to think of Swift as a man predisposed by his humanist education and his convictions as an Anglican divine to adhere to the traditional and compromising view as against either of the modern extremisms. It will be difficult for us now to avoid believing that the *Voyage to the Country of the Houyhnhnms* was therefore more probably than not an assertion of this middle view against its contemporary enemies, and it will be harder than it would be without such an argument from the age to the author to the work, to resist any interpretations of its details that may be necessary to make them accord with that theory of Swift's intentions.

This is likely to be our reaction, at any rate, until we reflect on the peculiar character of the argument we have been persuaded to go along with. There are many arguments like it in the writings of modern critics and historians of ideas in other fields (those who have interpreted Shakespeare in the light of 'the Elizabethan world picture', for instance); but they all betray, I think, a fundamental confusion in method. The objection is not that they rest on a false conception of historical periods. There is nothing intrinsically illegitimate in the mode of historical writing that organizes the intellectual happenings of different ages in terms of their controlling 'climates of opinion', dominant tendencies or ruling oppositions of attitude or belief; and the results of such synthesizing efforts are sometimes – as in A. O. Lovejoy, for example – illuminating in a high degree. The objection is rather to the further assumption, clearly implicit in these arguments, that the unifying principles of histories of this type have something like the force of empirically established universal laws, and can therefore be used as guarantees of the probable correctness of any interpretations of individual writings that bring the writings into harmony with their requirements. That this is sheer illusion can be easily seen if we consider what these principles really amount to. Some of them amount simply to assertions that there was a tendency among the writers of a particular time to concentrate on such and such problems and to solve them in such and such ways. There is no implication here that this trend affected all writers or any individual writer at all times: whether a given work of the age did or did not conform to the trend remains therefore an open question, to be answered only by independent inquiry unbiased by the merely statistical probabilities affirmed in the historian's generalization. But there are also principles of a rather different sort, among which we must include, I think, the formula of Swift's critics for the dominant conflict about human nature in his time. These are best described as dialectical constructs, since they organize the doctrinal facts they refer to by imposing on them abstract schemes of logical relationships among ideas which may or may not be identical with any of the various classifications and oppositions of doctrines influential at the time. Thus our critics' characterization of Swift's age and of Swift himself as a part of that age derives its apparent exhaustiveness from a pattern of general terms – the concept of 'Christian humanism' and the two contraries of this – which these critics clearly owe to the ethical and historical speculations of Irving Babbitt and his school. Now it may be that this scheme represents accurately enough the distinctions Swift had in mind when he conceived the fourth voyage; but that would be something of a coincidence, and it is just as reasonable to suppose that he may have been thinking quite outside the particular framework of notions which this retrospective scheme provides. We must conclude, then, that this whole way of using the history of ideas in literary interpretation is misconceived. From the generalizations and schematisms of the synthesizing historians we can very often get suggestions for new working hypotheses with which to approach the exegesis of individual works. What we cannot get from them is any assurance whatever that any of these hypotheses are more likely to be correct than any others that we have hit upon without their aid.

I should now like to invite the reader's criticism, in the light of what I have been saying, on another view of the intellectual background and import of the fourth voyage (or a considerable part of it at least) which I shall attempt to argue on the basis merely of ordinary historical evidence, independently of any general postulates about Swift or his age.

Whatever else may be true of the voyage, it will doubtless be agreed that one question is kept uppermost in it from the beginning, for both Gulliver and the reader. This is the question of what sort of animal man, as a species, really is; and the point of departure in the argument is the answer to this question which Gulliver brings with him into Houyhnhnmland and which is also, we are reminded more than once, the answer which men in general tend, complacently, to give to it. Neither he nor they have any doubt that only man, among 'sensitive' creatures, can be properly called 'rational'; all the rest – whether wild or tame, detestable or, like that 'most comely and generous' animal, the horse, the reverse of that – being merely 'brutes', not 'endued with reason'. The central issue, in other words, is primarily one of definition: is man, or is he not, correctly defined as a 'rational creature'? It is significant that Gulliver's misanthropy at the end is not the result of any increase in his knowledge of human beings in the concrete over what he has had before; it is he after all who expounds to his Houyhnhnm master all those melancholy facts about men's 'actions and passions' that play so large a part in their conversations; he has known these facts all along, and has still been able to call himself a 'lover of mankind'. The thing that changes his love into antipathy is the recognition that is now forced upon him that these facts are wholly incompatible with the formula for man's nature which he has hitherto taken for granted – are compatible, indeed, only with a formula, infinitely more humiliating to human pride, which pushes man nearly if not quite over to the opposite pole of the animal world.

What brings about the recognition is, in the first place, the deeply disturbing spectacle of the Houyhnhnms and the Yahoos. I can find nothing in the text that forces us to look on these two sets of strange creatures in any other light than that in which Gulliver sees them – not, that is, as personified abstractions, but simply as two concrete species of animals: existent species for Gulliver, hypothetical species for us. The contrast he draws between them involves the same pair of antithetical terms (the one positive, the other privative) that he has been accustomed to use in contrasting men and the other animals. The essential character of the Houyhnhnms, he tells us, is that they are creatures 'wholly governed by reason'; the essential character of the Yahoos is that 'they are the most unteachable of brutes', without 'the least tincture of reason'. The world of animals in Houyhnhnm-land, in other words, is divided by the same basic difference as the world of animals in Europe. Only, of course – and it is the shock of this that prepares Gulliver for his ultimate abandonment of the definition of man he has started with – it is a world in which the normal distribution of species between 'rational creatures' and irrational 'brutes' is sharply inverted, with horses, which he cannot help admiring, in the natural place of men, and manlike creatures, which he cannot help abhorring, in the natural place of horses.

This is enough in itself to cause Gulliver to view his original formula for his own species, as he says, 'in a very different light'. But he is pushed much further in the same misanthropic direction by the questions and comments of his Houyhnhnm master, acting as a kind of Socrates. What thus develops is partly a reduction to absurdity of man's 'pretensions to the character of a rational creature' and partly a demonstration of the complete parity in essential nature between men and the Houyhnhnmland Yahoos. There is of course one difference – unlike the Yahoos, men are after all possessed of at least a 'small proportion', a 'small pittance' of reason, some in greater degree than others. But I can see no clear signs in the text that this qualification is intended to set men apart as a third, or intermediate, species for either Gulliver or the reader. For what is basic in the new definition of man as a merely more 'civilized' variety of Yahoo is the fundamentally irrational 'disposition' which motivates his habitual behavior; and in relation to that his 'capacity for reason' is only an acquired attribute which he is always in danger of losing and of which, as Gulliver says, he makes no other use, generally speaking, than 'to improve and multiply those vices' whereof his 'brethren [in Houyhnhnmland] had only the share that nature allotted them'.

It is clear what a satisfactory historical explanation of this line of argument in the voyage would have to do. It would have to account for Swift's patent assumption that there would be a high degree of satirical force, for readers in 1726, in a fable which began with the notion that man is preeminently a 'rational creature' and then proceeded to turn this notion violently upside down, and which, in doing so, based itself on a division of animal species into the extremes of 'rational creatures' and irrational 'brutes' and on the paradoxical identification of the former with horses and of the latter with beings closely resembling men. Was there perhaps a body of teaching, not so far brought into the discussion of the voyage but widely familiar at the time, that could have supplied Swift with the particular scheme of ideas he was exploiting here? I suggest that there was, and also that there is nothing strange in the fact that it has been hitherto over-looked by Swift's critics. For one principal medium through which these ideas could have come to Swift and his readers – the only one, in fact, I know of that could have given him all of them – was a body of writings, mainly in Latin, which students of literature in our day quite naturally shy away from reading: namely, the old-fashioned textbooks in logic that still dominated the teaching of that subject in British universities during the later seventeenth and early eighteenth centuries.[1]

It is impossible not to be impressed, in the first place, by the prominence in these textbooks of the particular definition of man which the voyage sought to discredit. *Homo est animal rationale*: no one could study elementary logic anywhere in the British Isles in the generation before *Gulliver* without encountering this formula or variations of it (*Nullus homo est irrationalis*) in his manuals and the lectures he heard. It appears as the standard example of essential definition in the great majority of logics in use during these years at Oxford, Cambridge and Dublin; and in most of those in which it occurs, it is given without comment or explanation as the obviously correct formula for man's distinctive nature, as if no one would ever question that man is, uniquely and above all, a rational creature. It is frequently brought in many times over, in various contexts, in individual textbooks: I have counted a dozen or so occurrences of it in Milton's *Art of Logic*, and many times that number in the *Institutionum logicarum ... libri duo* of Franco Burgersdijck (or Burgersdicius), which was one of the most widely used and also one of the longest lived, of all these writings – it appeared in 1626 and was still prescribed at Dublin when Edmund Burke went there as a junior freshman in 1744.[2] I shall have some more to say of Burgersdicius, or 'Burgy' as Burke called him, presently; but it is worth noting that he provides us, in one passage, with the very question on which much of the fourth voyage was to turn and with the answer Swift

1 There are useful descriptions of many, though by no means all, of these in W. S. Howell, *Logic and Rhetoric in England, 1500–1700*, Princeton University Press, 1956.
2 See T. W. Copeland (ed.), *The Correspondence of Edmund Burke*, vol. 1, University of Chicago Press, 1958, pp. 4, 7–9, 21, 28.

was *not* to give to it: 'Quaerenti enim, Quale animal est homo? apposite respondetur, Rationale.'

Not only, however, was the definition omnipresent in these books, but there is some evidence that it was thought of, in Swift's time, as the special property of the academic logicians. Locke, for instance, calls it in his *Essay* 'the ordinary definition of the schools', the 'sacred definition of *Animal Rationale*' of 'the learned divine and lawyer'; it goes, he implies, with 'this whole *mystery* of *genera* and *species*, which make such a noise in the schools, and are, with justice, so little regarded out of them' (III, iii, 10; vi, 26; iii, 9). And there are other later testimonies to the same effect; among them these opening lines of an anonymous poem of the period after *Gulliver*, once ascribed to Swift – *The Logicians Refuted*:

Logicians have but ill defin'd
As rational, the human kind;
Reason, they say, belongs to man,
But let them prove it if they can.
Wise Aristotle and Smiglesius,
By ratiocinations specious,
Have strove to prove with great precision,
With definition and division,
Homo est ratione preditum;
But for my soul I cannot credit 'em.[1]

But the logicians had more to offer Swift than the great authority which they undoubtedly conferred on the definition 'rational animal'. They could have suggested to him also the basic principle on which the inverted animal world of Houyhnhnmland was constructed, and consequently the disjunction that operated as major premise in his argument about man. Whoever it was, among the Greeks, that first divided the genus 'animal' by the differentiae 'rational' and 'irrational', there is much evidence that this antithesis had become a commonplace in the Greco-Roman schools long before it was taken up by the writer who did more than any one else to determine the context in which the definition *animal rationale* was chiefly familiar

1 The *Busy Body*, no. 5, 18 October 1759. Both the ascription to Swift, which occurs in a note prefixed to this first known printing of the poem, and the later ascription to Goldsmith seem to me highly dubious.

to Englishmen of Swift's time. This writer was the Neoplatonist Porphyry of the third century, whose little treatise, the *Isagoge*, or introduction to the categories of Aristotle, became, as is well known, one of the great sources of logical theorizing and teaching from the time of Boethius until well beyond the end of the seventeenth century. There is no point in going into the details of Porphyry's doctrine: what is important for our purpose here is the new sanction he gave to the older division of animal species through his incorporation of it into the general scheme of differentiae for the category of substance which was later known as the *arbor porphyriana* or Porphyry's tree, especially in the diagrams of it that became a regular feature of the more elementary textbooks. Here it is, set forth discursively, in the crabbed prose of Burgersdicius (I quote the English version of 1697, but the Latin is no better). In seeking the definition of man, he writes, we must first observe that:

Man is a substance; but because an angel is also a substance; *that it may appear how Man differs from an angel,* substance ought to be divided into corporeal and incorporeal. A man is a *body*, an angel *without a body*: but a stone also is a *body*: that therefore a man may be distinguished from a stone, divide bodily or corporeal substance into animate and inanimate, that is, *with or without a soul*. Man is a corporeal substance animate, stone inanimate. But plants are also *animate*: let us divide therefore again corporeal substance animate into *feeling and void of feeling*. Man feels, a plant not: but a horse *also feels*, and likewise other beasts. Divide we therefore animate corporeal feeling substance into rational and irrational. Here therefore *are we to stand*, since it appears that every, and only Man *is rational* (*Monitio Logica: or, an Abstract and Translation of Burgersdicius His Logick*, London, 1697, pp. 13–14, second pagination).

And there was, finally, one other thing in these logics that could have helped to shape Swift's invention in the fourth voyage. In opposing man as the only species of 'rational animal' to the brutes, Porphyry obviously needed a specific instance, parallel to man, of an 'irrational' creature; and the instance he chose – there were earlier

precedents for the choice[1] – was the horse. The proportion 'rational'
is to 'irrational' as man is to horse occurs more than once in the
Isagoge; and the juxtaposition, in the same context, of *homo* and *equus*
was a frequently recurring cliché in his seventeenth-century followers,
as in the passage in Burgersdicius just quoted: other species of brutes
were occasionally mentioned, but none of them nearly so often. And
anyone who studied these books could hardly fail to remember a
further point – that the distinguishing 'property' of this favorite
brute was invariably given as whinnying (*facultas hinniendi*); *equus*, it
was said again and again, *est animal hinnibile*.

To most Englishmen of Swift's time who had read logic in their
youth – and this would include nearly all generally educated men –
these commonplaces of Porphyry's tree, as I may call them for short,
were as familiar as the Freudian commonplaces are to generally
educated people today, and they were accepted, for the most part, in
an even less questioning spirit, so that it might well have occurred to
a clever satirist then, that he could produce a fine shock to his readers'
complacency as human beings by inventing a world in which horses
appeared where the logicians had put men and men where they had
put horses, and by elaborating, through this, an argument designed
to shift the position of man as a species from the *animal rationale*
branch of the tree, where he had always been proudly placed, as far
as possible over toward the *animal irrationale* branch, with its enormously less flattering connotations. But have we any warrant for
thinking that this, or something like it, was what Swift actually had
in mind? It is clearly possible to describe the voyage as, in considerable part at least, an anti-Porphyrian satire[2] in the genre of the poem

---

1 E.g., Quintilian, *Institutio oratoria*, VII, iii, 3, 24. For the contrast of man and
horse in Porphyry see especially Migne, *Patrologiae*, 64, col. 128 (Boethius'
translation) '*Differentia esta quod est aptum natum dividere ea quae sub eodem
genere sunt; rationale enim et irrational, hominem et equum quae sub eodem genere
sunt animali dividunt.*'
2 Since this essay was first printed, my colleague Edward Rosenheim has
pointed out (*Modern Philology*, vol. 60, 1962, pp. 109–10; cf. his *Swift and the
Satirist's Art*, University of Chicago Press, 1963, p. 100 n.) that this description
of the fourth voyage as an 'anti-Porphyrian satire' needs some clarification.
How, he asks, 'are our own opinions changed by Swift's discrediting the
definition of man to be found in such texts on logic as that of Narcissus Marsh?
Is the reader's skepticism being chiefly directed against the texts themselves?

I quoted from earlier, *The Logicians Refuted*. But is there any evidence that Swift planned it as such?

That the Porphyrian commonplaces had been known to him in their full extent from his days at Trinity College in the early 1680s we can hardly doubt in view of the kind of education in logic he was exposed to there. Among the books which all junior freshmen at Dublin in those years were required to study or hear lectures on, we know of three in which the Porphyrian apparatus and examples had a prominent place: the *Isagoge* itself (which was prescribed by the statutes of the College to be read twice over during the year), the older logic of Burgersdicius, and the newer *Institutio logicae* of Narcissus Marsh. It is true that Swift, according to his own later statement, detested this part of the curriculum, and it is true that on

---

(Crane's phrase, "anti-Porphyrian satire" suggests that he may think so.) Or, on the other hand, is the satire directed against the substance of the proposition itself without particular concern for the contexts in which it has appeared?'

My phrase, I must acknowledge, clearly invites the construction Rosenheim puts on it. It does seem to imply that just as the targets of Swift's satire in Part III of *Gulliver* were the experimenters and projectors of the Royal Society, so, in much the same sense, his targets in Part IV were the academic logicians of the Porphyrian school. My actual view of the relation between the voyage and these logicians, however, is quite different from this and much closer to the view Rosenheim himself expounds in the latter part of his essay. Like him, I regard the fourth voyage, not as an attack on either logicians or logic (low as was his opinion of this subject), but as a satirical 'homily' directed against a much more nearly universal object – namely, that form of human pride which the late Arthur O. Lovejoy once called 'the generic pride of man as such' (*Essays in the History of Ideas*, Johns Hopkins Press, 1948, p. 63), the pride that springs from the imagined superiority of man as a species over all other living creatures in some major aspect of his nature.

For Swift in the fourth voyage, the chief foundation of this pride was the almost universally prevalent conviction, which the academic logicians in the tradition of Porphyry and his Greek and Roman predecessors did so much to keep alive, that the essence of man – and hence of all men – is contained in 'that definition *animal rationale*'. He had only to prove the falsity of this, and he had knocked out one of the great supports – perhaps the greatest support – of man's pretension to unique eminence in the animate world. This – I think Rosenheim would agree with me – was the major task he set himself in contriving his fable of Gulliver among the Houyhnhnms and the Yahoos, to the end of shocking his readers into that attitude of philosophic misanthropy ('not in Timon's manner') which consisted in thinking less exaltedly of themselves and expecting less of virtue and sense from their fellow creatures.

one examination in the 'philosophy' course (specifically Physica), in
his last year, his mark was *male* (he had a *bene* in Greek and Latin).
But this was an examination in a more advanced part of the Aristo-
telian system, and it is likely that he had fared better in the earlier
examination in logic, since he had evidently been allowed to proceed
with his class. It is possible, moreover, to infer from his occasional
use of logical terms in his later writings that, abhorrent as the subject
was to him, the time he had been compelled to spend on it as a
junior freshman was not a total loss. He at least remembered enough
of it to allude familiarly in different places to such things as a 'long
sorites', 'the first proposition of a hypothetical syllogism' and the
fallacy of two middle terms in a single syllogism;[1] and if this was
possible, there is good reason to suppose that he had not forgotten
the much simpler Porphyrian points about genera, species, and
definition, 'rational' versus 'irrational' animals, men and horses
which he had been introduced to at the same time.

The crucial question, however, is whether he had these notions of
the logicians actively in mind when, in the 1720s, he conceived and
wrote the *Voyage to the Country of the Houyhnhnms*. And here it will
be well to take a fresh look at the two much-quoted letters about
Gulliver's Travels which he sent to Pope in 1725, just after that work
was completed. In the first of these, that of 29 September, after having
told Pope that his chief aim is 'to vex the world rather than divert it'
and that he hates and detests 'that animal called man', he goes on to
remark: 'I have got materials towards a treatise proving the falsity of
that definition *animal rationale*, and to show it should be only *rationis
capax*. Upon this great foundation of misanthropy, though not in
Timon's manner, the whole building of my Travels is erected; and
I never will have peace of mind till all honest men are of my opinion.'
In the second letter, that of 26 November, he desires that Pope and
'all my friends' will 'take a special care that my disaffection to the
world may not be imputed to my age, for I have credible witnesses
... that it has never varied from the twenty-first to the f—ty-eighth
year of my life'. He then adds a passage which has been read as a
retraction of the judgement on humanity expressed in the first letter,

1 See J. M. Bullitt, *Jonathan Swift and the Anatomy of Satire*, Harvard University
Press, 1953, p. 73. Cf. also Swift, 'A Preface to the B—p of S—m's Introduction' (IV 53–84).

although the final sentence makes clear, I think, that it was not so intended: 'I tell you after all, that I do not hate mankind; it is *vous autres* [Pope and Bolingbroke] who hate them, because you would have them reasonable animals, and are angry for being disappointed. I have always rejected that definition, and made another of my own. I am no more angry with—than I am with the kite that last week flew away with one of my chickens; and yet I was glad when one of my servants shot him two days after.'

The casual references in both letters to 'that definition' – *animal rationale*' and 'reasonable animals' – which Swift tells Pope he has 'always rejected' have usually been interpreted by his modern critics as allusions to such contemporary philosophical or theological heresies (from Swift's point of view) as the 'optimism' of Shaftesbury or the 'rationalism' of Descartes and the deists. It is surely, however, a much less far-fetched conjecture, especially in view of the familiar textbook Latin of the first letter, to see in 'that definition' nothing other or more than the 'sacred definition' of the logicians which had been inflicted on him, by thoroughly orthodox tutors, in his undergraduate days at Dublin.

I find this explanation, at any rate, much harder to disbelieve than any other that has been proposed; and all the more so because of another passage in the first letter which is almost certainly reminiscent of the Trinity logic course in the early 1680s. It is the famous sentence – just before the allusion to – 'that definition *animal rationale*' and leading on to it – in which Swift says: 'But principally I hate and detest that animal called man, although I heartily love John, Peter, Thomas, and so forth.' Now to any one at all widely read in the logic textbooks of Swift's time two things about this sentence are immediately evident: first, that the distinction it turns on is the distinction to be found in nearly all these books between a species of animals and individual members of that species; and second, that the names 'John, Peter, Thomas, and so forth' are wholly in line with one of the two main traditions of names for individuals of the species man that had persisted side by side in innumerable manuals of logic since the Middle Ages: not, of course, the older tradition of classical names – Socrates, Plato, Alexander, Caesar – but the newer tradition (which I have noted first in Occam, although it doubtless antedates him) that drew upon the list of apostles – Peter, John, Paul,

James, Thomas, in roughly that descending order of preference. (Other non-classical names, like Stephen, Catharine, Charles, Richard, also appear, but much less frequently.)

We can go further than this, however. For although all three of Swift's names occur separately in various texts (Thomas least often), the combination 'John, Peter, Thomas, and so forth' was an extremely unusual one. I have met with it, in fact, in only one book before 1725; and I have examined nearly all the logics, both Latin and English, down to that date for which I can find any evidence that they had even a minor circulation in Britain. The exception, however, is a book which Swift could hardly have escaped knowing as an undergraduate, since it was composed expressly for the use of Trinity College students by the then Provost and had just recently come 'on the course' when he entered the College in 1682 – namely, the *Institutio logicae*, already referred to, of Narcissus Marsh (Dublin, 1679; reissued Dublin, 1681). Early in the book Marsh gives a full-page diagram of Porphyry's tree, with its inevitable opposition of *animal – rationale – homo* and *animal – irrationale – brutum*; and here, as *individua* under *homo*, we find 'Joannes, Petrus, Thomas, &c.' And a little later in the book the same names are repeated in the same order as individual specimens of *homo* in Marsh's analytical table for the category *substantia*.

Was this combination of names, then, Marsh's invention? There is one further circumstance which suggests that it may well have been. We know from his own testimony,[1] as well as from internal evidence, that the source on which he based the greater part of his Dublin logic of 1679 was his own revision, published at Oxford in 1678, of the *Manuductio ad logicam* of the early seventeenth-century Jesuit logician Philippe Du Trieu. Now of the two passages in the Dublin book that contain Swift's three names, the first – the diagram of

---

1 See his preface 'Ad lectorem' in the 1681 issue (it is missing from some copies but can be found in the Cambridge University Library copy and in that belonging to Archbishop Marsh's Library, Dublin); also the entry for 20 December 1690, in his manuscript diary. I owe this latter reference to Mary Pollard, of Archbishop Marsh's Library. For the rather complicated bibliographical history of Marsh's *Institutio logicae* (the title was altered to *Institutiones logicae* in the reissue of 1681), see her article, 'The Printing of the Provost's Logic and the Supply of Text-books in the Late Seventeenth Century', in *Friends of the Library of Trinity College, Dublin; Annual Bulletin*, 1959–61.

Porphyry's tree – has no counterpart in the Oxford book of 1678, although it has in Du Trieu's original text, where the names are 'Petrus' and 'Joannes'. It seems likely, then, that Marsh first thought of the combination 'John, Peter, Thomas, and so forth' when he revised his earlier revision of Du Trieu for his Trinity students in 1679; and this is borne out by what he did at the same time with the other passage – the table of substance. This he retained almost exactly as it had been in Du Trieu except for the names under *homo*: here, where in 1678 he had reprinted Du Trieu's 'Stephanus, Johannes, Catharina, &c.', he now wrote 'Johannes, Petrus, Thomas, &c.' Which would seem to imply a certain sense of private property in these particular names in this particular combination.

It is somewhat hard, then, not to conclude that Swift was remembering Marsh's logic as he composed the sentence, in his letter to Pope, about 'John, Peter, Thomas, and so forth'. But if that is true, can there be much doubt, in view of the Porphyrian context in which these names appear in Marsh, about what tradition of ideas was in his mind when he went on to remark, immediately afterwards, that 'the great foundation of misanthropy' on which 'the whole building' of his *Travels* rested was his proof – against Marsh and the other logicians he had been made to study at Trinity – of 'the falsity of that definition *animal rationale*'?[1]

(261–82)

C. J. Rawson

'Gulliver and the Gentle Reader', in M. Mack and I. Gregor (eds.)
*Imagined Worlds: Essays on Some English Novels and Novelists in
Honour of John Butt* 1968

'"Tis a great ease to my conscience that I have written so elaborate and useful a discourse without one grain of satire intermixed': this, from the Preface to *A Tale of a Tub* (I 29; see also I 32), outdoes even Gulliver's claims to veracity in its cheeky outrageousness. That

[1] I have discussed some further aspects of the subject in a brief article, 'The Rationale of the Fourth Voyage', in R. A. Greenberg (ed.), *Gulliver's Travels: An Annotated Text with Critical Essays*, Norton, 1961, pp. 300–307, and in a review of two papers on Swift and the deists, in *Philological Quarterly*, vol. 40, 1961, pp. 427–30.

'Provocative display of indirectness' which Herbert Read (in a fine though somewhat unfriendly phrase) saw in *Gulliver* governs also the mad parodic world of the *Tale*: the seven prefatory items followed by an Introduction, the signposted chapters of digression (one of them in praise of digressions), the pseudo-scholarly annotation (with the 'commentator' sometimes at odds with the 'author'), the triumphant assimilation into the notes of Wotton's hostile exegesis, the asterisks and gaps in the MS, the promise of such forthcoming publications as *A Panegyrick upon the World* and *A General History of Ears*. The 'author', a creature of mad and monstrous egotism, confides his private problems, and draws garrulous attention to his literary techniques. The obvious point of this marathon of self-posturing is to mock those modern authors, 'L'Estrange, Dryden, *and some others*' (1 32n.) who write this sort of book straight. At the same time, the *Tale* has a vitality of sheer performance which suggests that a strong self-conscious pressure of primary self-display on Swift's own part is also at work; the almost 'romantic' assertion of an immense (though edgy, oblique and aggressively self-concealing) egocentricity. Swift's descendants in the old game of parodic self-consciousness are Romantics of a special sort, like Sterne and (after him) the Byron of *Don Juan*. If the *Tale's* 'digression in praise of digressions' looks back to, and mocks, things like L'Estrange's 'Preface upon a Preface'[1] it also looks forward to Sterne's 'chapters upon chapters', and it is not for nothing that Tristram thinks his book will 'swim down the gutter of time' in the company of Swift's.[2] Whatever the ancestry of the technical devices as such, the parodic intrusions of Swift's 'author' have a centrality and importance, and are made by Swift to carry a strength of personal charge, which seem to be new.[3] In Sterne and Byron, self-conscious forms of parody and self-parody openly become a solipsistic exercise, an oblique mode of

1 See E. W. Rosenheim, Jr, *Swift and the Satirist's Art*, University of Chicago Press, 1963, p. 62.

2 *Tristram Shandy*, vol. 4, ch. 10; vol. 9, ch. 8.

3 For a most useful survey of this 'self-conscious' mode of writing, see W. C. Booth, 'The Self-Conscious Narrator in Comic Fiction before *Tristram Shandy*', *PMLA*, vol. 67, 1952, pp. 163–85. There is a good deal of this kind of writing shortly before Sterne, not necessarily derived from Swift, and my point does not *primarily* concern an 'influence'. See also Booth, *The Rhetoric of Fiction*, University of Chicago Press, 1961, p. 229.

self-revelation and self-display, and a reaching out to the reader on those terms. Swift has in common with Sterne, against most pre-Swiftian practitioners of 'self-conscious narration', the imposition of an exceptional immediacy of involvement with the reader. The narrators are not, of course, the equivalents of Swift or even Sterne: but each is an 'I' of whose existence and temperament we are kept unremittingly aware, who talks to the reader and seems to be writing the book, and through whom the real author projects a very distinctive presence of his own. Swift and Sterne also share a kind of intimate, inward-looking obliquity which sets them off, say, from their master Rabelais, who like them projects a formidable presence, but whose boozy companionable exhibitionism amounts to an altogether different (and more 'open') manner. This obliquity (more or less instinctive in Swift, more coyly self-aware in Sterne) perhaps takes the place of an overt self-expression which Augustan decorum, and whatever personal inhibitions, discouraged.

There are certainly important differences. When the 'author' of the *Tale* asserts, 'in the integrity of my heart, that what I am going to say is literally true this minute I am writing' (I 22), Swift is exposing the trivial ephemerality of modern writers. Similar remarks from Sterne (or, in a way, from Richardson) proudly proclaim the immediacy of their method of writing 'to the moment' (Richardson, Preface to *Sir Charles Grandison*). When Swift's 'author', again, asserts the importance of the reader's 'putting himself into the circumstances and postures of life, that the writer was in, upon every important passage as it flowed from his pen', so that there may be 'a parity and strict correspondence of idea's between the reader and the author' (I 27), Swift is attacking modern garrulities of self-revelation which for him amount to indecent exposure. In Sterne such remarks, however fraught with all manner of Shandean indirection, are real tokens of relationship. Tristram wants to tell you everything about himself, because he and Sterne enjoy his character (including the irony injected into it by Sterne, and of which Sterne's parodic performance is a part) as a rich fact of human nature. Both want to get the reader intimately involved:

As you proceed farther with me, the slight acquaintance, which is now beginning betwixt us, will grow into familiarity; and

that, unless one of us is in fault, will terminate in friendship. –
O *diem praeclarum!* – then nothing which has touched me will
be thought trifling in its nature or tedious in its telling
(*Tristram Shandy*, vol. 1, ch. 6).

The difference is not simply a matter of parody, for that exists in
Sterne too. Swift's 'author', like Sterne's, often addresses the reader
and invokes 'all the friendship that hath passed between us' (1
131). At the end of the *Tale*, he has no more to say but thinks of
experimenting on how to go on writing '*upon nothing*', 'to let' (in
a phrase Sterne might have used) 'the pen still move on':

By the time that an author has written out a book, he and his
readers are become old acquaintance, and grow very loth to
part: so that I have sometimes known it to be in writing, as
in visiting, where the ceremony of taking leave, has employed
more time than the whole conversation before (133).

Neither this, nor Sterne's passage, is quite straight. That both are in
some sense ironic need not be laboured. But Sterne's irony is of that
puppyish, clinging sort which prods, cajoles, sometimes irritates the
reader into a participation which may be reluctant and grudging, but
which is also primary, direct and real. Swift's words assert the same
intimacy, but the actual effect of the Swiftian acidity at the end of
the 'author's' innocent sentence would *appear* to be to sever the link,
to achieve not intimacy but an alienation. Sterne's irony is one of fond
permissive indulgence; the egotism, though mocked, is freely played
with, and the reader offered hospitality within it. In Swift's characteristic sting, the friendly egotism freezes into a stark reminder of the
fact of mockery or parody of egotism, and (more than parody though
by way of it) the claim to friendship with the reader becomes a kind
of insulting denial.

   There is thus, in this parody, a tartly defiant presence (that 'self-
assertion' which Leavis diagnosed)[1] which seems to differentiate it
from more normal modes of parody, whose formal business it is to
mock books. It is a truism that Swiftian parody, like that of many
writers who choose to make their most serious statements about life

1 See *The Common Pursuit*, Penguin Books, 1962, p. 80.

through the medium of allusions to books, is usually more than parody in that, in various directions, it transcends parody's limiting relation to the works parodied. *A Modest Proposal* is both more and other than a mockery of those economic proposals whose form it adopts. The real concern is with matters with which the parodic element has such as no necessary connexion: the state of Ireland (rather than economic projectors) in *A Modest Proposal*, human pride (rather than popular travel-writing) in *Gulliver*. The problem some-times arises of just where the dominant focus lies: a parodic energy may blur a more central intention, and there may be a hiatus between a local parodic effect and the main drift of the discourse. An aspect of this, to which I shall return briefly, is that teasing fluctuation, or bewildering uncertainty, of *genre* which critics have noted in some of Swift's works, and which gives a curious precariousness to the reader's grasp of what is going on. The *Tale* differs in a formal sense from *A Modest Proposal* and *Gulliver* in that the 'modernity' which it attacks finds one of its main symptoms in the kind of book that is being parodied, so that the congruence between parody and the 'real' subject is particularly close. Even so, it would be wrong to suggest that this 'real' subject is merely a matter of silly or offensive stylistic habits, like garrulousness or digressiveness. The cumulative effect of the *Tale's* formidable parodic array is to convey a sense of intel-lectual and cultural breakdown so massive and so compelling that the parodied objects, as such, come to seem a minor detail. This in no case makes the parody expendable. The manner of the hack-author, bland proposer or truthful boneheaded traveller are essential to the effects Swift is creating, and not merely as means of highlighting satiric intensities through disarming naïveties of style. My last ex-ample from the *Tale* shows how parody of friendly gestures from author to reader not only mocks modern garrulousness and all the intellectual slovenliness that goes with it (as well as capturing inci-dentally a typical social absurdity), but puts the reader himself under attack. This 'Satire of the Second Person', in H. W. Sams's useful phrase,[1] is not primarily a matter of *satirizing* the reader, but of making him uncomfortable in another sense, as a person we are rude to is made uncomfortable. Swift, as much as Sterne, is reaching out

1 See *English Literary History*, vol. 26, 1959, pp. 36–44.

to the reader, and the alienation I spoke of does not in fact eliminate intimacy, though it destroys 'friendship'. There is something in Swift's relations with his reader that can be described approximately in terms of the edgy intimacy of a personal quarrel that does not quite come out into the open, with gratuitous-seeming sarcasms on one side and a defensive embarrassment on the other. Such a description can only be a half-truth. And, like many of the examples I shall be discussing, the passage is much lighter than any account of it can be. It is a joke (a good one), and playful. But it is attacking play, and its peculiar aggressiveness is a quality which I believe to be not merely incidental but pervasive in Swift's major satires, whether parody is present or not. What is involved is not necessarily a 'rhetoric' or thought-out strategy, so much as an atmosphere or perhaps an instinctive tone. This is not to mistake Swift for his masks, but to say that behind the screen of indirections, ironies and putative authors a central Swiftian personality is always actively present, and makes itself felt.

Consider a scatological passage in *Gulliver*. I do not wish to add here to the available theories about the scatology and body-disgust as such. Psychoanalysts have examined it; C. S. Lewis says, sturdily, that it is 'much better understood by schoolboys than by psycho-analysts'[1]; another critic says the 'simplest answer is that as a con-scientious priest [Swift] wished to discourage fornication';[2] others say that Swift was just advocating cleanliness, mocking the over-particularity of travel-writers, or doing no more any way than other writers in this or that literary tradition. But most people agree that there is a lot of it, and it has been a sore point from the start. Swift knew it, and knew that people knew, and early in Book I he has a characteristic way of letting us know he knows we know. Gulliver had not relieved himself for two days, and tells us how in his urgency he now did so inside his Lilliputian house. But he assures us that on

1 See 'Addison', *Essays on the Eighteenth Century Presented to David Nichol Smith*, Clarendon Press, 1945, p. 1.
2 I. Ehrenpreis, *The Personality of Jonathan Swift*, Methuen, 1958, p. 39, on *A Beautiful Young Nymph Going to Bed*. Ehrenpreis also lists parallels from other writers. See also R. M. Frye, 'Swift's Yahoo and the Christian Symbols for Sin', *Journal of the History of Ideas*, vol. 15, 1954, pp. 201–17, and Deane Swift's *Essay* (1755), pp. 221 ff.

future occasions he always did 'that business in open air', and that the 'offensive matter' was disposed of 'every morning before company came' by two Lilliputian servants. Gulliver thinks the 'candid reader' needs an explanation, so he tell us this:

I would not have dwelt so long upon a circumstance, that perhaps at first sight may appear not very momentous; if I had not thought it necessary to justify my character in point of cleanliness to the world; which I am told, some of my maligners have been pleased, upon this and other occasions, to call in question (XI 29).

It is Gulliver and not Swift who is speaking, but it is Swift and not Gulliver who (in any sense that is active at this moment) has had maligners. Gulliver does have enemies in Lilliput, notably after urinating on the palace-fire, but the reader does not know this yet, and it is difficult not to sense behind Gulliver's self-apology a small egocentric defiance from the real author. This would be true whether one knew him to be Swift or not: but it comes naturally from the Swift whose writings, and especially *A Tale of a Tub*, had been accused of 'filthiness' (William King, *Some Remarks on The Tale of a Tub*, 1704), 'lewdness', 'immodesty' and of using 'the language of the stews' (William Wotton, *A Defense of the Reflections upon Ancient and Modern Learning ... with Observations upon The Tale of a Tub* (1705). (Swift called it being 'battered with dirt-pellets' from 'envenomed ... mouths'[1]). Swift's trick consists of doing what he implies people accuse him of, and saying that this proves he isn't like that really: the openly implausible denial becomes a cheeky flaunting of the thing denied, a tortuously barefaced challenge. This self-conscious sniping at the reader's poise occurs more than once: a variant instance of mock-friendly rubbing-in, for the 'gentle reader's' benefit, occurs at the end of book 2, chapter 1, where the particularity of travel-writers is part of a joke.

A related non-scatological passage, which Thackeray praised as 'the best stroke of humour, if there be a best in that abounding book',[2] is Gulliver's final farewell to his Houyhnhnm master, whose hoof he offers to kiss, as in the papal ceremony (see also 1 71,

1 1 5. Swift was not at first known to be the author.
2 *English Humourists*, Everyman's Library, 1949, p. 32.

and Rabelais, *Gargantua* chs. 2, 33; *Pantagruel*, ch. 30). (Gulliver seems to have leanings that way: he also wanted to kiss the Queen of Brobdingnag's foot, but she just held out her little finger – XI 101).

But as I was going to prostrate myself to kiss his hoof, he did me the honour to raise it gently to my mouth. I am not ignorant how much I have been censured for mentioning this last particular (XI 282).

Since the passage occurs in the first edition, Gulliver or Swift could hardly have been censured for mentioning this before. 'Detractors' would be presumed by the reader to object that human dignity was being outraged, and Swift was of course right that many people would feel this about his book in general. But this is not Gulliver's meaning at all, and the typical Swiftian betrayal that follows gains its real force less from mere surprise than from its cool poker-faced fanning of a reader's hostility which Swift obviously anticipated and actually seemed on the point of trying to allay:

Detractors are pleased to think it improbable, that so illustrious a person should descend to give so great a mark of distinction to a creature so inferior as I. Neither have I forgot, how apt some travellers are to boast of extraordinary favours they have received. But. . . .

Thackeray's praise ('audacity', 'astounding gravity', 'truth topsy-turvy, entirely logical and absurd') comes just before the famous 'filthy in word, filthy in thought, furious, raging, obscene' passage (*English Humourists*, pp. 34–5): it is perhaps appropriate that such coarse over-reaction should be the counterpart to a cheerful complacency in the face of the subtler energies of Swift's style.

The mention of travellers in the hoof-kissing passage brings us back to parody, but emphasizes again how readily Swiftian parody serves attacking purposes which are themselves non-parodic. Edward Stone's view that this reference is proof that Swift is merely joking at the expense of boastful travellers misses most of the flavour of the passage.[1] (One might as easily say that the main or only point of the passage is to guy a papal rite. I do not, of course, deny these secondary

1 See 'Swift and the Horses: Misanthropy or Comedy?', *Modern Language Quarterly*, vol. 10, 1949, p. 374 n.

jokes, or their piquancy.) But parody is important, almost as much in its way as in the *Tale*. Gulliver is an author, who announces forthcoming publications about Lilliput (I 47–8, 57) and Houyhnhnmland (I 275) – which is a common enough device – and whose putative authorship of the work we are actually reading, as well as being the source of many of its most central ironies, enables Swift to flaunt his own self-concealment in some amusing and disconcerting ways.[1] A portrait of Gulliver was prefixed to the early editions, and in 1735 this acquired the teasing caption 'Splendide Mendax' (Horace, *Odes*, III xi 35). The elaborate claims to veracity in 'The Publisher to the Reader' and in the text itself gain an additional piquancy from this. The 1735 edition also prints for the first time Gulliver's letter to Sympson, which, as prefatory epistles go, is a notably unbalanced document, providing advance notice of Gulliver's later anti-social state and by the same token giving a disturbing or at least confusing dimension to the sober opening pages of the narrative. Gulliver's announcement in the letter that *Brobdingnag* should have been spelt *Brobdingrag* (I 8) belongs to a familiar kind of authenticating pretence in both fiction and prose satire, but in so far as we remember it later it does make it slightly unsettling to read *Brobdingnag* with an *n* every time it occurs in the book. It is clear that these devices, though not meant to be believed, are not bids for verisimilitude in the manner, say, of Richardson's 'editorial' pretence or the countless other tricks of fiction-writers before and after Swift (the correcting footnote, the manuscript partly missing or lost, the discovered diary, the pseudo-biography). Nor are they quite a matter of pure hearty fun, as in Rabelais, meant to be enjoyed *precisely as* too outrageous to be believed. For one thing, Swift's celebrated 'conciseness' is too astringent. It is also too close to the idiom of sober factuality, and some people were literally taken in.

We are hardly expected to take *Gulliver's Travels* as a straight (even if possibly mendacious) travel story. But the sea captain who claimed

---

1 Real concealment seemed a necessity, with such a subversive book, though Pope told Swift on 16 November 1726 that people were not worried by 'particular reflections', so that he 'needed not to have been so secret upon this head' in (*Correspondence*, III 181). In any case, *simple* anonymity or pseudonymity would have served the practical purpose. Swift's authorship soon became fairly well known anyway.

to be 'very well acquainted with Gulliver, but that the printer had mistaken, that he lived in Wapping, and not in Rotherhith', the old gentleman who searched for Lilliput on the map, the Irish Bishop who said the 'book was full of improbable lies, and for his part, he hardly believed a word of it'[1] (though some of these readers may have been more *ben trovati* than real) do tell a kind of truth about the work. Swift's whole ironic programme depends on our not being taken in by the travel-book element, but it does require us to be infected with a residual uncertainty about it; and these instances of an over-successful hoax fulfil, extremely, a potential in the work to which all readers must uneasily respond. This is not to accept the simpler accounts of Swiftian betrayal, which suggest that the plain traveller's, or modest proposer's, factuality lulls the reader into a false credulity, and then springs a trap. With Swift, we are always on our guard from the beginning (I believe this is true of sensitive *first* readings as well as later ones), and what surprises us is not the fact of betrayal but its particular form in each case. But if we are on our guard, we do not know what we are guarding against. The travel-book factuality, to which we return at least at the beginning and end of each book (even the end of book 4, in its strange way, sustains and elaborates the pretence) is so insistent, and at its purest so lacking in obvious pointers to a parodic intention, that we really do not know *exactly* how to take it. What saves the ordinary reader from being totally taken in is, obviously, the surrounding context. (The very opening of the narrative, from the 1735 edition onwards, is coloured by the letter to Sympson: but even before 1735 one would have needed to be exceptionally obtuse to think, by the end of the first chapter, that one was still reading a travel-book.) But not being taken in, and knowing the plain style to be parodic, does not save us from being unsure of what is being mocked: travel-books, fictions posing as travel-books, philosophic tales (like *Gulliver* itself) posing as fictions posing as travel-books.[2] Bewilderment is increased by the uncertainty of how much weight to give, moment by moment, to the fact of parody as such and to whatever the style may be mocking,

1 See *Correspondence*, III 180, 189; see also M. M. Rossi and J. M. Hone *Swift or the Egotist*, Folcrope, 1934, pp. 330, 411.
2 See R. Quintana, *Swift: An Introduction*, Oxford University Press, 1962, pp. 53 ff., 158 ff.

since the parody as we have seen is continuously impregnated with satiric purposes which transcend or exist outside it, but which may still feed on it in subtle ways. And we cannot be sure that some of the plainness is not meant to be taken straight, not certainly as factual truth, but (in spite of everything) transiently as realistic fictional trimmings: at least, the style helps to establish the 'character' of the narrator, though this 'character' in turn has more life as the basis of various ironies than as a vivid fictional personality. No accurate account can exhaust the matter, or escape an element of giddy circularity. The proper focus for Swift's precise sober narrative links is paradoxically a blurred focus, because we do not know what to make of all the precision. The accumulation of unresolved doubt that we carry into our reading of more central parts of *Gulliver's Travels* creates, then, not a credulity ripe for betrayal, but a more continuous defensive uneasiness. This undermining of our nervous poise makes us peculiarly vulnerable, in more than the obvious sense, to the more central satiric onslaughts.

The parodic element, though not primary, is never abandoned. At the end of book 4, when any live interest in travel-writers may be thought to have totally receded in the face of more overwhelming concerns, Gulliver keeps the subject alive with some tart reminders of his truthfulness and the mendacity of other travellers. The practice is commonplace, but again there is nothing here either of Rabelais's friendly outrageousness as he refers to his 'histoire tant veridicque', or his or Lucian's corresponding frank admission that they are telling monstrous lies, or the honest workmanlike concern with verisimilitude that we find in, say, *Erewhon*.[1] Gulliver says:

Thus, gentle reader, I have given thee a faithful history of my travels for sixteen years, and above seven months; wherein I have not been so studious of oranament as of truth. I could perhaps like others have astonished thee with strange improbable tales; but I rather chose to relate plain matter of fact in the simplest manner and style; because my principal design was to inform, and not to amuse thee (XI 291).

This passage, which belongs with the well-known (and perhaps

1 See Rabelais, *Pantagruel*, ch. 28, *passim*; Lucian, *True History*, I, 2 ff.; Butler, *Erewhon*, chs. 9–29.

somewhat more light-hearted) remark to Pope about vexing the world rather than diverting it, emphasizes Swift's fundamental unfriendliness by a characteristic astringency (that tone is partly Swift's though Gulliver may overdo it), and by a use of the second person singular which is aggressively contemptuous. This probably parodies or inverts the common use of 'thee' and 'thou' in addresses to 'gentle readers', where, so far as the pronoun is not merely neutral, intimacy or familiarity is the point. But one can also compare places where an author treats his reader with mild aggressiveness, as when Burton opens his long preface to *The Anatomy of Melancholy* by proclaiming his freedom to tell or withhold information which the reader wants: in fact, the passage hardly has a Swiftian tang, and Burton ends the preface by earnestly requesting 'every private man ... not to take offence' and by presuming 'of thy good favour, and gracious acceptance (gentle reader)'.[1] Fielding's usages range from warm friendliness (*Tom Jones*, book 18, ch. 1), through a more ruggedly admonishing but still friendly tone (book 9, ch. 7), to a partial identification of the reader with 'a little reptile of a critic' (book 10, ch. 1): but even here there is an initial comic relaxation (the comparison with Shakespeare and his editors), and the later concession to the reader that perhaps 'thy heart may be better than thy head'; and when Fielding takes stock of his relations with the reader in book 18, ch. 1 he warmly disclaims any intention to give offence.[2]

But Swift's use of 'thee' is the hostile one ('thou' and 'thee' were also often addressed to inferiors),[3] where familiarity, so to speak, has bred contempt. And what we sense in Swift's attack is not the grand public voice of the Satirist, which is, for example, Pope's voice.

1 'Democritus Junior to the Reader', *The Anatomy of Melancholy*, Everyman's Library, 1932, vol. I, pp. 15, 123.
2 Contrast Gulliver's use of this convention: 'I never suffer a word to pass that may look like reflection, or possibly give the least offence even to those who are most ready to take it. So that, I hope, I may with justice pronounce myself an author perfectly blameless; against whom the tribes of answerers, considerers, observers, reflecters, detecters, remarkers, will never be able to find Matter for exercising their talents' (XI 293). This hardly pretends to be a friendly, or even a plausible, gesture from Swift, though it is, of course, amusing.
3 For both these uses, see *OED*, 'Thou', *pers. pron.*, 1*b*, and 'Thou', *verb*.

When Pope uses the hostile 'thee' in the *Essay on Man* (e.g. book 3, lines 27 ff., 'Has God, thou fool! worked solely for thy good. . . . Is it for thee the lark ascends and sings? . . .'), it is Man he is addressing, not the reader. Swift's refusal of the 'lofty style' in the *Epistle to a Lady* rests on an old notion that ridicule is more effective than lambasting ('Switches better guide than cudgels'), but he has a significant way of describing what the raillery does: it 'nettles', 'Sets the spirits all a working'. 'Alecto's whip' makes the victims (here specifically 'the nation's representers') 'wriggle, howl and skip': the satirist makes clear that the whip is to be applied to 'their bums', and that he will not be deterred by the smell.[1] Nothing could make clearer the note of quarrelsome intimacy that is the hallmark of Swift's satire. It may not be very attractive, but it is not meant to be: and it has a unique disturbing effectiveness.

Gulliver's angers (whether nagging tartness, as in the passage under discussion, or ranting fury) reflect a cooler needling offensiveness from the Swift who manipulates the 'switch'. The chapter, and the volume, end with Gulliver's onslaught on pride, and his petulant instruction to all English Yahoos 'who have any tincture of this absurd vice, that they will not presume to appear in my sight'. It is Gulliver and not Swift who is speaking (here it is important not to confuse the two: saying this has almost become a nervous tic among critics), but there is really no sufficiently vivid alternative point of view that we can hang on to at this final moment. I shall return to this, and to what Gulliver actually says, later. What I want to stress here is that the final chapter begins with a needling defiance and the openly unfriendly intimacy of a petty insult, and ends with quarrelsome hysteria. The hysteria is Gulliver's and Swift seems in control. But the quarrel with the reader is one which Swift has been conducting through Gulliver, even though, when Gulliver becomes acutely unbalanced, there is an incomplete (at least a not quite literal) Swiftian commitment to what the quarrel has come to.

Gulliver is sometimes called a gay book. Arbuthnot seems to have started this when he said 'Gulliver is a happy man that at his age can write such a merry work' (*Correspondence*, III 179). His letter is joyful about the success of *Gulliver*, and tells of the Captain who

[1] *Epistle to a Lady*, lines 139 ff. (*Poems*, II 634–7).

claimed to know Gulliver, and the old man who looked up his map. Arbuthnot loved 'mischief the best of any good natured man in England' (*Correspondence*, III 120), and is full of happy complicity in Swift's success and the bonus of a hoax. Pope and Gay were also 'diverted' by the reception of the book (III 181, 182). Part of the 'merry' seems more Scriblerian in-joke than sober description. But the book really is merry, and one thinks of witty fantastications like the joke about the handwriting of ladies in England (*Prose Writings*, XI 57),[1] or the charming comedy of the Lilliputian speculations about Gulliver's watch (XI 35), which Johnson praised.[2] Such things are very funny, with mild satiric overtones, but without being unduly charged with needling obliquities or any blistering intensity. This is true even in some cases where we should expect Swift to be very hostile. Much of the folly of scientists in book 3 is treated thus, the flappers, the substitution of things for words, the mathematical obsession which makes the Laputans describe

the beauty of a woman . . . by rhombs, circles,
parallelograms, ellipses and other geometrical terms,
(XI 163)

(a joke which is not without bearing on our own habit of reducing women's shapes to 'vital statistics'). *Gulliver* has a notably unbuttoned way of giving itself over to local eruptions of mood, but it may be that the very fluctuations of tone invite us (though it will not do to be too solemn) to reconsider the whole nature of the 'merriment'. Swift obviously enjoyed the comedy of incongruity that runs right through the work (the Lilliputian troop on Gulliver's handkerchief, various Houyhnhnm postures, the She-Yahoo embracing Gulliver): this comes through plainly in his letter to Motte discussing illustrations to the book (*Correspondence*, III 257–8). But a good deal of this grotesque comedy, notably in Brobdingnag, is close to being rather painful. The hailstones as big as tennis-balls, the huge frog, the monkey which takes Gulliver for one of its own (XI 116 ff.) have an undeni-

---

1 The clinching joke, though not the passage as a whole, is Swift's. See R. W. Frantz, 'Gulliver's "Cousin Sympson"', *Huntingdon Library Quarterly*, vol. 1, 1938, pp. 331–3.
2 Boswell, *Life of Johnson*, ed. G. Birkbeck Hill and L. F. Powell, Clarendon Press, 1934, vol. 2, p. 319.

able science-fiction humour, but Gulliver is throughout in peril of his life. This is even truer of the slapstick comedy of the bowl of cream (XI 108): not only is it fraught with painful possibilities for Gulliver, but it reflects a crude and bitter malevolence in the court dwarf. J. M. Bullitt speaks well of Swift's 'seeming merriment' as reflecting 'an almost compulsive desire to separate himself from the intensity of his own feelings'[1] and the margin between high-spirited fun and more disturbing purposes is sometimes a thin one. If notions of the jest as a breaker of tensions, a disguised means of attack, or a showy (*vive la bagatelle!*) shrugging-off of painful feeling seem too ponderous to impose on some (not all) of these passages, they are not foreign to Swift's manner as a whole, and come into his thinking about satire:

All their madness makes me merry....
Like the ever-laughing sage,
In a jest I spend my rage:
(Tho' it must be understood,
I would hang them if I cou'd)
(*Epistle to a Lady*, lines 164–70; *Poems*, II 635)

And if the self-humour in these verses forbids us to take the passage at its literal intensity (as it forbids us to take at *their* literal intensity the 'hate and detest' and 'drown and world' passages in the letters to Pope expressing the 'misanthropy' behind the *Travels*) (*Correspondence*, III 103, 117), yet the self-humour is plainly not of the kind that cancels what is said. I imagine, indeed, that the self-humour may in some ways be more disturbing than the plain uncompromising statement would have been without it. In dissociating the thing said from the full violence of the saying, the ironist both unsettles the reader and covers himself. Since we have here no firm alternative viewpoint to give us our bearings, we can only know that the ironist means part of what he says, but not exactly how large, or quite what sort of, a part; and so do not know what defenses are called for. More important, obviously half-meant self-undercutting statements of this kind ('I would hang them if I could', 'I hate and detest that animal called man') are more uncomfortable than if they had been wholly meant, for then we might have the

1 *Jonathan Swift and the Anatomy of Satire*, Harvard University Press, 1961, p. 7.

luxury of dismissing them as ranting folly. In just this way, our consciousness of Gulliver's folly makes us paradoxically more, not less, vulnerable to the onslaughts on our self-esteem in book 4. Had Gulliver been presented as sane, we should (since again there is no real alternative voice, and no firm norm is indicated) have had to identify him with the satirist behind the mask, and so have been enabled to reject both as totally outrageous. As it is, we reject what comes from Gulliver, and are left with that disturbingly uncertain proportion of it which comes from Swift. It is precisely Gulliver's distance from Swift that permits the Swiftian attack to look plausible. Much of the humour of *Gulliver's Travels* has this effect, not really of attenuating (still less of belying) the Swiftian attack, as some critics hold, but of lending it that self-defensive distancing which makes it viable. Gulliver's solemn habit of trotting and neighing, fully aware of and undeterred by people's ridicule (XI 279), releases the whole situation from any possibility of Swift himself seeming solemn.

The same may be said, the opposite way round, of those jokes at the expense of the Houyhnhnms, which are sometimes said to prove that *Gulliver's Travels* has an anti-Houyhnhnm message: their per-plexed 'gestures, not unlike those of a philosopher' (XI 226) when they try to understand Gulliver's shoes and stockings, their language which sounds like High Dutch (IX 234), their way of building houses, threading needles and milking cows (XI 274). The first thing I would note is that humour about the Houyhnhnms is never of a destructive tartness: contrast some of the anti-Lilliputian jokes. It also makes the Houyhnhnms (otherwise somewhat stiffly remote, or so some readers feel) seem engagingly awkward and 'human', and Swift has a note of real tenderness in some of the passages, the description of the Houyhnhnm dinner-party for ex-ample (XI 231–2). Irvin Ehrenpreis, in a fine account of this humour, says that Swift is smiling at his own 'whole project of bestowing concrete life upon unattainable abstractions' and 'warning the sophisticated reader that [he], unlike Gulliver, appreciates the comical aspect of his own didacticism'.[1] The concession conforms to the

1 See 'The Meaning of Gulliver's Last Voyage', *Review of English Literature*, vol. 3, 1962, p. 35.

normal method of the work: one of its effects is to make it more difficult for the reader to answer back.

But the humour has other resonances too. One Houyhnhnm absurdity that some critics make much of is their complacent notion that man's physical shape is preposterous and inefficient for the purposes of life. This is a nice joke when we think of a Houyhnhnm mare threading a needle. But it turns to a cruel irony not at the Houyhnhnms', but at mankind's, expense, when Gulliver's Houy-hnhnm master assumes that men are anatomically incapable (despite their impulses) of fighting the destructive wars Gulliver tells him about. Gulliver replies with an exuberant assertion to the contrary that displays a moral fatuity which also has its comic side:

I could not forbear shaking my head and smiling a little at his ignorance. And, being no stranger to the art of war, I gave him a description of cannons, culverins, muskets, carabines, pistols, bullets, powder, swords, bayonets, sieges, retreats, attacks, undermines, countermines, bombardments, sea-fights; ships sunk with a thousand men; twenty thousand killed on each side; dying groans, limbs flying in the air: smoke, noise, confusion, trampling to death under horses' feet; flight, pursuit, victory; fields strewn with carcases left for food to dogs, and wolves, and birds of prey; plundering, stripping, ravishing, burning and destroying. And, to set forth the valour of my own dear countrymen, I assured him, that I had seen them blow up a hundred enemies at once in a siege, and as many in a ship; and beheld the dead bodies drop down in pieces from the clouds, to the great diversion of all the spectators (XI 247).

This enthusiastic fit is obviously funny. It is funny partly because of the concreteness with which Gulliver generalizes, the entranced particularity with which he evokes not a real battle which happened but some sort of common denominator of war. The effect is instruc-tively different from that of a scene in *Nineteen Eighty-Four* which seems to make some of the same points, and which (like other things in that novel) may have been distantly modelled on Swift.[1] An entry

1 See *Nineteen Eighty-Four*, Penguin Books, 1954, pp. 10–11.

in Winston Smith's diary describes a war-film with a ship full of refugees being bombed, and a 'wonderful shot of a child's arm going up up up right into the air', and a greatly diverted audience applauding and 'shouting with laughter'. Smith says the film is very good, and talks of 'wonderful' scenes as Gulliver might. To this extent he is conditioned by the awful world of 1984, but he is struggling for his mental freedom (writing the diary is itself punishable by death), and he suddenly breaks off to think of his account as a 'stream of rubbish'. The scene does not become funny, because Smith is, in a deeper and partly unconscious sense, disturbed and pained by it, instead of being in Gulliver's fatuous trance of grotesque delight. Orwell drives the painfulness home by having Smith say that there was in the audience a prole woman who 'suddenly started kicking up a fuss and shouting they didn't oughter of showed it not in front of kids they didn't'. That there should be, within the situation itself, this glimpse of a hurt and protesting normality does not offer much reassurance: but it reaches out to the reader in a kind of complicity of despair. Neither Orwell nor the reader can stand apart from the narrator, or from the rest of the humanity described, and there can be no question of laughing anything off.

The incident in Orwell, however representative (it is in its way as representative as Swift's passage, and of similar things), is a vivid specific occurrence (though only a film), to which a pained immediacy of reaction on Smith's and on the reader's part is natural and appropriate. In Gulliver's account, even when, as at the end, he seems to turn to specific occurrences, there is a comic lack of distinction between the general and the particular, and Gulliver's all-embracing celebration has a callous yet oddly innocent absurdity. The comic note, and the fact that the horror is so diffused, ensure that no immediacy of participation by the reader in the things described is possible, or expected. For obvious reasons there is no complicity between the reader and either Gulliver or any member of the applauding crowds. Nor is the grim high-spirited comedy a congenial idiom for any complicity between the reader and Swift: the reader has, rather uncomfortably, to laugh *at* Gulliver, without having anyone very much to laugh *with*. Gulliver's folly is at this moment the moral folly of complacent acceptance, not, as later, the medical folly of unquestioning repudiation, of mankind. But there can be no

question of Gulliver's folly, or Swift's comic sense, cancelling or
seriously attenuating the point about war and attitudes to war which
the passage makes: one of their effects, as with other examples of
Swift's humour, is to remove Swift's angry attack from the plane of
rant. Yet we are not, I think, very actively horrified at Gulliver's
feelings, as we should have been if they had been Winston Smith's.
In a novel, or in life, we should be revolted by his callousness. But
we cannot, here or elsewhere, respond to him as a 'character'. He is
too absurd and two-dimensional. There is a detachment of the
character from what he reveals to us which is part of the whole
satiric formula of *Gulliver's Travels*, and which the humour here
reinforces. We think less about Gulliver than about war, and what
Swift is telling us about our attitudes to it. The message is disturbing,
and for all the fun, Swift is not, anymore than elsewhere, being very
friendly.

The tense hovering between laughter and something else, the structural indefiniteness of genre and the incessantly shifting status and
function of the parodic element, the ironic twists and countertwists,
and the endless flickering uncertainties of local effect suggest that one
of Swift's most active satiric weapons is *bewilderment*. It is perhaps not
surprising that this weapon should have backfired, and that there
should have been so much doubt and disagreement both about the
unity of the work, and the meaning of its final section. One of the
risks, but also rewards, of the attacking self-concealments of irony is
that they draw out their Irish bishops. But we are all, inevitably,
Irish bishops in some degree: and the Swift who sought to vex the
world may well be deriving a wry satisfaction from our failures to
pin him down, although he might not consent to know us in Glubbdubdrib (XI 197). What one means by 'unity' is too often rather
arbitrary, but there is perhaps a broad over-all coherence in the
consistency and progression of *Gulliver's* onslaught on the reader's
bearing and self-esteem. But it is a tense and rugged coherence,
and no neatly chartable matter, and any more 'external' unities of
formal pattern or ideology seem ultimately inseparable from, and
possibly secondary to, those satiric procedures and tones which
create the commanding impact of the Swiftian voice. An attachment
to schematic patterns *per se*, of the kind for which books 1 and 2

provide such a brilliant model, seems to have had two results. One has been a tendency to wish either or both the other books away. The other has been a quest to discover in the work as a whole some things of the geometrical shapeliness that exists between the first two books. The exercise easily becomes disembodied even when its limitations are partially recognized: it hardly seems to matter much that books 1 and 3 deal with bad governments, while books 2 and 4, in alternating pattern, deal with good governments.[1]

There are of course some broad structural facts of considerable significance, such as that we are led through three books of allegorical societies which are in principle translatable into real life (with a mixture, as Thomas Sheridan put it, of good and bad qualities 'as they are to be found in life'),[2] and which provide a solid background of 'realistic' evidence of human vice, into the stark world of moral absolutes of book 4; and that the Struldbrugs at the end of book 3 are a horrifying climax which prepares us for this. The specific fact that the Struldbrugs give a terrifying retrospective deepening to the Houyhnhnms' fearlessness of death is only one aspect of their disturbing importance: their chief force, at first meeting, is to put the concerns of the narrative once and for all on an entirely new plane. Again, the fact, noted by Case and others[3] that the incidental persons in the narrative links between the four main episodes tend to become nastier and nastier, provides an important progression, not perhaps because the reader senses it as a progression (unless it happens to be pointed out), but because the evil of sailors and others (the 'real' men) in books 3 and 4 provides a relevantly documented and depressing background to the main preoccupations of those books. (The Portuguese captain and his crew are an exception to which I shall come later.) The point about these patterns is not that they are neat and flawlessly progressive (they are not), and not merely that they fit in with the 'themes' (though they do): it is that they have an effect *as we read*, without our necessarily being aware of them *as*

1 See A. E. Case, *Four Essays on Gulliver's Travels*, Princeton University Press, 1945, p. 110.
2 See *The Life of the Rev. Dr Jonathan Swift*, 2nd edn, 1787, p. 433.
3 See A. E. Case, *Four Essays*, p. 121; J. Horrell 'What Gulliver Knew', *Sewanee Review*, vol. 51, 1943, pp. 492–3; S. H. Monk, 'The Pride of Lemuel Gulliver', *Sewanee Review*, vol. 63, 1955, p. 56.

patterns. After all, the real point about even the special relationship between books 1 and 2 is not the arithmetical piquancies, but the unfolding irony about human self-importance.

This self-importance, or pride, is at the centre of the work's concerns. A principle that is sometimes overlooked in discussions not only of structural shape but of ideological themes is that these things make themselves felt, if at all, through the reader's continuous submission to *local* effects, which means in this case exposure to the Swiftian presence at close quarters. Ideologically, *Gulliver's Travels* revolves round the familiar Augustan group of concepts, nature, reason and pride. Its position is basically a commonplace one, but it bears some restating because some ironies of characteristic force and stinging elusiveness proceed from it. Nature and reason ideally coalesce. Nature is ideal order, in all spheres of life: moral, social, political, aesthetic. Deviations from this are unnatural, as murder or any gross misdeed might, in our own idiom, be called an unnatural act. If one said that the deed came naturally to one, one would be using the term in a different sense. Such other meanings were also of course available to Swift, and I shall argue that the interplay between ideal and less ideal senses provides an important irony. Reason is the faculty which makes one behave naturally (in the high sense), makes one follow Nature and frame one's judgement (and behaviour) by her just and unerring standard. So More's Utopians (in some ways ancestors of the Houyhnhnms) 'define virtue to be life ordered according to nature, and that we be hereunto ordained of God. And that he doth follow the course of nature, which in desiring and refusing things is ruled by reason',[1] and the Houyhnhnms believe a somewhat secularized version of the same thing (XI 248). The terms nature and reason are often in fact interchangeable. Where this is not so, they may complete one another: nature teaches the Houyhnhnms 'to love the whole species', reason to distinguish between persons on merit (XI 268). The Houyhnhnms, etymologically 'the perfection of nature' (XI 235), combine nature and reason in the highest sense.

1 *Utopia*, trans. Ralph Robinson, Everyman's Library, 1951, p. 85. For an excellent discussion of More and Swift, see J. Traugott, 'A Voyage to Nowhere with Thomas More and Jonathan Swift: *Utopia* and *The Voyage to the Houyhnhnms*', *Sewanee Review*, vol. 69, 1961, pp. 534-65.

Their virtues are friendship, benevolence, decency, civility, but they have no ceremony or foolish fondness (XI 268). This means that they have both emotions and propriety, but that neither is misdirected or excessive. They would have understood Pope's phrase in *The Temple of Fame* (line 108) about 'that useful science, to be good'. Their morality is pervaded by an uncompromisingly high (and instinctive) common sense and utilitarianism, and what might be called an absolute standard of congruity or *fittingness*. Thus they cannot understand lying because speech was made to communicate (XI 240), or opinion, because there is only one truth and speculation is idle (XI 267). It follows that behaviour which offends against this unerring standard is readily seen as deviation or perversion. (This is a suggestion which Swift exploits very fully and painfully.) Even physically, the Houyhnhnms are rational-natural, for (thanks partly to their simple diet, Nature being, as Gulliver knows from some 'insipid' meals, 'easily . . . satisfied' – XI 232) they are never ill, illness being a deviation from the natural state of the body. For a comic boiling-down of this mind–body ideal, one might cite Fielding's deist Square, who 'held human nature to be the perfection of all virtue, and that vice was a deviation from our nature, in the same manner as deformity of body is'.[1] Swift had his tongue in his cheek about some Houyhnhnm notions of the 'natural' standard of mind-body integration, as when the Houyhnhnm master, in a passage of not very flattering but entirely delightful comedy, considers our physical shape unsuited for the employment of reason in 'the common offices of life' (XI 242): but Swift *is* seriously suggesting that luxurious eating habits are a cause of human physical degeneracy, so that morality and physical

1 *Tom Jones*, book 3, ch. 3. I hasten to say that I do not believe that the Houyhnhnms are therefore a satirical skit on the deists (or that Square, as one might just as easily 'prove', was a skit on the Houyhnhnms), though the rationalisms have points in common. A. O. Lovejoy's 'The Parallel of Deism and Classicism', *Essays in the History of Ideas*, Capricorn Books, 1960, pp. 78–98, makes abundantly clear that many basic assumptions about Nature and Reason were the common property of deists and non-deists alike. (My discussion here is indebted to this and other essays in Lovejoy's book.) This may be the place to say categorically that in my view Swift treats the Houyhnhnms mainly seriously and not mockingly, and that the recent arguments to this effect by Sherburn, Crane, Rosenheim, W. B. Carnochan, and others have put criticism of *Gulliver's Travels* back on the right lines.

health are causally related and not only (as apparently for Square) by analogy. Nature ideally is one, and her laws pervasive.

In *Gulliver's Travels*, however, there is a gap between Nature and 'human nature', in an actual sense, which would make Square's complacency untenable, though his *rationale* is perfectly applicable to the Houyhnhnms. The Houyhnhnms are not complacent in Square's sense because in them the ideal and the actuality are fully matched. Actually, Square's remarks also concern an ideal and, like other forms of philosophical 'optimism', logically allow for an uglier reality: but, given the ugly facts, Swift (and Fielding) would see a monstrous impropriety in putting the matter that way at all. Mankind is guilty of a collective deviation from nature and reason at every level, and this Unreason, by the familiar buried pun, becomes in *Gulliver* (as in *A Tale of a Tub* or *The Dunciad*) a vast and wicked madness: the congruence between madness and moral turpitude is one of the most vivid and inventively resourceful themes of Augustan satire. Scientists, or those of a certain sort, are one of the traditional examples. They delve into what nature keeps hidden, and they seek to pervert nature (in such cases the word slides easily from an ideal sense to something approaching 'things as they are') into something other than it is, 'condensing air into a dry tangible substance', 'softening marble for pillows and pin-cushions', arresting the growth of wool on sheep (XI 182).[1] The phrase 'natural philosophy' provides an exploitable pun (Fielding said natural philosophy knew 'nothing of nature, except her monsters and imperfections' – *Tom Jones*, book 13, ch. 5), and when Gulliver explained to the Houyhnhnm master,

our several systems of *natural philosophy*, he would laugh that a creature pretending to *reason*, should value itself upon the knowledge of other people's conjectures, and in things, where that knowledge, if it were certain, could be of no use (XI 267–8).

Science becomes divorced from usefulness and good sense. The Laputans are 'dextrous' mathematicians on paper but have no idea

1 These wonderfully apt examples are adapted from Rabelais, *Fifth Book*, ch. 22, as is noted in W. A. Eddy, *Gulliver's Travels. A Critical Study*, Russell, 1963, pp. 161–2. Jean Plattard's notes to the *Cinquiesme Livre*, Paris, 1948, pp. 324–5, show that Rabelais was literalizing a series of adages of Erasmus. See also the account of Lucian's *True History* in Eddy, p. 16.

of 'practical geometry' (XI 162). Natural philosophy is thus at least doubly unnatural, in that it variously violates nature, and in that it is the irrational pastime of creatures who pretend to reason. This is routine perversion, built-in to the situation. It exercised Swift, and Pope, *as* perversion. But there are further perversities. One is the encroachment of science on government. The Brobdingnagians stand out from the 'wits of Europe' in not having 'reduced *politics* into a *science*'. Unlike us, they have no books on 'the *art of government*', and despise mystery, refinement (a term which, as in many other satires of Swift and Pope, has familiar suggestions of dishonesty and other vices, as well as folly: 'heads refined from reason' – see *The Dunciad*, book 3, line 6), and intrigue (XI 135). The Laputans, on the other hand, like our mathematicians, have a 'strong disposition' to politics (XI 164), and the Academy of Lagado has a school of political projectors (though that, by some characteristic reversals, has crazed professors trying to do genuine political good, as well as schemes which hover uncertainly between outright folly and a sort of mad good sense – XI 187 ff.). What, Gulliver asks, is the connexion between mathematics and politics? Perhaps it is that 'the smallest circle has as many degrees as the largest', so that it might be thought that managing the world requires 'no more abilities than the handling and turning of a globe'. But he thinks the real explanation is

a very common infirmity of human nature, inclining us to be more curious and conceited in matters where we have least concern, and for which we are least adapted either by study or nature (XI 164).

This professional perversion or unnaturalness has connexions with a whole series of ironies about perversity in the professions and occupations of men. The Yahoos are of a 'perverse, restive disposition' (XI 266), and Swift seems to see human perversity as a thing of almost unending coils of self-complication. But before coming to this, the main outline may be summarized thus.

In the nature–reason dialectic at its simplest and purest, every vice is readily resolved into a violation of nature, and therefore into a peculiarly culpable form of unreason. The greed, quarrelsomeness, ambition, treachery and lust of men, as we encounter them throughout the *Travels*, are in an elementary sense unnatural by definition.

This unnaturalness is prone to almost infinite refinements, and therefore as we shall see open to a painful and varied series of ironic expositions. But the over-riding unnaturalness, which becomes unbearable to Gulliver at the end, is that the 'lump of deformity, and diseases both in body and mind' called man, should be 'smitten with pride': pride, in the assumption itself, in the face of so much folly, that man is a rational animal, the pride of having any self-esteem at all (as Gulliver, though perhaps not Swift, might more extremely put it), and (in the special case of scientists and their like) the pride of impiously tampering with God's creation and the normal state of things. Pride, which governs the mad scientists of book 3 (and the philosopher experts – XI 37, 103–4); the puny self-importance of the Lilliputians in book 1, who play at men; and that of men, which emerges by extension in book 2, is the most deeply unnatural of all the vices because, as the other vices prove, there is nothing to be proud of.

This diagnosis of mankind is an Augustan commonplace, and many important elements of it may be found not only in an earlier humanism but also in various old traditions of classical and Christian thought. But Swift refines on it by a number of characteristic ironies which serve to undermine any comfort we might derive from having to contend with a simple categorical indictment of mankind, however damaging. Whichever way we interpret book 4, man is placed, in it, somewhere between the rational Houyhnhnms and the bestial Yahoos. He has less reason than the former, more than the latter. The Houyhnhnms recognize this in Gulliver, though they think of him, and he eventually thinks of himself, as basically of the Yahoo kind. A Houyhnhnm state may be unattainable to man, but there are norms of acceptable, though flawed, humanity which do not seem, in the same way, beyond the realm of moral aspiration: one-time Lilliput (XI 57 ff.), modern Brobdingnag, the 'English Yeoman of the old stamp' (XI 201), the Portuguese captain. These positives must be taken gingerly. Ancient Lilliput and the old Yeoman are no more, Brobdingnag is hardly a European reality, there are not many like the Portuguese captain and his crew, although some other decent people make fleeting unremarkable appearances. Still, they are there, and at worst, we reflect, we are still better than the Yahoos. But in conceding this assurance, Swift also takes it away. This is not just in the dramatic strength of the parallels between them and us, which culminate in the 'objective' test of the female Yahoo's sexual craving for Gulliver (XI 266-7). There are qualities in which Gulliver is actually inferior: 'Strength, speed and activity, the shortness of my claws, and some other particulars where nature had no part' (XI 260). Swift can be more or less playful with those 'usual topics of *European* moralists' (XI 137) about a man's physical inferiority to animals, and an earlier speech of the Houyhnhnm master, already referred to, has its rich comic side (XI 242-3). But it is a point meant to be taken note of, and recurs with some insistence. There is no mistaking the tartness with which we are told, in a further twist, that the Yahoos (to whom men are physically inferior!) are superior in agility to asses, though less comely and less useful in other respects (XI 272-3). This is a Houyhnhnm view, but we need not suppose that Swift meant it literally in order to sense that he is having another snipe at the human form divine.

But more important is the assertion that man's portion of Reason, which theoretically raises him above Yahoos in nonphysical matters, is in fact something 'whereof we made no other use than by its assistance to aggravate our *natural* corruptions, and to acquire new ones which nature had not given us' (XI 259). The notion that men use their reason to make themselves worse rather than better was not invented by Swift (see R. M. Frye (p. 390, fn. 2), pp. 208-9) but it disturbingly weakens the contrary assurance that it is after all by virtue of our reason that we are better than the Yahoos. It is a Houyhnhnm comment, but so are the contrary ones (XI 234, 256, 272). No one else tells us much either way. It recurs in various forms. Gulliver comes to realize that men use reason 'to improve and multiply those vices, whereof their brethren in this country had only the share that nature allotted them' (XI 278). When men are under discussion, linguistic usage on the subject of reason and nature tends to change: reason multiplies vices, nature allots them. In an earlier passage there is even an unsettling doubt as to whether reason in this case really *is* reason. It occurs after the cruel irony in which the Houyhnhnm master supposes that, odious as men are, Nature has created their anatomy in such a way as to make them 'utterly incapable of doing much mischief' (XI 247), to which Gulliver replies with the account of war which I discussed earlier. The master then says he hates Yahoos but cannot *blame* them any more than he would blame 'a *gynnah* (a bird of prey) for its cruelty',[1] but as to man,

> when a creature pretending to reason, could be capable of such enormities, he dreaded lest the corruption of that faculty might be worse than brutality itself. He seemed therefore confident, that instead of reason, we were only possessed of some wuality fitted to increase our natural vices (XI 248).

This possibility, that man's reason is not reason, is not entertained. It goes against the run of the book's argument. But it is characteristic of Swift to place it before us, as an alternative (if only momentarily viable) affront. Either we have no reason, or what we have is worse than not having it. The irresolution saps our defences, for we need to answer on two fronts. At the same time, neither point is true to the book, which does concede (notably through several comments of the Houyhnhnm master himself) that Gulliver is both better and more rational than the Yahoos. Swift is needling us with offensive undermining possibilities even while a moderately comforting certainty is being grudgingly established. Of the two negative, undermining streams of argument, the dominant one is that which says we do have reason, but that it makes us worse. Its most intense manifestation occurs with Gulliver's description of the Yahoos' horrible smelly sexuality. The passage incidentally shows how germane the term reason is, in ways we might not automatically expect, not merely to the concept 'good morals' but also to the concept 'virtuous passions'. It drives home how the most unlikely vices tend to equal unreason (or, in the perverted human sense, not *unreason* but reason):

> I expected every moment, that my master would accuse the Yahoos of those unnatural appetites in both sexes, so common among us. But nature it seems hath not been so expert a schoolmistress; and these politer pleasures are entirely the productions of art and reason, on our side of the globe (XI 264).

---

[1] This is an illuminating parallel to Swift's remark to Pope on 26 November 1725 about the kite (*Correspondence*, III 118). I have briefly discussed interpretations of this controversial letter in a review in *Notes and Queries*, vol. 209, 1964, pp. 316–17.

Though this has special resonances in the context of *Gulliver's Travels*, and a true Swiftian tang, it is also the classic language of primitivism, which is in fact a minor theme of the work. The Houyhnhnms are in some respects prelapsarian innocents, ignorant of at least some forms of evil, and with no bodily shame or any idea of why Gulliver wears clothes. They also have no literature, but a high oral tradition in poetry and knowledge (XI 235, 273–4). Utopian Lilliput and the old English Yeoman are idealized pre-degenerate societies, and Swift's concern with the idea of the degeneration of societies has often been noted. But there is the contrary example of Brobdingnag, an advanced and largely good society which, by a shaming and pointed contrast with Lilliput and England, has emerged from an earlier turpitude (XI 138).[1] The Yahoos prove that there is no idealization of the noble savage: and though the Houyhnhnms do have a primitivist element, the high ideal of Nature associated with them embodies some key-values of civilized Augustan aspiration. This may partly proceed from a not fully resolved duality in the conception of reason both as civilized achievement and as corrupting force, not to mention the sense, perhaps a tending against both others, of a spontaneous rightness which 'strikes ... with immediate conviction' (XI 267).

But, if so, the confusion is not really Swift's. The fact is that both the language of ideas on these matters, and ordinary English idiom, make available these various senses. Nature and reason were all-purpose terms, and Swift, who was not writing a logical treatise (although it has been shown that he was, in a manner, refuting logical treatises),[2] was only too ready, as we have seen, to exploit the ironic possibilities offered him by the language. His whole style in this work thrives on what from a strictly logical point of view is a defiant (and transparent) linguistic sleight of hand. The textbook definition of man as *animal rationale* simply refers to that reasoning faculty which was supposed to distinguish men from beasts – to borrow Locke's

1 The passage runs pointedly against the Lilliputian (XI 60) and English (XI 201–2) examples. All rather strikingly have grandfather–grandchildren references. The contrast may reflect Swift's interest, noted by some critics, in a cyclical theory of history (e.g. XI 210), but such force as it has on the reader *as a contrast* is simply to the discredit of England.

2 See pp. 363–85. [Ed.]

phrase in *Essay Concerning Human Understanding* (book 4, ch. 17, p. 1). Swift's 'disproof' consists of tacitly translating a descriptive definition into a high ethical and intellectual ideal, and then saying that man's claim to reason is fatuously and insufferably arrogant.[1] The often-quoted formulation in the sermon 'On the Trinity' that 'reason itself is true and just, but the reason of every particular man is weak and wavering, perpetually swayed and turned by his interests, his passions and his vices' (IX 166) shows that Swift is perfectly aware of semantic distinctions when he wants to be. It can also stand as an acceptable boiling-down of much that is said about human unreason in *Gulliver's Travels*. Swift's concern here, however, is not to boil the issue down to its commonplace propositional content, but to exploit the damaging ironies by all the verbal means which the language puts at his disposal.

The double standard by which the words nature and reason tend to be used in a debased sense when they refer to men, and an ideal sense when they refer to Houyhnhnms, lies at the heart of this. The dreadful thing is that man is neither natural in the high sense, nor (like the Yahoos, as the quotation about 'politer pleasures' showed) in the low. If we then grant that this double unnaturalness is itself natural to man, we find him becoming unnatural even to this nature. Suggestions of multiple self-complicating perversity exist in the accounts of all men's occupations and professional activities. One might instance the Laputan reasoners, who are 'vehemently given to opposition, unless when they happen to be of the right opinion, which is seldom their case' (XI 163); the Admiral who 'for want of proper intelligence . . . beat the enemy to whom he intended to betray the fleet' (XI 199); the kings who protested to Gulliver in Glubbdubdrib

> that in their whole reigns they did never once prefer any
> person of merit, unless by mistake or treachery of some
> minister in whom they confided: neither would they do it if

---

1 See I. Ehrenpreis, 'The Meaning of Gulliver's Last Voyage', *Review of English Literature*, vol. 3, 1962, p. 34. In some ways, *animal rationis capax* is not really very different from *animal rationale* in the low-pitched textbook sense. Bolingbroke may have this partly in mind when he says the distinction 'will not bear examination' (*Correspondence*, III 121).

they were to live again; and they showed with great strength
of reason, that the royal throne could not be supported
without corruption (XI 199).

the politician who 'never tells a *truth*, but with an intent that you
should take it for a *lie*', and vice versa (XI 255).[1] Most elaborate is the
chain of ironies about the unnaturalness of the law. It is unnatural
that laws should exist at all, since nature and reason should be
sufficient for a rational creature. Other related perversities are: that
while meant for men's protection, the law causes their ruin; that
(for a variety of discreditably tortuous reasons) one is always at a
disadvantage if one's cause is just; that lawyers use irrelevant evidence,
and a jargon which no one can understand (which among other
things runs against the reiterated principle that speech is only for
communication); that lawyers, who are expected to be wise and
learned, are in reality 'the most ignorant and stupid' of men (XI
248–50). A major irony running through this is that man is unnatural even to his own natural unnaturalness. Assuming that moral
perversion is natural to the species, it becomes, in this sense, natural
for judges to accept bribes. But it is even more natural for judges to
be unjust, so that

I have known some of them to have refused a large bribe from
the side where justice lay, rather than injure the *faculty*, by doing
any thing unbecoming their nature or their office (XI 249).

One becomes unnatural to one's lesser natural iniquities when a
deeper iniquity competes with them. The concept of Nature is
debased by an ever-declining spiral into whatever depths mankind
might perversely sink to. Whatever these depths, Gulliver can follow
the spiral downwards and (both in his naïve complacent phase and in
his later disenchanted misanthropy) accept them as natural. The
spiral has almost endless possibilities, and the reader for much of the

1 Physicians provide a monstrously concrete example of nature turned upside
down. The basis of the reversal is the perfectly fair notion, discussed earlier,
that health is the 'natural' state of the body: 'these artists ingeniously considering that in all diseases nature is forced out of her seat; therefore to replace her
in it, the body must be treated in a manner directly contrary, by interchanging
the use of each orifice; forcing solids and liquids in at the anus, and making
evacuations at the mouth' (XI 254).

time has not even the comfort of feeling that there is a rock-bottom. But there is at the end, something like rock-bottom, a final insult to the nature of things which Gulliver finds completely unbearable:

My reconcilement to the Yahoo-kind in general might not be so difficult, if they would be content with those vices and follies only which nature hath entitled them to. I am not in the least provoked at the sight of a lawyer, a pickpocket, a colonel, a fool, a lord, a gamester, a politician, a whore-monger, a physician, an evidence, a suborner, an attorney, a traitor, or the like: this is all according to the due course of things: but, when I behold a lump of deformity, and diseases both in body and mind, smitten with *pride*, it immediately breaks all the measures of my patience; neither shall I be ever able to comprehend how such an animal and such a vice could tally together. The wise and virtuous Houyhnhnms, who abound in all excellencies that can adorn a rational creature, have no name for this vice in their language, which hath no terms to express any thing that is evil, except those whereby they describe the detestable qualities of their Yahoos; among which they were not able to distinguish this of pride, for want of thoroughly understanding human nature, as it shows itself in other countries, where that animal presides. But I, who had more experience, could plainly observe some rudiments of it among the wild Yahoos (xi 296).

Pride, the complacency of thinking that man is a rational animal, now becomes the 'absurd vice' which is the final aggravation of all our iniquities, the ultimate offence to nature. Yet even pride, the ultimate unnaturalness, is itself part of 'human nature' ('for so they have still the confidence to style it',[1] says Gulliver to Sympson, p. 7), so that we may wonder whether we really have after all reached rock-bottom, or whether there is yet another opening for still deeper unnaturalness to be revealed. But things do stop here, and in this final impasse the only possible response, dramatically, is Gulliver's mixture of insane hatred and impotent petulance as he forbids any English

[1] But this parenthesis may refer to the word 'degrading', and not to the phrase 'human nature'.

Yahoo with 'any tincture of this absurd vice' ever to appear in his sight.

The book ends here, with Gulliver a monomaniac and his last outburst a defiant, and silly, petulance. We are not, I am sure, invited to share his attitudes literally, to accept as valid his fainting at the touch of his wife (XI 289) and his strange nostalgic preference for his horses. He has become insane or unbalanced,[1] and I have already suggested one reason why, in the whole design of the work, this is appropriate: it makes his rant viable by dissociating Swift from the taint of excess, without really undermining the attack from Swift that the rant stands for. It is Gulliver's manner, not Swift's, which is Timon's manner, as critics are fond of noting, which means that he (like Lucian's or Plutarch's Timon),[2] and not Swift, is the raging recluse. But his are the final words, which produce the taste Swift chose to leave behind: it is not great comfort or compliment to the reader to be assaulted with a mean hysteria that he cannot shrug off because, when all is said, it tells what the whole volume has insisted to be the truth.

It is wrong, I think, to take Gulliver as a novel-character who suffers a tragic alienation, and for whom therefore we feel pity or some kind of contempt, largely because we do not, as I suggested, think of him as a 'character' at all in more than a very attenuated sense: the emphasis is so preponderantly on what can be shown through him (including what he says and thinks) than on his person in its own right, that we are never allowed to accustom ourselves to him as a real personality despite all the rudimentary local colour about his early career, family life and professional doings. An aspect of this are Swift's ironic exploitations of the Gulliver-figure, which to the very end flout our most elementary expectations of character consistency: the praise of English colonialism in the last chapter, which startlingly returns to Gulliver's earlier boneheaded manner, is an example. The treatment of Gulliver is essentially *external*, as, according to Wyndham Lewis, satire ought to be.[3] Nor is Gulliver

1 Conrad Suits does not think so: 'The Role of the Horses in *A Voyage to the Houyhnhnms*', University of Toronto Quarterly, vol. 34, 1965, pp. 118–32.
2 Lucian, *Timon, or the Misanthrope*, Plutarch, *Life of Antony*.
3 See R. C. Elliott, *The Power of Satire*, Oxford University Press, 1960, pp. 225–6.

sufficiently independent from Swift: he is not identical with Swift, nor even similar to him, but Swift's presence behind him is always too close to ignore. This is not because Swift approves or disapproves of what Gulliver says at any given time, but because Swift is always saying something *through* it.

Gulliver in his unbalanced state, then, seems less a character than (in a view which has much truth but needs qualifying) a protesting gesture of impotent rage, a satirist's stance of ultimate exasperation. Through him, as through the modest proposer (who once offered sensible and decent suggestions which were ignored), Swift is pointing, in a favourite irony, to the lonely madness of trying to mend the world, a visionary absurdity which, in more than a shallow rhetorical sense, Swift saw as his own. At the time of finishing *Gulliver*, Swift told Pope, in a wry joke, that he wished there were a 'hospital' for the world's despisers.[1] (If Gulliver, incidentally, unlike the proposer, does not preach cannibalism, he does ask for clothes of Yahoo-skin – XI 236 – and uses this material for his boat and sails – XI 281). But Gulliver does not quite project the noble rage or righteous pride of the outraged satirist. The exasperated petulance of the last speech keeps the quarrel on an altogether less majestic and more intimate footing, where it has, in my view, been all along. Common sense tells us that Swift would not talk like that in his own voice, but we know disturbingly (and there has been no strong competing voice) that this is the voice he chose to leave in our ears.

Still, Gulliver's view is out of touch with a daily reality about which Swift also knew, and which includes the good Portuguese Captain. Gulliver's response to the Captain is plainly unworthy, and we should note that he has not learnt such bad manners (or his later hysterical tone) from the Houyhnhnms' example. But we should also remember that the Captain is a rarity,[2] who appears only briefly; that just before Gulliver meets him the horrible mutiny with which book 4 began is twice remembered (XI 281, 283); that the first men Gulliver meets after leaving Houyhnhnmland are hostile savages (284); and that just after the excellent Portuguese sailors there is a hint of

1 *Correspondence*, III 117; see W. B. Carnochan, 'The Complexity of Swift: Gulliver's Fourth Voyage', *Studies in Philology*, vol. 60, 1963, pp. 32 ff.
2 'O, if the world had but a dozen *Arbuthnetts* in it I would burn my travels' (*Correspondence*, III 104). Don Pedro may, in this sense, be an Arbuthnot.

the Portuguese Inquisition (288). The Captain does have a function. As John Traugott says, he emphasizes Gulliver's alienation and 'allows Gulliver to make Swift's point that even good Yahoos are Yahoos'.[1] But above all perhaps he serves as a reasonable concession to reality (as if Swift were saying there *are* some good men, but the case is unaltered), without which the onslaughts on mankind might be open to a too easy repudiation from the reader. In this respect, he complements the other disarming concessions, the humour and self-irony, the physical comicality of the Houyhnhnms, Gulliver's folly, and the rest.

Even if Swift is making a more moderate attack on mankind than Gulliver, Gulliver's view hovers damagingly over it all; in the same way that, though the book says we are better than the Yahoos, it does not allow us to be too sure of the fact. (The bad smell of the Portuguese captain, or of Gulliver's wife, are presumably 'objective' tokens of physical identity, like the She-Yahoo's sexual desire for Gulliver.) This indirection unsettles the reader, by denying him the solace of definite categories. It forbids the luxury of a well-defined stand, whether of resistance or of assent, and offers none of the comforts of that author–reader complicity on which much satiric rhetoric depends. It is an ironic procedure, mocking, elusive, immensely resourceful and agile, which talks at the reader with a unique quarrelsome intimacy, but which is so hedged with aggressive defenses that it is impossible for him to answer back.

Finally, a word about the Houyhnhnms. It is sometimes said that Swift is satirizing them as absurd or nasty embodiments of extreme rationalism. Apart from the element of humour, discussed earlier, with which they are presented, they are, it is said, conceited and obtuse in disbelieving the existence or the physical viability of the human creature. But, within the logic of the fiction, this disbelief seems natural enough. The Lilliputians also doubted the existence of men of Gulliver's size (XI 49), and Gulliver also needed explaining in Brobdingnag (XI 103–4). In both these cases the philosophers are

1 'A Voyage to Nowhere with Thomas More and Jonathan Swift: *Utopia* and *The Voyage to the Houyhnhnms*', *Sewanee Review*, vol. 69, 1961, p. 562. For another useful perspective, see R. S. Crane, 'The Rationale of the Fourth Voyage', in R. A. Greenberg (ed.), *Gulliver's Travels. An Annotated Text with Critical Essays*, Norton, 1961, pp. 305–6.

characteristically silly, but everybody is intrigued, and we could hardly expect otherwise. Moreover, Gulliver tells Sympson that some human beings have doubted the existence of Houyhnhnms (XI 8), which, within the terms of the story (if one is really going to take this sort of evidence solemnly), is just as arrogant. More important, the related Houyhnhnm doubt as to the anatomical viability or efficiency of the human shape (apart from being no more smug than some of Gulliver's complacencies *in favour* of mankind) turns to a biting sarcasm at man's, not at the Houyhnhnms', expense when, as we have seen, the Houyhnhnm master supposes that man is not capable of making war (XI 247).

The Houyhnhnms' proposal to castrate some younger Yahoos (XI 272-3) has also shocked critics. But again this follows the simple narrative logic: it is no more than humans do to horses. Our shock should be no more than the 'noble resentment' of the Houyhnhnm master when he hears of the custom among us (XI 242). To the extent that we *are* shocked, Swift seems to me to be meaning mildly to outrage our 'healthy' sensibilities, as he does in the hoof-kissing episode. But in any event, the Houyhnhnms get the idea *from* Gulliver's account of what men do to horses, so that either way the force of the fable is not on man's side. The fiction throughout reverses the man–horse relationship: horses are degenerate in England (XI 8, 295), as men are in Houyhnhnmland. Again, I think man comes out of it badly both ways: the Yahoos of Houyhnhnmland make their obvious point, but the suggestion in reverse seems to be that English horses are poor specimens (though to Gulliver better than men) because they live in a bad human world. At least, a kind of irrational sense of guilt by association is generated. We need not suppose that Swift is endorsing Gulliver's preference of his horses to his family in order to feel offended about it. At many (sometimes indefinable) points on a complex scale of effects, Swift is getting at us.

The Houyhnhnms' expulsion of Gulliver belongs to the same group of objections. It seems to me that some of the sympathy showered on Gulliver by critics comes from a misfocused response to him as a full character in whom we are very involved as a person. The Houyhnhnm master and the sorrel nag are in fact very sorry to lose Gulliver, but the logic of the fable is inexorable: Gulliver is of the Yahoo kind, and his privileged position in Houyhnhnmland was offensive to some, while his rudiments of Reason threaten (not without plausibility, from all we learn of man's use of that faculty) to make him a danger to the state as leader of the wild Yahoos (x1 279). The expulsion of Gulliver is like Gulliver's treatment of Don Pedro: both episodes have been sentimentalized, but they are a harsh reminder that even good Yahoos are Yahoos.

The main charge is that the Houyhnhnms are cold, passionless, inhuman, unattractive to us and therefore an inappropriate positive model. The fact that we may not like them does not mean that Swift is disowning them: it is consistent with his whole style to nettle us with a positive we might find insulting and rebarbative. The older critics who disliked the Houyhnhnms but felt that Swift meant them as a positive were surely nearer the mark than some recent ones who translate their own dislikes into the meaning of the book. But one must agree that the Houyhnhnms, though they are a positive, are not a *model*, there being no question of our being able to imitate them. So far as it has not been grossly exaggerated, their 'inhumanity' may well, like their literal *non*-humanity (which tells us that the only really rational animal is not man), be part of the satiric point: this is a matter of 'passions'.

They are, of course, not totally passionless.[1] They treat Gulliver, in all personal contacts, with mildness, tenderness and friendly dignity (x1 224 ff.). Gulliver receives special gentleness and affection from his master, and still warmer tenderness from the sorrel nag (283). Their language, which has no term for lying or opinion, 'expressed the passions very well', which may mean no more than 'emotions' but does mean that they have them (226). In contrast to the Laputans, who have no 'imagination, fancy, and invention' (163), but like the Brobdingnagians (136), they excel in poetry (273–4), though their poems sound as if they might be rather unreadable and are certainly not enraptured effusions.

But their personal lives differ from ours in a kind of lofty tranquility, and an absence of personal intimacy and emotional entanglement. In some aspects of this, they parallel Utopian Lilliput (60 ff.),

1 See G. Sherburn, 'Errors Concerning the Houyhnhnms', *Modern Philology*, vol. 56, 1958, pp. 94–5; W. B. Carnochan, 'The Complexity of Swift: Gulliver's Fourth Voyage', *Studies in Philology*, vol. 60, 1963, pp. 32 ff.

and when Gulliver is describing such things as their conversational habits ('where there was no interruption, tediousness, heat or difference of sentiments'), a note of undisguised wishfulness comes into the writing (see the whole passage, 277). W. B. Carnochan has shown, in a well-taken point, that such freedom from the 'tyrant-passions' corresponds to a genuine longing of Swift himself (op. cit., p. 27). I do not wish, and have no ability, to be psychoanalytical. But in a work which, in addition to much routine and sometimes rather self-conscious scatology (however 'traditional'), contains the disturbing anatomy of Brobdingnagian ladies, the account of the Struldbrugs, the reeking sexuality of the Yahoos and the She-Yahoo's attempt on Gulliver, the horrible three-year-old Yahoo brat (XI 265–6), the smell of Don Pedro and of Gulliver's family and Gulliver's strange relations with his wife, one might well expect to find aspirations for a society which practised eugenics and had an educational system in which personal and family intimacies were reduced to a minimum. Gulliver may be mocked, but the cumulative effect of these things is inescapable, and within the atmosphere of the work itself the longing for a world uncontaminated as far as possible by the vagaries of emotion might seem to us an unattractive, but is surely not a surprising, phenomenon.

But it is more important still to say that the Houyhnhnms are not a statement of what man ought to be so much as a statement of what he is not. Man thinks he is *animal rationale*, and the Houyhnhnms are a demonstration (which might, as we saw, be logically unacceptable, but is imaginatively powerful), for man to compare himself with, of what an *animal rationale* really is. R. S. Crane has shown that in the logic textbooks which commonly purveyed the old definition of man as a rational animal, the beast traditionally and most frequently named as a specific example of the opposite, the non-rational, was the horse.[1] Thus Hudibras, who 'was in logic a great critic', would

> undertake to prove by force
> Of argument, a man's no horse.[2]

1 See pp. 363–85. [Ed.]
2 *Hudibras*, pt 1, canto 1, pp. 65, 71–2. See Ehrenpreis, op. cit. (p. 413, fn. 1), pp. 23 ff., for further illustration of the relevance of logic books. (The lines

422   Hugh Kenner

The choice of horses thus becomes an insulting exercise in 'logical' refutation. The Yahoos are certainly an opposite extreme, and real man lies somewhere between them. But it is no simple comforting matter of a golden mean. Man is dramatically closer to the Yahoos in many ways, and with all manner of insistence. While the Houyhn-hnms are an insulting impossibility, the Yahoos, though not a reality, are an equally insulting *possibility*. Swift's strategy of the under-mining doubt is nowhere more evident than here, for though we are made to fear the worst, we are not given the comfort of knowing the worst. 'The chief end I propose to my self in all my labours is to vex the world rather than divert it': and whatever grains of salt we may choose for our comfort to see in these words, 'the world', gentle reader, includes *thee*.

(51–90)

Hugh Kenner

from *The Counterfeiters: An Historical Comedy* 1968

As Cicero twines other words about *humanitas* – *comitas, facilitas, mansuetudo, clementia, doctrina, litterae, eruditio* – he seems to unfold and explicate the assumption that civilized people will already under-stand *humanitas* to subsume them all. To be fully human is to be all these things. And it is possible not to be fully human: possible, and fatally easy: when, like Turing's computer, you have been taught chains of answers out of a program, like the busy impostors castigated in *A Tale of a Tub* who have 'become *scholars* and *wits*, without the fatigue of *reading* or of *thinking*': indebted to *indexes*, and *systems and abstracts*; to *quotations* 'plentifully gathered, and booked in alphabet'; to 'judicious collectors of *bright parts*, and *flowers* and *observanda's*,' and thus, in a few weeks, 'capable of managing the profoundest, and

---

from *Hudibras* were pointed out to me by J. C. Maxwell before Ehren-preis's article appeared.) Another specified example of the non-rational animal was the ape. That Gulliver should have been taken by a Brobdingnagian monkey for one of its kind (XI 122) gains an additional piquancy from this. Swift uses the horse, unlike the monkey, as an opposite, not as a parallel, but man is the loser both ways.

most universal subjects. For, what though his *head* be empty, provided his *common-place-book* be full' (*A Tale of a Tub*, ch. 7). It is this man, *mutatis mutandis*, that Turing says you cannot tell from a man. As Vaucanson's duck implies, while we do not see the mechanism, an egg and ducklinghood, so a Turing Machine, suitably instructed, implies the long flowering of *humanitas*. And the other impostor, *homo non humanus*, is the observer schooled to regard with disciplined niceness the present instant: the empiricist on whose 'sublime and refined point of felicity' Swift memorably rounded, calling it 'The serene peaceful state of being a fool among knaves:'[1] Lemuel Gulliver, for instance, who observes, observes, observes, and is one of the most insidiously sympathetic characters in fiction. For it is attractive to be relieved of the obligation to seem, in the traditional sense, civilized: not to have to undergo the long slow process of shaping one's taste and judgement, but only to invest one's formative years in 'navigation, and other parts of the mathematics', and having to be sure read during one's leisure hours on shipboard 'the best authors ancient and modern', to take refuge behind a clean face, a well-brushed coat, and the assertion, in every crux, that one has verified one's facts.

Generations of readers have been playing Turing's game with Gulliver since 1726 without being quite able to decide whether he is human or not, so thoroughly does he play the dehumanized observer. He is the complete empiricist; he is empiricism itself, trousered and shirted: empiricism elevated into a life style, and rendered capable of a language that surprisingly resembles English. This language differs from English in a few trifling particulars. It has little syntactic variety; subjects tend to come before verbs and objects after them, while qualifying phrases are linked to substantives with diagrammatic accuracy. It is nearly devoid of figuration; it seems unaware of the vast suggestive resources of English idiom; it will only assert, as though the natural operation of the mind were a sequence of assertions. And it abridges its labors with audible relief whenever it can incorporate an expression of number. In fact it will only explicate what it cannot quantify; there are eight expressions of quantity in the

1 *A Tale of a Tub*, ch. 9. This book becomes much less puzzling once we realize how much of it is a counter-empirical tract.

first three sentences, which carry the author through all the seminal years of his life. Even courtship is quantified: 'Being advised to alter my condition,' writes Gulliver, 'I married Mrs Mary Burton, second daughter to Mr Edmond Burton, hosier in Newgate Street, with whom I received four hundred pounds for a portion.' 'With whom I received' is delicious.

If we heard this in the course of Turing's Game, would we decide straightway that we were dealing with the machine? We might; and we might be ill-advised. We might equally well say that we are dealing with a man who lacks what the ancients called *pietas* ('dutiful conduct towards the gods, one's parents, one's family, one's bene-factors, one's country'). Of *pietas* Gulliver displays only occasional rudiments. He does not mention God, of whom he seems not to have heard, not even when he tells us of the mercy to which he confided himself at the time of his first shipwreck: he confided himself, he says, 'to the mercy of the waves'. His family seldom sees him. His benefactors are chronicled and forgotten. No web of sentiment and obligation draws him tighter, as the years pass, into a system of human affection; we read very near the end how 'as soon as I entered the house, my wife took me in her arms and kissed me, at which, not having been used to the touch of that odious animal for so many years, I fell in a swoon for almost an hour': no doubt checking his watch as he fell. An ancient would also find him lacking in *paideia*, that elusive incorporation into one's mind of the viable past, to draw near which is to incorporate that which we are. Of this process, so far as he has dabbled in it, Gulliver has two things to say: that he spent three years at Emmanuel College, Cambridge, and that while a young man at sea he read the best authors. Two sentences only are devoted to his dealings with that complex mental heritage which distinguishes *homo humanus* from the barbarian: and an account of no more than two sentences is adequate to the results, so far as we can judge them.

And we can judge a great deal; we are meant to judge a great deal; to judge Gulliver; to sharpen our mental apprehension on him. For Swift's great irony amounts to this, that whereas Gulliver fancies himself the accidental emissary of the human race to parts unknown, and hence the perpetual observer and recorder, it is Gulliver himself for the most part who is constantly under observation. Swift was the real inventor of Turing's game, the object of which is to see what we can tell about a man if we have reason to wonder whether he may be an artifact. The three positions in the game are occupied, respectively, by Gulliver; by ourselves, who are presumably human, partakers in *humanitas, homines humani*; and by various other creatures who may or may not be human, or quasi-human, but are as apt in empirical disciplines as Gulliver himself, and a good deal readier to spot an inconsistency. They observe him at least as closely as he them, and more than once he is put to the trouble of formally explaining human values to them, he who has so little notion of what it may mean to be human. This great chattering booby, this casually programmed talking machine, he is *our* spokesman, *our* ambassador, the player who must prove that he is human while a giant or a horse occupies the observer's seat. And yes, he is our representative; we have no right to complain, for he represents a modern ultimate, carrier and incarnation of the values we really value: notably accuracy, cleanliness, and the power to adjust. Compared with Swift's, Turing's formulation of the game seems almost trivial.

The Gulliver we can see is quite as peculiar as the Gulliver the beings in the book see. The most evident thing about him is surely his utter ignorance of everything save navigation, a little applied mathematics, and medicine (though as ship's physician he seems unashamed to report that the crews are perpetually sick). Civilization is memory; if we know more than our fathers, they are (in T. S. Eliot's phrase) that which we know. History, the classics, the works which we have learned to call humane letters, as indispensable to our cultural identity as are our private memories to our personal identity, all of these are as if unknown to him. It is surely no accident that his journey draws motif after motif from the *Odyssey*, which for all we can tell he has never read; nor that he spends nine pages on the Struldbrugs, who live forever, first rhapsodizing over the thought of an earthly immortality, then dismayed at a spectacle of eternal decreptitude, all the while unaware of the attention that has already been devoted to this theme: never having heard of the fate of the Sibyl of Cumae, or of the miseries of Tithonus. The Brobdingnagians never remind him of the Cyclops, nor the Houyhnhnms of the Centaurs, who were the wisest creatures in Greece. All that cycle of classical narrative which forms a moral terminology among civilized men has never existed for him. Our attention may be distracted from these lapses by their consonance with the style, which an empirical hygiene has purged of classical allusion on the ground that literary tricks impede the record of observation; to say as much is to say that we ourselves, unless the words remind us constantly of the classics, forget their relevance. We have made a long step toward our own dehumanization in putting them aside in a special place, to be tended by surly men called scholars and never to be touched except when the mood is, as it never seems to be, just right.

And Gulliver resembles ourselves in this too, that he has learned to regard history as a spectacle. He falls in with some sorcerers who have the power to summon up out of the past 'whatever persons I would choose to name, and in whatever numbers among all the dead from the beginning of the world to the present time, and command them to answer any question I should think fit to ask'. It is a philosopher's dream; and Gulliver dreams of entertainment. He desires to see Alexander the Great at the head of his army, and is entertained with this vision, on a wide screen and no doubt with stereophonic sound. And on being privileged to question Alexander the pupil of Aristotle, he asks him only this, whether it is true that he was poisoned. His next request is to see Hannibal crossing the Alps, elephants and all; and his question for Hannibal, when the star steps forward out of this spectacle, is a technological one: is it true that he employed vinegar to dissolve inconvenient rocks? Hannibal assures him that, no, he had no vinegar. Clearly Gulliver has an eye for minutiae: he has missed a brilliant career as a classical scholar. Clearly too, he has no notion at all of what the past has to teach. All is fact, corporeal fact; there are no moral facts, there is no drama, there is no *paideia*.

And that is the reason for his very poor showing when, in the second and fourth books, in the court of Brobdingnag and before the talking horses, he undertakes the Psalmist's challenge, 'What is man?' If there is one being in the world who has no notion of the scope of that question, that being is Gulliver. He thinks that man is a rational animal. A computer is likewise a rational animal, most rational; and so are Swift's horses, animals – and rational too. There is really no point in Gulliver's competing with them, but compete he does.

We have our first sight of Turing's Game in the second book, when the learned men of Brobdingnag set themselves the problem, what is this creature that has come among them? We readers think we know that it is a man. But the Brobdingnagians know what a man is: a man is a being like themselves, seventy feet tall. And they are able to pick up this specimen, and examine it, and note its hominoid shape, and puzzle over the fact that it seems capable of learning their language; and they conclude that what they are dealing with is a *relplum scalcath*; very learned words of theirs, which may be interpreted into learned words of ours, *lusus naturae*; which words may be further interpreted, a flaw in the continuity of nature: something that has no business existing. It is amusing to reflect that a computer, since it works by natural laws, is not a flaw in the continuity of nature at all. *It* has a right to exist, in the same universe with the magnetic poles and the rotating earth, the cherry stones that remember how to make cherries and the glaciers that shear off the sides of mountains. It is ourselves who have no strictly natural business existing here. One can imagine the forces of natural evolution eventually producing a computer. It is harder to imagine them producing even Gulliver.

The learned men of Brobdingnag, when they decide that Gulliver has no business existing, are perhaps misled by his size. The King of Brobdingnag, however, plays the game under Turing conditions, attending to the other player's conversation, not his stature. And the more Gulliver talks to him, the more the King becomes convinced that if indeed Gulliver speaks for a race of beings like himself, then that race has no business existing; it is 'the most pernicious race of little odious vermin that nature ever suffered to crawl upon the surface of the earth'. This is Gulliver's fault, perhaps, since he talks so much about wars and plagues and poisons; he has been, we may be tempted to decide, badly programmed. If we think that, let us attend to how he fares among the horses.

For among the horses Turing's Game has assumed clearer contours. Gulliver comes among them a being quite different from themselves: he goes on two legs, he has no hooves. But he resembles rather closely a species with which they are already familiar, a species of beings that also goes on two legs, and lacks hooves. This species is greedy, and filthy, and vicious, and cannot be taught to speak; so as the Greeks listened to the speech of aliens, and heard only what sounded like *bar bar bar*, and called them barbarians, so the Houyhnhnms listening to the sounds of the filthy creatures on their island seem to have called them after the most prominent sound to be heard, *Yahoo*. And as the Turing player must decide whether a man can be told from a machine, so the talking horses must decide whether Gulliver can be distinguished from a Yahoo.

Like a computer, he seems strangely tidy; they can observe no organs of generation, nor of excretion, since they do not understand that they are not looking at his hide but at his clothes. And like a machine, he does not eat what the animals do; Yahoo food he shuns, as a Univac would shun hamburgers. So they listen to him speak; and the first thing they must do is teach him their language, which he has little difficulty in learning. This suggests that he is less like a Yahoo than he is like themselves, since the Yahoos cannot be taught anything of this kind.

And now, very strangely, the positions in the Turing Game are shifting; for Gulliver has had to learn the horses' language, which is a grave disadvantage. The Houyhnhnms naturally do not see it as a disadvantage, but we can. For he must use a speech devised by rational animals, exactly as someone who wants to talk to a computer must use Fortran or some other computer language, and avoid entangling the rules of Fortran with attempts at metaphor, hyperbole, synecdoche or hypothetical expressions. The language Swift devised for the Houyhnhnms is, like the various Universal Languages projected in his time, an early form of Fortran; and its first peculiarity is that all expressions have their face value (what would be the point of wanting to deceive a computer?). All expressions are of two sorts: they either say the thing that is, or the thing that is not; and there is no more purpose in saying the thing that is not, than there is in supplying a machine whose time is costing you five hundred dollars per hour with inaccurate data.

We can see that there is no way for this language to accommodate hypothetical expressions, since to 'suppose' that so-and-so is true is to entertain the usefulness of saying the thing that is not; nor can it entertain metaphors, since my love is not a red red rose unless I have made a serious mistake; nor can it manage qualifiers, since either the bare assertion is accurate, needing no adjustments, or inaccurate, and open to reconsideration. You cannot commence the Apostles' Creed in such a language, since it can have no meaning for 'believe', and no term for the God whom no one has seen; and as for believing *in* God, what sense can be attached to that? You might believe God, but that is a tautology; of course you believe Him, if He says anything, because when no one says the thing that is not you believe whatever is said.

Under this handicap, then, Gulliver sets out to explain what it is to be human; under a double handicap, what is more, since his mental habits are those of an empiricist, who pretends not to be human anyway. That is no doubt why he learns the Houyhnhnms' language so well. And handicapped alike by the intractable language and his own incomprehension (which we can guage by the fact that he never once complains about the intractability of the language) he sets out to expound human affairs: a chronicle of uncomprehended externals. So he explains, for instance, the religious conflicts of Europe as vicious disputes over whether the juice of a certain berry be blood or wine, or whether it be better to kiss a post, or to throw it into the fire. (Swift is playing a double game here, as so often, but let it pass.) The more he talks the more confused he grows, and the more ashamed; the more convinced, indeed, that he is at bottom no more than the creature he seems to resemble, a Yahoo. By the time he has decided that the Yahoos are his brethren he has learned the perfect code of Yahoo behavior; so that when he finally sails away from Houyhnhnmland, Swift in a flight of imagination worthy of the proprietors of Buchenwald has him make the sails of his boat out of Yahoo skin: young and fresh Yahoo, because the old one's skins are too tough.

And all this time his hosts have been imposing on him a set of values proper to rational animals. They have four cardinal virtues, temperance, industry, exercise and cleanliness, a code accessible alike to the reader of *Playboy* and to Professor B. F. Skinner. The traditional human virtues would be meaningless among rational animals for whom the thing that is not can have no saying, and for whom adaptation to the beneficences of nature is ultimate truth. For fortitude implies privations to be met, and justice implies the workings of the unjust, and prudence the bitter need to choose between conflicting goods, and wisdom the insufficiency of either information or shrewdness.

The Houyhnhnms, moreover, educate their young in strength,

speed and hardiness; there is no need to educate them in anything else, since all else comes naturally. They educate them with judicious impartiality, since the bond between parents and offspring is purely biological, and the obligation purely rational. They regulate births with care, on eugenic principles, matching the strength of one parent with the comeliness of the other. They thread needles, these horses, and they milk cows: what a feat of Swift's, to make us believe *that*! And they have no imaginative literature as we understand it; their poetry makes exact comparisons (because one says the thing that is, and hence takes one's satisfaction in tautologies), and it praises Friendship, Benevolence, and athletic prowess: the oddest derivation from Pindar ever conceived: fancy Diagoras of Rhodes yawning through an encomium in Houyhnhnmese. Had some Homer appeared among them, they would have banished him as a pernicious fabulist. For it is clear how Swift made them up. He borrowed their bodily form from that of the centaur, purified it toward equinity by removing that awkward human thorax, and set them down in what is unmistakably Plato's *Republic*. And Gulliver, though he has read the best books ancient and modern, recognizes none of this.

For virtue, said Socrates, is knowledge, and can be taught; and knowledge is what you know already, if you draw it out of yourself systematically, as the geometrical proof was drawn out of the boy in *Meno*. That is the computer's virtue: knowledge. It has no other virtue except method. It is the perfect rational animal. We build it, then we program it, and what we teach it can be said to be potentially known, so perfectly adapted are those propositions to its inward structure. We keep it clean, and applaud its industry and exercise, and never think to notice its temperance, so free is it from impulses incompatible with its own well-being. The computer, the third partner in Turing's Game, is the newest incarnation of an old dream, the dream of Socrates who fancied that reason and method delineated the contours of an ideal world, if only poets with their lewd imaginings and unmeasured statements could be prevented from muddling things up. The penchant for composing poetry is a Platonic manifestation of original sin, traceable in equal parts to the laziness which generates muddled statements, and the desire to soothe oneself with postulations of the thing which is not.

And Gulliver resolves to spend the rest of his life, back home among the English Yahoos, modelling his impulses yet more per- fectly on those of the noble Houyhnhnms. This last Odysseus, at the end of his journeyings, frequents the stables only of his Ithaca, and talking for hours on end with a pair of horses, does his poor best to fulfill yet another ancient scripture, one of which doubtless he has never heard: the mysterious tradition preserved by the Pyrrhonist chronicler Sextus Empiricus, that Odysseus at the end of his life was metamorphosed into a horse.[1]

And the oddest thing about this odd book is the effect it has had on generations of readers, who have looked up with dismay from the fourth part and concluded, not that Gulliver was mad, but that his author was. The Yahoos, they decide, must be meant for human beings; but what dreadful beings! The Yahoos are themselves, are ourselves, they decide, but how dreadful of Swift to say so! Playing yet one more hand of Turing's Game, reader after reader has ex- amined Yahoo, and examined man, and decided that they are identi- cal; and examined Gulliver, and examined man, and decided that they are also identical. The reader is deceived by two counterfeits. The Yahoo is not human at all; Gulliver is not human enough. Gulliver, for whom the Fortran of the horses is the last word in explicit rationality, even becomes a two-legged reasoning horse before our very eyes, without our thinking to protest that something is badly amiss; and we permit ourselves without protest to ascribe to a man who must have been mad, even though he was a clergyman of the Established Church of Ireland, what is by its own premises the only extensive work of English literature written by a horse. (127–42)

1 The Loeb Classical Library, *Sextus Empiricus*, vol. 4, p. 149.

A Modest Proposal

Hugh Sykes Davies

from 'Irony and the English Tongue', in B. Vickers (ed.), *The World of Jonathan Swift* 1968

Another useful prolegomenon to the study of 'keys' and codes in irony depends on the fact that it is by no means the only mode of expression which makes use of them. It shares them with allegory and metaphor, and some of the keys and codes used in irony can be studied more easily if they are compared with the processes met with in these other forms of expression. For example, in all three modes one of the most widely used keys to the existence and de-coding of a coded message is the presentation to the receiver of a statement which, if taken to be uncoded, *en clair*, is manifestly incompatible with its context in the rest of the utterance. Thus the reader of *The Faerie Queene* sets out with a gentle knight pricking across a plain in company with a fair lady for a distance of twelve Spenserian stanzas. In the thirteenth (so closely did the writer follow a Platonic notion of the magic in numbers) he learns that they have come to a cave called '*Errours den*'. Now all the proper nouns so far encountered have been in italic type; 'Errour' too is in italic, and though it is not at the beginning of a line it begins with a capital letter, so that it must be taken as some kind of proper noun. But the reader also knows, since he must be acquainted with English to be reading the poem at all, that 'Errour' is an abstract concept, and one which is not usually associated with so concrete a thing as a den, the haunt of a wild animal: 'Errour', taken *en clair*, is incompatible with its immediate context. He is thus warned that the use of the word in this passage is different from that which he usually encounters, and he is thereby prepared to regard the abstract concept as being, for the nonce, also a creature or person of some kind. This enables him to de-code the message conveyed in the set of signals about a filthy hag of serpentine aspect, with a long knotted tail and a large horrible progeny. They are all both creatures of a sort, and abstract concepts, the nature of which can readily be de-coded from various puns and other verbal signals. This is, with many variations, the rather tedious method of allegory. It is worth noting, by the way, that the Greek word from which irony comes was one of the words which in ancient Greek meant what we now mean by allegory; and also that allegory is one of the possible vehicles for satire, as in Orwell's *Animal Farm*, where the 'keys' are of the same type as Spenser's '*Errour's den*'. There is, for example, a horse called 'Napoleon', which is not, as both my usual bookmakers have assured me, a possible name for a real horse in English.

Metaphor uses keys and codes in a less tedious, and more varied manner. For example, the reader of Yeats's *A Prayer for my Daughter* hears in the first five stanzas of a father's natural forebodings and wishes for his infant daughter, and in the sixth he is told of his wish that she should become 'a flourishing hidden tree'. Now all the other things that he has wished for her have been good or in some way favourable. It is therefore most unlikely that this wish is meant literally, since for a girl to grow up into a tree would be neither usual nor wholly pleasant for her parents. The reader is thus warned that the expression is not to be taken literally, and that it is in some sort of code, the essence of which is that only those aspects of a tree's existence which might be pleasant for a girl are to be taken as being desired for her. The following lines confirm the rightness of this de-coding, and guide it more closely. The verse ends, for example, with the wish that the girl should 'live like a green laurel', and specifies the 'likeness' in the line 'Rooted in one dear perpetual place'.

As an example of the difference between key and coded signals in irony, we may take Swift's *Modest Proposal*. The first eight paragraphs of the pamphlet are concerned with the unhappy state of the Irish poor and their children, and they establish in the reader's mind, by the normal mode of communication, the writer's deep concern for their sufferings, and his indignation with those responsible for them. When, therefore, in the next paragraph he advances the suggestion that they should be fattened, sold and eaten, the reader has been quite sufficiently alerted to the incompatibility of such a course with the writer's real feelings, and warned that the message must not be taken at its face value. He has been assured, moreover,

that the writer himself is not a cannibal: his knowledge of the tasti-
ness of children's flesh, he carefully explains, has come to him at
second hand from 'a very knowing American of my acquaintance in
London' (XII 111). There is, moreover, the plain fact that in the
society which uses the English language – and used it in Swift's
time – cannibalism is generally frowned on, save under certain
extreme conditions such as shipwreck, war in the jungle and Outward
Bound endurance courses. Indeed English law discountenances it even
under these extreme conditions, if the verdict in Stevenson's case
may be taken as representing the last word of our lawyers on the
subject. This incompatibility of the particular proposal with everything else that can be learnt about the writer and his background,
both from the text itself and from its context, is the key which warns
the reader of the need for de-coding, and suggests to him how it
should be done: that what the writer really means is that the children
of the Irish poor should *not* be eaten, as, in a manner of speaking,
they actually are being eaten, by the English – including the reader.

A Modest Proposal also illustrates very clearly the compatibility
between irony and metaphor – a compatibility to be expected from
the similarity between their basic modes of communication. For the
initial suggestion that the children should be eaten is immediately
followed by this metaphor which itself provides a key to the correct
de-coding of the ironic message:

I grant this food will be somewhat dear, and therefore very
proper for landlords; who, as they have already devoured most
of the parents, seem to have the best title to the children
(XII 112).

And towards the end of the pamphlet, this key is repeated, with a
very slight variation in the choice of key-word:

For, this kind of commodity will not bear exportation; the
flesh being of too tender a consistence, to admit of long
continuance in salt; *although, perhaps, I could name a country,
which would be glad to eat up our whole nation without it*
(XII 117).

In both of these passages, it is the metaphor which provides the
key to de-coding the ironic signals. But it must be observed that if

metaphors are to carry out this function, they must obey the general law for keys of codes: they must not themselves be in code. That is to say, they must be so commonplace that there will be no risk of their being taken literally, and in this respect Swift's metaphors are very different from the tree-metaphors in Yeats's poem, for they (despite some slight reference to the Daphne-laurel myth) are essentially novel and exploratory, as are most of the metaphors of modern poets. Both of the key-words used by Swift here have long histories of use in very much the same sense which makes them effective warnings of the existence of coded signals in *A Modest Proposal*. The first, 'devours', occurs in a famous description of the Devil in the Bible. He is said to go to and fro in the earth, like a roaring lion, seeking whom he may *devour*, and it is, of course, understood that the Devil, for all his faults, is no cannibal. It is men's souls, not their bodies, that he is roaring for. The phrase has acquired something of proverbial currency and force, and may well have exercised some influence over the whole lexical history of this word. Shakespeare uses it often in this metaphorical sense; 'time' and 'pestilence' devour, so do wars and the sea; good deeds past are 'scraps devoured', and so on. In Milton, the scythe of Time devours, and so do death and war. Swift himself used the same word in such contexts as these:

The utmost favour a man can expect from them is, that which Polyphemus promised Ulysses, that he would devour him the last (*A Tritical Essay*, 1 249).

... there is hardly any remainder left of dean and chapter lands in Ireland; that delicious morsel swallowed so greedily in England under the fanatic usurpations (xii 185–6).
(The synonymy of 'devour' and 'swallow' used in this special sense can be extensively paralleled in Shakespeare, Milton, etc.)

As for 'eat up', there are examples by the score in the same predecessors: in Shakespeare, for example, 'Appetite, a universal wolf,'| So doubly seconded with will and power,|Must make perforce a universal prey,|And last eat up itself'. 'He that is proud eats up himself'; 'if the wars eat us not up, they will'. This group of nearly synonymous metaphors was, in fact, already so commonplace that none of these words could be misunderstood, or be taken literally, and the conventional mode of de-coding them was a clear pointer to the de-coding of the more elaborate coded signals which they accompany. Indeed there is a sense in which *A Modest Proposal* can be regarded as a deliberate expansion of these conventional metaphors, with all their associations; all it does is to take them literally, and so suggest that they are, in the particular case, much more nearly true in the literal sense than their habitual users might care to believe. (140–43)

Acknowledgements

For permission to use copyright material acknowledgement is made to the following:

For the extracts from 'Andrew Marvell' and 'Cyril Tourneur' from *Selected Essays* by T. S. Eliot to Faber & Faber Ltd, Mrs Valerie Eliot and Harcourt Brace Jovanovich, Inc.; for the extracts from 'The Oxford Jonson' and '*Ulysses*, Order and Myth' by T. S. Eliot from *Dial* to Mrs Valerie Eliot and Faber & Faber Ltd; for the extract from *Ulysses* by James Joyce to The Bodley Head and Random House Inc.; for the extract from the 'Introduction to "Pansies"' from *The Complete Poems of D. H. Lawrence* edited by Vivian de Sola Pinto and F. Warren Roberts to the Estate of the late Mrs Frieda Lawrence, Laurence Pollinger Ltd and the Viking Press Inc.; for the extract from 'Introduction to *The Words Upon the Window-Pane*' from *Explorations* by W. B. Yeats to Mrs W. B. Yeats, Mr M. B. Yeats, Macmillan & Co. and the Macmillan Co., New York; for the extract 'Swift as an Ecclesiastical Statesman' from *Essays in British and Irish History in Honour of James Eadie Todd*, edited by H. A. Cronne, T. W. Moody and D. B. Quinn to Frederick Muller Ltd; for the extract from 'D. H. Lawrence and Expressive Form' from *Form and Value in Modern Poetry*, originally published in *Language as Gesture* by R. P. Blackmur, to Harcourt Brace Jovanovich, Inc. and George Allen & Unwin Ltd; for the extract from *Attitudes towards History* by Kenneth Burke to Hermes Publications; for the extract 'Swift' from *Poets of Action* by G. Wilson Knight to Methuen & Co. Ltd; for the extract from *The Prose Style of Samuel Johnson* by W. K. Wimsatt Jr to Yale University Press; for the extract from 'Addison' by C. S. Lewis from *Essays on the Eighteenth Century Presented to David Nichol Smith* to the Clarendon Press, Oxford; for the extract 'Jonathan Swift' by Louis A. Landa from *English Institute Essays* to Columbia University Press; for the extract 'The English Dog' from *The Structure of Complex Words* by William Empson to the author, Chatto & Windus Ltd and New Directions Publishing Corporation; for the poem 'Hypocrite Swift' from *Collected Poems 1923-1953* by Louise Bogan to Peter Owen Ltd and Farrar, Straus & Giroux Inc.; for the extract from 'The Excremental Vision', chapter 13 of *Life Against Death* by Norman O. Brown, copyright © 1959 by Wesleyan University, to Wesleyan University Press and Routledge & Kegan Paul Ltd; for the extract from *The Exclusions of a Rhyme* by J. V. Cunningham to The Swallow Press

Inc.; for the extract from the Foreword to *Werke*, vol. 6, by Georg Lukács to Herman Luchterhand Verlag; for the extract 'Swift and the Comedy of Evil' from *Swift: The Man, His Works and the Age* by Irvin Ehrenpreis to Methuen & Co. Ltd and Harvard University Press; for the extract 'Literary Satire – the Author of *A Tale of a Tub*' from *Jonathan Swift* by Herbert Davis to Mrs Herbert Davis; for the extract from 'Swift and Kafka' from *Strains of Discord* by Robert Martin Adams to Cornell University Press; for the extract 'The Quixote Theme' from *Theme and Structure in Swift's Tale of a Tub* by Ronald Paulson to Yale University Press; for the extract 'James Joyce: Comedian of the Inventory' from *Flaubert, Joyce and Beckett: The Stoic Comedians* by Hugh Kenner to the author; for the extract from 'Swift's *Description of the Morning*' from *English Poetry* by F. W. Bateson to Longman; for the extract 'Jonathan Swift: The Poetry of "Reaction"' from *The World of Jonathan Swift* by Geoffrey Hill to Basil Blackwell & Mott Ltd; for the extract 'The Sin of Wit' from *Jonathan Swift: A Critical Introduction* by Denis Donoghue to Cambridge University Press; for the extract 'Alice in Wonderland' from *Some Versions of Pastoral* by William Empson to the author, Chatto & Windus Ltd and New Directions Publishing Corporation; for the extract from 'Personal and Political Satire in *Gulliver's Travels*' by Arthur E. Case to the author and Princeton University Press; for the extract from *Politics versus Literature: An Examination of Gulliver's Travels* from *The Collected Essays, Journalism and Letters of George Orwell Volume 4* by George Orwell to Miss Sonia Brownell, Secker & Warburg Ltd and Harcourt Brace Jovanovich, Inc.; for the extract from *A Rhetoric of Motives* by Kenneth Burke to the University of California Press; for the extract 'The Houyhnhnms, the Yahoos and the History of Ideas' by R. S. Crane from *Reason and the Imagination: Studies in the History of Ideas 1600–1800* edited by Joseph A. Mazzeo to Routledge & Kegan Paul Ltd and Columbia University Press; for the extract 'Gulliver and The Gentle Reader' from *Imagined Worlds* by C. J. Rawson to the author; for the extract from *The Counterfeiters: An Historical Comedy* by Hugh Kenner to the Indiana University Press; for the extract from 'Irony and the English Tongue' from *The World of Jonathan Swift* by Hugh Sykes-Davies to Basil Blackwell & Mott Ltd.

Select Bibliography

Editions: Collections

Herbert Davis *et al.*, *The Prose Writings of Jonathan Swift*, 14 vols., Blackwell, 1939–68.

Harold Williams, *The Poems of Jonathan Swift*, 3 vols., Clarendon Press, 1937; 2nd edn, 1958.

Harold Williams, *The Correspondence of Jonathan Swift*, 5 vols., Clarendon Press, 1963–5.

Herbert Davis, *Jonathan Swift: Poetical Works*, Oxford University Press, 1967.

Editions: Individual Works

Herbert Davis, *Drapier's Letters*, Clarendon Press, 1935.

William A. Eddy, *Gulliver's Travels, A Tale of a Tub, Battle of the Books, etc.*, Oxford University Press, 1933.

A. C. Guthkelch and David Nichol Smith, *A Tale of a Tub*, Clarendon Press, 1920; 2nd edn, 1958.

Eric Partridge, *Swift's Polite Conversation*, Deutsch, 1963.

Harold Williams, *Journal to Stella*, 2 vols., Clarendon Press, 1948.

Editions: Selections

W. A. Eddy, *Satires and Personal Writings*, Oxford University Press, 1932.

John Hayward, *Selected Prose Works of Jonathan Swift*, Cresset Press, 1950.

Edward Rosenheim, Jr, *Selected Prose and Poetry*, Holt, Rinehart & Winston, 1959.

Herbert Davis, *Jonathan Swift: Poetry and Prose*, Clarendon Press, 1964.

Philip Pinkus, *Jonathan Swift: A Selection of His Works*, St Martins Press, 1965.

Books on Swift

John M. Bullitt, *Jonathan Swift and the Anatomy of Satire*, Harvard University Press, 1953.

Henry Craik, *The Life of Jonathan Swift*, Murray, 1882; 2nd edn, Macmillan, 1894.

Herbert Davis, *Jonathan Swift: Essays on His Satire and Other Studies*, Oxford University Press, 1964.

Nigel Dennis, *Jonathan Swift*, Weidenfeld & Nicolson, 1964.

Denis Donoghue, *Jonathan Swift: A Critical Introduction*, Cambridge University Press, 1969.

Irvin Ehrenpreis, *The Personality of Jonathan Swift*, Methuen, 1958.

Irvin Ehrenpreis, *Swift: The Man, His Works, and the Age*, vol. 1, *Mr Swift and His Contemporaries*, Methuen, 1962, vol. 2, *Dr Swift*, Methuen, 1967.

William Bragg Ewald, Jr, *The Masks of Jonathan Swift*, Blackwell, 1954.

Oliver W. Ferguson, *Jonathan Swift and Ireland*, University of Illinois Press, 1962.

Denis Johnston, *In Search of Swift*, Hodges Figgis, 1959.

Louis A. Landa, *Swift and the Church of Ireland*, Clarendon Press, 1954.

John Middleton Murry, *Jonathan Swift: A Critical Biography*, Cape, 1954.

Martin Price, *Swift's Rhetorical Art*, Yale University Press, 1953.

Ricardo Quintana, *The Mind and Art of Jonathan Swift*, Oxford University Press, 1936; 2nd edn, Methuen, 1953.

Ricardo Quintana, *Swift: An Introduction*, Oxford University Press, 1955.

Edward W. Rosenheim, Jr, *Swift and the Satirist's Art*, University of Chicago Press, 1963.

Leslie Stephen, *Jonathan Swift*, Macmillan, 1882.

Brian Vickers (ed.), *The World of Jonathan Swift*, Blackwell, 1968.

Milton Voigt, *Swift and the Twentieth Century*, Wayne State University Press, 1964.

Kathleen Williams, *Jonathan Swift and the Age of Compromise*, University of Kansas Press, 1958.

Books Containing Discussions of Swift

Robert Martin Adams, *Strains of Discord*, Cornell University Press, 1958.

James L. Clifford and Louis A. Landa (eds.), *Pope and His Contemporaries*, Clarendon Press, 1949.

James L. Clifford (ed.), *Eighteenth Century English Literature*, Oxford University Press Inc., 1959.

Michael Foot, *The Pen and the Sword*, MacGibbon & Kee, 1957.

Paul Fussell, *The Rhetorical World of Augustan Humanism*, Clarendon Press, 1965.

Hugh Kenner, *The Stoic Comedians*, W. H. Allen, 1964.

Hugh Kenner, *The Counterfeiters*, Indiana University Press, 1968.

Marjorie Nicolson, *Science and Imagination*, Oxford University Press, 1956.

Sheldon Sachs, *Fiction and the Shape of Belief*, University of California Press, 1964.

Ernest Lee Tuveson (ed.), *Swift: A Collection of Critical Essays*, Prentice Hall, 1964.

Books and Articles on Particular Works

A Tale of a Tub

Phillip Harth, *Swift and Anglican Rationalism: The Religious Background of 'A Tale of a Tub'*, University of Chicago Press, 1961.

Ronald Paulson, *Theme and Structure in Swift's 'Tale of a Tub'*, Yale University Press, 1960.

Emile Pons, *Swift: Les années de jeunesse et le 'Conte du Tonneau'*, Strasbourg, 1925.

Miriam Starkman, *Swift's Satire on Learning in 'A Tale of a Tub'*, Princeton University Press, 1950.

Poems

Marius Bewley, *Masks and Mirrors*, Atheneum, 1970.

C. J. Horne, 'From a Fable Form a Truth: A Consideration of the Fable in Swift's Poetry', in R. F. Brissenden (ed.), *Studies in the Eighteenth Century*, Australian National University Press, 1968.

Maurice Johnson, *The Sin of Wit: Jonathan Swift as a Poet*, Syracuse University Press, 1950.

A Modest Proposal

Donald C. Baker, 'Tertullian and Swift's *A Modest Proposal*', *Classical Journal*, vol. 52, 1957, pp. 219–20.

Louis A. Landa, '*A Modest Proposal* and Populousness', *Modern Philology*, vol. 40, 1942, pp. 161–70.

George Wittkowsky, 'Swift's *Modest Proposal*: The Biography of an Early Georgian Pamphlet', *Journal of the History of Ideas*, vol. 4, 1943, pp. 75–104.

Gulliver's Travels

William A. Eddy, *Gulliver's Travels: A Critical Study*, Princeton University Press, 1923.

Irvin Ehrenpreis, 'The Origins of Gulliver's Travels', *PMLA (Publications of the Modern Language Association of America)*, vol. 72, 1957, pp. 880–99.

Robert C. Elliot, *The Power of Satire: Magic, Ritual, Art*, Princeton University Press, 1960.

Samuel Monk, 'The Pride of Lemuel Gulliver', *Sewanee Review*, vol. 63, 1955, pp. 48–71.

Books and Articles on Swift in Relation to Other Writers

John Fletcher, 'Samuel Beckett et Jonathan Swift: vers une étude comparée', *Annales publiées par la Faculté des Lettres de Toulouse*, 1962, pp. 81–117.

David P. French, 'Swift and Hobbes – A Neglected Parallel', *Boston University Studies in English*, vol. 3, 1957, pp. 243–55.

Bertrand A. Goldgar, *The Curse of Party: Swift's Relations with Addison and Steele*, University of Nebraska Press, 1961.

Phyllis Greenacre, *Swift and Carroll: A Psychoanalytic Study of Two Lives*, International Universities Press, 1955.

Edwin Honig, 'Notes on Satire in Swift and Jonson', *New Mexico Quarterly Review*, vol. 18, 1948, pp. 155–63.

P. D. Mundy, 'The Dryden–Swift Relationship', *Notes and Queries*, vol. 193, 1948, pp. 470–74.

James Preu, 'Swift's Influence on Godwin's Doctrine of Anarchism', *Journal of the History of Ideas*, vol. 15, 1954, pp. 371–83.

John F. Ross, *Swift and Defoe: A Study in Relationship*, vol. 2, University of California Publications in English, 1941.

John Traugott, 'A Voyage to Nowhere with Thomas More and Jonathan Swift: *Utopia* and *The Voyage to the Houyhnhnms*', *Sewanee Review*, vol. 69, 1961, pp. 534–65.

Ira O. Wade, *Voltaire's 'Micromegas': A Study in the Fusion of Science, Myth, and Art*, Princeton University Press, 1950.

Index

Extracts included in this anthology are indicated by bold page
references